A TASTE OF TORMENT

SHADOW HILLS ACADEMY: RELENTLESS
BOOK ONE

STACEY TROMBLEY

A Taste of Torment

Shadow Hills Academy: Relentless / Book one

Copyright © 2022 by Stacey Trombley

All rights reserved.

No portion of this book may be reproduced in any form without written permission from the publisher or author, except as permitted by U.S. copyright law.

This is a work of fiction. Any resemblance to actual persons, places, or events is coincidental.

Exterior cover design https://trifbookdesign.com

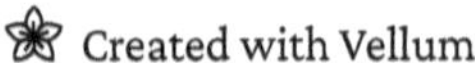 Created with Vellum

A TASTE OF TORMENT

SHADOW HILLS ACADEMY: RELENTLESS
1

STACEY TROMBLEY

I

I'LL FIND THE DEVIL AND MAKE HIM PAY

PASSING through the wrought iron gates toward the intimidating Shadow Hills Academy is like taking my first steps toward hell, but I walk with my head high, because torment or not, I'll find the devil and make him pay.

"You sure about this?" My mother's voice is quiet as she wraps her arm over my shoulder.

"Yes," I lie.

I lean into her touch, even though public affection is a tad cringe worthy just before I start a new school. Right now, I couldn't care less. I've never been super close to my parents, but this summer... well, we needed each other.

Truth is, I've never been alone a day in my life. It just wasn't my parents I relied on most. As I strain my neck to look up at the ugly brick spires of this stupid school, I realize that will end today.

This year, my sister won't be with me.

It's quiet out here. The surrounding mountains and forest are eerily still, as if no living soul were around for miles. I know that's a falsehood and there will be crowds of people once I enter the building, but for the moment, there's utter silence. Today is the first day of school, but I'm the only one arriving the old-fashioned way, it seems.

It's not like most of these *things* travel by car.

"We've gone through this," my father says calmly. "Candice can make her own decisions."

"But if they're not for the right reasons—" Mom pulls me into her arms and buries her face in my hair. I understand my mother's fear because I feel it too. Dark shadows press in from the back of my mind. Memories I'd rather forget. Attending this school will force me to face those shadows again.

"I just want to make sure you're not having second thoughts," she says. "You can always change your mind."

"I know," I whisper. "Thanks."

Maybe next week, I'll call her crying and ask her to pick me up. But for now, I'm sticking to my undoubtedly reckless decision. Being an active member of the magical community has always been dangerous, which is why my parents let us make that choice.

For the last three years, I'd chosen to avoid all things supernatural.

That changed when one of these monsters took something precious from me.

Avoiding this place now would be admitting defeat. It would be giving up on justice for her.

I could go to nearly any high school in the world, but I chose the one where literal demons reside—where my sister's killer is hidden behind pretty brick walls and wrought iron windows—because I have something to prove. To myself and the monsters within.

Mom finally releases me, and I smooth out my blue plaid skirt that falls nearly to my knees.

Dad offers me a fist. I roll my eyes but complete his fist bump.

"Remember, if you have any trouble at all, we can put in a call to the Blackthorns," he says.

"No," I say too quickly and then force a smile. "I'm a big girl. I don't want to ask for help from *them*."

"You used to be friends," he reminds me.

I swallow and then avert my gaze so he won't see the whisper of fear that washes over me. Yes, I used to be friends with *him*, the boy that now haunts my nightmares.

Curved talons crunch into the stone walkway of an otherwise normal neighborhood. Thick, scaled skin covering long, muscled limbs. Pitch-black, bottomless eyes.

I push away the memories before they overwhelm me.

That monster was my best friend. A boy both sweet and shy.

Normal.

Except, that was the biggest lie of all.

And that's why I won't let the disguise of this place lull me into a sense of ease.

It looks like any other snooty prep school for the annoyingly wealthy, and I now fit the part perfectly too in a blue plaid skirt, white button up top, and matching knee-high socks. My dark hair is a tad curly and trimmed to my shoulders.

The difference is, I really am what I appear to be.

Human. Weak. Vulnerable.

Utterly terrified.

I unfold my wrinkled acceptance letter with tense fingers.

Candice Montgomery,

It is with great pleasure that I write to inform you that you have been accepted into the Minor Program at Shadow Hills Academy!

Great pleasure, my ass. Schools like this begrudgingly accept a few non-magic students per year. I may have some roots in the magical community, but that doesn't mean I'll fit in.

My mother's bottom lip trembles as she nods. I give her one last tight hug, followed by another fist bump to my father, and then I march up the steps toward my worst fear and most challenging ambition.

I PUSH open the massive stone doors to the school without hesitation and am greeted by a rush of chaos. There's a large crowd gathered in the main lobby; so much so that it's hard for me to shove my way in. Luckily, the crowd is distracted by something at the front of the room, and once the door opens far enough, I slip in barely noticed.

High above, curved wooden accent beams decorate the domed ceiling. The floor is checkered marble, and the people surrounding me are all well-groomed with tailored uniforms, perfectly fitting each body.

The pretentious boarding school vibes continue inside, I see.

Most of the girls are tall and willowy, somehow still

with luscious curves. The boys are even taller, with thick muscled frames. Their skin is flawless and smooth over sharp cheekbones.

I wrinkle my nose and resist the urge to look down at my too long skirt and the button I can't keep fastened around my chest.

I didn't have time to have my uniform tailored due to my *expedited acceptance.*

But what difference would it make to have a tailored uniform? It's like being surrounded by airbrushed models, not a single flaw on their luminescent skin. I may as well run with my frumpiness and make the most of it.

I need to find the hall to administration so I can get my schedule and get to my normal Minor classes with the other weak students. Maybe I'll be able to breathe there.

There are several open walkways in this main hall. One reads: **Portals.** My stomach sinks. Definitely not that way.

Another, **Elite Hall.** That's arguably worse.

Arena. Nope.

Administration.

As I track my path toward my destination, I finally find the source of all the attention, and my stomach drops to my feet. Three figures stand on the platform between two spiral marble staircases.

The breath freezes in my lungs when my gaze falls on the demon heirs.

Jarron, Trevor and Beatrice are the most powerful students at this academy. The pride and joy of Shadow Hills.

From here they look... well, ethereally beautiful but otherwise normal. Human.

But I know better. Maybe better than anyone else here.

These demons keep their true forms hidden, even from other supernaturals. Because knowing and understanding are two very different things.

I work to keep my heartrate steady in this throng of supernaturals that can sniff out a weakling in a millisecond.

"There are three spots open," someone whispers. "Who do you think they'll pick?"

I try to ignore the whispering, but my curiosity is peaked and I follow the girl's gaze to two framed lists on the wall between the staircases.

"Their inner circle?" I ask smoothly, or at least that's what I'm going for. My fingers are trembling, so I doubt they're fooled.

The blond girl flicks a brow. "You new, or what?"

The brunette next to her nods. "They're announcing now."

"Thanks," I say and continue past. Leave it to me to arrive during an announcement by the very people I'm most afraid to face.

A red glow flutters up and down in front of the framed parchment on the left side, finishing a name in lovely swirling calligraphy.

Prince Jarron Blackthorn.

I swallow. Each prince gets to name three students to be part of their "inner circle."

It's a public declaration of the most popular and powerful students. You're in or you're out, and everyone knows where you stand. They want you to know.

My gaze rises, almost involuntarily, and I freeze when I find the pitch-black stare of Jarron Blackthorn pinned right on me. The cold bite of magic hits my spine. Every muscle tenses, frozen in place.

The room seems to hush—or maybe that's just my mind shutting everything out but the predator before me.

He knows I'm here.

I try to remember the kind boy that once wore this skin. He's older now, more man than boy, but I try to focus on that memory of our friendship and not the one of a stalking beast that carved its talons through my sister's flesh.

It doesn't work. My mind and body both remember the terror. My sister and I both survived that night, but it changed us.

I haven't seen Jarron since.

And now his magic is holding me hostage. I clench my jaw, working hard not to show my panic.

I don't know if it's my sheer determination or if he lets me go, but I finally rip free from his spell and I immediately duck between the bodies surrounding me.

"I'd do anything to have them pick me," a boy murmurs as I shove the rest of the way through the crowd.

"You're a literal pick me." The girl next to him laughs.

"For them? Hell yeah."

My teeth chatter, panic building in my chest. The rest of these students desperately want attention from the other-worldly prince. I want anything but.

Yes, he's powerful. Yes, he's sexy as hell.

But that beautiful face hides the soul of a monster.

2

FRESH MEAT

THE DISTANT CHATTER of the crowd fades into nothing as the door to administration clicks shut behind me. A set of middle-aged white women in cardigans stare in my direction.

After an awkward beat of silence, the woman in a pink cardigan scuttles forward and forces a smile while the woman behind her remains unmoving.

I pause, mind going blank for a moment. Is that... fear?

Do these middle-aged secretaries *fear* me? Confusion swirls in my mind, blocking out the panic I was battling.

"Hello," I say sweetly. "Mr. Vandozer told me I'd get my class schedule here today."

"Yes, of course," the woman says without looking me in the eye. Her bottom lip is trembling. She pulls out a folder. "Candice Montgomery, correct?"

I nod.

"You'll—You'll find everything." She pauses, staring down at the folder in her hands. "Everything you need in here, dear. Including a map of the school and your dorm number." She swallows.

It's an odd feeling for a stranger to fear me, particularly when I know I hold no power over them in the slightest. For them to fear me when I still fear others.

Is it because of the nature of my admittance?

The headmaster himself signed the paperwork after I persuaded him that it was in his best interest to accept me last minute. Blackmail is such an ugly word, but it's quite beautiful in practice.

So, yeah, I threatened the headmaster to get into the school, but that was with information about *events* that have taken place here. Mysterious deaths aren't overly uncommon at places like this, and I know of at least two that were swept under the rug to protect Elite students. Students that would rip me to shreds without a second thought if they knew I was threatening to expose them.

I'm not stupid enough to release the information, but Mr. Vandozer doesn't know that.

"Thanks," I say one more time, stomach squirming. I don't even have the heart to ask her for help to my first class with the way her fingers tremble.

Her lips part, like she wants to say more, but I flee from the room, too confused and overwhelmed to bother with anything more.

As more students stroll by, chatting idly, their eyes practically glowing with ungodly power, I have a new thought. The secretaries were horrified, scared out of their wits. And I can't imagine they're like that all the time. They know the manner of monsters that roam these halls.

They couldn't possibly fear me.

But they could fear *for* me.

I STAND in the hallway alone. Several students pass by like bees buzzing in a hive. After a few deep breaths, I force my body to calm enough for me to examine the paperwork the nervous secretary gave me.

On the front of the red folder is an elaborate coat of arms, with a crown on top and a serpent in the middle.

"*Human*," someone mutters in my direction.

My eyes flare. I don't even know which of the beings passing said it but it sure gets my butt moving a little farther down the hall.

I find a quiet corner to collect myself.

Only once my fingers have stopped trembling do I allow myself to flip through the papers.

Right up front is a map—which I've already memorized from the website— and my schedule. On the other side is a brochure showcasing smiling kids with shining white teeth. One of them has suspiciously long canines.

Where worlds collide, power is at your fingertips.

Even after studying the map, I find I'm still lost. There's supposed to be a stairwell near here, but where? I spin around.

There was an open house last weekend, and many students moved into their dorms a few days early. But if I'm honest, I was too cowardly to show up before I absolutely had to, which means now I have to wing it quickly.

"Need help?"

I spin to find a short girl with skin a few shades darker

than mine, large brown eyes, and long black hair pulled into a sleek ponytail. She smiles kindly.

"Uh, yeah. I guess so." I hand her my schedule.

"You're new right?"

I nod, trying not to be too obvious in my examination of the kind girl. She's not a demon—I don't think. Maybe a fairy? A witch?

"We don't get many new students that aren't timid freshman." She chuckles. "Brings a new meaning to fresh meat, if you know what I mean." She wiggles her eyebrows, still staring at my schedule like she's memorizing it. God, please don't let me have a vampire stalker in my first five minutes here.

Her gaze slowly rises to mine. "You do know what I mean, right?"

"Yeah."

Her eyes narrow. "Okay, good, 'cause I mean, I know you're human—you are human, right?" She leans in, her eyebrows furrowed.

This time, I allow a small smile and nod. I mean, I'm mostly human. I don't have any magic or anything, but my great, great, great grandmother was half-fae and half-demon, and my family has worked as scientists in the magical community for generations, so we're well aware of what's around us. It's just that, me and my sister have always stayed away from it all.

Well, almost always.

Neither of us had spoken to a magical being in three years—until this summer, when she made a choice that altered both of our fates.

"Yeah, humans are pretty rare here," the girl chatters away. "But you, like, know what this place is, right?"

"Yes, I know what this place is. Hell itself. I'm out of my league. Yada, yada. I get it." I force my steely determination to resettle into my bones. This place terrifies me, and I hate feeling this way. But I will conquer this school like I've conquered every other goal I've set for myself. I do not fail.

She shrugs. "Human or lesser magical being makes little difference. It's usually more to do with the knowledge. Humans get too freaked out when they learn about all the secrets in their world." She wiggles her fingers at me. "Most of us don't have much power. There are only a couple students here you should watch out for."

I nod and instinctively peer around the corner to watch the students scatter through the hall. One of them has horns. Another is two feet tall. "I'm well aware." I sigh and force my attention back on the girl, allowing the last of my jitters to leave my body.

"Oh, good. Come on, your first class is this way." She curls her arm in mine and pulls me down the hall—farther away from the crowd at the entryway, to my immense relief.

"I'm Janet, by the way. What's your name?"

"Candice," I answer.

She nods. "So, what brings you, a human, to this school?" she asks as we bound up a set of stairs.

I shrug. "My parents work in potions."

"Oh! Awesome."

"What about you? What order are you?"

"I'm a betweener. Half-troll, half-witch, and not the strong parts of either."

"Troll?" I ask. "Sorry, I mean—" Is it offensive to be

surprised at someone's heritage? Or maybe she'll find it flattering that she doesn't look at all like a troll?

She waves me off. "Don't worry about it. Get it all the time. Luckily, the smell didn't pass down to me, and my Brazilian complexion from my papai's side helps hide the color." I note the slight green tint to her skin. I doubt a human would ever notice.

Now out of direct danger from the heirs, I allow myself the chance to examine everything. The mahogany trim and sleek marble flooring. The thick doors with numbers labeled on every window. It's an ivy league high school cliché.

Only those that already know will see the differences in this part of the school.

The lights are a dull yellow, casting odd shadows around. Many of the creatures here prefer darkness, so bright lights aren't common. Perches sit near the ceiling for the pixies. Gemstones hang over every doorway.

It just makes the place feel even creepier.

I head down another hall, still arm in arm with my new half-troll bestie. We turn a corner to a large corridor, where there are more students hanging around chatting casually. Apparently, these are students uninterested in the drama below.

I take in a long breath and note that it feels normal here. No pressure of suffocating magic, and no predator gazes rousing my fear instincts. "It's much calmer up here."

Janet nods quickly. "Yeah, you want to stay away from the craziness on the north side of campus. I don't know how much you're up on magical politics, but those kids by the stairs? Bad news."

"The demon heirs. Yeah."

Janet shrugs. "They're not literal demons. You know, heaven and hell or whatever. But they're from a world that's dark and scary, where the creatures have inspired some of the darkest human legends."

None of that is news to me, but I let her ramble on.

"I mean, they might be cool as hell," she continues. "I doubt it—I just wouldn't know—but they're so powerful it's not worth the risk for those of us considered lesser, ya know?"

"But," a high-pitched voice chimes in from my right. I spin but don't see anyone. "If you can get on their good side," the voice continues around the other side of my head, "you're set for life."

"Hey, Lola!" Janet says to no one, so far as I can tell. Something buzzes in my ear, and I automatically duck away from it. Luckily, I know better than to swat at what I assume is a pixie.

"Stop, Lola. You're freaking her out."

"A new human?" the pixie says, darting around again. I twist but then hear a *thwap* against the door just past Janet, and a tiny body drops to the ground.

"Oh my god!" I drop to my knees immediately and help the tiny pixie into my palm. Janet stifles a laugh.

"Yep. Never better," the pixie says as she stands. Her wings begin vibrating and pick up speed until she lifts off my hand, hovering right in front of my nose. Her shiny purple wings flutter so quickly they blur together. She's maybe six inches tall, with dark brown skin and black hair pulled into two puffy pigtails on either side of her head. "Oh, hmmm, I smell something else. You're not totally human, are you?"

I swallow and shake my head slowly. "I'm like one-tenth fae."

"Oh, fun! What species?" Lola asks.

"High fae," I tell her. Which are basically elves but with stronger magic. I'm not a big fan of even those kinds of creatures. They don't treat humans as equals.

"Of course." She pouts, and I shrug.

High fae are the most common fae species to breed outside of their kind. I mean, imagine a six-inch fairy breeding with a six-foot creature? And trolls, minotaurs, and centaurs are all a bit too animalistic to be attracted to humanoid beings. Usually.

"I don't have any magic at all, though."

"No biggie. What's your first class?" Lola asks.

"History of Worlds," Janet answers for me. "Super easy if you're already up on the supernatural world. You've got a lot of newbie classes, actually. Next is astronomy with Mr. Kovit in the planetarium—best place on campus for a nap. Then, potions. You should be good at that, right? That's your parents' profession."

I nod.

"Hey, so," Janet says, her arm wrapping in mine again, "let's meet back at the main office for lunch hour. Don't worry about today; it'll be a cakewalk. They really just want to make sure people can find their way around. After classes are done for the day, we'll show you around Minor Hall and to your dorm and stuff."

"That'd be great." I force another smile.

I don't tend to make friends very quickly— apparently my resting bitch face game is a little too good— so it's an incredible stroke of luck to find two sweet girls that want to be my friend this quickly. But even so, the knot in my stomach remains. I never wanted to be part of this world. And yet, here I am, taking History of Worlds, potions, and Occult Ethics.

I just have to hope enrolling in this magical school isn't the worst— and final— mistake of my life.

3

DEALING WITH SUPERNATURALS 101

JANET WAS RIGHT, the classes so far have been basically nothing. In Portals 101, the teacher gave us a handout about basic portal safety and then gave a quick run-down of the worlds that have portals directly into this school.

That part made me feel super icky, but it is what it is.

Earth is sort of a neutral territory for the supernatural world. Since there are no massively strong magic users native to this world, most supernaturals feel safe traveling here for trade, education, and political alliances. And there are only a few schools even on this planet where creatures from different planets commingle.

Next, I had astronomy, which was a bit extravagant for a high school class but in a good way. We sat through a presentation in the planetarium, lounging in cushioned chairs in a completely dark room, craning our necks to stare up at a domed ceiling that's spelled to show the stars while the teacher rambled about space facts. It was great.

In my potions class—chemistry, according to my public

records—the teacher went over basic supplies, which I know backward and forward. I'm in a beginner's class, which means I can pass that class in my sleep.

In the second half of the day, I will wade deeper into the magical aspects of school here. Not that my schedule has much more than the basics, but I do have one self-defense class in the arena.

My only stressful moments, so far, have been trying to find my way between classes. Most of the time, Janet or Lola would show up to nudge me in the right direction.

They're a little extra, but I actually really appreciate the help. They're not scary or powerful. They're just curious and a bit over eager. So far—if I forget Jarron picking me out of the crowd in my first moments here—my experience at Shadow Hills has not been as miserable as I'd expected.

Well, until I walk into the lunchroom.

I shiver as the rush of magic settles over me like a blanket. Power is palpable here, with so many supernaturals gathered in one place. Walking past the packed tables feels like walking through water.

The ceiling is like two hundred feet high and covered in glowing stalactites and sparkling gemstones that create a pixilated image of a galaxy.

It's easy to spot and identify most species grouped at the very mundane rectangular tables. Pixies dart here and there, there is a table of trolls—only four take up the whole section that would have room for at least eight human-sized creatures.

Then, there's the popular kids.

There are three separate tables filled with obviously Elite students. The beautiful and powerful fae, with their designer jewelry and embellished uniforms, bright eyes, pointed ears, and immaculate hair. The hot wolf shifters—the jocks of the supernatural world, of course. And the demon royals. There are three royals, but they have an entourage of other supernaturals gathered around them.

I swallow and shift my gaze away from them immediately.

This is the only time that every student gathers into one place, aside from special events. Since I won't have access to the top dorms where the strongest students spend most of their time, this will be my one chance daily to mingle with my actual suspects.

And it's already making my palms sweat.

I hate, hate, hate feeling out of control. Hate feeling like if someone wanted to harm me, or make me do something, they could. And I couldn't stop them.

That's the feeling I've spent my life running from.

"You alright?" Janet whispers as we take a seat at an empty table on the far left of the massive hall. I nod quickly.

"You are a little pale," Lola adds.

A small boy with dark green skin sits beside Janet and says nothing. He just stares at me.

He's little but still definitely a troll.

"I'm fine. Just overwhelmed." And damn if that ain't the truth.

"Hey, Stevie, can you go grab an extra plate for Candice so she doesn't have to walk all the way up there?"

The little green boy hops up without a word.

"What, magical food doesn't just appear on the table?" I joke.

Lola snorts. "I wish."

In the middle of every table are what I think are empty candle holders with flat tops. As Lola circles around the tallest of the three and then drops onto her butt, I realize they're pixie perches.

Janet shrugs. "Spelled food never tastes as good as real food anyway and holds almost no nutrients."

"Besides, they make all the students walk through the arch up front to get their food."

"Right!" Janet says. "That helps them keep an eye out for injuries, illnesses, and spells. Tomorrow, you'll definitely have to enter."

"Oh," I say stupidly. "Okay."

"It's no big deal. You won't even notice the magic. It's just a check to make sure there's no issue with bullying."

"Or slaves," a girl with horns two seats down chimes in and then shivers.

"Oh hush, Romera. We're trying not to scare her."

"Slaves?" I repeat.

"Well," Janet says slowly, "when you put such a large mix of magic levels together, some beings take advantage of others. With potions or spells or glamours. And yeah. It's obviously frowned upon. By making students go through the archway every day, they can make sure that's not actively happening."

"Right," I say, but my stomach twists. I may not be able to keep any food down today. This new information does not increase my confidence in this place.

The little green boy rejoins us with a bowl of soup and a roll.

"Thank you," I tell him, as he slides the plate in front of me.

"That's it?" Janet exclaims. "She's gonna starve."

"It's perfect," I chime in quickly. "My stomach couldn't handle much more than this anyway."

Janet examines me. Then, she nods sharply. "I've got a ton of snacks in the dorm. I'll hook you up later when we're safe from all this." She waves vaguely.

"And we have dinner in the dorm common rooms, so we'll be safe there." Lola wiggles, and her wings tinkle just slightly. My lips twitch. She's adorable.

"You'll love Minor Hall," Janet says. "We're kind of the outcasts, but it's perfect for people like us. You'll feel safe there, trust me."

I give her a small smile and allow that spark of hope to grow.

"This is my half-brother, Stevie, by the way. He's a freshman."

"Nice to meet you, Stevie." His gaze drops to the floor, and he doesn't at all respond to my greeting. But I don't take it as an insult. He's shy; I'm cool with that.

Slowly, I force myself to take a sip of the reddish-brown stew. It's salty and bland, but I suppose that's not a bad thing. It'll go down easy, which is all I need.

Janet and Lola chat away about some of the school drama, and I zone it out entirely. The bread, unlike the soup, is delicious. Soft and buttery. I devour it quickly.

Janet scarfs down a sandwich with some kind of dark slimy meat—I don't dare ask what it is—as she chats about the flings this summer. So-and-so dumped so-and-so. Some girl got mad that her ex hooked up with someone else. Seriously, basic high school drama. It's almost comedic how normal it all feels.

Around the lunchroom, there are myriads of different species. Some are massive, some are tiny. Some appear entirely human, just really pretty, and some definitely could not pass for normal if they went out in public—scales and horns and unnaturally colored skin.

Now that the attention isn't on me, I do find myself curious about it all. I know a lot of details about the supernatural world. I've lived in and around my parents' successful business as potions masters. I've seen trolls and witches and fae and pixies. It's just that, with the exception of Jarron's family, I haven't spent much time with them.

A cold chill drops over me suddenly. I release a quick breath and a puff of white comes out. I freeze. Did me thinking his name call him or something? Can he read my mind? Dammit, maybe he *can* read my mind.

"What are you doing here?" His low voice is smooth as fresh snow, but the bite is just as cold.

I sit up straight, and I brace myself for what I know I'll find.

Lola and Janet stare over my shoulder, as if the big bad wolf himself were standing behind me. And he is, kind of. I spin to find dark brown eyes, so damn hypnotizing it should be a sin. I lick my lips and immediately hate myself for it.

Three students stand beside our table.

Two guys, gorgeous as hell itself, and a girl that could be walking anime. But it's the tallest of the three that snags my attention and won't let go.

Jarron's face is sculpted like a golden statue, perfect cheek bones and smooth bronze skin. His hair is longer than the last time I spoke with him several years ago. The curls dip down over his forehead, almost reaching his lashes.

There is no kindness in his severe expression. No longing, no hopefulness. Only the look of a predator with prey in its sights.

"Awww, look. A pretty lost lamb," Bea says.

I wrinkle my nose at the girl clinging to Trevor's arm.

Bea, short for Beatrice.

Her hair, black as night, is braided down her back, and her skin is pale. She may as well be a gothic snow white, with a button nose, and full red lips. She probably doesn't even have to put on makeup—the magic makes her that beautiful.

She's technically non-royalty, from the same world as Trevor and Jarron, but she's been courting Trevor for so long most consider her a princess. We've met, but she doesn't seem to remember me.

"Candice is anything but a lost lamb," Trevor murmurs. My attention shifts to him. His skin is several shades darker than his brother's but they share the same sharp cheek bones and deep dark eyes. He crosses his arms, but then peers up at his brother who's predator gaze has not left me for even an instant.

"What are you doing here, Candice?" Jarron says. His baritone voice sends a shiver down my spine.

The energy in the room has turned tense. All the chattering has stopped, and the attention has turned to the demon royals—and me.

These three are more than popular. They're the center of this school's universe.

They're from a family with so much power that no one else can stand against them. Once you're on their radar, your choice is bow before them or die.

I bite the inside of my lip, and then I force a smile to cover the anger swirling in my chest. "Aren't you happy to see me?"

Miss Snow White curls a lip in disgust. "Met a few weakling friends, already, have you?"

Anger curls in my gut at the looks Bea gives Janet and Lola. "Don't talk to them like that," I spit, maybe harsher than I should give then fact that this girl could suck the breath from my lungs with half a thought. But truth is, those girls behind me are kind and vulnerable and I'll be damned if I let any other innocent people be hurt while I'm here, no matter what it costs me. I'll do what I can to protect my new friends.

Bea's eyes widen but she doesn't immediately react so I change the subject quickly. "We were just about to go check out our dorms." I say then glance down at my wrinkled slip of paper. "Could you point me to Minor Hall? I'd so appreciate the help." I spin the words so sweetly there isn't a person on the planet that would believe it was sincere.

Jarron narrows his eyes, his lips parting.

"You *would* be in Minor Hall." The Demoness laughs then points lazily down the hall behind us. "Take the first stairway to the right. Another right and it's in that hall somewhere." She waves her hand haphazardly.

"Thanks!" I chirp and hop to my feet immediately, desperately seeking a way out of this conversation.

"Wait," Jarron's low voice calls after me, but I don't stop, don't even pause. I rush down the aisle, away from the demons. A set of footsteps pound behind me, almost louder than my heartbeats. As pathetic as it is, I'm not ready to face the devil I once knew.

"Candice." His command has enough force that it sends a jolt of discomfort down my back. I grimace, but after a pause, I continue walking. Just as I make it to the lobby outside the cafeteria, Lola and Janet catch up with me. Lola flies in front of my face. Janet curls her arm in mine.

"What the hell?" Lola squeaks, darting to avoid me running face first into her wings.

"You did *not* tell us you know Prince Jarron," Janet whisper yells.

"I don't."

"It sure seemed—" Janet's voice trails off into a squeal as a heavy shadow settles over all three of us. A hand snakes around my arm. The breath catches in my throat as my body whips to face the demon prince's dark stare.

"Candice," he says softer this time, but his shadow magic still pulses from him, demanding he be heard. "Talk to me," he adds. "Please." The final word is hoarse. He almost sounds *desperate*.

Shock ricochets through me. I swallow and then nod, unable to even speak without my knees giving out. He glances at my shocked friends and then gently guides me out of the lobby and into the hall. Eyes of every shape and size follow us, but out here, no one is in ear shot.

"What are you doing here, Candice?"

I cross my arms, trying to avoid shivering in his presence. I hate feeling small, feeling weak. And how could I help that in the presence of someone this powerful? "What does it matter?"

He stares at me, incredulous. "The last I heard from you, you wanted nothing to do with me because of what I am. You said you swore off everything magical. Then, you just show up years later, out of the blue, and think I shouldn't even be curious?"

"You can be curious, but it doesn't mean I'll tell you anything." I shuffle my feet.

"Are you kidding?" he hisses.

I shrug. I know I'm being unfair, but it's weird for him to care this much. Or at all, really. I'm not sure what to make of it. I hate how his power makes me feel, and this is the only way I know how to hide it.

"Did our friendship mean anything to you at all?" His voice has dropped so low it's almost a whisper.

I swallow and stare down at my shoes as I shuffle them awkwardly. "It did once," I admit. I knew Jarron years ago. And yeah, we were friends. But that was before I knew he was a demon prince.

Well, no. I *knew*. But it was before I knew what it *meant*. What it felt like to be near someone that powerful. Before I saw his true form, and before he almost killed Liz.

"What are you doing here, Candice? Tell me, and if you never want to speak to me again, I'll honor it. But tell me why." He rubs the back of his neck.

He seems almost insecure. Which is basically the exact opposite of what I expected. It's disarming, in a way. I feel guilty for talking to him so harshly for no reason except my own insecurities.

I don't want to be part of this world, his world. I don't want to feel like a meaningless bug next to a commanding prince, but I'm not here for what I want. I'm here for what I need. And I need information.

"Did you hear about what happened to Elizabeth?" The words come out as a whisper.

He pauses. "I heard something. I wasn't sure exactly what happened. Is she okay?"

"No." I'm barely able to force the word from my lips. "She's dead."

Jarron freezes, and so does the entire room. Literally. A chill washes over everything. Ice crackles, inching up the walls. When I breathe, it comes out in a puffy white cloud.

I force my gaze to meet his. "And I'm here," my voice becomes more sure, more determined, "because the person who killed her goes to this school."

4

SUSPECT NUMBER ONE

"Who?" Jarron growls.

"I don't know, but I'm going to find out." I don't tell him what I do know—that it was almost certainly a demon that killed my sister.

He glances over his shoulder to the cafeteria, where the entire school watches us curiously. "How do you know it was someone here?"

"She died in the Forest of Nails, three miles north of campus. And her journal says she was seeing someone here. Someone powerful. I'm going to piece it together and find out who did it."

Even if it means facing the devil that was once my friend. Even if it means killing a being a thousand times stronger than I am.

He nods slowly, his shoulders still slumped. "I'll help."

I blink. "No."

"Yes," he says. "I'm not going to just sit around while you search out someone who killed your sister. Someone who could just as easily kill you. You need an ally. Someone to protect you. I can make sure *no one* touches you."

I shiver at the power in his voice. The demand. He wants to protect me?

Or at least, that's what he wants me to think.

My lips part, but I can't tell him that he is my first suspect. Elizabeth had a big crush on him until we found out about his magics and he hunted her, hurt her.

Then, years later, she started dating a demon at this school and wound up dead? Yeah, I don't believe in coincidences.

It's still hard to imagine Jarron hurting her. It's hard to picture the boy who used to climb trees with me, and left dandelions on my front porch, as the demon capable of remorselessly killing my sister. But I sure as hell can imagine the monster inside of him committing a terrible crime like that.

He hurt her once before, after all. It may have been a minor injury, but it was purposeful.

I shiver as the image of Jarron's true form pops into my mind. Scales dark as night, horns that curl over his head and bat-like wings. It doesn't even sound that bad when described, but seeing it...

No human can stand up to creatures like that. Their magic slices into your very bones and whispers how weak you are. How insignificant.

It was the face of a monster that could kill a human without a second thought.

"Let me help you," he says, so low it's almost a growl. "I swear not to get in your way and only to protect you. Besides, if you suspect someone powerful is to blame, then you'll need access. Access a new human will not have—but I will."

I mean, he's not wrong. Here, we're sorted into halls based on our strength levels. I'll be in the Minor Hall with most of the freshman and weakest supernaturals. The most powerful are in the Elite Hall. Which is where all of my suspects will gather and party and bathe and do pretty much everything except attend classes and eat lunch. "You can get me access to the Elite Hall?"

His eyebrows rise, a shadow falling over his face. "Yes."

My lips part as I consider him.

"I'll get you access and make sure the most powerful trust you. They'll want to be your friend and tell you all of their dark secrets in only a matter of days."

I frown. "How can you do that?"

"Trust me." He smiles.

I pause but then finally nod. I'll accept his help because he's right. I need it. "But you realize that when I find out who did this, I'm going to kill them. No matter who it is—"

"Yes," he agrees. "I will welcome their death."

5

VULNERABILITY IS THE WORST

THE MOMENT JARRON reenters the cafeteria with his long purposeful strides, Lola and Janet rush forward. They cling to me like we'd all barely survived a traumatic experience, and they guide me out the back doors.

The chill wind rushing over my skin is a shock at first, then I welcome the cool breeze on my warm cheeks. A few miles behind us are green rolling mountains. The sun is high over clear blue skies.

Lola buzzes ahead toward the patch of trees behind an open field. To the left is a massive arena that's like a mix between a college football stadium and the colosseum. It's made of old stone, with columns and torches, but with a dome ceiling made of metal and glass.

Janet stops at the first set of trees, but my attention is still on the arena.

"What the hell was that?" Lola asks.

I swallow and shift my gaze back to my new friends.

"Long story," I whisper.

"People are going to be talking about that all day."

I groan and slump down into the grass, back leaning against the rough bark. "I have to go there next," I tell them, pointing to the arena.

Janet sighs and nods. "You're in the lowest level class, though, so you won't be faced with anything too tough."

We sit still, not talking for a few minutes while I force myself to relax. Jarron confronted me about my reasons for being at this school. He's now the only one who knows why I'm here.

I'm not sure why I even told him. I should have just lied.

"So, how do you know Jarron?"

I sniff, pulling my mind back into focus. I have a job to do here. A purpose. I'm out of my league, I know, but I've never been one to back down from a challenge. "His parents know mine."

"Sounds like the super, simplified version," Lola chimes dramatically.

I shrug.

"Also, how the hell do your parents know the king and queen of the Under World?" Janet asks.

I press my lips together. "They're potions masters. They have some important clients."

Janet presses her palm to her mouth. "Yeah," she mumbles, then drops her hand. "I would have expected like Olivia Rodriguez and Jennifer Aniston, important. Not other-world-royalty important."

"Wait!" Lola shrieks. "Candice Montgomery. Your parents are *the* Montgomerys?"

Janet gasps.

I roll my eyes. "They're not that big of a deal."

"Are you kidding? They're famous. Didn't they help the goblin heir take back her kingdom by brewing a spell that tricked a mountain troll into thinking he was an owl for a full week?"

I snort. "Yeah, but that's more funny than impressive."

"No, it's impressive!"

"And funny," Lola chirps. "Which actually makes it more impressive."

"Right?" Janet says. "They're not like mafia potions masters; they're creative and sometimes even silly. They're like the epitome of mad scientists."

"Mad scientists usually try to take over the world, don't they? My parents just help people." And yeah, their 'help' has made some major political changes throughout several different worlds but still. They're my parents, and all they did was brew a potion that tricked a troll.

And stopped a war.

And ended a thousand-year monarch.

I cross my arms. All right, my parents are badass. I admit it. But they're my parents, and it's not like I've trained to follow in their footsteps. Yes, I've been around magic and potions since I could walk, so I'm above average, even in the supernatural world, but I'm just a *mostly* human teenager with *mostly* human parents.

"Give me the run down on self-defense classes," I blurt out, mostly to change the subject but also because my palms are sweating just thinking about entering that arena.

I don't allow myself to enter a place where I don't have some sort of upper hand. That's my thing. Back at my old school, I wasn't the most popular, but boy did I know all the secrets there were to know about everyone.

I didn't do drugs, but I knew who did. I didn't do much hooking up, but I knew all there was to spill about who did.

My parents made sure I had adequate self-defense training from a young age because even if we decided to stay out of the magical world, they knew we'd be vulnerable just living in their home if we didn't train.

So, we trained.

I could hold more than my own in a regular school. Not that I used it for much more than volleyball and field hockey —and the one time I gave Jimmy and Dominic both bloody noses for harassing Liz during gym class—but I held enough confidence that no one messed with me.

I'm brutal, for a human.

It's just that, here, my form of brutality is not enough. Not nearly enough. I'm like a middle schooler hopping onto the field with professional football players—without a helmet. If I push the wrong buttons, I'll be pummeled quickly.

I hate that feeling.

So, in theory, I should be fine in a remedial self-defense class, but...

Janet shrugs. "It's not a big deal. You can wear regular clothes. You'll literally be with a bunch of freshmen. Some will have magic but nothing too strong. Only Minor and Major class supernaturals at most. And day one, she'll probably make you lift weights or play a stupid 'ice breaker' game or something."

I swallow. That doesn't sound too terrible. "When do the stronger supernaturals train?"

"There are always multiple classes going, but they keep them very separate. Upper level students usually take the lower arena—there's three levels in there—where there are more wards. You'll be in the main area that's just like an open field of nothing. They'll teach you to block and break basic holds. Nothing too big."

"But don't wander," Lola says seriously, her face suddenly in mine, wings beating so quickly they're a blur of silver and purple. "Those higher-level kids will be around."

"Right," Janet says. "I would suggest going to the bathroom during lunch period so you can avoid even using the bathrooms in there."

Lola does a little twist and then plops down on my shoulder. "Ugh, do you remember the time Rebecca got spelled in the stall and came out panting like a dog and running on all fours?"

Janet groans. "That was terrible. There are some bullies in the high levels."

"Yeah, but if she knows Jarron, people won't mess with her."

Janet shrugs. "Maybe, but it also puts a target on her back. Especially for the girls who trail after him."

I narrow my eyes. "What do you mean by girls who trail after him?"

"Well, I mean, boys too but—"

My eyes flare. "Not what I meant." She was implying something and she knows it.

Janet gives me an annoyed look. "No one knows anything about you, and your first day here Jarron's running after you? Rumors are bound to fly that you're competition."

I scoff. "I'm a magicless human in Minor Hall. I'm not competition for anyone."

Lola spins like she finds the fluttering leaves more interesting than this conversation. Janet raises her eyebrows but then finally shrugs. "Maybe not, but that won't stop people from talking."

6

LOVE POTIONS CAN SUCK MY DUCK

Janet and Lola were right; defense class was as uneventful as all the rest. The teacher introduced herself and took us on a quick tour of the arena, which is ridiculous by the way. State-of-the art, three levels, surrounded by major magical wards so the building won't take damage even with full-on magical battles.

We walked around the highest viewing level of the basement arena, where the higher level students have class, and we watched from the balcony as their purple and blue and silver magic soar toward targets.

The teacher treated us like toddlers who might get spooked over our own shadow, which was both annoying and appreciated. I guess this is what I get for taking all the freshman courses.

Most of the students in my class are freshman witches, but there are a couple surprising additions. Two half-goblin boys and a wolf shifter. Even though he's the size of child, shifters are strong. *I'm going to be sparring with a wolf shifter.*

Runt or not, that scares the crap out of me.

I survive the first day without incident though, so I'll take it as a win.

Mythic Literature, Occult Ethics, and Numerology 101 are all back to boring basics. Reading, ethics, and math with a slight supernatural twist.

Even after such an easy day school wise, I'm utterly exhausted by the time the bell rings to signal the end of classes. I don't rush out because I know the halls will be worse than the classroom and I don't actually know where I'm going yet.

"Candice?" a tinkling voice calls before I'm even at the classroom door. She soars over the heads in the packed hall. Though I'm drained, I find myself smiling every time I see her.

I'm not sure how I got so lucky to have met such attentive, sweet people so quickly.

"Hey, Lola, you're here in record time."

She beams. "When classes are over, I'm always the fastest out."

I enter the swamped hall, the chatter bouncing off the walls. I watch a few of the supernaturals walk by; several sets of eyes drift to me and stick.

I frown. I might be the new girl, but it's the first day of school. Is it really that big of a deal? I feel like the reactions are getting progressively worse throughout the day. Janet comes rushing up, breathless. "Ready? I'm so excited to show you Minor Hall!"

"Ew," someone mutters as they pass by.

"Can't wait," I tell her. Janet wraps her arm in mine and guides me through the crowd. She pushes through a metal door and into a quiet stairwell. We rush up three levels and then into a hall that smells vaguely of sewage. Only a few students are around us now.

Our feet squeak on the icky linoleum flooring—just like my time at public school. Out the window, though, is a nice view of the rolling hills and a pretty garden with a domed awning. Everything here is shaded for light sensitive supernaturals.

We eventually reach an open rusty iron gate right in the middle of the average looking hall with a crooked sign that reads, "Welcome to Minor Hall! Those who do not belong will suffer greatly."

I run my hands through my hair. *That's cheery.*

"The archways are spelled to burn the skin off your body if you don't belong," Lola tinkles joyfully.

Well then. I ignore the pit in my stomach and try to convince myself it's not so bad.

As horrific as it sounds, I know the spell is made to protect us. Minor students are the most vulnerable. The ones without protection.

More powerful students are not allowed in our private quarters for good reason, and a potent spell is the only way to ensure we're truly safe. Even from demon royalty... *for example.*

I can't resist wincing as I walk through the passage. The zing of magic makes me gasp, but then I'm through. And in only a few feet we're in a larger corridor. The hall is brightly lit, covered in rounded glass. Outside there are a couple pretty basic maple trees and a few patches of wildflowers.

"That's it." Janet wipes her hands dramatically. "Now, you're safe from anyone powerful."

I close my eyes and try to convince myself she's right. We're safe. I can relax here.

There's a large fireplace, blazing with multicolored flames, and a painting of an open field with a massive black void looming over it.

I raise my brows at the image but don't have time to examine it for long. The ceiling is at least fifty feet high with patchwork stones and discolored glass. There are several sets of open archways lining the path, all made from spiraling cobblestone.

The sound of excited chattering comes from down the hall but halts the moment I step into the next room. A boy with horns peeks out from one of the archways then darts back out of sight.

"Welcome to the Minor dorms!" Lola announces in a squeaky high voice, her arms spread wide.

"Looks like everyone is excited to have me," I mutter, eyeing a group of four girls huddled in the corner, watching me in tense silence.

"Oh, they'll warm up to you," Janet assures me. "You're just the topic of like *all* the rumors since lunch. No one is quite sure what to make of you."

My eyebrows furrow. "What kind of rumors?"

"Oh, you know... You're a dark sorceress hellbent on world domination. You're a potion master's kid that slipped Jarron a love potion. You killed a man in Reno once. The usual." Lola shrugs. I almost smile—almost. But the whole potion thing kind of gets under my skin.

"They think I gave him a love potion?"

"They're dumb rumors. People just like to be dramatic. You've obviously got some kind of history with the bad-boy prince, and your parents are potions masters. It's a large leap, but people like to chatter." Janet shrugs. "It'll blow over quickly. Trust me."

I twist my fingers together and force a smile.

"Come on, I'll show you around."

Janet weaves me in and out of the various rooms of Minor Hall. There's a decent sized dining hall filled with scuffed-up, round wooden tables, a small library, a game room, and a TV room filled with mismatched couches. It feels like a super outdated summer camp.

Most of the students here are small in stature or timid. There are a couple pretty girls with horns and a boy so large I assume he's part giant.

Even though everyone hushes when I come near, and whisper the moment I'm out of earshot, the weight I'd felt in the halls and in the lunchroom is noticeably absent.

Even to many of these creatures, I'm weak. But this is the kind of weakness I can make up for with my intelligence and skill. The difference between me and fae, demons, and wolf shifters? Not so much.

If things really do calm down, I think I could find myself feeling at home here.

This part of the school is reserved for the weakest of all students. Most freshman live here, but there's also a whole set of dorms for the upper classmen that remain in Minor Hall. With special permission, or testing out, each student has the opportunity to access a new hall, each one a step up. Major Hall is a bit stronger than Minor but still on the weak side of things. Some of the more dangerous creatures are never allowed to be in Minor, no matter how weak or young. Which is what I assume is happening with the runt shifter in my defense class who's in Major Hall despite being a rather weak freshman.

As a human senior, I'll certainly remain in Minor Hall throughout my time here, which I don't intend to be long. Janet is a senior, and Lola a junior. Both have told me they'll remain in Minor Hall until they graduate too.

It doesn't really matter to me one way or another. I don't care if people think I'm weak. I only care that they're right.

The moment I figure out who hurt my sister and get my revenge, I'll be back to normal human school and none of this will matter.

Janet flops onto a massive U-shaped leather couch in the middle of the common room. "My room is down that way," Janet points to the right, "and yours is down that one." She motions to the hall entrance next to it. "We'll be close. And we can totally hang out in any of the common areas."

I sit beside her. "That's good."

I know I'm not the easiest person in the world to befriend. My list of flaws are a mile wide. I'm fearful of this place, and it makes me act very defensively. But these two have accepted me instantly and treat me like an equal. I don't think they'll ever truly understand how significant that is and how much I'll burn the world down if anyone hurts them. And I've only known them for a single day.

"It's cool in here," I admit, looking up at the mismatched colored glass on the ceiling and names carved into the wood, even in hard-to-reach places.

"I mean, it's the outcast hall," Janet says with a sigh, slumping even further until she's practically lying on it. "We get the least luxuries and instead get noses turned up in our direction. But once we're behind these gates, we're safe. I mean, other than a few freshmen here that act like they're better than us and can't wait to test out, we're a big dysfunctional family."

Lola lands on my shoulder. "Jerks in this section of the school are few and far between. Just ignore them and you'll love it here."

"I already do," I say. "You guys have made it— bearable. I really want to thank you for being my friend. I don't have many of them and it... it means a lot."

"So you like it here?" Janet grins.

"More than I expected to, for sure."

"Did you expect to hate it?" Lola sits, legs folded beneath her. Her wings still buzz.

"Pretty much."

"Then, why did you come?" Janet asks.

"Long story." I shrug. "I just never liked being surrounded by people I know are more powerful than me. Makes me feel like I have no control over what happens to me." It's a feeling I've worked to avoid for a really long time.

"Then you'll love it in Minor Hall."

I smile. Unfortunately, I can't just fall into the comfort of Minor Hall because there's no way my sister's killer resides here. They're in Elite Hall, almost certainly.

My stomach twists as I think back on my conversation with Jarron.

In order to get justice, I'll have to face my fears, as well as beings I stand no chance against. Like Jarron. But I know everyone has a weakness. So long as I keep under the radar and don't make any serious enemies, I'll have time to unravel the mystery and then find the chink in my villain's armor.

Janet scootches in, leaning close. "Okay, now, spill the tea. How do you know Jarron?"

Lola squeals and flutters to my inside shoulder so all three of us are crowded together. "Yes, yes, yes. You have to tell us."

I sigh. "It's not some big story. We knew each other as kids. I haven't seen him in three years."

"Three years?" Lola asks.

"Okay, but like, what kind of relationship did you have? Because I swear, I've never seen him look at anyone like that. Ever."

"Like what?" I try to picture what she's talking about. What about that conversation was significant? Other than that *"please."* Which, if I'm totally honest with myself...

I shake my head. Nope. Not being honest with myself, got it.

"He *chased* you," Lola says, as if that means something to me.

"Jarron doesn't chase anyone," Janet says, her voice hushed and reverent. "You come to him or you don't get to interact with him. It's like he doesn't care about anyone or anything. Except, apparently, you."

"It's not like that."

"Are you sure? Because it's hard for me to imagine Jarron doing that... ever. A wolf shifter, sure; they act on whims. Fae? Could be random fits of jealousy over anything at all. But the steely demon prince? Uh-uh. If he didn't care, he wouldn't have followed you. Or called for you. He wouldn't have even looked in your direction."

I can't argue with them about any of this because I really don't know Jarron. Not anymore. Instead, I explain our past interactions matter-of-factly. "His parents were two of my parents' clients. They came into the shop a lot, and we played. Trevor was there too. My parents had a vacation house on the same island as his, and we spent a couple summers playing together."

Lola sucks in a breath. "Myre Island?"

I nod.

Janet stills. "Maybe we were wrong to assume you'd stay in Minor Hall. If your parents have a house on Myre Island—"

"Not anymore. They sold it when we refused to go anymore."

"We?"

I press my lips together. I have to stay calm. "Me and my sister. Once Jarron and his brother grew into their power, it was different. We didn't feel safe with them anymore. We decided we didn't want to be the weak ones in our friend group."

"Where's your sister now?"

Acid swirls in my belly. Emotion stings my throat. I'm not sure how to deal with this. How much truth should I tell them? I hadn't planned to bring Elizabeth up at all, but now, how could I lie? How could I hide the emotions welling up inside all the time?

"She died. This summer," I whisper the awful words. I hate saying them. I hate admitting it. My sister is dead, and every time I think about that fact, I want to burn the world to the ground.

Janet winces. "That's terrible."

"I'm so sorry!" Lola says, her wings shuddering.

I nod and try for a sad smile. "It's okay." I mean, it's not. But that's what you're supposed to say, right?

"Is that why you came back here?"

"What?" I ask much too quickly, anxiety crawling in my chest.

"To honor her. Prove that you're good enough."

"Oh," I mutter. "Yeah. I guess so. She was opening up to the supernatural world more than I was in the last year. When she died, I decided to give it a chance." My stomach sinks. I don't like lying to people who are sincere. I want to tell them the truth. But could I really be honest about how I daydream of shoving a dagger through someone's eye socket? The face is different each time, but in my mind, that person did it. They killed her. And it feels good to steal their life in return.

I swallow. I'm pretty sure I'm a terrible person, but I don't even care. Maybe I'm as evil as the demons running this school.

But the difference is, no one knows it.

7

When Magic is Currency Human Life is Worthless

I turn quiet once the sun sets and eventually excuse myself to my bedroom to be alone. Janet and Lola give me sad smiles and kind words of encouragement.

I'm glad I told them about Liz, even if it's only a partial truth.

They'll at least understand that I'm not okay sometimes.

Once I saw the dark sky taking over, it hit me that this is my first night in a boarding school without her. Usually, during our first time at a new school, we'd lay in one of our beds together, chatting about every moment of our day for hours.

Every person we met—the cute boys and nice girls, the jerks to stay away from, and the mean bully girls. The teachers or classes that were going to be difficult and the ones that would be cake.

Some of those things, I could talk with Janet and Lola about, but I've only known them for a day, and I'm keeping so much from them—it's not the same.

So, heart heavy, I sneak away into my bedroom to spend time with Liz in my own way.

My bedroom is cramped and smells dingy. There's one small window, but the curtains hanging on one wall are so long that it gives the illusion it's massive. There are two twin sized beds with stiff mattresses and red sheets. My roommate is a sophomore witch, named Corrine. Janet told me she's a little snooty but she won't cause any harm.

She doesn't so much as look in my direction when I enter the room, so that's fun.

But that's fine with me. It might be a little awkward but at least I'll have some quiet time.

I pull out my plush blanket and wrap it around my shoulders. This is the same blanket I've had since our first year in boarding school. Liz had one too. It's now sitting abandoned on her bed at home.

A bed she only slept in a few times in the last three years.

I only have a few pieces of her left, and the biggest one is staring up at me from my lap. I've read the stupid journal four or five times over since it showed up on my bedside table at home.

That's when I knew the investigation was over.

I think my parents thought it would be a comfort for me, a way to feel connected to her again. In some ways, they were right, but I'm certain they didn't expect me to obsess over it.

I've studied it, taken notes. Read and reread. For hours on end.

I stare down at the pink leather journal with silver gel pen doodles all over it.

The pages are worn and covered in scribbled handwriting that I sometimes struggle to read. On the front page is her name, *Elizabeth Montgomery*, embellished with stars and flowers and swirls in varying colors and dated from our last day of middle school, when our parents gifted us each a journal. Mine remained empty until this summer. Elizabeth's is around three-quarters full.

I'd never even realized she wrote in her journal until after her death. The journal was turned in to the investigators, and that was the first time I'd seen it since we unwrapped them together.

But then, her murder case was deemed "unsolvable." That's a word that truly gets under my skin. The case isn't unsolvable, they just don't want to deal with the repercussions of investigating a powerful supernatural.

That's the problem with this world. With enough magic, you can get away with anything. The rulers of the Under World could demolish the earth if they decided to. No mortal investigators want to risk their wrath, not for one human girl.

Someone of no consequence.

So, if the trail led them toward someone too *dangerous*, they'd drop the case faster than a hot potato and pretend the evidence didn't exist. Which is what I assume happened in my sister's case.

My parents hired an independent investigator, after the official investigation was dropped. At least this way, if they found the killer, they'd know never to work with them again. Maybe they'd brew their own brand of revenge.

I heard that discussion in the middle of the night a few weeks after we found her body.

Except, after a week—a *week*—they dropped their investigation too and refused to tell me why.

They told me all the sappy stuff about mourning and celebrating her, remembering the good yada yada yada. Her journal turned up in my room without a word that week.

And I took matters into my own hands. I spent an entire night pouring over her words. I learned she was dating someone new, someone who "reigned supreme," at a nearby magical academy.

I also found a half-completed application to Shadow Hills Academy inside the investigator's box, left abandoned in our closet.

I'd crossed her name off the application and filled it out for myself. It had been a full two weeks past the admissions deadline, so I'd sent in a *personal* note to the headmaster along with it.

And that brings me to now. Sitting in my cold, dingy dorm room in a magical school, holding my dead sister's journal.

Liz wrote less than fifty short entries in it, which means only major events or times she was feeling especially emotional made her pull it out. I find myself wondering if she purposefully hid that she wrote in it or if I'd just never noticed.

The first three entries are sappy and silly. She talked about her first year of regular human school and how she sometimes missed being part of the supernatural world— something she never mentioned to me. She admitted that I was right; we were better off using our talents to get ahead in the human world where we could be some of the most influential women in whatever field we decided to enter, instead of being barely tolerated in the magical world.

Our parents are famous potions masters, which is cool. But we had still witnessed them be threatened over and over, called unimportant and weak. We've had our house ransacked by trolls after our parents refused to help them murder a enemy family. We'd lived with bodyguards for an entire year in sixth grade because of kidnapping threats from a rival potionist.

That's the truth of how we became friends with Jarron and Trevor.

We saw them every once in a while, usually only one at a time, when their parents would make a quick trip into the shop for a meeting.

Dozens of guards would show up, blocking off the whole block. When I was a child, I didn't realize how bizarre that really was. That was when they were only occasional clients. But when the royal family of the Under World chose my parents for a regular contract, it nearly cost us our lives.

A witch potionist believed she deserved the contract simply due to the magic in her blood, and she tried to force my parents to back out of it by threatening Liz and me.

We had no idea it was happening at the time. We just thought our parents were being paranoid, but come to find out, the car accident, house fire, and Liz's stomach virus that year were not freak accidents. The witches plan backfired, of course, when the underworlders got involved.

In order to protect their investment, the royal family made their presence known in our lives for several months until the threats magically disappeared.

Poof.

In fact, I haven't heard a peep about that witch since.

This is only one piece of why Liz and I separated ourselves from the supernatural world entirely. I was getting ready to start high school and Liz, a year behind me, was still in Junior High.

We were at an age where we were just beginning to realize the truth of the world our parents are so deeply intrenched in.

We began to see the magic swirling around us and how it was used against us regularly. We saw how even our friends would change—literally—when their magic became stronger and stronger.

I refused to be afraid of what was around every corner. I refused to care about people I wasn't safe with. People who would eventually realize how minuscule we were, in the grand scheme of things, and leave us behind.

Our parents gave us the option of going to a boarding school instead of staying at home, and they were noticeably relieved when we chose to leave the magical world. So we found a boarding school we could attend together.

Liz and I loved it. It was thrilling to feel powerful for once.

We never fit in to the posh crowd, which was fine by me, but we had our own form of power. A power I quickly became addicted to.

Liz has a few entries about our first couple weeks in England. Being parted from our parents was hard on us both, but it was exciting to see the world and be out on our own.

Liz thrived on the attention. She had a group of girl-friends that followed her around like puppies, and boys treated her like royalty. We had our share of enemies, but I stood by my sister and protected her. Over and over.

And yeah, I may have brewed a potion or two in the middle of the night to enforce our reputation. It didn't take long for people to fear us.

During summers, we'd spend time with our parents abroad, instead of going home where we might be at risk. One summer, we went to Kenya, and last year, Indonesia. This summer we were supposed to go to Canada, but that never happened.

Neither of us had spent more than a week at our home since we left Myre Island.

Until this summer. I stayed longer in Detroit for an internship, and Liz went home three weeks sooner. In those weeks, I've learned from her journal, Liz met someone new.

A powerful supernatural that made her feel like she was "on fire with passion." Someone who could change the game for her.

Someone she never named.

Not to me, our parents, or in her journal.

Liz disappeared the day after I came home, and we didn't find her body until two weeks later—in the forest two miles from this campus.

Just like Liz, I feel like I'm on fire—except instead of passion, I'm burning with rage.

Clenching my jaw tight, I flip to her final journal entry. Because clearly, I'm a masochist.

JUNE 4TH

. . .

I'VE ALWAYS BELIEVED *what Candice told me—we'll never really belong in the supernatural world. Those creatures will never treat us like equals.*

We will always be at their mercy.

But I don't believe those things anymore.

I feel strong for the first time in my life. I feel in control.

He makes me feel that way. He lights me up from the inside and tells me tales of what we could be together. I love the sound of his voice and the vision he has for our future. Together, we can be powerful. His mark would lend me his strength and make me like him. We just have to wait for the right time, and then I'll be able to achieve all the things I was too afraid to wish for.

It won't be easy, I know. And my sister is only one obstacle, but I can't give this up. I won't.

He is my future.

He knows how to make me one of the most powerful creatures in this world. Able to make others bow down at my feet. I can feel it, stirring in my blood already. The truth.

I cannot wait to ascend.

xo Liz

I CLENCH MY JAW.

I cannot wait to ascend.

Those words grate against me. The anger is so palpable I feel like I could grow claws like a shifter and rip apart the world. My sister met a high-level supernatural who at least told her he *intended* to bond to her.

A marking, on a human, isn't usually permanent. It's a

temporary showing of belonging. It's one-part animalistic ownership and one-part protection. It gives them just a taste of magic and connects the two creatures while the mark remains.

Most humans, male or female, would love to be marked.

But that's not what my sister was talking about.

No, whoever she was dating—for *two weeks*—was promising to bond to her. Basically, the supernatural version of marriage, except worse. Bonds cannot be broken. It's a permanent combining of two souls. There are only three or four known species capable of such a bond with a human.

Nightshades, which are extremely rare, and none of them are within five hundred miles of us.

Demons from the royal line of Oriziah, like Jarron and Trevor.

And Sphinx, which haven't been seen on Earth for two centuries.

Which is why I'm almost certain my culprit is a demon.

A bonding like that can make a human supernatural. But they'll never be as powerful, like my sister seems to claim in her journal. *He knows how to make me one of the most powerful creatures in this world.*

He lied to her. I don't even know how he could have convinced her of this. We know very well that a bonding does not make the two parties equal. It's a small river of magic connecting the two. Small bits of magic. Bonding with an immensely powerful being like Jarron would have made her strong. Very strong, compared to a human. She could stand against a vampire, probably, but not a strong shifter or nearly any high fae.

She knew this. We were taught this many times.

So, what could he have said to make her believe otherwise? That, somehow, he could *ascend her*—a term usually only used by fanatic humans obsessed with magical beings. Fanatics that worship vampires and become their blood bags willingly just for the chance that they might be turned. Fanatics that follow fae around like groupies.

The term *ascend* implies supernaturals are a higher form of being. It implies everything I've always hated about the magical world.

They believe humans are a lesser form of being.

They believe magic makes them more worthy.

Screw that. And screw them for believing it.

I lie back in my bed and stare at the uneven beige ceiling. Whoever brainwashed my sister and then killed her is going to know what it feels like to be helpless. If it's the last thing I do.

8

THE RIGHT TOOLS

"*Potions*," the willowy professor drawls dramatically, "is an underrated portion of magic in this world. Hop across a portal to the Radial Plane and you'll find a society in which those gifted in potion making are regarded as spiritual leaders and even gifted by the gods."

I shift in my seat, inwardly groaning. Another day of sitting through dragged-out lectures. Every instructor feels the need to give an inspirational speech defending their passion for their subject.

This teacher is a witch, with tattoos all the way up her stick-thin arms and her hair twisted into an intricate updo of braids. The wall behind her is faux brick, covered in shelves stacked to the ceiling with jars of hundreds of different magical ingredients—some of them still living.

All right, so it's a little different from human school.

In a human school, I'd be wearing a white lab coat and eye protection. The walls would be solid white and the tables cold metal.

Here, I'm in a dark room instead of bright white, the tables are made of stone and our experiments are completed in copper cauldrons instead of beakers and Bunsen burners.

"There tends to be a fundamental misunderstanding of what potion making is," the teacher continues, pacing back and forth at the front of the room. "It is not only medicinal, and it is not only for the weak. The purpose is not to make up for some perceived lacking but to expand our understanding of how different forms of matter interact and how those interactions can be used to create great change."

She stops and whips around to face the class. "Potions is the breeding between art and science."

"And magic," someone mutters.

The teacher freezes, a horrified expression on her face. After a long, awkward beat, she begins a short walk down the aisle, passes my row, and stops next to a boy with thick arms and plump lips. "What did you want to add?" she asks softly.

He grimaces. "Nothing. Just—"

"Yes?"

"Potions is magic too. That's all."

"I see. Please defend your assertion."

The boy's eyebrows rise. "It's a form of magic?"

"Theoretically."

"You need magic to do it."

"Do you?" she asks. When the boy just stares helplessly, she continues, "Can someone with no magic brew a potion?"

"They need to use some kind of magic, right?"

"Do yourself a favor, boy. Next time, do not speak about what you know nothing of."

His shoulders slump, an annoyed frown on his lips.

The teacher marches back to the front of the class and selects three jars, placing them in a line on the table beside the smoking cauldrons. "These ingredients are Majoram, moss from the Twisted Forest, and ginger root. If I were to combine these three ingredients into a base of silver and water, brewed for three days, what would I create?"

I frown, considering the three ingredients. It would have to be a simple potion, but they're fairly potent ingredients. "A protection spell?" I ask.

"Yes. A spell that would rebound any offensive magic for several minutes."

That sounds impressive.

"Now, if I were to invite any human off the street and have them do the honors of combining and stirring the ingredients, what would happen?"

"Theoretically, it would turn out the same," I answer.

The teacher turns to face me and sets her hand on her hip. "How do you know?"

"Because I could complete that potion, and I have no magic."

There's a surprised gasp somewhere behind me.

"None at all?"

I shake my head. "Nothing usable."

She nods. "So, then, how can you create magic? A might protection potion?"

"Because the magic is in the ingredients."

"Correct!" she says loudly. "Any human is capable of completing most potions. There is certainly a level of talent and intuition involved in potion making, but that is not a form of magic we recognize. Potion making does not require magic. Magic is simply an ingredient in our experiments. So, let me ask this: if a potion requires no magic, is it easy?"

No one answers. We all know the answer is no. Potions is one of the hardest fields.

"Potions making is a form of magic that can change worlds, and yet anyone can learn it. It requires patience and dedication, a blend of intuition and knowledge. But even the weakest in magic can become powerful with time. Do not, I repeat, do *not* underestimate a talented potionist. Even a human can wreak magical havoc. You just need the tools and the desire to make your enemy burn."

9

THE PLOT TWIST I SHOULD HAVE
SEEN COMING

My lips part as I enter the lunchroom at the start of my second week. Something is very different. No pulsing magic pressing down on me. No intimidating beings sizing me up.

"Where is everyone?" I ask as we walk toward the front archways to grab our lunch. Half the tables are empty.

"Isn't it nice?" Lola exclaims, flutters through the air, her wings glowing slightly. "I love when the Elite give their big announcements during lunch period."

"Big announcements?"

"Yeah," Janet says. "The final inner circle is being announced."

Lola shrugs.

I twist my lips and follow Lola and Janet up to the bars of food and under the magical archway. I hold my breath as I pass under the spell revealer. Nothing happens. No zing or pulse of magic like in Minor Hall. Nothing at all.

"I thought they already had their lists up?" I ask as I browse the food options. I find the soup and rolls Stevie got

61

me yesterday, as well as a large option of salad and fruits. Grainy breads that shimmer silver—fae food, I assume. There's also a whole section of meats. Some are literally raw. Some steaming and brown.

"Yeah, I guess they're making a change."

"After a week?" I ask. "Talk about fickle."

They chuckle.

I grab a quarter rotisserie chicken and roasted potatoes. With no Elite around to make me nervous, I can eat a nice meal with no worries.

Maybe I should be at the announcement to get an idea of the social dynamics of my suspects, but this is too pleasant to miss. We take our seats at our usual table. Stevie, Romera, and even my roommate, Corrine, sit nearby, as well as a few other Minor Hall students I haven't met yet.

I enjoy my flavorful chicken and potatoes, and for a little bit, I can pretend everything is back to how it used to be. Liz is off with a boy somewhere, and we're at a regular school away from the politics and dangers of the supernatural world.

I have new friends, but that's a good thing. School is easy. I'm going to get into a great college to study politics and become someone important in the world.

That's it. That's the life I want.

I finish off my plate while Janet and Lola chatter about the school's drama. Corrine pipes in a few times, hinting about a boy who's apparently obsessed with her but only smirks when the others ask her any questions about him.

Janet eventually rolls her eyes and leans in to whisper, "She's probably making him up."

Belly full, I stretch and take another look around the

room. The lunch period is a full hour, and it doesn't take nearly that long to eat. I wonder what most students do with the rest of the time.

A crowd of whispering girls enters the lunchroom and sits with a group of Major students. They begin a frantic chatter, filled with joy and laughter. Someone got good news, I guess.

More students enter, a few obviously on the more powerful end. They ignore the lesser students.

"I'm gonna go grab my extra credit homework from the potions hall before it gets unruly in here," Lola says, buzzing up to hover in front of us.

"Okay, see you after classes," Janet chimes with a smile. Lola flutters away quickly.

"We should probably find something to do too. It'll get a little hectic in here soon, as the Superior and Elite students make their way back. There's always someone with hurt feelings, and they make it everyone else's problem."

I nod and follow. Most of the other Minor students have the same idea, and slowly, the weaker students filter out while the stronger students enter.

A tall and willowy blond girl marches past us. Her crystal blue eyes find me in the crowd and darken, a glare of utter hatred. *Okay?*

"What was that about?" Janet asks.

I shrug.

"That's her," someone whispers from a group of boys passing.

I stop walking, pulling Janet to a halt beside me.

"What the hell?" Janet mutters.

My mind jumps to my conversation with Jarron then to the announcement that just happened. My stomach sinks.

"Oh no." I rush forward, hoping I'm wrong. I had not even remotely considered this, and I should have. Dammit, I should have realized.

"What?" she squeals, skipping to keep up with me.

I practically drag her all the way down the hall until we reach the chattering crowd standing by the list of the demon royals' chosen inner circle. The framed lists are too far for us to read from here.

"Congratulations."

I twist to face Bea, Trevor's girlfriend. Her arms are crossed, and her smile is smug.

"Congratulations for what?" Janet whispers urgently.

"You thought she'd stay in Minor Hall, didn't you?" Bea says sweetly to Janet. "You thought you had another outcast for your dwindling friend group. That's sweet."

Janet tenses. Her arm is still wrapped in mine, but her face is slack, eyes big.

"I'm not leaving Minor Hall," I say, voice low. I squeeze Janet's arm.

Bea's eyebrows rise. "Why would you stay in Minor Hall if you're part of the inner circle? No one has ever done that."

I frown, too shocked by her words to respond.

"Holy. Crap," Janet exclaims, her voice only barely over a whisper now.

I pull her farther into the crowd; I need to see the names. Need to see this for myself.

"He named you part of his inner circle," Janet says flatly, and I know she's trying to hold back her emotions. "I *knew* there was more there than you let on."

I swallow. The words are too small to make out. The calligraphy is obnoxiously detailed, making it even harder.

Finally, I'm able to read Jarron's list. The bottom name is not mine. I swallow. The next name is not mine.

"Oh my God. He put you first."

I cling to Janet as tightly as I can manage, my fingers digging into her forearm. It must hurt, but she doesn't react. I swear my knees might buckle here and now. Finally, I find my name.

In the first spot. ***Candice Montgomery***

Honestly, I'm more mad at myself. I should have realized. Should have seen this coming. Jarron knows I need to get into Elite Hall. He told me he'd get me in. Of course he'd add me to his list. He has three people he can name that will get special treatment just for befriending him.

A shadow falls over me, and everything goes quiet. I clench my hands into fists as I force myself to face the powerful demon breathing down my neck.

"Hello, sunshine."

The gaze of dozens of supernatural beings weighs down on me, making it hard to breathe.

A dimple appears on Jarron's right cheek alongside a crooked grin. "Would you like to go somewhere to chat?" His voice is so low it's a near rumble. He peers down at me through long lashes, hands in his pockets as if he were completely at ease.

It gets under my skin.

There are still hushed whispers, but those nearest lean in, listening closely. I glare at a few students that step in closer to us. "Somewhere else would be good." I turn quickly to Janet. "I don't know what is happening, but I have to..."

"Right." She forces a smile, her eyes unfocused. "Sure, yeah, go talk." She shakes her head. "My god. You're going to talk to the *heir of the Under World* alone." She blinks rapidly like reality is just catching up to her.

I've known her for barely more than twenty-four hours, so I find it surprising how much I care what she thinks. I care how she feels. I want to explain this to her. I want her to know that whatever is happening here was not my plan nor my desire. I want to stay with her and the other outcasts in Minor Hall. But I have to do this.

"Are you going to be okay?" she asks, her eyebrows pulling down.

I press my lips into a thin line, unsure how to answer that question. Will I be okay? Am I safe with Jarron? Honestly, I don't know. But I'm going to have to pretend. Because if I want to play this game, it's going to get dangerous.

I nod quickly. Then, on a whim, I pull her into my arms for a tight hug. "Thank you for caring and for being my friend so quickly. It's not going to stop because of," I pull back and wave vaguely, "whatever this is."

"Okay," she whispers. Then, I turn and follow the demon prince down the hall while the crowd quietly observes.

10

YOU REALLY DO THINK I'M A MONSTER, DON'T YOU?

I CROSS my arms and keep my back to the entrance of the room until I hear the door click behind me. Jarron moves so quietly I can't even tell he's here until his shadow settles over me.

"I'm not moving to Elite Hall," I whisper, then I force myself to face him. His eyes are so soft it disarms me for a moment. Then, I pull in a deep breath and channel my anger. My determination. *Don't let him get under your skin.*

"You don't have to," he says, eyes still searching my face with quiet awe. I look over his shoulder just to stop examining every inch of his ridiculously beautiful face.

"Are they even going to believe it?" I ask quickly. "I get the reasoning. I need to get into Elite Hall, and this will give me access to... probably everything. But is it necessary? The first spot? Will people even believe it? Why would you or anyone else add me—a human, one that's not even that pretty—to their inner circle?"

Jarron frowns. "One, you are beautiful. And two, there

67

are many reasons to add someone to an inner circle. Power and prestige are not the only reasons."

Sure, I'm decent by human standards, but by theirs? Fat chance. "What do I have that you'd want?"

One of Jarron's brows flicks up, and his lips curve into a grin. "You'd be surprised."

I roll my eyes but turn away to hide my reddening cheeks. I'm certainly not used to Jarron flirting with me. Not like this anyway. He was fairly shy when we were friends.

He's obviously changed quite a bit.

Jarron rolls his shoulders. "No one will question you being in my inner circle... if we're dating." His tone is so calm, his words so matter of fact, for a moment they do not compute in my mind.

My blood turns cold as the reality of what he'd suggested finally settles. "Dating," I repeat flatly, barely hearing the word.

"You do know the meaning of the word, yes?"

I whip my attention back to him, anger settling my mind. "Don't be a jerk."

His smile grows. "That, I cannot promise."

"You're going to pretend to date me so I can investigate my sister's death?"

"Yes." He puts his hands in his pockets casually. Hell, he looks good in his dress clothes. He's wearing black slacks and a white button up shirt under a grey vest. His sleeves are rolled up casually—why are guys' forearms so attractive?

He wears an expression so damn smug it's giving me a stomachache.

I bite the inside of my cheek. This is not at all what I'd expected, and I'm not sure what to think about it. On the one hand, it'll work. I'll have the chance to get all kinds of close with my potential suspects, including Jarron. And being part of the in-crowd could even draw the killer to me. But is that a good thing? Yes and no. I'm going to have to be prepared at all times.

And it will be extremely awkward to pretend to date someone I'm *not* interested in. Someone I can't get close to.

I'll have to keep two secrets from Jarron, all while pretending to date him.

First, that he's my number one suspect in my sister's murder.

Second, that I'm utterly terrified of him.

"Why?" I ask. "Why would you do that?"

That's how my sister's murderer got to her, isn't it? Wooed her and promised to make her powerful.

"Many reasons. But most of all, I want to help you. If someone in this school killed a person I care about, I will destroy them."

Care about. He hasn't seen my sister in three years. "You cared about Elizabeth?" I ask dubiously. Unless he has seen her recently.

For the first time, Jarron's smile slips. He pauses this time, watching me with haunted eyes as dark as the Under World. "You really do think I'm a monster, don't you?"

My lips part, but Jarron leaves without waiting for a response. He walks from the room quietly. We both know the answer to that question.

II

DATING A DEMON WAS NOT PART OF THE PLAN

"Oh my God!" A tiny body and fluttering wings slam into my chest. "Is it true? I haven't gone to look myself. Are you part of Jarron's inner circle?" Lola asks frantically.

I sigh. "Yeah, I guess I am." More lying. I'm not ready for it. I was hoping this would be my refuge. Instead, I have to keep this ridiculous mask up at all times.

Janet separates from me and stands quietly, watching with concern. "What happened?"

I press my lips together. "Well, you were right. He's—" I really don't know how to do this. God, this is embarrassing. "He wants to date me." I'm dizzy the moment the words leave my lips.

"OMG, are you going to faint?"

My eyelids flutter. "I think I need to sit down."

Janet hooks her arm in mine and guides me to the common room, and the three of us flop down onto one of the uneven couches.

"Do you need water?" Lola asks.

I try to swallow, but my mouth and throat are dry. I wince.

"Water coming up!" Lola says and flies off around the corner.

I press my palms to my eyes. And try to force my body to calm. Dating Jarron, the demon prince. My once friend and possibly my sister's murderer.

"I guess it was wishful thinking," Janet murmurs, looking off to the other side of the room.

"What?" I whisper.

"That we'd get another Minor lifer to hang with. There's only five of us, you know that? Five seniors still in Minor Hall. Every cool new person that shows up leaves us behind and never looks back."

I purse my lips.

"I mean, I'm happy for you and all. It's just…"

I nod. "It's the outcast hall. It's only fun when there's someone else to share it with."

She gives me a sad smile.

I squeeze her hand. "I know you don't believe me, but I really do not intend to leave Minor Hall. I like it here. I feel safe, and I need that. Especially if I'm going to be spending time in Elite Hall. And I like you. You and Lola. My first day would have been literal hell without you. I want to be your friend. Even if… even if…" I swallow, unable to finish the sentence.

"You're dating a literal prince?"

"A *demon* prince."

Grunting grabs our attention, and Janet and I both turn to find little Lola carrying a water bottle larger than her entire body by the bottle cap, wobbling to and fro as her little wings struggle to keep them in the air. "Here I come!" she squeaks.

I snort a laugh and reach out to take it from her gently. "Thank you."

Lola drops to the couch, panting heavily. "You're. Welcome," she says between breaths.

I take a sip. Cool water soothes my throat and eases the tension in my chest.

"So, tell us again how you don't know Jarron that well?"

I allow a small smile. "Okay, yeah, I knew him. But I didn't—" I look up at the mismatched glass above our heads. "My sister had a crush on him, so it's really weird to think he'd be into me now."

"Oh, yeah. I could see that."

"But also, you don't say no to him," Lola adds. "He's like drool worthy hot."

My heart clenches. "He is quite attractive." To be honest, that's part of the problem.

Jarron is model hot. I've never put a lot of stock in what I look like. I'm vaguely attractive by human standards. It never mattered to me that I wasn't the turn-heads kind of beautiful like my sister.

But going to school here is like living in L.A. When you're surrounded by models, singers, and actresses, it's hard to feel beautiful.

Still, that wouldn't bother me if dating the hottest guy in school wouldn't put a microscope on me. Half the whispers will be jealous complaints of how Jarron couldn't possibly be into me when there are dozens of incredibly gorgeous options not only ready but eager to jump his bones.

"So, you were friends before," Lola prompts. "Like how close? Tell us about it."

"Like childhood best friends. We explored the island together and caught lightning sprites by the fae portals. He led me through a pretty deep cave one time, and we found this super cool underground waterfall. It was... it was really amazing."

"That sounds romantic," Janet says, wiggling her brows. Lola's body shimmers purple.

"It wasn't. Not really. I was thirteen, and we didn't—well, *I* didn't think of it that way."

"Maybe he was trying to woo you even then."

I laugh. "Yeah, I don't think so. I don't know when—" I shake my head. It doesn't matter because it's not real. None of it is real.

And to be perfectly honest, there is a very real possibility that Jarron wants to pretend to date me so he can kill me the way he killed my sister.

You really do think I'm a monster, don't you?

I want to believe in Jarron. I really do want to believe that he could remain good. That he could still be the boy I cared about. That I shared my secrets with.

The sad look in his eyes from today will haunt me for a while.

I just can't let those hopes and that guilt overrule my better judgement. There's a chance—a small one—that he could be the sweet boy I knew, and there's also a chance—a good one—that he really is a monster.

I2

IF A DEMON MUST PUBLICLY CLAIM YOU, FLOWERS AREN'T THE WORST OPTION

A GENTLE KNOCK on my door drags me from a restless sleep.

My limbs are stiff and heavy as I twist in the small, lumpy bed. I groan and turn over, hiding from the early morning light streaming through the window, despite the curtains being drawn tight. Leave it to Minor Hall to get paper-thin curtains. It's not like any vampires would be in this hall.

"What was that?" Corrine, my roommate, asks, her voice much more chipper than anyone should be at first light.

I groan. "Don't know. Don't care." The clock says it's 7:15 a.m. I do not intend to get my sorry butt out of this bed until precisely 8:15 a.m. Fifteen minutes before my first class.

The knock is louder the second time. "Delivery!" a voice calls.

"Delivery?" Corrine squeals. She hops up to open the door and squeals again at the sight of a massive bouquet of calla lilies so dark they look black at first glance but are really shades of purple and red. "Ohmegod!" She lifts the flowers by the vase. The petals loom over her head, getting stuck in strings of her hair.

A few students crowd our doorway from the hall. Apparently, the delivery, even this early in the morning, caught some people's attention.

"Who the hell would send you flowers?" I grumble, wiping the sleep from my eyes. I don't think I'll be getting any more sleep this morning. A fact I am not remotely happy about.

"Not me," Corrine says. "You."

After a pause, where my brain shuts down and reboots, I throw my hands over my face. *Dammit.* The events of yesterday come crashing back down on me. *I'm fake-dating the demon prince. Right.*

"Candice," she reads the card, slow and sultry. "I feel like the luckiest person alive that I get a second chance at getting to know you. I'll be saving you a seat at lunch. Love, Jarron."

More squeals. This time, Corrine is not alone; several of the students in the hall are swooning with her. People I don't even know.

God, why did he have to make a spectacle?

I groan. I know why. Because in the supernatural world, you show your intentions openly. Everyone knows who you belong to. He's claiming me as his in the most human way he can manage. The other options are more *barbaric.*

He must know they'd go over very badly with me if he tried. There will be no marks left on my body, permanent or not.

I get up and slam the door on the gawking onlookers and then curl back up into bed, pretending this didn't just happen.

Corrine slips from the room without another word, probably to go gossip with the other students. Curled up in the fetal position, I weigh my options. I could go out there now, deal with the barrage of attention that's going to come at me no matter what I do and at least get some breakfast and maybe a cup of coffee before classes start. Or I could hide away in here, mind spinning through all the unpleasant things of the past and present. I'll be anxious and angry by the time I get up and get to class, but at least I'll have forty-five less minutes of attention to deal with.

It's tempting, but it's another thing that has power over me. I won't let it. So, I'll take the high road and reclaim every bit of power I may wield.

I toss my blanket back before I change my mind and dress quickly. I throw some product into my hair but don't bother with make-up. I could spend hours perfecting my appearance, but I'd still be lackluster compared to the others, especially the Elite girls.

I refocus my mind, then I exit my bedroom. There are still a few students whispering in the hall, who freeze and stare wide-eyed as I march past, but the rest have dispersed.

I enter the Minor food hall and more silence greets me, despite the fact that there are nearly fifty beings watching me. I ignore the looks and walk up to the warming trays full of meats and eggs. There are also two platters, one filled with pastries and another of fruits.

I fill my plate to overflowing. One, I'm hungry. Two,

breakfast is my favorite. Three, if I'm expected to sit with the Elite, I doubt I'll eat even a bite for lunch.

"When do you think she'll move out?" someone whispers nearby.

"Today, probably."

"I dunno, she might stay here. If he drops her in a week, what's the point in going through all the trouble?"

My stomach gives an anxious squeeze at that, which is exceptionally stupid. We're not even really together; of course he's going to drop me.

"Candice!" a sweet voice calls, and I whip my attention to a tiny pixie waving at me from the far table. I smile and head her way. Janet is there too, her head still low.

"We heard about the flowers," Lola purrs. "It's so swoon worthy."

I force a smile, but it's stiff. "Still not sure what to think about it all."

"You'll still be our friend, right?" Lola asks.

"Of course! Honestly don't expect it to last long anyway. We—we're not really compatible."

Lola shrugs, her curls bouncing, then takes a bite of her tiny muffin. Crumbs fall to the table as she mumbles, "Lots of humans have relationships with sups."

I quirk a brow, and then I begin to shovel food into my mouth. Janet watches my sloppy performance, and her lips curl into a smile. "Lola's right. It can happen."

I shrug. "Just not getting my hopes up. Not sure the Under World will be thrilled to have me as a queen."

"Maybe not at first, but if you were to be mated, you'd gain magic."

"Some, but not a lot. And they'd be mad 'cause it would

make him weaker." I hold up my hand. "*Way* too soon to be talking about this stuff. It's a long shot. I'm not getting my hopes up. The end." I wouldn't want that anyway. Even if Jarron's and my relationship were real—which it's not—and even if by some miracle we fell deeply in love and stayed together through all the ups and downs and we mated and married, I'd still be the weakest of them all. Stronger than a human, weaker than a demon. It's not enough to take away that icky feeling of being vulnerable at all moments of the day.

We finish off our breakfasts in silence, and I work to ignore the whispers still floating around me.

"Jarron's note," Janet and Lola lean in as if I'm about to spill some big secret, "said he'd be holding me a seat at lunch. Which I guess means I'm going to have to ditch you guys."

Janet looks down at her plate to hide a frown.

"Are you afraid?" Lola asks.

"Terrified." Sitting with Jarron will mean sitting with all the top Elites. At least three demons and several other massively powerful supernatural students will all be there.

"You'll be fine." Lola hops onto my shoulder.

"Yeah, Jarron would kill anyone who even thought about hurting you," Janet says.

I grimace.

"I mean it. Even though I'm pretty sure you're under-valuing his feelings for you, even if it wasn't that big of a deal to him, by pure pride alone, he'd have to make sure no one impedes on his territory."

"Great, a supernatural pissing match in my honor. That'll be great."

"Whatever you want to call it, it'll keep you safe."

"Yeah, from everyone except Jarron."

13

THE MOST POWERFUL HAVE NO RULES—AND THAT'S EXACTLY THE PROBLEM

ALL DAY, people gawk at me. Between classes, I simply hold my books tightly against my chest, focused straight ahead. *Ignore the whispers. Ignore the sneers.*

Lola eats up every second of the attention. Janet is quiet.

She doesn't believe I'm not going to leave them, but she remains by my side. I guess it'll just take time to convince her to trust me.

I walk into the cafeteria, and it feels like everyone is watching. The room stills, waiting. My heart thunders in my chest, cheeks warming.

I'm so not ready for this.

But this is my chance to solidify my place with the Elites so I can find the killer. I'm a spy. Playing a part. The demon prince's girlfriend. I don't know how to play that part, but I suppose it doesn't matter. I just have to keep my head up and pretend not to be disgusted by the Elites.

No problem.

"You got this," Lola says, holding her tiny fist out. I smile and fist bump the pixie as gently as possible.

"Good luck," Janet whispers.

"Thanks. I'll see you guys for dinner tonight. In Minor Hall."

"You sure?" Lola asks. "He might want you to go to Elite Hall for—"

"Don't care." Lunch is all I have in me for today. "I'll be back to hang with you guys after class. Promise."

"If you say so," Lola says, fluttering in front of my face. Then, she twirls away, dancing with all attention on her. That is, until I take my first step forward.

I walk with my chin high, toward the demon prince, whose eyes are just for me. His expression is unreadable. As I approach, he stands slowly, carefully, like he's taking care not to spook me. I would never admit that I appreciate it.

He pulls out the chair next to him, and the breath sticks in my lungs.

I release it as I take the seat.

"Welcome." Jarron's chest is puffed out. He's proud to share his friends, his place, I guess? I look around, and all I see are narrowed, glowing eyes and grim expressions.

Powerful beings sizing up their newest rival.

"It's about time Jarron gets a girl," Trevor says with a wink.

I glare at him. At least Trevor, I know. His words seem to break the ice with the table of high-level supernaturals.

"We always welcome a little extra beauty in our circle," says a boy with silver eyes and a big grin. He's the only person at the table that seems at ease. "Helps to offset the grisly beasts we spend our time with." He nudges a demon with short red horns next to him.

"Uh, thanks?"

"Get used to the compliments," a girl with dark hair says. "Stassi's shameless flattery has no end."

"It's his best quality." The blond I recognize from yesterday beams at him.

Stassi winks at her. She shifts her gaze back to me, and her frosty blue eyes instantly harden. *Would ya look at that? Looks like I have a new president of my fan club.*

"So, is it true?" the girl says, barely hiding disgust. "Are you really dating?" One of her brows flick. I note her pointed ears. The fae princess from the Frost Court I've heard about, I presume.

I can't help but notice her perfect body, but I don't let them linger because I don't want to be creepy. She's wearing a tight, light blue shirt covered in clear gemstones. Gemstones are her worlds currency, meaning she may as well be wearing diamond-covered clothes.

Her blond hair is in perfect ringlets.

"Do you have a problem with that, Aurie?" Jarron says, his voice near a rumble.

Another girl down the table chuckles. Her skin is darker, with sharp features and plump lips. She has tattoos circling her wrist, which marks her as a witch. Her smile, though seemingly sincere, exposes sharp canines. I'm not sure what order she's mixed with, but she's certainly no ordinary witch.

She's not particularly feminine—in fact, she's wearing slacks instead of skirts like the rest of us—but she's still beautiful enough that I have a hard time looking away.

These girls are exactly the kind of females the realms would expect Jarron to go for. Stunning and powerful. The kind of girls that probably expect to woo him eventually.

The demon royals have always been known to be open in their mate choosing—even a weak human is a possibility. But every prince is strongly encouraged to marry powerful to increase the magic in their line, or at the very least, not dilute it.

So, though he's technically allowed, no one would be particularly pleased if Prince Jarron bonded to a human.

Trevor sits with Bea at the end of the table. There are two other demons between the demon princes. One male, one female. On the other end of the table are three more silver-eyed jock-type boys. Wolf shifters.

"Of course not. Just want to know where we stand." Aurie smiles, her frosty gaze turns to me. "We are the most powerful students in the school. With us, there are no rules."

My eyebrows rise. I don't tell her that that's exactly what I'm afraid of.

"Need anything, just say the word," the fae brunette says.

I don't respond, partly because there isn't anything I could ask for. The only thing I want is my sister's killer in the ground, but that has to stay a secret for now.

"She's like a deer among wolves," someone mutters, and I suck in a breath. Do I look that out of place? I'm trying to keep my heart-rate under control, my expression calm, but I don't seem to be succeeding.

"Like a deer in headlights." Someone laughs.

My chest tightens. Jarron slings an arm over the back of

my chair and releases a low rumble from his chest. "Careful," he says, so low it sends a shiver down my back.

The others exchange looks. Dubious and amused. They don't expect me to last. I shouldn't be annoyed by that. Unlike what Lola said earlier, humans don't usually last long in relationships with strong supernaturals. The humans either die, skimp off out of fear, or the supernatural simply gets bored and drifts toward someone more like them.

There are a few success stories, but they're the exception, not the rule.

Good thing I don't intend to stick around long either. Just long enough to figure out which one of them killed my sister.

My gaze turns sharper as I examine them each as suspects. I will not be another victim. They don't know it, but I'm not a doe. I intend to bite back.

"This is my brother," Aurie says, nodding to one of the boys I'd assumed was a wolf shifter. On closer inspection, his glowing stare and pointed ears. He's fae.

"We're Frost Court royalty."

"Congratulations," I mutter. Auren squints momentarily, but then her expression smooths into one of casual confidence.

"So, Candice, what's your story?" one of the shifters asks, a built male with dark skin.

I shrug.

"Her parents are potions masters," Jarron answers for me. "The Montgomerys. Ever heard of them?"

The shifter's sucks in a breath. "Everyone's heard of them."

"Our parents go way back," I answer awkwardly. There, at least I've said something.

"That, they do," Trevor adds.

"Ohhh! That's who you are," Bea adds, her bright red lips pouting slightly. "I can't believe it took me that long to figure it out!"

I grimace.

"It's been three years, Bea," Trevor says, "She hasn't changed that much."

Bea shrugs. "I just forgot she existed." Even back then, Trevor and Bea were joined at the hip. Childhood arranged marriage that's turned out quite well.

I snort, and Jarron glares at her. "At least she's honest," I mutter.

Jarron leans in close. "She most definitely did not forget you existed," he whispers, low enough for the others not to hear.

I frown. Does that mean he thinks she could be a suspect? My sister's journal makes it clear it was a male she was dating, but what if she were seeing Trevor behind Bea's back? That would explain why she was so secretive. Bea could have discovered them and killed her out of jealousy. It's a pretty decent motive.

It also makes me turn my attention a little tighter to the girls in front of me. They're still eyeing me like a piece of meat they intend to devour.

I know essentially nothing about these supernaturals. I'm going to have to dig to find out their stories. Each and every one. What do they want? What are their goals? Who are their allies? Their targets?

I mentally note that for my first project. I'll ask Jarron,

Janet, and Lola about these students. I'll have to dig into the drama and rumors and history between all of them. That way, when I do get a break in my case, I'll have the context I'll need.

I like this plan because it means I can lay low for a bit while I uncover what I can.

My hammering heart tells me I'm a coward, but my mind tells me it's logical and fits my story anyway. I'll be the scared human crushing on the impressive demon prince.

I'll have to deal with some alone time with Jarron still, of course, but that's survivable.

I think.

It's the longest half hour of my life, sitting at this table surrounded by beings who could not only end my life with a flick of their wrist and half a thought but would enjoy doing it.

"Do you want to go for a walk?" Jarron finally asks, his voice smooth and casual.

I barely restrain an audible sigh of relief. I thought I was going to be stuck here for the rest of the lunch hour. My nod is slow.

The room seems to hush as Jarron rises and holds out his hand for me.

My stomach flips, the moment I slide my hand against his smooth skin. Hundreds of stares follow our stroll out of the room.

The moment we're out of the cafeteria, Jarron drops my hand.

"Outside?" he asks.

I cross my arms and nod. It's still pretty warm out, even here in Idaho, but it won't stay that way long. Snow could be on the horizon at any moment.

The sky is a soft blue, and the green-covered mountains tower over the valley. We're in the middle of nowhere out here.

We exit the school and pass under a covered walkway with glass shading the stones. Protection from the sun for any Under Worlders.

The breeze tosses my hair back. To our left is a large window leading right to the cafeteria. Meaning those hundreds of students are still watching, some of them pressed right up to the glass.

I groan, and Jarron chuckles.

"You'll get used to it."

"Kinda doubt that."

His smile slips. "Do you hate it here that much?"

We walk down a trail leading to a small garden, and soon, I can no longer feel the eyes boring into my back. "Kinda," I admit.

He's quiet for a few more minutes. We pass under a white willow, and my fingers graze the glossy leaves.

"You could leave if you want. I'll find her killer and make them pay. I promise."

I snort. "I'm not leaving."

He nods. "Didn't think so. Figured I'd offer anyway."

I look up into the leaves above. Though there's a glass dome above the garden, it doesn't feel like it. The breeze still blows, the sun still warms my skin. It's pretty here.

"We should..." He rocks back on his heels. "Maybe talk

about the logistics." He leans against the bark of the large tree, again with his hands in his damn pockets.

"Like?"

"Well, if we're dating, there's going to be expectations."

I nod. Rules. Boundaries. I like that idea. "Okay. What did you have in mind?"

"You should eat lunch with us and spend at least an hour in Elite Hall after classes every day."

"No."

His eyebrows rise. "No?"

"No, I'm not coming to Elite Hall every day. I'll give you lunch. And I get that I'll have to come to Elite Hall sometimes, but not every day."

"So, how often? Three days a week?"

I pause to consider then tentatively nod.

"And one weekend night. Two hours minimum."

"What?" I squeak.

"It'll be expected of a dating couple. To be honest, that is a modest amount of time. Those two hours can be spent in public, the library, or my room."

I cough. His room? *What the hell am I getting myself into?* I close my eyes and let the smell of lavender ease my anxiety.

"You have control over this Candice. If you want to back away from this plan, we can. It'll be harder, but I fully intend to get to the bottom of it. If you want to be in Elite Hall to be part of the investigation—"

"Yes, I want to be part of it. It's just—" I'm not going to get into this with him. Not now. "I'll just need a little time to adjust. This first week, let's take it easy. I'll sit with you at lunch and spend one hour in Elite Hall. To be determined."

"Deal. Let's plan on Saturday. We can take a trip into the Forest of Nails if you want. Do a little digging there. Only if you want."

My stomach twists, gazes cast to the ground. The Forest of Nails is where my sister died. He wants to check out the scene, I guess.

And yet, the idea of going into the forest alone with him seems like an unwise choice. "No, I don't think so."

There, I'll leave it at that and hope he assumes I'm just nervous about facing my sister's place of death. Which I am. But that's not the reason I don't want to go.

He examines me for a beat and then nods. "Have you seen…" He trails off, brow furrowing.

"What?"

"The autopsy?" he asks gently.

I swallow. "It's confidential. My parents wouldn't tell me anything about it either."

Jarron nods. "I'll look into it. What else made you decide it was someone here?"

"Her journal. And a half-completed application for admission here."

His eyes narrow. "She didn't want anything to do with supernaturals either."

"No, she didn't."

"Anything else I should know? That's enough for me to get started, but if there's anything else that can lead me in the right direction…"

I shake my head. I wouldn't share anything else with him even if I had it. Jarron seems to get that I don't fully trust him. He knows that just because I'm here, doesn't mean I'm all of a sudden team-demon. He's a means to an end, and I'm—

I don't know what I am to him. But I suppose I'll figure that out eventually. For better or worse.

14

DEAR DIARY

A DAY *in the life of a demon prince's girlfriend: Wake with a pounding headache, my dead sister's journal still clutched in my hands. Shovel food into my mouth while my peers stare mercilessly. Listen to rumors and assumptions and criticism constantly.*

"She literally has zero magic; how is she even at this school?"

"Ew, she thinks she's better than us, doesn't she? No magic but a prince likes her tits and her parents have money, so clearly she's superior."

"She's such a pick-me."

Go to class and try to pretend those words don't get under my skin. Focus on studying, even though the subjects are simple and the tasks too easy.

Sit among predators during lunch and don't eat a bite because my stomach is in knots while they slide in veiled threats and insults like I'm too dim to understand.

"Humans have the softest skin. Delicious."

"Nah, she's not my type. I don't have a thing for little girls with big doe eyes and not a thought in their head."

"Helplessness is sexy, didn't you know?"

Chide myself for how unsafe I am. How terrified I am of being alone with him.

Spend every moment terrified he'll kill me the way he killed her.

Hide away in Minor Hall with my only two actual friends, watching movies and taking notes in my journal, while the rest of Minor Hall avoids me like the plague. Reread my sister's last few journal entries and contemplate all the things I did wrong.

"Did she resent me for pushing her out of the supernatural world?"

"If I hadn't taken that internship, would she have told me about her boyfriend? Would I have noticed the signs?"

"Did I put her down too much? Suck away her confidence in her own strength and leave her vulnerable to the first predator to walk into her life with the promise of power?"

Fall asleep after hours of torturing myself.

Wake with a pounding headache and do it all over again.

15

EVERYTHING IS A COMPETITION HERE, EVEN FRIENDSHIP

"You okay? You look so stressed out."

I glance up to Janet and Lola watching me, concerned expressions etched onto their faces. We're sitting in the game room because it's the only place I don't get bothered by the whispers. Janet and Lola are doing their homework, but mine was done before I even left class, so I flip through my nearly empty purple journal, pondering all my life choices.

"Yeah, I'm good," I answer quickly and then wrack my brain for an excuse. I should be deliriously happy, right? Dating a prince they all think I actually like. Meanwhile, I'm wondering if he'll drain my blood the moment I let him corner me. "All the whispers and stares have been getting under my skin." There. That's true and understandable.

I only have to waste another hour or so before I can excuse myself to hide away in my room and obsess over my sister's journal some more. Fun.

"Yeah, people are so annoying," Lola says with a tinkle. "Like, get over it already."

"It's only been a few days. People here live for drama, and you're just the 'it thing' right now."

I nod absently and flip another page. Once I saw that Liz had been using the journal our parents gifted us, I dug through my drawers and found my own. I'll need somewhere to write my notes about my investigation, why not the forgotten purple leather monstrosity? It feels symbolic, somehow. My sister kept her secrets in her journal. I'm going to expose them in mine.

Her secrets put her in the grave, and my research will bring her to justice.

"Hey, I could use your help with something," I blurt out to my new friends.

"Of course. Anything," Janet says.

"I feel super out of sorts here. I don't know much of anything about the Elite I sit with at lunch. Could you help me get the lay of the land? Spill the tea about the powerful people?" *Did that sound casual enough?*

Lola squeals. I blink back my surprise, and flinch as she flutters up into my face.

"You're speaking Lola's language." Janet chuckles. Then, she reaches out and lifts her palm until she's gently lifted Lola out of my face.

"Yeah, sorry. You said spill the tea, and I just couldn't contain my excitement." She tinkles again, purple sparks of magic fluttering down to the table.

"So, what do you want to know?" Janet asks, shutting her charms workbook and sliding it away.

"Uh, could you give me a rundown of the Elites I sit

with? Oh! What do you know about Jarron's inner circle? No one has really talked much about that." I should know who else was on the list, right? I didn't even pay attention to the names below mine. They could be anyone.

"Yes!" Janet says. "So, Stassi and Laithe are the two others on the list."

"You bumped Manuela off," Lola says excitedly.

"Manuela?" I think back to the scary witch from lunch. I liked her. She's intimidating, but she didn't give off 'I'd like to kill you' vibes like some of the others.

"Yep, she's a badass witch with dryad blood."

I blink. "Dryad? Really?"

Lola flutters her wings, and I'm guessing that means yes. I knew she was something more than witch, but I wouldn't have guessed dryad. They're incredibly rare.

"She's dating a wolf shifter, but they're really low key. I don't know of any big drama involving her other than that. They've been on-off for a couple years."

"Stassi," I say, thinking through the other two names she said. "That's the flirty wolf shifter?"

Lola nods. "Oh, yes! I love him. He's so sweet." Her cheeks glow purple. Is that a pixie blush? I resist the urge to grin at her.

Stassi is very complimentary. I suppose a lot of girls like that.

"He's super funny too."

He didn't seem like the kind of person Jarron would want to spend time with, given how reserved he seems to be.

"Stassi has had several big romances; most have ended badly."

I twist my lips. A shifter can't bond to a human, promising them power. They can mate with humans, but not in the same way. The human stays a human.

"And the other one in his inner circle?"

"Laithe. He's some sort of lesser demon. I don't know the specific species, but he's linked with Jarron magically."

"Linked magically?"

"Kind of like a platonic bond? I don't know much about it, but Laithe is only here because of Jarron. He's basically sworn to protect him. They're very close."

Interesting.

"He doesn't have any drama either. Laithe is reserved like Jarron. They keep to themselves."

"Others at the table—well, there's Auren, the fae princess. She's nice, but she's been trying to seduce Jarron for years."

Nice? I'm not so sure about that assessment. I'm not surprised, however, to hear she's been pursuing the highly sought after demon prince.

"And her best friend, Mia, is fae too, but not royalty. They have drama galore. We could talk for days about those two and their conquests."

"Another time." I chuckle. "Anything I should know about the shifters? There are tons of them, and they don't seem all that friendly."

"Oh, yeah. They tend to be super territorial and even controlling sometimes. There are three different packs here. You'll notice who groups together with whom. Males do not intermix with males from other packs."

"Well, except the occasional hook up." Lola tinkles a laugh.

"Sure, but in general, the conflicting packs do not get along. Never get between their scuffles."

Like I'd ever be stupid enough to do that.

"Most of the shifters at your table are from the Silverback pack in northern Montana. The one with the head alpha."

I nod. That's the most powerful pack in the world right now since their alpha got universal status—meaning he is the alpha over all the other alphas. That status can change at any time, though. Power changes are frequent in the shifter community.

Lola flutters over and lands on my shoulder. "The wolves won't bother you while you're with Jarron. It's the girls you have to watch out for. If things don't work out with Jarron, that's when you should be wary of the shifters."

I sigh.

"Well, not only girls. Just mostly."

"Everything with the Elite is about competition," Janet explains. "They all vie for more influence by getting close to the strongest, like Jarron. The wolf shifters all want a powerful female for a mate, so they're all pursuing Auren because she's the strongest female in school—aside from Bea, maybe. You know about Bea, right? She's basically already married to Trevor, Jarron's brother."

"Yeah, I'm well aware of that stuff."

They nod. "Jarron's the biggest target, for sure. The girls all want to get close to him, and definitely a few boys do too. But no one has ever really been successful. He's always been so cold to everyone. That's why your relationship is so shocking. You're the first person he's shown any real emotion toward."

I bite my lip. "Thanks. That's a lot of information. It'll help me a lot." I force a smile and stand. "I'm gonna head to bed." While all of this is still fresh in my mind and I can scribble a bunch of notes into my research journal.

"But I have so much more drama to tell you about!"

I laugh. "I'll take all the drama. But give it to me in bits, please."

"Oh, fine!" Lola sighs and slumps down to the tabletop.

"See you in the morning?" Janet smiles.

"Definitely. Tomorrow, I'm supposed to spend the day with Jarron in Elite Hall." I give them an exaggerated grimace.

"So exciting! You'll have to tell us all about it."

"Do you think they'd let you take pictures?" Lola says with a laugh.

I chuckle and bid them goodnight. I don't let myself dwell too much on what Saturday will be like. I thought entering the school was like walking into hell. Walking into Elite Hall will be like entering the devil's den.

16

THE DEVIL'S DEN

"Good morning, sunshine," Jarron says smoothly as he approaches.

I lean back against the marble staircase in the main hall of the school, trying my best to hide his effect on me. Good and bad.

Jarron stops a few feet away, his hands clasped behind his back.

"Hi," I say quietly. *Could I be more awkward?*

"Ready?" He smirks.

Not at all. I nod.

Jarron guides me through the south wing and up several sets of stairs. We don't talk as we walk, and I find myself examining the changes in architecture on this side of campus. The ceilings are higher; the molding is more elaborate and brighter. Soon, I notice shiny stones occasionally embellishing the lights.

We turn one final corner, and I stare wide-eyed at a massive archway at least fifty feet tall. It's solid gold, with stunning jewels twisting and turning all the way up and around, making it look like sapphire vines are protecting the entrance.

"Welcome to Elite Hall."

"This is unbelievable."

Jarron chuckles. "It's a bit ostentatious for my tastes. But you know how supernaturals are."

"Is it as elaborate inside?"

"More," Jarron mutters, annoyance clear in his tone.

One part of me is excited to see it, experience it. One part of me knows I'm going to hate how it makes me feel so small.

And that's the goal.

This kind of luxury is created to showcase how much weaker beings do not belong. People like me are meant to feel *unworthy*.

Jarron walks forward and then stops, waiting for me to finish gawking at the golden archway. He silently holds out his hand.

My breath catches in my throat. He's beautiful. Powerful. Strong. And he's looking at me like I hold something precious to him.

I'm not sure what that could mean for me.

Maybe if that terrible day never happened, things would have been different. If he hadn't shown me what it feels like to be utterly powerless.

But honestly, I'd already been prepared for the time our paths would split. I knew they would. *The weak human and the impossibly powerful, handsome prince.* That's not a friendship that can last forever. So, even if he hadn't shown me the monster beneath his skin, I likely would have just made the move first. Hurt him before he could hurt me.

Now, I'm putting myself in a position to undo it all.

But I'm going to follow it through because it's what I must do.

I cling to Jarron's hand as we enter Shadow Hills Academy's Elite Hall.

17

WHY DO ONLY BEASTS SEEM TO UNDERSTAND THAT LIBRARIES ARE THE WAY TO A GIRL'S HEART?

JARRON WAS NOT EXAGGERATING. This place is gagging-ly extravagant.

The domed ceiling is a hundred feet tall. Panels of tinted glass showcase the sky above.

Against the far wall is an incredibly beautiful mural that says: **The best way to predict the future is to create it.**

Jarron's fingers are still curled around mine, gently guiding me through the hall. It's surprisingly bright. I expected elaborate and shiny but dark. Jarron is from the Under World, where there is no light at all.

"Doesn't the light bother demons?" I ask, unable to hold back my curiosity.

"Not here. There are spells in every room to keep us comfortable. This is the only place I've been since my magic manifested that I've been able to feel the sun without discomfort. As much as we Under Worlders love shadows, I'd miss the feel of the sun on my skin if I were to return home."

"Yeah, I could see that." Before his power manifested, Jarron was a—mostly—normal kid. While on Earth, he appeared as a human, able to play out in the sun with the rest of us.

He spent months of his life on Earth, away from the darkness of his world. I couldn't imagine what it would be like for the sun to all the sudden feel like it was suffocating me.

"The comfort of the sun is perhaps the only luxury I'd be hard pressed to give up. Although, there is something here you may like."

He tugs my arm, and I follow him through a corridor to the right until we come to a room with massive windows showcasing a lovely field of black flowers. A few students sit in various cushioned chairs clustered together and stop chatting as we pass.

He guides me down a narrow hall and a metal spiraling staircase, where the light darkens and the air cools, then into a dimly lit room with a rustic feel. A dim glow comes from two hanging industrial lights and a massive fireplace at the far end.

To the left is brick wall covered in shelves of jars, with different shades of liquids, and a counter, with several small cauldrons and a few machines. There are six bar top tables around the room, with dark metal chairs.

The chattering quiets as we enter, but I ignore the stares and instead pay attention to the vibe of the room. It's like an old speakeasy, and I love it.

"You'll like this," he tells me, ignoring the others. He releases my hand for the first time and sets to work combining several of the liquids from the unmarked glass bottles and then pours his steaming concoction into a black metal mug.

I frown, trying to figure out what potion he's making. Potions aren't an uncommon leisurely indulgence for the supernatural world. Sleep potions, relaxers, hallucinogens. Any kind of desirable effect humans use drugs for, we can recreate with a potion that doesn't come with addiction or debilitating side effects. But Jarron's ingredients seem nonsensical. There's no magic in any of them.

His smile is as big as I've seen as he hands me the cup. The smooth metal is warm against my palm.

"What is it?" I ask, cautiously taking the beverage.

"A chai latte."

"No way." My lips part as I examine the creamy liquid. The steam stings my nose in the most pleasant way.

"Try it," he says smugly, crossing his arms.

The delicate mixture of cream and spices makes my mouth water but even so, I twist my lips. It puts me in a very vulnerable situation, to accept a potion from a powerful being. The gaze of the other students press in on me, though and I consider that the risk is likely worth the reward.

Very, very slowly, I lift the cup up and tilt it back. Warm frothy liquid reaches my lips, and the flavor zings through my mouth.

I gasp. It's the most glorious thing I've ever tasted. "How?" I breathe.

Jarron's smile widens, eyes alight with joy in a way I haven't seen since we were kids. I realize, as I watch him, that I miss it. I miss him.

I hadn't allowed myself to feel that because I was so

determined to stay away; I wouldn't allow feelings to make me weak.

The night Jarron changed, when he became a full-fledged demon—his pitch-black eyes and predator form—there was nothing left of the sweet boy I knew. I saw that truth. Felt it. And it terrified me.

So, to me, the boy I knew died, and a demon took his body. That's how I thought about him. But now, I'm faced with the truth that I was at least partially wrong.

"Magic," he says.

I chuckle. "How did you know how to make it?" Chai was always my favorite growing up, but he wasn't ever a fan, so I don't see why he'd learn the recipe.

"Trevor still drinks it sometimes." He shrugs. "You can take it with us. There's a lot more to see."

Jarron takes me back down the hall and up to the brightly lit main level.

"The dorms are that way." He points toward the bright sunroom we passed earlier. "The common rooms are all this way."

This is so much larger than Minor Hall, despite housing less than half the number of students. "Where are you taking me now?"

"You'll see."

And I did. At the end of the hall, I found us on the edge of a massive staircase spiraling down. We are at the top of a five-story library. Each level has a wide circle balcony with mahogany railings and walls covered in books.

"Good lord," I whisper.

Jarron is smiling again. "Anything you want to know about anything can be found here. Even hidden information. Ancient spell books. The secrets to power hidden around this world and many others."

"Think there's something here that will help us understand my sister's death?"

He purses his lips. "Not without more information. I'm still waiting to hear back about the autopsy. Should be in within a few days if my source pulls through."

"Really? It's that easy?"

"Everyone wants to do me a favor." He shrugs.

"The wonderful life of a demon prince."

"Something like that," he mumbles, his shoulders slumping. He averts his gaze and runs his fingers over a set of books against the wall.

I narrow my eyes. "What does that mean?"

He crosses the balcony and leans against the railing, staring down at the walls and walls of books below, as if they hold some treasure he's been searching for but no longer believes is attainable. I wait, and when he finally looks at me again, my eyebrows rise in a silent prompt to go on.

"There are definitely benefits. But—"

"But what?"

"Nothing ever feels real," he says, his voice low. "When every single person you meet wants something from you, they tend to never look past the surface. It's hard for me to trust that anyone actually likes *me*. They want my power but don't care about who I am as a person."

I swallow, trying to ignore the pit in my stomach. Is he talking about me? Am I using him the same way so many others do? Did I prove his insecurities right when I walked away from our friendship three years ago?

Or am I thinking too much into this?

"Anyway." Jarron gives a gentle shake of his head, just enough to ruffle the edges of his dark hair. "Once we get the autopsy, we may have a better idea of where to start looking. If there were any substances in her system. Residue of magical dust. I don't know. Lots of options."

My lungs seize. It's very hard to hide my reaction to the absolute terror rolling through me at the thought of seeing a report of how my sister died. Seeing pictures. I clench my jaw, heart pounding.

She was my sister. The one person I told everything to. And now, she's just a report in someone's filing cabinet Jarron has to promise favors to get access to.

"Do you want to walk around down there?" Jarron nods to the rest of library.

My lips part. "Um, no."

His eyebrows rise.

"Not right now. There's a lot of people down there."

"Right. Not ready to face—" he cuts off, like he determined his last word was not a good idea. "People," he finishes.

I'm curious what he was about to say. *Suspects? Powerful supernaturals? His friends? My rivals?* That replaced word could really tell me a lot about his mindset.

"We could go to my room," he says gently, avoiding eye contact.

I pause, unsure how to respond. A whole thirty minutes of walking through Elite Hall probably isn't enough time together to convince people we're in a real relationship. He initially suggested *two hours*. But I'm also not ready to face my suspects.

He nods slowly. "Want another drink?" he asks, motioning to my empty mug. I'd downed the drink before we even reached the library.

My shoulders relax ever so slightly. "Sure."

We head back to the speakeasy, which is still fairly empty. I watch as Jarron makes me another piping hot beverage, followed by something dark red and topped with cinnamon for himself.

We sit on a red velvet bench in front of the low flickering fireplace.

Silence stretches awkwardly, and I'm now a bit disappointed I didn't choose to explore the library. Here, we're alone. Which is kind of what I wanted but also... not. I don't know what to talk to Jarron about. We were friends once. Really close friends.

But it was during that weird time between childhood and adolescence. We've changed in foundational ways.

"I have something for you," Jarron mutters after several minutes of strained quiet.

"Oh?"

He pulls his hand from his pocket and reveals a small stone. His eyes shine with amusement, and joy? A very undemonic expression, to say the least.

I frown and lean in to examine the stone between his fingers. It's an uneven glossy silver. "Mithril?" I whisper.

He nods, lips twitching.

We used to go searching for the legendary metal on Myre Island as kids. We never found any, but it was fun to pretend. "Where did you find it?"

"There's a tunnel through the mountains to the south of here, where dwarves used to roam and occasionally weld.

The mines are abandoned now, but there's a few tiny remnants of their treasure."

That's the kind of thing that Elizabeth would have been fascinated by too. Is that how he lured her into the Forest of Nails? The promise of rare, shiny objects?

"Do you want it?"

"No," I say quickly but immediately regret it. Maybe it's the right choice—don't let him know I have an interest in something he can use against me later. Not that I'd let him. But I do also really want to check out the metal. It's spelled and nearly indestructible.

I shouldn't even be surprised that the next morning, that same stone, inside a pretty black box, was delivered to my bedroom in Minor Hall.

18

JARRON ISN'T THE ONLY DEMON I'VE GOT TO CONFRONT

I cling to the handwritten note delivered to me mid-potions class.

Request for meeting. *Mr. Vandozer's office, 12 p.m. Today.*

I bite the inside of my lip as I stand outside of the headmaster's office. Yep, the headmaster I blackmailed into admitting me to his school for supernaturals. I've had meetings with principles in the past, but I usually knew the reason before I walked in and had a plan in place. Using magic potions at a human school was pretty easy since I could always just claim ignorance. *Wow, I can't believe that happened! What do you think could have caused all of Brenda's hair to fall out over night?*

I couldn't get away with any of those things here.

But I haven't used any potions. I haven't done anything against the rules. So, I don't even know what to expect. I knock on the door.

"Come in," a deep voice bellows.

I push open the thick mahogany door and force my chin up. I will not show any weakness. Demon royalty my age are one thing, but a demon with the same power, many years older? There's nothing I'd trust this man with.

If I can even call him a man.

He does look like one, though. The man behind the desk has a sharp jaw and generally handsome features, despite the whisper of a beard. I don't know how old he is, exactly— he could be a hundred, he could be thirty. Demons live to be a few hundred years old, so the fact that he looks to be in his early twenties is pretty meaningless.

His gaze is sharp as he takes me in. I resist the very strong urge to curl my lip.

"Hello, Candice." Mr. Vandozer says smoothly. His voice has a gravelly quality to it and an overall sense of authority that sends a chill down my spine. It's a common tactic used against beings of strong magic, to keep them reminded of his power. To keep them in their place.

I'm not even close to a threat, so the weight of his magic on me is more than unnerving.

"You don't have to magically influence me," I mutter. "I'm human."

He flinches. Then his shoulders relax and so does the pressure in the air. I didn't realize how much he was using until it waned.

"Sorry. Habit." His expression tells me he's not at all sorry.

"So, what do I owe the pleasure?" I ask, still holding tightly to the note.

"Why don't you sit, Miss Montgomery."

Inwardly groaning, I obey without comment.

He examines me closely. I refuse to squirm.

"I invited you in today just to check-in." He tilts his head innocently. "Make sure you're comfortable."

I flick a brow. "Yep. Perfect. Guess I can go now, then." I begin to stand.

He clears his throat, and I smirk. I knew it wasn't that simple.

"I get the feeling you do not like me, Miss Montgomery. Or perhaps you are simply under the impression that I do not like you, given the note you sent along with your application."

I flop back into the chair. At least we're over the fake pleasantries and onto the elephant in the room.

"I am not concerned with your information. If you think it's the first time someone has tried to blackmail me or this school, you'd be wrong. There are other ways of dealing with those kinds of threats than bowing to commands."

My muscles tense. Was that a threat?

"I did not admit you out of fear. I admitted you because you are the exact kind of student we want at Shadow Hills."

I flinch. The hell? "Humans?" I ask incredulously.

"You are not strictly human, are you?" he asks with a tone that implies he knows exactly what's in my blood.

I narrow my eyes. What difference does that make? "I have zero magic."

"And how much magic do your parents have?"

"None. Or close to it."

"And yet, they are two of the most famous potionists in history."

I blanch. History? Really?

"You'd be correct in assuming we pride ourselves on recruiting the most powerful young supernaturals to our school. It increases our clout and our ability to develop world class facilities and renowned teachers. But there are very few top schools that commit to also developing weaker supernaturals. It is one of our core philosophies that even the weak can become powerful. You do not need to have a strong level of magic to be influential in the magical community. Your parents prove that. We want the best possible students on both ends of the spectrum."

I'm a potential feather on his cap. If I can have any kind of success in potion making like my parents, I'd make this school look good. I suppress a sigh.

"Okay, so you want me here. Cool. Anything else you'd like to discuss?"

"Yes, there is one other thing. According to my records, you have only passed through our spell blocking arches in the lunch hall once this week."

Oh. Right.

"There have been rumors spreading about you, and though I don't have any actual concerns, please be sure to pass through the arches, even if you decide not to eat our food. It's an important part of public perception."

I give him a sharp nod.

"You are dismissed."

I stand immediately and rush for the door, ready to be done with this conversation as quickly as possible.

"But Miss Montgomery?"

I pause, hand still on the door handle.

"I hope, in time, you'll learn that there are many ways to become powerful. If you come to trust me, I can help you achieve your true potential."

I9

A DEVIL ON HIS THRONE

Jarron is the picture of arrogant comfort, leaning back in the small metal chair like it's his throne and everyone else should grovel at his feet. His elbows are draped over the armrest carelessly. His eyes are hooded.

My heart thuds as I approach.

His lips curl into a smile when his dark gaze lands on me.

"Everything okay?" I ask, taking my seat between him and another demon at the Elite lunch table.

"Jarron's in a *mood*," Auren says, her smile bright like she likes it. I can't help but glare at her. Jarron's lips twitch, but he says nothing.

"What kind of mood?" I ask uncertainly.

He drapes his arm over the back of my chair and leans in. "Nothing you need to be concerned about."

I'm not convinced, but as more Elite join the table chatting idly, my shoulders relax.

"Would you like something to eat?" Jarron asks casually, his fingertips glide gently over my forearm.

I shrug. I've gotten used to not eating much during lunch lately. I'm inevitably too distracted and nervous to eat while surrounded by predators. But my conversation with Mr. Vandozer comes to mind.

"You better go up anyway," Stassi says, with an uncharacteristically serious tone.

"Don't want another visit from the gracious Mr. Vandozer," another one of the wolves says with a wide grin.

My brows rise. I guess I'm not the only one the headmaster has been chatting up.

"Perception is reality," Mia says with a smug smile.

Auren's face is impassive as she shrugs, acknowledging my unasked question. "It's hard to believe you two are really an item with the way you always keep each other at arm's reach." Her icy glare cuts into me. A rumble reverberates from Jarron's chest, and I turn to see him glaring at Auren.

My stomach sinks. We've only been "dating" for a week, but if people really are questioning our relationship, we'll have to change something. And that something will very likely be unpleasant for me.

Jarron slides his chair out and stands, holding out his hand.

I take it and then rise slowly, meeting his intense stare. We walk hand in hand toward the rows of food at the very back of the cafeteria. Jarron glances back at the table of his peers, a challenge in his eyes, just before he passes through the magical arch. I don't know what would happen if someone were spelled. Would an alarm go off? Would they turn purple? Would sparks fly?

I'm not sure I'll ever know because, again, nothing happens when I walk through. My shoulders relax until I notice Jarron watching me closely.

"Were you nervous?"

I shrug. "Not really, but it's weird to have the whole school anticipating something. The what-ifs tend to make their way in no matter what."

He nods, seemingly content with that answer, and then we grab plates and browse through the rows of available food.

"So, does the whole school really think you've spelled me?" I ask.

"The other way around, actually."

I blink, but then I remember the rumors about me using a love potion on him. I clench my jaw. Of course they would think that. Why else would the sexy and powerful Prince Jarron desire a plain Jane human girl?

"They didn't say *that* at the table."

"No, they know better. It would be my duty to rip them to shreds for implying I was weak enough for you to manipulate me."

My brow furrows.

"So, instead, they twisted it around. They're seeking to get under my skin or yours. Auren's been spreading the rumors, and I'm growing quite annoyed." His voice lowers until it's a near growl.

"If you know she's spreading the rumors, why don't you do something about it?"

"She doesn't know that I know. I'm giving her the opportunity to reverse course or double down."

I press my lips together. If she doubles down... "What

exactly does 'rip to shreds' mean?" Is it a figure of speech or—

He gives me a knowing look, and the implication sends a shiver down my spine. *Literal, or close to it. Got it.* I take a bowl of the same brownish soup from my first day and a roll. Jarron examines my plate. "You don't eat much," he comments. "I seem to remember you having a larger appetite."

My cheeks warm. "Lunch isn't my biggest meal. I spend more time... thinking than eating."

"I see."

"Don't worry. I eat more than enough during breakfast and dinner."

He grunts but says no more. Meanwhile, he covers his plate in suspiciously rare meat. I've never had the stomach to ask about a demon's diet. They drink blood. I think? But perhaps that isn't all they eat of their prey.

I hold my chin high as we walk back to the table. The cafeteria is hushed, everyone silently gawking.

They're wondering, *How? If not for a spell, then why?*

Who am I that Jarron would want me?

I'm no one, I want to tell them. *Just the ghost of vengeance, and I'll be gone soon.*

Auren's eyes are even icier than usual when we take our seats back at the Elite table.

"Proud of yourself, are you?"

"Careful," Jarron growls.

I'm tired of being the lost sheep. I may be prey, but I'm

not willing to let that fear become me. I take a bite of my soft roll and hold back a moan. Jarron stills, his attention shifting to me with a quirk of his brow. Okay, maybe I didn't hold it back as well as I thought.

My cheeks redden.

"Is that a new sound to your ears, Jarron?" Manuela says, her voice like a purr.

The table giggles.

"Oh, he's heard plenty." Auren sits up straighter. The giggling settles.

"Perhaps not to his liking, however." Manuela's words find their mark, and Auren flinches.

The chuckles are muted this time.

This is not the direction I expected this conversation to go, but I'm certainly learning from it. *Auren and Jarron have been intimate.*

That news is not supposed to bother me.

"It is certainly something different when it's with someone you actually *like*," Trevor says.

Jarron rolls his eyes at his brother. "Don't sink to their level."

"Is it not true?" Trevor shrugs.

"It's none of their business," he barks.

Trevor nods in my direction. "She seems interested. Maybe you should consider not leaving her in the dark the next time. Learning of this sort of thing in front of enemies is not exactly ideal."

Jarron turns to me, his expression concerned, then nods. His features smooth into indifference. "Advice taken," he whispers.

Trevor nods and then turns back to Bea, his nose grazing the side of her neck. Bea giggles.

"Enemies?" I ask.

"There is a fine line between friend and foe, at least in our world," Manuela says. "Never forget that."

I consider her words. Not that it's a stretch for me to say these people are my enemies, but for Trevor to claim them as such did surprise me.

There's a fine line between friend and foe.

Supernaturals hoard power, apparently even in the form of friends. The more strength your friends have, the more you have. But they are also your competition.

I recall what Jarron said about not trusting that anyone likes him. Is this what he meant? Every friendship, every relationship, is a business transaction. There's no real comradery or affection.

They care about his strength and nothing more. It makes me reconsider my thoughts on his inner circle.

"Well, this conversation has been very illuminating," I mutter before taking a sip of my bland soup.

"Learn to read between the lines, little human, and every conversation will be illuminating." Manuela's smile exposes her canines.

"Her name is Candice," Jarron growls. "Use it or leave."

Manuela holds up her hands, exposing sharp nails. There is no hint of fear in her arrogant smile. "No nick names, got it."

"*Little human* is not a nickname," he says, voice low with power. "Do not test me." The warning fills the air like electricity.

The table stills, tension thick. I get the feeling Jarron doesn't use his magic very often. The hair on my arm rises.

"Except you," he whispers, the pad of his thumb drifting down my jaw. "You can test me anyway you like."

My heart pounds like a damn jack rabbit, and I know he can hear it.

His inhuman eyes, narrowed in on me, make my skin crawl. His magic still hovers in the air around his "friends." And I realize that this is why I'd avoided him for so long.

Because this being next to me is not the Jarron I knew. Not the boy I cared for. I didn't want my memories ruined by the fear I knew I'd experience.

What I didn't expect, however, was how much I'd like it.

20

DID THE PRINCE OF THE UNDER WORLD JUST BLUSH?

TODAY, when Jarron invites me back to Elite Hall, I take him up on it. Maybe it was the implications during lunch that people are questioning our relationship. We need to be more convincing, right? I shouldn't keep avoiding hanging out with his people.

I shouldn't keep avoiding being alone with him.

So, I pass up on the comforting safety of Minor Hall and head into the wolves' den, where my destiny is hidden in the shadows.

"Look who it is," a wolf boy with long dreads purrs, but then his lips curl into a grin.

"The little—" a ginger boy begins—another wolf shifter based on his silver eyes. His attention shifts to Jarron, wide with panic.

"Hey, Candice." Stassi grins. "You look ravishing today, as always." He winks at me.

My lips part in surprise, but Stassi just turns his attention back to the other wolves. "Not that hard."

The first wolf chuckles. "Hey, Candice," he says, copying the exact cadence, but not in a mocking way—I don't think.

Jarron's shoulders relax.

His hand rests on the small of my back and guides me down the spiral stairs to the speakeasy room. There are a few groups of supernaturals clustered around the bar top tables. At one table, three small girls have their noses in textbooks. At another, two boys and a girl are playing a card game. A group of boys stand in the corner chatting idly. I don't recognize any of them.

We approach the fireplace at the end of the room, but the bench we sat at before is occupied by a couple sucking face. Jarron clears his throat, and the couple scurries away.

"That was not nice."

"Did you expect a demon to be polite?"

"No," I say quietly. "But I'd expect the Jarron I once knew to be."

He examines me and takes a seat on the bench, waiting for me to join him. I swallow and then sit a few inches from him.

"Am I really that different? From whom you knew before?" He leans his elbows on his knees casually, examining the fire.

"Sometimes," I admit. "But not always in a bad way."

"Not always," he repeats, tasting the words. "What don't you like?"

My heart picks up speed. "I don't know," I whisper. Which is only partially true.

I find I do like the aggressive part of him more than I'd have thought. The Jarron I knew was generally quite sweet and attentive. Adventurous. He had lots of ideas and ambitions, but not in a take-over-the-world kind of way.

This Jarron is different.

He isn't evil, the way I'd anticipated—at least in any way he's shown me so far. He's more reserved, which is kind of strange to me because he's basically the king of this school. He could do anything he wants and even the headmaster would be hard pressed to stop him.

So why is he so quiet? So aloof? Why does he have no real friends?

Other than my secret fear that he's the one who killed my sister, I have no reason to question his goodness. He's more mature, which isn't a bad thing.

Honestly, the only thing I *don't* like is how his power makes me feel.

But he doesn't hold that power over people. He simply is—in a way he can't control.

"Tell me what you want from me, Candice. I'll give you whatever you need."

I ignore the pleasant twist in my belly. "I need answers."

He nods. "I'm working on it."

We quietly watch the flames flicker while other Elite students chatter behind us.

"Did it bother you?" he asks eventually. "The conversation at lunch today?"

"Why would it?"

He shrugs. "Just what Trevor said."

I sniff and sit up straighter. "Well, Trevor thinks we're really in a relationship too. Right?"

His lips part. "He does. But he also knows me better than the rest."

I'm unsure what he means by that but decide not to dwell too much on it. "I just mean, he thinks talking about your relationship with Auren would bother me because he thinks we're together."

"So, it didn't. It didn't bother you?"

I shake my head, but the bitter taste of the lie settles on my tongue.

"And it wouldn't matter to you to know that we dated."

I meet his gaze, controlling my expression as tightly as I can imagine. "You can tell me if you want. It's helpful to know the dynamics during our ruse."

There's a flash of disappointment in his eyes. Barely there before his features smooth back into his mask of indifference.

"We dated," he says, voice bare of emotion. "For a few weeks, freshman year. I was exploring my newfound power. She's the kind of girl I thought I should want. She cured me pretty quickly of those notions."

"Was she mean?"

"She was exactly as she is now. Vain and superior. It became very clear she only liked me for the way it elevated her status."

I watch the fire flicker and pop. "Have you dated anyone else?"

"No."

I frown. It's been three years. In the time since we were friends, he's only had one very short-term girlfriend he didn't even really like. Or maybe he did like her, and that was the problem. "Not all supernatural girls are like that, I'm sure."

"Maybe some are less obvious about it, but *all* supernaturals are like that. The wolves, the fae, the lesser demons, even Manuela. The only ones who care some are Trevor and —well, I suppose Laithe is an exception."

I resist the urge to tell him that I care. I did once, but now—now, I'm using him just like everyone else. "Well, mortals aren't much better."

He shrugs. "I have limited experience with humans, so maybe I've just been lucky."

His heavy gaze settles on my neck, and I still, not daring to turn in his direction.

"Or maybe you've just been unlucky in your experience with supernaturals. Or maybe you need to seek out a different sort." I force myself to look at him again. "You surround yourself with the most powerful, the most ambitious. Aren't those the most likely to use you?"

"That's the conundrum, isn't it?"

"What?"

"I need a strong partner. It's not only expected but a requirement for me personally. To keep my interest, I need ferocity in a partner. I admire ambition and drive."

A random thought crosses my mind, and I smirk.

"What?" he asks, noting my expression.

Ignoring the flutter in my stomach, I meet his stare with a taunting challenge. "Are you secretly a submissive?"

Jarron's eyes flare dramatically, and I chuckle.

"Did I just make the prince of the Under World blush?" I nudge him with my elbow. I would not be surprised to learn that demon sex life includes chains and whips, but I would be surprised to learn the demon prince is the one who prefers being chained.

A strange expression crosses his face, and he takes in a

long deep breath, eyeing the ceiling. He's tense, something warring in his mind. Then, he rolls his shoulders and the tension drains away.

"I want a matched partner," he says, forcing a calm tone. "If I must be submissive a time or two, that wouldn't bother me."

This time, I cannot ignore the flutter as it drifts lower.

"You're a switch. Got it."

This time, he gives me an incredulous glare. "Miss Montgomery," he says, his eyes full of amusement, his pitch rising into a mocking tone, "you are quite knowledgeable in worldly ways." He tsks like a reprimanding teacher. Or maybe he's trying to mimic my mother. Either way, I laugh deep and hearty, only a tad embarrassed at the turn this conversation took.

Jarron's expression turns serious as he watches the laughter die quickly.

"What?" I finally whisper.

"It's good to hear you laugh," he says quietly. "I've missed this."

I surprise myself when I answer. "Me too."

After a while longer of sitting and chatting in front of the fire, Jarron stands and offers me his hand. I stare at it for a few moments.

"Do you ever think about before?" I ask him. Maybe it's a stupid question. He's not the one that avoided me for years. The one that chose not to be his friend anymore.

"All the time."

I swallow and take his hand.

"Why? What were you thinking about?" he asks as we walk through a shadowy corridor.

"The time I got stuck in a riptide." I stare down at my grungy boots squeaking over the shiny white marble flooring.

He nods absently. I don't finish telling the story and neither does he. We both remember it clearly, and there's nothing more to be said. He saved me from drowning, and I was mad at him for it.

Mad because I was determined to do it myself. I hadn't wanted his help. It didn't matter that I'd needed it. I'd been trying to swim out of the tide for twenty minutes already, and he'd offered his help several times. He'd held out his hand to me, begging me to accept it.

I was so stubborn. I'd needed to prove I could do it myself.

I was near collapsing, choking on water, unable to keep my head up when he finally ignored my wishes and grabbed me. He'd towed me back to shore, even though he was exhausted too.

He didn't have his full demonic power then, but he was still stronger than the average boy. I'd probably be dead otherwise.

I'm a stubborn fool. That's deep in my blood. Something that will never change.

He walks me through the hall and down another. I stop paying attention to where we're going, my mind lost in thought until we stop in front of a set of sleek black double doors.

"I have something to show you," he says quietly. Was that a thread of nervousness in his voice?

"What is this?"

He stares down at me, shadows covering half his face. "My room."

My heart sinks, eyes flashing to the door and back. "Your room?" Why am I so utterly terrified of his room? *Because being alone with a literal demon makes you vulnerable.*

Part of me still suspects he killed my sister, after all.

Or maybe because I don't trust myself.

"You don't have to go in," he says slowly. "But—"

"Yes, I do," I answer, defeated. I cannot be this much of a coward.

Jarron's hand flashes up to my face, and I flinch, but my eyes fly back open when I feel his gentle caress. His fingers wrap around my chin, pulling my gaze up to his. "You always have a choice. Always."

I swallow.

"If you want to stop dating, we can. If you want to keep your distance from me, you can. I will find a way for you to do your research without me if that's what you need. If you want to keep this up but not go into my room or touch me or kiss me ever, we can make that work. I don't care what those people think about you and me. I don't. They can go touch grass. You and I will only be what we make it, not them."

I blink rapidly. His voice holds such conviction. He means it. Believes it. He doesn't care about perception at all. He only cares what I want. What a strange revelation.

I shake my head and step back from his hold. Uncertainty twists through my mind.

"Tell me what you want, Candice."

"What do you have to show me?"

He glances at the door then back down. "The autopsy."

My chest is so tight, my next breath is painful.

I obviously can't read that out in public. Maybe I shouldn't read it in front of him either, though. I squeeze my eyes shut, and soon, I find myself sucking in panicked breaths.

He steps closer, but this time, he does not touch me. "Tell me what you need, Candice. I'll make it happen."

I resist a groan of frustration but then solidify my determination. "Let's go inside."

21

I'M REALLY MORE OF A TAYLOR SWIFT KINDA GIRL

Jarron pushes open the doors and then waits for me to enter. My chest is still tight as I step over the threshold.

My vision adjusts quickly to the darkness, allowing me to take in the massive room. This is not a dorm bedroom like mine. This is an apartment.

Two shiny black doors line the left wall. I'm not sure where they lead, but I'd guess at least one is a closet. There is a set of tinted glass doors on the back wall, which leads to a large, shaded balcony.

The rest of the room is massive. A four-poster bed with a black silk canopy over top is pressed against the right wall. There's a pile of books and papers covering the ground in the far corner that I lift a brow to.

The left corner has a wet bar and table with chairs and a vast selection of liquids I'd bet are not generally legal for minors. Not that demons have such laws. In the other corner is a fireplace surrounded by shelves of books and knickknacks. There is so much space between areas they each feel like separate rooms.

"This is ridiculous," I mutter.

Jarron chuckles darkly. "I know."

I walk forward to peer out the glass doors. The patio is covered in gorgeous black tiles, dozens of cushioned chairs, and a fire pit. "Looks like the perfect spot for a party."

"I don't do much entertaining. To be honest, I don't like people much."

I laugh at that. "We have that in common." I turn back to him. "Isn't it expected, though? Flaunt your wealth and power to those below you."

He gives me a half-grin. "Most of the Elite's assumes I do and they're just not invited. They don't bring it up because they don't want to showcase that they're not in enough to know about my parties."

I snort.

"What's with this?" I ask, nodding to the random pile of books and papers scattered in the corner.

He shrugs, hands in his pockets, and his gaze settles firmly on me. "I'm not a very tidy prince."

"Everything else is pretty pristine."

"Cleaners come in three times a day to pick up after me unless I turn them away. It took weeks of training to get them to leave my one corner of chaos be."

Amusement warms my chest. I sit on the ground next to the mess. Somehow, this makes me feel more comfortable. A reminder that Jarron is still human-ish. I run my fingers over the leather covers of the books and debate picking up his scattered handwritten notes.

Jarron sits on the edge of his bed, just watching me.

"Anything private in here?" I ask.

"I'm not concerned about keeping anything from you."

My stomach gives an uneasy twist. Is that because I'm not a threat?

Ignoring the unpleasant thought, I gingerly pick up a pile of papers and begin to sort through them. Scribbled notes on what seem like totally random subjects. Theoretical physics, black holes, a book titled *History of Man*. "Researching something?"

"Just things I find interesting." He reclines on his bed, and I have to resist the urge to look up at his stretched-out figure.

A few of the papers are sketches. A tall tower, a surprisingly elaborate forest, a sandcastle, a set of hands tightly gripping a book. Nothing super artsy but still pretty good.

I pause on a sketch of the moon.

"I've tried drawing the sun, but I cannot get it right."

I pick up another book. "*Anna Karenina*?" I mock.

He shrugs. "Trevor likes it. It's alright."

Another book is the *Art of War*. I flick a brow at that. "You would."

I notice his lips curl from the corner of my eye, but I continue to resist looking at him. I flip through the book, curious. I've seen it before, and I've read summaries of some of the passages on the internet. I've never read the actual thing.

"You can borrow it if you want. I honestly think you'd like it."

I shut the book and shrug but keep it tight in my grasp.

"Want me to play some music?" he asks casually.

I smirk. "Is this the part where you play Clair De Lune

and we bond over our ancient taste in music? 'Cause I'm really more of a Taylor Swift kinda girl."

He snorts. "We're the same age."

"So, no classical music, then?"

"I can play some jazz from the twenties. Is that old enough?"

"I'm good." I look down at the book in my hands. "You really don't mind me just rummaging through your things?"

He sits back up. "Not really. I figure it might help…"

My brow furrows. "Help?"

"Take your mind off the reason we came in here. If you don't want to face it, we don't have to."

I press my fist to my mouth and then slide it away quickly to cover my panic. Honestly, I'd forgotten about the autopsy. Or maybe he's right; I allowed myself the distraction so I could forget.

"You're welcome to rummage through my books and notes any time."

"Noted," I say much more quietly than I'd intended.

Jarron doesn't speak again. He just sits, waiting for me.

"Where is it?" I finally ask.

He nods toward a manila folder sitting on top of the shining black table by his bed. I blink rapidly. It was right there the whole time.

He opens his mouth to speak, but an embarrassed anger stirs quickly, and I snatch the folder from the table. I don't know why I do it. Maybe because Jarron keeps being so nice and considerate and it's making me feel weak. Making me feel like the damsel he must protect, and I don't ever want to be that person.

Without leaving my spot on the ground, I flip it open straight to the picture of a limp hand covered in blood.

The sound that escapes my lips is pathetic, even I can tell that, but I have no control over it. Her nails are painted dark blue with tiny little dots to look like stars. I'd painted those.

My hands clench into fists, and I barely manage to hold back a sob.

I close the folder and force breath after breath through my lungs. Jarron doesn't move for a full minute as I work to control myself. Tears still well in my eyes, my chest is still tight, but I'm not actively sobbing, so that's good news.

"I can tell you what's in it if that helps."

I swallow. "I need to see it myself. But it might take some time."

Jarron nods. I sniff back my tears, which, to my horror, cover my cheeks and run down to my nose. I wipe away what I can.

I knew it would be hard to see, but I didn't expect it to come on that quickly or intensely.

"You looked through it already?" I ask, holding the folder up. I remind myself that this is why I'm here. And I refocus on the demon in front of me. There's still a chance he is the one that did this. I can't let my guard down. I need to believe it's possible or I run the risk of falling into the same trap as Elizabeth.

"Yes," he says calmly.

"Did you find anything interesting?"

Jarron slides down from the bed to sit on the cold stone floor. He holds out his hand, requesting the folder but not taking it. "May I?" His voice is so gentle I nearly shiver. I hand him the folder.

He carefully thumbs through the stack of papers inside the cursed folder, holding the information about my sister's death, then he pulls out one single slip and hands it to me.

I sniff again and then take the report. There's a date and a few signatures.

"Toxicology report," he tells me.

Breathing still comes with difficulty, but I try to force my brain to obey. Finally, I find the words.

Present in blood: Atropine; Residual sortilege.

"What does it mean?" I ask. Though I have a base understanding of the words—atropine is a toxin that can cause hallucinations, and sortilege is just a word for physical evidence of magic—I don't have any context for what it could mean. The residue could mean a glamor or influence, but I couldn't say exactly how.

"Because her body was found over a week after her death, it's hard to say. The residue was slight, just enough to know something happened. It could have been as small as a magical barrier, like the ones we pass here daily."

"But then, wouldn't the trace have been gone entirely after a week if it were such a small source?"

"Theoretically, yes. So, we can assume a larger amount of magic was used on her, but it's still very vague. There's more though."

I swallow. "Just tell me."

He pulls out another sheet of paper but then hesitates. "It's a picture, but she's not in it."

"Okay," I whisper.

He hands me the image of a forest. There are scorch

marks all over the ground, chunks missing from trees, dirt and rocks everywhere, as well as splatters of red.

I frown. *What the hell happened there?*

He hands me another image.

A small card among the rubble, similar to a tarot card, but it's a character I've never seen. It's a genie? A scary-looking, purple being with golden cuffs and middle eastern style dress.

"What's this?"

"I wasn't sure at first, but I've done a little bit of digging, and it turns out it's a calling card of sorts."

"Calling card?"

He nods. "For a set of games. Very illegal, very immoral, very secretive."

"What sort of games?"

His expression is grim. Silence stretches between us so long I'm ready to strangle him.

"What?" I force out of my dry lips, the sound coming out shrill and pathetic.

"They're called the Akrasia Games. They're a sort of magical *Hunger Games*. Several contenders, only one survivor."

"So, you suspect," I say, glancing back down at the two images, "somehow, Liz was forced into these games?" My bottom lip trembles. So many questions fly through my mind. Who would do that? Her boyfriend? Who runs them? Why? What happens to the winner?

"The games aren't well known. They're very secretive, and so, most of what I've learned is speculation. But from what I understand, no one is ever forced into these games. They choose it."

"Excuse me?" I straighten. "You're suggesting my sister volunteered for this?" I slam my forefinger into the image of the destroyed forest.

Jarron holds his palms up. "I'm only telling you what I've learned from the investigator's findings. It's possible this was all a decoy by the killer. There are still some inconsistencies. But if the authorities and your parents believe it, it does explain why they'd drop the investigation."

This isn't at all what I'd expected to learn. I ignore my stomach twisting in all the worst ways and clear my throat. Logic—I need to use logic right now. I need to get to the bottom of this. Even if she was part of this barbaric competition, there are still so many people to blame. I need to know who.

"Tell me what you know."

Jarron puffs out his chest, like he's preparing for a battle. "The games are legendary. Supposedly run by an ancient jinn." He nods to the calling card.

"Are jinn even real?"

"Not that we know of. There are many supernatural species still being discovered, and the legends are prevalent in certain parts of this world. Many believe they did exist but died out. Some believe there was simply one powerful being that called themselves a jinn. We don't know. But that's, at the very least, their mascot of sorts."

"Okay," I say. The genie's eyes are deep black and harsh. It's not a kind drawing.

"Ten contestants are recruited, all from a level three or lower. The winner is promised power beyond imagining."

I curl my lip in disgust. "So, they prey on weak supernaturals and promise them lies to get them to kill each other for sport. That's what you're telling me?"

Jarron nods, his eyes soft. I don't want his sympathy.

"And conveniently, no one knows who runs these games or if they're even real."

"Correct."

"So, how many other bodies did they find here? Were there nine others beside my sister?"

"No," Jarron whispers. "Your sister was the only one found."

I frown. "The hell—"

"That's the part that bothers me the most. It sounds more like a cover up to me. Why else would there be no other bodies?"

Some of my anxiety eases at that thought. Somehow, it's easier for me to believe some psychotic asshole murdered my sister in cold blood than to believe she fought—willfully or not—in this terrible competition with other supernaturals. Did she kill before she died? Was she injured and forced to continue fighting?

She would have been so scared.

I shake my head from those thoughts. A cover up is a simpler and easier-to-digest answer.

"Do you think the whole scene was orchestrated, then? They damaged the forest and left the card just to cover her murder?" To be honest, that sounds like a lot to cover up one murder of an ordinary human girl. I know our parents are famous potionists, but we don't have that much influence.

Jarron shrugs. "I don't have any firm theories, just doubts."

I nod and hand the papers back to him. "I guess we should have taken a trip to the forest after all."

"I went," he says, voice low. "Last Sunday. I took a few pictures, but I couldn't find anything remotely like this."

I frown. It's all very odd. "These games, they've taken place before, I take it?"

"There's scattered evidence of them taking place over the last few hundred years at least."

"Do you have that evidence? Are there books on the subject? Can you get your hands on them?"

"I don't know of many books, but I'll gather what I can. And asking around about it may backfire, but I will see what I can do."

My mind is still spinning so rapidly I can't tell which way is up.

"Would you like to sit outside for a little bit?" Jarron asks softly.

"Fresh air sounds nice," I admit. I stand on wobbly knees, and Jarron tenses, like he's unsure if he should touch me, help me. But I force my legs to obey and manage to walk out onto the patio on my own two feet.

The air is frigid, and a chill sweeps over me immediately, but it also soothes my tight lungs. Jarron flicks his wrist, and the table to the right alights in a small blue flame, warming the area.

I shift closer to the warmth with a small smile.

"Can I ask you something?" Jarron whispers after a while.

I sniff, hands out to the warmth of the flame. "Sure."

"Why did you swear off all things magical?"

I pull in a quick breath. *Why did you leave me?* That's what he's asking.

I bite my lip, heart hammering. I try my best to explain my insecurities. "When the people you spend time with are a million times stronger than you, it makes you vulnerable. I realized I had no control with people like you. I hate that feeling."

He's quiet for a long time. The wind rustles in the trees beyond the open balcony. The mountains in the distance have a scattering of snow along the top.

"You don't really think I'd hurt you, do you?" he says eventually.

My heart skips a beat. Jarron is still a suspect in my sister's murder, but mostly because I have so little to go on.

The pieces fit, a bit too well for comfort.

But one look in his eyes tells me to trust him.

I'm just not sure I should believe my stupid heart. "I don't know," I whisper. A truth that pains me. I want to believe him. I want this friendship back.

Jarron stops, twisting so quickly I barely see it happen, and then he grips my chin with a featherlight touch. My breath catches, staring into his bottomless black eyes. "I swear, I will not let anyone harm you. Not even me." His voice is gravelly, desperate.

I try to ignore the flutter in my chest.

"I hate this," I whisper, more truths finding their way to the surface. "I hate feeling powerless. Weak."

Jarron releases my chin and straightens. "Candice, if only you knew how much power you have over me, you'd never feel weak again."

22

WILL JARRON TELL ME HE LOVES ME BEFORE HE STRANGLES ME TO DEATH TOO?

I STARE at Elizabeth's journal—her bubble letters and cute doodles on the edges. I miss her so much it's literally painful. And it's so much worse because I can't tell anyone the things I'm feeling.

I would have told her, though. She'd have understood. She'd have told me how to deal with this.

I flip through the pages and pages filled with her thoughts, her feelings, her hopes and dreams. The image of her limp, bloody hand flashes through my mind.

I turn another page, but her words end. One week before her death is her last entry.

My chest aches when I come to the empty pages. The parts she was supposed to be filling in now, and for years to come.

The parts that were taken from her.

The overwhelming need to talk to her hits me again and I sniff back the welling tears.

I glance to the pen on the bed a few inches away, and I

swallow. Maybe I can talk to her again. She just won't be able to talk back.

I pick up the pen and flip a few more pages. I'll leave a few blank, to represent what should have been. What she lost. I pick an empty page and begin to write.

I miss you so much, Elizabeth. I want to talk to you, hear you, see you, hug you. I want you to have the life you were supposed to have.

A tear sneaks down to the tip of my nose. I wipe it away quickly.

I feel so alone here, even with a "boyfriend" and some real, sincere friends. I'm still so damn alone. Because I can't let anyone see what's really inside. The hate and the fear and the confusion. It's like a hurricane inside my chest that I have to hide at all times. It's exhausting.

I read your words, and sometimes it makes me feel closer to you, but other times it makes me feel even more confused. Because those wonderful things you were feeling, I'm afraid to feel them too. I'm afraid I'm falling into the same trap you did.

I came here for revenge. I came here to find the bastard that hurt you and destroy him. I cannot rest until I do that.

And now, I'm here. I'm working on uncovering the mystery surrounding your death. I intend to do that. But

I'm also slipping into this abyss that terrifies me. I don't know where it leads.

He gave me flowers, just like your crush did. He's sent me letters, just like yours did. He smiles at me and tells me I'm beautiful—just like yours did before he killed you.

I CHOKE ON A SOB.

WILL *Jarron tell me he loves me before he strangles me to death too?*

23

IF JUSTICE HAS NO HOLD ON THIS PLACE, I'LL HAVE TO CREATE MY OWN

I WAKE WITH A THROBBING HEADACHE.

Elizabeth's journal is still in my grasp, as usual.

Will Jarron tell me he loves me before he strangles me to death too?

My stomach sinks but not in the way I'd expected. Not out of fear. Out of guilt.

I can't tell if I'm being stupid for continuing to doubt Jarron. My heart honestly believes he is good and kind and sincere. But that doesn't make sense with what I know about demons.

And my sister was misled. Yes, she was a bit more of a hopeless romantic. She was more naïve and trusting, but she wasn't dumb.

What if I'm being naïve too? What if Jarron's pretty face and pretty words are manipulating me just like Elizabeth?

Or what if... what if it's all real? What if he is good and kind? What if he really cares and will help me find Liz's killer? What if Jarron really does have feelings for me?

I shake my head. For some reason, that's the harder thing to believe.

I pull my body out of bed and ignore the continued ache in my chest. Liz's laughter echoes through my memories. I miss her so much it physically hurts.

This plan of mine hasn't worked out how I'd anticipated. I didn't plan to like it here. I didn't plan to have friends. I didn't plan to want to let my guard down.

Maybe I should have anticipated some of those things. In my mind, though, I was a heartless machine, here for one goal, and being a human with feelings in the between time wasn't part of the plan.

Reality has different plans, clearly.

I head into the Minor Hall common room. The happy chattering dims the moment I enter, but I don't have the heart to care today. I keep my gaze focused on the dry scrambled eggs and pile them onto my plate.

My emotions are all over the place these days, but I need to make sure I take care of myself. I refuse to let this place have that much power over me. I refuse to let my sister's murderer kill me too, even if it's just through depression.

I won't do it.

Sometimes, that stubbornness is the only thing that pulls me out of bed in the mornings. The anger in my gut is my fuel.

Here, there are too many people stronger than me. Even in Minor Hall, nearly every student I come across has more magic or physical strength than I do. Little Lola could sprinkle a bit of dust on my head and put me to sleep in a moment. Janet is short but has superhuman strength in those limbs and could crush my skull if she really wanted.

Those wizard boys chuckling at me in the corner could cast a spell to make me kill myself with very little chance I could resist.

Of course, those are the sorts of things the enchantment archways are supposed to stop. Any student who uses that kind of magic on another would be expelled, and possibly charged in the interdimensional court system, depending on who they harmed and how badly. Someone from Elite Hall harming someone in Minor Hall would almost certainly be swept under the rug. They'd be expelled, but they'd get into another supernatural school on another continent or world, and all would be well for them.

True justice has no hold on this place.

"You okay?"

I blink and register Janet watching me with a worried expression. I force a smile as we sit in our usual spot.

"Yeah, you look off," Lola says quietly.

I pull in a long breath through my nose. "Bad night, I guess."

"Anything you wanna talk about?"

"Have you ever heard about the Akrasia Games?"

Janet chokes on her bite of bacon. Lola's wings stop fluttering, and she drops gently onto her butt. "You're not thinking about…"

The glare I give her must be impressively horrible because she jerks back like I've smacked her. I soften my expression. "I don't even know what they are," I say quickly. "But I, well, there's someone that suspects my sister may have been involved."

Janet and Lola are quiet for a few minutes. Then, Lola hops up and lands on my shoulder, leaning in to whisper. "The games are forbidden to talk about in Minor Hall because it's almost always Minor students that join. The winners are promised power by some icky supernaturals; no one knows who, though. But in order to win, they have to kill the other contestants. There are said to be spectators, and bets are made. It's a source of entertainment."

I bite my lip, letting her words settle in my mind. Was my sister in these games? How? Why?

Lola flutters back to her perch, but neither of my friends touch their food again until several minutes later when I force my own fork up to my mouth. Stubbornness wins over my anxiety-filled stomach.

"Why do people enter?" I could guess, but I want more clarity.

"Weak students are sometimes bullied into it. Most seek it out because they don't want to be weak anymore. Or there is something they desperately want but can't get without magic."

"Some say the magic is a false promise. Some say the winner gets a single wish granted."

I frown. "Like, from a genie?"

Lola shrugs. "That would make sense. There's no real proof they even exist, but lots believe they do."

Janet gives me a pitying look. "If your sister was... It's hard to say what her motives could have been."

I force another few bites down my throat, and then I toss the rest. It's enough to live on, I tell myself. "Did you know that Jarron dated Auren?" I blurt out. The other day, they started telling me a little bit of the drama, but they conveniently missed this part.

Lola gasps, a tiny sound.

Janet nods. "It wasn't very long, but she's the only female he's been known to be with. Until you."

"I really don't like her," I admit. "Tell me all the things."

They seem excited about this new subject and wiggle in to spill what they know.

They tell me about the rumors surrounding her. She's royalty from the fae realm, of course, but she's trapped on Earth since the portals were all destroyed a year ago. Several fae have been abandoned here, but she and her brother are some of the most notable.

She's been dating a wolf shifter on and off but still follows Jarron around, hoping he'll change his mind eventually. She's apparently really nice to most Minor sups, though. She and Janet did a project together in charms one year, and she treated her like an equal.

That makes me reconsider the devil horns I picture on her every time I see her now. She's just power hungry, not evil—and maybe even just desperately trying to find a place to belong now that she's been displaced from her own world.

Still not a fan of her tactics but, it does help me understand her a bit better.

"I'm glad she has some redeeming qualities," I say, and Janet smiles.

"I totally get why you don't like her," she adds. "I wouldn't in your situation either."

We pack up and head to our classes. I'm getting the hang of everything—mostly. I've become an early favorite to the witch that teaches potions. It's easy, and I don't have to spend much time focusing on the lessons.

Madame Terry doesn't care in the slightest when I spend

my time reading ahead and checking out additional materials on creating new potions from the back of the class while others are working on remedial potions. She's invited me to join a more advanced class and doesn't understand why I declined. I don't want something that's going to take too much of my focus from what I really want to do: find my sister's killer.

There are some perks to being good with potions, though, and I intend to use what little strengths I do have. I'm just not sure how yet. I'll figure it out.

I'm not allowed to use any magic that manipulates a student's free will, but I am allowed to use defensive spells and potions. I haven't told anyone about the research I'm doing, not even the teacher, but based on the knowing looks she gives me, I get the feeling she's got an idea.

So, when I slip into my lower-level potions classroom early in the morning to check out a new book from the tiny library and found a new book sitting conspicuously on top of the shelf, I slid it beneath my other books without delay.

Madame Terry winked at me as I departed.

I take my seat in History of Worlds and flip open the new books.

POWER TO THE POWERLESS. Major Defenses for Minor Supernaturals.

I blink. That's a bit on the nose for what I'd been expecting. I suppose Madame Terry does know exactly what I'm after. Or maybe she's just heard about who I'm dating and expects this will be useful.

I crack open the book the moment Mr. Thomas begins droning on about the portals around the world and the creatures that have come through them to now reside in our society.

This is another class that's easy as pie because I learned this stuff when I was growing up, and this class is geared toward supernaturals or humans entirely new to the idea of multiple worlds. Some of the other students are trolls and barely understand the language. There are also a few young fae that knew there were other worlds when they came here but nothing about them. I'm one of two humans in the class, and that's probably half of the human population in the school.

I flip through the old textbook, only stopping to jot down the due date for an essay assignment. It's not a potions book, surprisingly, but there is a section of potions in here.

The book is specifically created for low magic beings going up against majorly strong beings. There are even a few inspirational stories about some of the most powerful non-magical beings in history.

Then, there are another three hundred pages with lists of spells and potions and charms and objects that can give strength to the those with limited magic.

Each page is dedicated to another form of magic that does not require base magic to acquire or use, but they are impressively advanced.

Some of the objects, I've heard of but are in the possession of influential supernatural families. Like Excalibur, a sword that has killed many wizards in the past. Now hidden away by the Chancellors, a society of wizards. Or the Gem of Oriziah, a stone that can only be used by the magicless because it steals the magic from any supernatural within a twenty-foot radius, which I know is held in the caverns of the Egyptian temples and protected by several societies of supernaturals.

There are lesser objects, though, that the book advises can be used to create spells for those lacking magic, like siphons or fae gemstones. Those can store magic for anyone to use—if they know how.

Finding those objects and learning to use them would take years of sleuthing and practice. Or lots and lots of money. The thought does inspire interesting ideas, though.

By the time I make it to my next class, I decide to focus on reading through the potions in the book since those will be the only reasonable things I have enough ability to use in this situation. If I were to stay in the supernatural world for long, I'd dedicate myself to mastering them all, but I won't be.

So, potions it is.

Potion one: flight.

My parents have made potions like this before. Or transportation potions. They're dangerous and tricky and only last a few minutes. Not quite worth my time.

Next, *truth potion.*

Potentially useful and something I'd already considered. I know the basics of how these work and what would be required, but I didn't have detailed instructions until now. I can't really use one of these until I have more to go on, though. If I were to give one to Jarron, he'd know the moment the spell ended, and if his answers lead me nowhere, I'll have lost the trust of my only Elite in.

Bad idea.

Third, *death potion.*

I blink. That's interesting. Of course, poisons are common, but that's not what this is. This is an instant and traceless potion that kills the one touched by the liquid. It does not need to be ingested, nor does it remain in the body. It leaves no trace. Its constitution is by far the lowest of any I've ever attempted—meaning it is an extremely condensed form and would take weeks to simmer down.

I've honestly never even heard of this potion, and I wonder if it's highly illegal. Have my parents made this potion before? They tend to be cautious people, but with those they trust—like the demon royal family—they'd have no problem breaking all the rules. If they have made something like this, they've certainly never mentioned it at the dinner table.

"Something more interesting than my class, Miss Montgomery?"

I shut the book in a heartbeat and give a sheepish smile to the dwarf standing in front of my desk.

"Sorry. It's potions homework," I say quickly.

"Well, you are not currently in potions class, are you?"

"No, sir."

"Put it away or I'll take it."

I nod quickly and put my book, along with my other notebooks, beneath my chair. That's not a risk I'm willing to take now that I suspect the book holds illegal spells that can honestly help me.

"Good," the dwarf teacher says—hell if I remember his name— "tell me the difference between sirens and mermaids."

"Both are humanoid supernaturals that live in water. Sirens are salt water only. Mermaids can survive in either.

Sirens don't have full tails, just webbed hands and feet; they also have hypnotic magic that mermaids do not. Their song can be deadly or simply hypnotizing, depending on their skill level and desire to cause harm."

"Are mermaids harmless, then? If they hold no magic."

I frown at that question. "They hold magic," I say slowly, "just not a hyper specific form. They can create spells the same as any witch, but most don't get that kind of education. They prefer solitude."

The instructor nods, content with my knowledge of the topic.

The professor rambles on, and I pretend to take notes, but instead scribble random thoughts about my situation.

Someone killed her. Was it him?

I sketch a few doodles onto the page.

If not, what does he want? Just to help? Am I a charity case?

In my next class, I keep my shiny new book hidden away in my bag and instead pull out my purple leather journal.

Each page has a name of an Elite student with whatever notes I've acquired about each. There's one I'd been putting off. I find an empty page and write his name in big bold letters.

Jarron Blackthorn.

Suspect.

The heir to the throne of Oriziah, the largest known Under World. The most powerful creature in this school, possibly on Earth.

One of the few beings able to bond to a human and make them powerful. A monstrous predator lies beneath his skin. A monster that will stalk humans as prey.

He says he cares about Liz.

Liz had a crush on him, but then his magic manifested, and he hunted her in demon form. He hurt her. Could he have done it a second time?

I stare down at his name. I have a hard time justifying my understanding of demons with the Jarron I know. Even Trevor, in the few times I've dealt with him, hasn't been what I expected. I thought they'd have changed. I thought I was going to face a being that looks like my old friend but is something so much different inside.

I expected evil calculation and dark aggression. Controlling behaviors and violent tendencies. But they're the same. They seem so human.

Is that just part of the act?

I write the big question: *Are demons cold calculated killers or capable of deep human emotions?*

Get a book on demon behavior, I write in firm block letters. A demand of myself. I have to understand what is usual for demons outside of Trevor and Jarron. It'll help me have a better sense of if I'm being manipulated or not.

The bell rings, and I drift through the halls, not really present. My mind is running through so many different things. Jarron. Trevor. Auren. The Games. Potions I can use for my revenge when I do figure out who the culprit is.

My foot catches on something. One moment, I'm upright, and the next, the floor is coming toward me way too fast. I barely manage to throw my hands out before I face plant straight into the pretty marble flooring. My knees hit first, though, and it sends a wave of pain shooting through my body.

Gasps, followed by laughter, rings out through the hall.

I clench my teeth tight and force myself from the

ground, body aching. Blood drips onto the back of my hand. My stomach sinks.

I sit up quickly and wipe the blood from my nose. *Perfect. Wonderful.*

Some of the laughter halts.

"Need help, Ascension seeker?"

I sneer in the general direction of the crowd, but I don't know who made the offensive comment. They basically called me the magical equivalent to a gold digger.

Anger swirls in my belly.

The moment I'm on my feet, something slams into my chest. I flinch, but there is no pain, only the light weight of a pixie pushing against me.

"OMG, are you all right?" Lola squeals, her wings fluttering.

"Yeah, fine," I force out.

"Come with me, we'll get you cleaned up before lunch. Jarron's gonna lose his shirt if he sees you bloody."

I rush after my pixie guide into the bathroom and stop in front of the mirror. There's only a small stream of blood from my nose that's already stopped. I pour water on a paper towel and do what I can to clean myself up but there's still a dark red stain on the collar of my white shirt that I have a feeling is not going to come out.

"What happened?" she asks as I work.

"Someone tripped me, I think. I don't really know. I was just walking one second, the next I wasn't. For all I know, I fell from my own damn clumsiness."

Lola nods frantically. "Good, that's the story you'll have to tell him, then. *'I'm just clumsy, oops. My bad.'*"

I frown. "Why lie? If someone did trip me, let them face

his wrath." My stomach clenches in disgust at the hypothetical villain twisting his mustache in my mind.

Lola's laugh is near hysterical. "Uh, well you could, but since you don't know who it was, you could end up with innocent blood on your hands."

"You think Jarron would kill someone for tripping me?"

Her eyes widen. "Not kill, no. Probably not. But remember, this is the supernatural world, where any threat is life and death."

I frown, but to be honest, I'm not sure I'd feel that guilty. But I guess we'll see. Either way, I can't hide the blood completely, and I'm going to be facing Jarron in a matter of minutes.

"Thanks for your help, Lola." I give her a smile, and her expression softens. "Let's go find Janet before she freaks too."

Lola flutters up near the lights. "Good idea." Then, she darts from the room and down the hall before I can even catch up. The chaos from my fall has already settled, and people are mostly minding their own business.

Maybe it won't be as big a deal as Lola was making it out to be.

Janet is bouncing on her toes in the lobby outside the cafeteria, though, and she squeals when she sees me. Her arms are around me suddenly.

"Jeez, dude, I'm fine."

"You sure?" she asks, pulling back and looking me all over. "I heard someone pushed you!"

I flinch. "Who told you that?" I ask, looking to Lola, who literally told me not to say that just minutes ago.

"A bunch of people were talking about it."

"Perfect."

I give Janet another reassuring pat on the arm, and we walk into the cafeteria together. Most of the room doesn't pay me any mind anymore, even today. Only a few people peer in my direction with concerned curiosity.

The room is fairly quiet but not silent.

Jarron's expression is casual as he looks up and meet my stare, and I try my best to keep my expression neutral. I really don't need him to make a scene over this.

His gaze darts to my shirt then back up, and the room chills in an instant. Every voice quiets as his magic settles over the space. I stop, the hair on my arms standing up straight.

"Go," I whisper to Janet and Lola. I'd be royally pissed if he acted out and hurt them. His reputation can take a dump if he's going to hurt people who care about me to keep it.

Jarron stands slowly, muscles tense. The room darkens. Like an all-consuming cloud is rolling past the sun.

He walks toward me, and I swear I can hear every pounding heart. Every terrified whimper as Jarron marches up the aisle until he's standing over me.

His eyes are pinned to mine. His fingers wrap gently around my chin, and he leans down. For a moment, I think he's going to kiss me, which makes no sense at all. Even so, my stupid, stupid heart flutters.

"What happened?" he asks.

I pull back from his grasp, looking down at the tiny spot of blood on my white shirt. "I don't know. I just fell."

"Bull shit," he spits.

I roll my eyes, my stupification gone. "I'm not lying. I don't know. I was walking, then I wasn't."

He straightens, and turns his burning gaze to the gawking crowd. "Who did this?" His voice is loud and quiet at the same time. Like a whisper magically amplified.

Several gasps ring out.

"Someone knows, and I'm going to find out."

No one moves. No one speaks.

"It's not a big deal," I whisper, ignoring the continued fluttering in my chest. Nope not supposed to be enjoying this. They all fear me right now—one flick of my finger, and I could destroy any one of their lives—and something about that power has always gotten under my skin. It's not that I want to cause someone pain, but knowing I can? It's intoxicating. Stupid, but it's my vice.

I know the kind of supernatural I'd be, and that's one of the reasons I didn't want to be around them. I couldn't even be mad when they took advantage of my weakness. I'd do the same.

His gaze lightens. "It is a big deal," he tells me, then leans in to murmur. "If they think they can get away with harming you, it puts us both in danger. I won't allow it."

Right, because this is more about his reputation than me. I shake my head. "If I knew who did it, I'd tell you."

He nods and then turns to face the bulk of the crowd. "Let me make one thing very clear," he says, violence in his tone, "she is mine. Anyone who dares touch her will suffer for a very long time."

He lets the threat linger, tightening over everyone in the room.

Then, he releases his magic altogether.

Everyone relaxes at once, and chatter rises into a crescendo as Jarron holds his hand out for me. He's still tense as we walk back to the table, his expression very clearly livid.

"Stupid bitch deserved it," someone says, her voice ringing out much clearer over the chaos than I assume was intended, and once again, the room stills.

I jerk my attention to Jarron—his eyes are pitch black, his expression an angry calm. It unnerves me. His body remains unmoving, but after three beats, a scream pierces the air.

Auren is standing stick straight, her face contorted into a grimace of terror. More ice crackles against the window-panes, and the room dims. Black swirling shadows creep through the air toward Auren—like a monster's claws, slowly stalking its victim.

I press my hand over my mouth and then slide it away quickly to cover my panic.

For the first time, fear strikes me. I don't know why I care, but somehow, I really don't want her harmed. But when I look into his black eyes, I don't see Jarron. I see the monster.

Pitch black eyes, no whites at all. His cheeks seem more sallow somehow. His expression is emotionless.

This is the demon prince I expected when I walked into these halls.

The demon that hurt my sister.

With trembling fingers, I place my hand on Jarron's fore-arm. He blinks and looks down at it. I swear, the room brightens slightly when he meets my stare. His eyes are still pitch black, but his expression is softer, filled with curious concern.

I shake my head ever so slightly.

His shoulders relax, and Auren collapses into her chair, panting. Three fae rush to her the moment the black magic recedes. They fuss over her, whispering frantically. The rest wait, several feet from the table, watching Jarron and I closely.

Jarron's attention doesn't leave me. "She deserves it and more." He tells me, but the demonic rage is gone. My Jarron is back.

"Maybe. But I think you made your point for now."

"Is that true?" he asks, turning back to Aurie, whose usually bright eyes are dim and red rimmed.

Her gaze darts between me and Jarron. Her hand is spread over her chest. She nods quickly, fear and embarrassment still clear on her face.

"I didn't hear you," Jarron says.

"Yes," she pants. "I'm sorry."

I grab Jarron's hand and pull him the rest of the way to our table. We sit right across from Auren as usual. Jarron's intense stare doesn't leave her, but she never looks up from the table.

One by one, the rest of the Elite retake their place at the table silently.

I don't know if she was behind my fall, but I do know she's been against me from the beginning. I know she's behind several of the rumors about me.

She is the opposite of a friend, so maybe I should have let it play out.

Maybe it's because Janet told me she's been nice to her. Or maybe it's simply because one harsh comment isn't enough to condemn someone.

Either way, it felt right to stop Jarron.

The table is quiet for the first few minutes. Then, finally, Jarron suggests we go get food. For the first time, I grab a chicken breast and pasta. A real lunch. *Look at me go.*

Jarron doesn't comment. He grabs one small red steak, and we head back to the table without comment.

At the fully awkward table, I eat happily. Why do I feel so much more comfortable when someone else is miserable?

"That was so hot," Stassi blurts out eventually. I flinch, but Jarron just snorts. I shake my head, not willing to dwell very long on Stassi's random compliments, and continue eating my chicken pasta.

"I'm not yours, by the way," I say between bites, side eyeing the demon prince beside me. Those words sounded good in the moment, but I do want to get my two cents in. He stops mid-bite.

Trevor snorts.

"If it keeps you safe, you are," Jarron says, his voice low and serious, but there's a glint of amusement in his eyes.

"I don't belong to anyone."

His fork clinks against the table. My body responds to the predator's attention with a shiver. "Do what you want; I won't stop you," he says seriously. "Our dating arrangement doesn't have to be monogamous. But me claiming you may keep you alive here. And I will never stand by while someone hurts you."

My smirk slips.

"That includes anyone at this table. Touch her in any way she doesn't explicitly request—or instruct anyone to touch her—and I will tear you apart in this very room. Do you understand?"

The wolves nod immediately. The girls quirk brows and

exchange glances and then finally, each nod. The demons narrow their eyes at the other supernaturals, as if they're there to police the others on behalf of their prince.

"Aurie," Jarron says, softer but still firm. She jerks her head up, eyes filled with tears. "I know what you've been doing, and it stops now. Do you understand?"

Her bottom lips trembles but she nods.

"You don't deserve her mercy."

"Trust me," I say, voice low. "She won't get it a second time."

Jarron's smile is cruel but pleased.

Aurie's nose wrinkles, the first sign of anger at the situation. For a moment, I thought she'd learned her lesson. Now, I think she'll double down on it. She'll cower beneath Jarron's stare, but mine? Not a chance.

I'm a human, not worthy of having any power over her. She won't accept it.

24

WHY ARE BAD IDEAS ALWAYS A GOOD TIME?

On Saturday, when I meet Jarron in front of Elite Hall again, there's something different about him. I expected him to be tense after yesterday's conflict. Someone tripped or pushed me, and we don't know who. But instead of tense and concerned, he's utterly calm as he waits for me in front of the entrance, hands in his pockets as usual.

"You look like you're in a good mood." I flick a brow, but the truth is, I feel more relaxed too.

"I am."

I purse my lips. "Odd, isn't it?"

"Not really."

He holds out his hand to me. "I'm glad you stopped me yesterday."

My lips part, unsure what to say to that. He's happy I stopped him? Would he have regretted hurting Aurie? And even if that's the case, does that really explain a good mood?

He takes me into the speakeasy room again and quickly makes us both warm beverages—me a ridiculously delicious chai latte and him something dark red—and we take our seats by the fire. Today, the room clears out as we sit. We are entirely alone.

Despite Jarron's good mood, it seems no one else is quite as comfortable as we are. I curl my legs up under me as we sit, back pressed against the armrest as I watch the flames flicker.

"Your big thing is control, right?" he asks.

My eyebrows pull down. "I guess so."

"Yesterday, you took control. I liked it."

I blink. That's what he liked? "I kind of worried it might make you look weak," I admit. It did feel good, but having his human girlfriend dictate his actions? Can't be a good look for a future world ruler.

He shrugs. "I'm not concerned about that. Yes, mercy can be dangerous, and Aurie may have deserved my wrath, but her actions *yesterday* were small. She got her warning. We'll see what she does from here."

I nod.

"And," he continues, "I like that you felt comfortable enough to stop me. That took courage most people don't have. Believe me, *you* did not look weak yesterday, and that matters significantly more."

I take a sip of my creamy beverage to hide my embarrassment.

"You've been a bit out of your element so far. Uncomfortable and unsure. It's all understandable, but I enjoy seeing the old Candice."

I look up at the ceiling and consider that. "What's the old Candice?" I ask finally. I know I've changed a bit, and being here has definitely thrown me off and made me an annoying, scared version of myself. But I'm curious what he thinks is the old me.

His wolfish smile is back. "You may not have magic, Candice, but I've never met a stronger person on the inside. You are incredibly shrewd and resilient and brave. Stubbornly so, which explains why you'd come to this school with plans of revenge."

I chuckle, but it fades quickly. "Magic or not, I'm going to kill who ever hurt her."

"Good," he growls.

"And I don't want you to do it for me."

He pauses, eyeing his own drink. After a minute, he asks, "How do you intend to do it?"

I shrug. "Depends on who it is. But I'll find a way." Maybe it'll require an illegal death potion. Maybe I'll find a way to weaken them and then strangle them to death the way they did her.

I strongly suspect my villain is a demon based on the context clues in my sister's journal, but I don't know for sure. Her lover was almost certainly a demon. There are only maybe three known supernaturals that could have mated with her in a way that would have made her more powerful, and only one of those species goes to this school. But there's still a small possibility her lover wasn't the one that killed her.

We let the silence stretch between us for several more minutes until our glasses are completely dry.

"There are different kinds of power," he mutters, seemingly to himself. "Magic is only one."

My lips curl into a cruel smile. This is a truth I've always known but have let myself forget sometimes.

"You are not weak, Candice. Don't ever let anyone make you feel that way."

I pull in a long breath, considering those words. I have done that, haven't I? I had some form of power yesterday, over Jarron. He was following my command.

But it's not enough.

Yes, it's nice to have Jarron as my shield, but I cannot rely on him. Even if he's being sincere, even if he had nothing to do with my sister's death, he is not a permanent solution.

We're not really dating. He is not planning to make me his bonded.

Even if this friendship is real and strong, he won't be around forever. I must stand on my own.

"I have another question for you." He fidgets with the empty mug in his grasp. His lips curl into a bashful smile. "We talked about how much time we'd spend together, and it's modest. But we haven't talked about PDA."

"As in public displays of affection?"

He nods slowly.

My lips part. "We hold hands, don't we?" A few times, as we've walked through Elite Hall. It's not a lot, I know, but—

"Do you think that's enough to convince them you're mine?"

My heart is suddenly jack hammering in my chest. We've now been *dating* for almost two weeks. "Has anyone said something? Other than Aurie." It's probably a stupid question. I know they've been talking.

He chuckles. "All the time."

"Really?"

He shrugs. "It's all joking, of course. Guys likes to rag

on each other, and shifters are extremely affectionate beings. It's strange to them to see a couple who barely touches."

My eyebrows rise as I consider that.

"I've told you before that we don't have to do anything you don't want to. I mean it. We don't ever have to touch if that's what you want. We don't ever have to be alone together. But the more we sell this, the easier it will be for you to fit in with the group. The more you fit in, the more people will come to you with their problems and offer secrets to get in with you. There are girls here that will do anything to be your best friend. If we make people believe this is real, that you could be a long-term addition to my life, you'll have the in you need to investigate anything and everything."

I swallow. "Well, what did you have in mind?"

He has a point. So far, everyone has kept me at arm's reach, unsure what my role really is, and I don't blame them. I have been a deer in the headlights.

But no longer. Anger is my motivation. I will find my footing here. They'll learn not to mess with me. Not because of who I'm dating but because of who I am.

The thought of being even closer with Jarron is unnerving. I'm not sure how much I can trust myself with him. He's beautiful. His voice gets under my skin in a way I simultaneously love and despise.

If only you knew how much power you have over me, you'd never feel weak again.

Problem is, he has power over me too.

"A kiss," he says in a near whisper, as if he's afraid that if he says it too loudly, it'll shatter my resolve. Afraid that I'll run from him, the way I did back then at the first glimpse of his true form.

"In public?" I ask, trying my darndest to keep my voice smooth and calm. I'm not sure if I succeed.

"In Elite Hall, at first."

I'm dizzy at those words.

"At first?" I say, trying to keep my tone playful.

His lips twitch. "There's an event coming up—two weeks from Saturday. A banquet we hold yearly as a sort of fundraiser. Some alumni will attend. Some potential new students. It's stiff and lame and all about keeping up appearances."

"And you want to—"

"I want," he muses, "to dance with you, flaunt you. And, yes, kiss you."

Holy crap monkeys. Why oh why did I put myself in this situation? Because the effect those words have on my body are all the proof I need that I am not equipped to keep Jarron from getting too close.

"And that's enough to convince people?" I ask, no longer at all successful at keeping my voice under control. I'm breathless, and there's no point in hiding it.

"It's a start. The biggest sell, will be in the little things. The things we can't plan. Small touches. Casual comfort together. Hanging out with the group together. Laughing."

"Well, the hanging out and laughing, we should be able to handle, right?"

"Now that we're a bit more comfortable, yes."

"But what kind of touches are we talking about?" I hold my breath, knowing the question is setting me up, but I have to know what I'm in for.

"We can practice," he suggests. He looks over his shoulder to ensure we're still alone. We are. "You can veto anything you don't like."

I wet my dry lips. *Bad idea. Bad idea. Bad idea.* "Good idea."

His eyes darken, and my heart races. He leans in closer and reaches up toward my face. My chest rises and falls rapidly, but the rest of my body is utterly still.

Starting at my collar bone with feather light touches, he runs his fingers along the side of my neck, then he gently pulls my hair over my shoulder.

I release a shaking breath.

"Is that okay?" he whispers.

"Mmhmm," I nearly squeak in response.

His fingers continue their journey, this time down the side of my arm, all the way to my wrist. I watch the slow movements, little swirls with his middle, forefinger, and thumb, dancing over the vulnerable skin of my inner wrist —the place he'd leave his mark if I let him. It sends shivers down my spine.

Then, he slowly hooks his finger into my palm. He examines the soft skin and smooth lines then curls his fingers between mine until they're intertwined.

"Is that it?" I ask breathlessly.

He pauses. "Do you want it to be?"

My breath hitches, and that's my only response. Because I don't know the answer. Yes. No.

Part of me wants to beg him not to stop. Which is kind of the problem.

He leans in until his nose just barely grazes my ear. "Candice," he whispers, and I swear I'm one step away from throwing my head back and whimpering like a simpering fool.

I leap up from the chair, panting like I've just run a marathon.

His eyes betray his surprise, but his lips curl into a smug smile.

"I think that's enough for now."

"Okay." He sits up straight then pats the spot beside him. "Practice is over." The *for now* is implied, or maybe that's just in my head.

25

SPEAK OF THE DEVIL

I walk hand in hand with the crown prince of the Under World through the bright foyer of Elite Hall. What in the world has my life become?

My calm demeanor has unfortunately shattered with the promise of more touching. I try to remind myself that I'm in control.

Never let anyone make you feel weak.

That includes Jarron.

Anxiety crawls through my body like a living thing, though, at the thought of kissing him. Is it because I fear him? Or because I want him?

Maybe both are true.

Our relationship wasn't ever like this before. We held hands sometimes as we ran through the forest. We even hugged a time or two.

But he did not touch me like *that.*

I shake my head. Nope, not gonna dwell on that, because if I go too far down that path, I might implode.

I remind myself that he may have done all these same things with my sister. Told her he'd make her queen of his world. He'd mark her, bond her. *Ascend her.*

Jarron hasn't said any of those things to me, but, well, it's still early, right?

My sister was only dating her lover for two weeks.

He fits all the clues in her journal. Plus, Liz had a major crush on him when we were younger. It would have been very easy for him to get into her heart. Two weeks would have been plenty of time.

We haven't uncovered much about the Akrasia Games, so I don't really know how they fit, but for all I know, that was a cover up. Maybe her boyfriend lost control and killed her on accident. Or a jealous rival killed her. Then, they placed her in the right position to make it look like she died by entering those dangerous and very illegal games.

If my parents believed it, that explains why they stopped searching for the killer. They wouldn't want to expose the way she died to the world, and in that case, there's no real villain. She did it to herself.

Yes, they could try to tear down the competition altogether, but that's a bigger endeavor than finding one murderer. This is an entire organization that investigators have been hunting for centuries.

But I refused to put the blame on Liz. Even if she did enter these terrible games, someone must have manipulated her into it.

Maybe her boyfriend pushed her to enter so she'd be worthy of him. In that case, he's still guilty, and I'll still tear him to bits.

Control. Power. Leverage. That's what I need now.

I'm only a human in a war with supernaturals. I have very few weapons in my arsenal. One of those is the element of surprise—that's about all I've got right now other than sheer tenacity.

But I know I can build up my knowledge. That's my next plan.

We approach a group sitting in the sunroom. Bea is on Trevor's lap as they chat idly with a few wolf shifters. Manuela is lounging back in her cushioned chair, arms crossed, not far from the group.

"Speak of the devil," Trevor says with a flick of his brow.

"Such an old joke," Jarron complains.

"Wasn't talking about you." Trevor's winks at me.

I grimace. "Hey! Asshole."

The whole group laughs, and my shoulders relax. Trevor isn't my biggest fan, but he's more of a friend than the others.

Friends. I want to have friends here.

That's how I find out if the demon holding my hand played a role in killing my sister or not.

"Where are you two headed?" Trevor asks.

"Back to your *room?*" Bea asks, wiggling her eyebrows.

Jarron holds back a smirk. "Not yet."

I press my lips together tightly. "Library," I say. Relax, stupid. Relax. "We're headed to the library first."

"So boring!" Stassi complains. "Hey, we strongarmed Trevor into having a party tomorrow night. Is the hottest couple in school going to grace us with their presence?" He leans forward, expression hopeful.

I look at Jarron.

"Up to you," he tells me.

I nod. I'm supposed to be dating Jarron and be part of the group. I've never been all that social. I don't mind people, but I don't seek them out. So, a party isn't exactly my forte, but it'll serve a purpose.

Jarron nods. "We're in."

"Yes!" Stassi throws a fist in the air.

"Girlfriend finally opening up, huh?" another shifter says.

"Getting one over on the ice princess will do that to a girl," Manuela says.

I roll my eyes, even though she's not wrong. It's not that I like Auren hurting, but yesterday's events did help me feel a bit more comfortable in this group. I'm beginning to understand my role.

"We'll see you around," Jarron mutters then tugs me by the waist to continue down the hall. "So, a party," he says the moment we're alone again.

I shrug. "Seems like a good idea given what we discussed earlier."

He nods. "It is. And yet, I'm still surprised you agreed to it."

"Well, maybe you don't know me as well as you think."

He chuckles. "Maybe not."

Jarron and I head into the library, and once again, I'm awe struck at its sheer size. I mean, I've been to bigger libraries but not *magical* ones. I wouldn't find *Art of War* or Jane Austen in these shelves—for that, I'd have to go to the school-wide library. Here, every book is based on magic.

Whether history of supernaturals, studies on different worlds, substances unknown to human scientists, creatures of the deep. Space monsters. Inter-dimensional travel. The options are endless.

Jarron shows me the general ropes and then sets me free to explore all I want. I have two things in mind. First, I search in the potions section and select an advanced collection of battle potions. These are the kinds of things I'll need to have on hand if and when I ever go head-to-head with a supernatural.

The kinds of things I can use to protect myself when some douchebag decides to push me around in the hallways again.

Then, I head to the level Jarron said was entirely dedicated to other worlds.

The more I know about creatures from the Under World, the better, so I spend a little time browsing the Oriziah section, specifically seeking books about the royal line.

There are a few volumes to select, but most of them are detailed descriptions of past rulers' reigns. I find one that acts as a general summary, which is exactly what I'm looking for. I flip through the pages before I commit and find the first half of the book is a historical overview, and the back half is cultural aspects and general characteristics. *Perfect.*

I take my two books and head back down to the ground level to meet Jarron. He's already sitting at a glass table, nose in a book. He looks up when I approach. "Find what you were looking for?"

I nod but offer no further explanation. I'd prepared one

if he asked why I was researching his kind, but he doesn't ask.

"What about you?"

He holds up the book he's reading. *A Legacy of Cruelty, Supernatural Effect on Earth's Magic-less Society.*

I tilt my head, trying to figure out what he's getting at with that one.

"There's a chapter on the Akrasia Games."

"Oh."

"I'll give it to you when I'm done if you want."

I nod and then flip open my potions book. I figure that's the safer of the two. This book is much more detailed and complex than the one my potions teacher gave me, but even so, I don't find a death potion quite like the other one.

I do find another potion of interest, though.

A magic nullifier.

The description tells me it will suppress a supernatural's magical ability anywhere from minutes to hours, depending on potency. And it doesn't need to be ingested.

Winner winner.

In a matter of seconds, this potion will make the magical being essentially mortal for the duration of the potion's affects. All I have to do is get the liquid on the target's face and it'll work.

It's complicated, mostly because the concentration is high. I need to brew the potion and then very carefully let it simmer for nearly a week to condense the magic so it can be used on the skin.

I recall what my defense teacher told us about supernaturals during our training—they tend to over-rely on their magic.

In this school, they put an emphasis on battling with and without magic, but that's not a common practice. Most supernaturals do not have strong physical abilities without their magic. Their slower speeds and less strength would throw them off completely.

This very well may be what I need.

There doesn't seem to be many limitations, except that earth-based magic is immune. That really only applies to witches. So, don't use it on Manuela or my roommate. Any other species? Fair game.

"Find something of interest?"

I can't help but stop my smile from spreading even wider. I search through the ingredient list. It's pretty extensive. It'll take a full three weeks to brew. But totally worth it.

I start jotting down notes to myself of what I'll need. Three quarters of them I can get in my potions class. But there are another five I'll struggle to get my hands on because they're rare ingredients only found in other worlds.

I make a second list, with those hard-to-find ingredients, and pass it to Jarron. "Think you could get these for me?"

He raises his eyebrows. "Finally taking after your parents, are you?"

I shrug. "Use my strengths to my advantage."

"Good girl." He folds the page, again not asking my intentions, and puts it in his pocket. "Give me two days."

I smile. I appreciate his respect of my privacy. His trust.

Content with my day's work, Jarron and I head back toward his room.

"What did you find about the Akrasia Games?" I ask as we head down the hall.

Something new crosses my mind. What-ifs I'd rather banish at this point, but I can't help it. My mind is still my most objective strength right now. Every possibility must be considered.

What if Jarron wooed my sister and convinced her that if she won the games, she could be his queen? What if he's now priming me to do the same?

My stomach twists.

Why would he do that? Other than some sadistic form of entertainment? No idea.

I don't even think this line of reasoning makes any sense. Why would he be so willing to openly date me if he was determined to bond to a powerful being? He doesn't seem to care what people think about him dating a human.

Unless he just gets off on getting our hopes up and then crushing them.

That's not at all the Jarron I know, I remind myself. But I barely know him.

The other book in my hand should give me a bit more insight into the reality of royal demons. Were my previous expectations about demons entirely false?

Jarron seems so surprisingly human. Is that all an act?

"Not much," Jarron answers my nearly forgotten question. "The story only told me what I already know. No one knows who runs the competition, how contestants are chosen, when or how often they happen. The book simply explains what they discovered after each of the events took place."

"Like?"

"Like, there are around ten weak supernaturals or humans who enter and they're made to fight inside a magical dome. They don't know for sure what happens to the victor, or if there even is one."

I frown. "Why would there not be a victor?"

"It's not outside the realm of reason for cruel supernaturals to lie to achieve their goals. We have no way of knowing if their promises are fulfilled or not. Maybe all the contestants die at the end. That would explain how they've kept the games so secret for so long. No survivors to tell their tale. Or maybe the victor is silenced some other way."

"Hmm."

We enter Jarron's room, and I take a seat on his plush couch in front of the already flickering fire.

"I could ask around. There's a chance I could get an in from influence alone. I only worry..."

"What?"

"It's public knowledge we're together. They'd have to be extremely selective on who they give any information to, even potential betters. I don't know if I'd be disqualified for being a human sympathizer."

I cross my arms and watch the fire. "Unless you wanted your significant other to enter."

Jarron jerks his attention to me, his face full of rage and confusion. "What?"

I shrug. "Elizabeth was dating someone powerful. Someone who apparently told her they knew a way to make her powerful too."

Jarron blinks.

"She mentioned in her journal that he promised to *ascend* her."

His expression of disgust is a relief if I'm honest.

"If you fell in love with a human but knew you couldn't

mate with her without weakening your reign, what lengths would you go to alleviate that conflict? To make it so you get the best of both worlds?"

He sits up straight. "Not this." He slams a finger into the book, the image of a magical dome scrawled on the page. "If I fell in love with someone too weak to keep my reign—which is not an issue I personally have, by the way—then I would choose not to mate with them. It's appalling to think they'd risk their love's life for power. In fact, I can't see how that's love at all."

I press my lips together tightly. "I agree," I whisper eventually. "But that doesn't mean someone else might not."

Jarron runs his fingers through his dark locks once and then leans his head against his palm. He remains that way for several minutes, the silence stretching.

"I'm happy you came here, Candice," he says flatly, dropping his hand and leaning back. "Happy to have the chance to get to know you again. But if I could go back and save her, save you from this—even knowing it would mean I'd never see you again—I'd do it in a heartbeat."

My heart aches. So would I.

And somehow, maybe I'm also happy to be here.

There's this broken place inside my heart that's been there long before Liz's death. It's a vulnerability I've desperately covered up by running away.

Inadequacy.

That's what broke my heart. When I realized I was nothing. Meaningless.

Inconsequential.

And while that hasn't changed, being here is teaching me to face this fear instead of run from it. And I'm beginning to find my footing in the world I was too afraid to face.

"I was a coward," I say, in part to myself but also to him.

I don't know what to make of Jarron. I don't know if I should trust him, I don't know why his touch nearly undoes me, but he was once my friend, and regardless of if he's a calculated killer now, I shouldn't have left the way I did then.

You're a monster.

"I was a coward when I ran away from you. And Trevor. And this world. That's the truth. I was too afraid to face the reality of where I fit into this universe. Where there are entire worlds full of beings with magic I can't even fathom."

Jarron swallows.

It's like, I'm standing in this between place. A crossroads. I'm living a life where my sister's death propelled me either into the path of a psychopath killer or helped me to rectify a great wrong.

If Jarron is what he seems, then I'm the biggest douchebag in the world for snubbing him three years ago.

If he is what I'm still petrified he is—a true demon, capable of lying and killing and enjoying every second of the manipulation—then... then I'm in big, big trouble.

"You're strong, Candice. Stronger than them. Stronger than me. It's about time you see it too."

"Thanks."

"I know you told me this isn't what you want, but I'm gonna offer anyway," he says slowly, deliberately.

I watch him as he prepares to make his speech. His eyelashes are low, fists tight over his thighs.

"You want to find your own strength, and I support that.

But you have more than you think you do. You could wield the greatest weapon in this world."

My eyebrows pull low.

"Me," he growls. "There are many different forms of power, and you have power over me. Think of me as a weapon that no one else has access to. A weapon only you wield."

I don't know how to respond to that.

He leans in close, chest rising and falling heavily. "I would make the world bow at your feet, Candice, if that's what you wanted. Just say the word."

The hair on my arms rises. That is what I want.

Maybe it's that tiny bit of demonic blood in my veins, but damn if those words aren't sweet as honey to my black soul.

"I'll keep that in mind," I tell him. Because it's not as simple as he claims. I wouldn't be the only one wielding that weapon. If I could hold him in my pocket like a damn Pokemon and use him as I please, it'd make sense. But this promise is complicated. And it also hinges on trust.

So, I'll keep his offer in mind, and maybe even test him a time or two. But I won't rely on it. Instead, I'm going to find power of my own. I'm going to prove that I'm not the deer in headlights.

I'm a viper in the grass. I just have to find my poison.

26

THE ROYAL LINE OF ORIZIAH

*THE DEMONIC ROYAL **line** comprises of all descendants of Emperor Illendia, the first demon of Oriziah believed to travel inter-dimensionally and the first known ruler to mate with an alien. These descendants now number in the thousands and are considered the ruling class on the planet of Oriziah, otherwise known as the Under World. The royal line numbers in the thousands, but Oriziah remains a monarch planet with far less within the line of succession.*

There are seven species of demons accepted as higher beings by the inter-dimensional courts, with many more listed in the Oriziah Constitution. These species have earned a reputation for savagery and violence in many of the portal worlds, but the royal line continues to stand out.

The royal line has two distinct forms: one that appears nearly entirely human—though, occasionally with pointed ears—and their demon form, which consists of leathery wings and curling black horns. They can change forms at will.

The magic of the royal line continues to be unrivaled by even beings from other planets, and since the onset of their rule, the planet of Oriziah has developed into a powerhouse within the inter-dimensional systems. They have established many core alliances with fae, witches, humans, dragons, and many others.

Unlike the other species of their world, the royal line has long been considered talented negotiators and fiercely loyal allies. Most still fear their power, but those they bond to have only sung their praises.

Rarely does a demon of this bloodline marry within their own species. Though this has added to their influence within the universe, it has also caused conflict on their own planet.

This dilution of their demonic blood has long been the source of unrest on their planet. The war of Amelisia was one such conflict. Three tribes from Amelisian mountains attempted to overthrow the royal line, claiming them "aliens" who are unfit to rule.

The resolution of this war is shrouded in mystery. Official inter-dimensional reports simply claim, "The royal line has successfully assured their constituents that their demon souls remain intact and strong. Their rule is secure once again."

Many critics of the Orizian royals claim the secret behind this conflict and its resolution is integral to understanding the true cruelty of their kind, and yet this secret has never been publicly revealed.

27

GOD DIDN'T GIVE ME POWER, SO I'LL BREW IT INSTEAD

AFTER POTIONS, I approach Madame Terry's desk. "I have a question." I blurt out.

She slowly peers up at me, brow arched.

"There's a potion I want to try out. It's advanced. And maybe not at all what I'm supposed to be doing in this class. I'm not even positive it's legal."

Legalities matter very little in the grand scheme of things, but in the school, they do. My parents have brewed many illegal potions in their days and never saw a sniff of trouble because they've always made sure to stay on the right side of conflicts. In the same way no one wants to investigate a powerful supernatural for wrongful deaths, no one wants to investigate the source of potions when it's connected to said influential supernaturals.

But the school is a different matter.

"What's this potion?"

"A nullifier," I tell her.

Her lips curl into a smile. "I like it. Do you have an ingredients list?"

I hand her the scribbled list of ingredients.

Her lips flatten as she reads. "I don't have all of this."

I nod. "Jarron is going to help procure some of them."

Without pause she pulls out a piece of paper from her drawer. She scribbles something at the top, then carves the swooping letters of her signature to the bottom and holds it out to me.

"What's this?"

"Independent study permission. You will have access to one of the labs in Under Hall, to be assigned when you arrive. It will be yours for the next three months to complete your independent project. It will be in addition to your work during this class, but it will also increase your GPA if you complete your project, and you'll have the ability to enter for scholarships or grants based on your success."

I shake my head. "I don't want any of that. I just want to make the potion for myself."

She shrugs. "If you have the chance to get recognition or additional resources, it's usually best to take advantage."

I bite my tongue because I can't tell her that my goal is to stay away from the supernatural world after this school year. I want every magical being to forget I ever existed. But then again, if I succeed in killing the person responsible for my sister's death, under the radar may no longer be an option.

That's something I haven't really considered. It only makes this potion more important.

I stare at the note. Under Hall, as in all the way down below the dungeons. Fun.

"There will be basic supplies available in the study hall, but take an inventory of what is there versus what you need and take whatever else from the stores here, plus the advanced materials you'll need to procure yourself."

"Thank you," I tell her. My heart is racing with both anxiety and excitement. This potion will take a minimum of three weeks to make, but it'll be massive if I can pull it off.

I'm not much closer to uncovering my sister's killer. Everything is so circumstantial.

But I am closer to regaining my power. I'm achingly close to being able to do something when I do find her killer.

IT TOOK Jarron less than forty-eight hours to get four of my five requested ingredients, but the last is taking a bit longer. He promised I'd have it by the end of the week, so I'm taking him on his word and starting the potion now. Unicorn bone meal is one of the last ingredients to go in, so I can live without it for ten days if I start now. If it comes any later, my potion will be ruined. I've told Jarron this, but I've also decided it's worth the gamble.

I want this potion yesterday.

So, now begins my countdown. The instructions say it will give me three full uses before it runs out, and that's a generous portion, assuming it'll be used on very strong demons.

I'm already preparing for the likelihood that I'll want to make a second batch, and I'm researching what other potions I want to begin. I've made a few useful basic potions in class that I've packaged up and saved for later use. One is a blood clotter, to save someone from bleeding out too quickly when injured. Another is a speed accelerator. It doesn't make you as fast as most supernaturals and is impressively short lived, but it's potentially useful all the same. And the last is a stunning potion that will shock the target in a fairly painful manner.

Jarron sits in the corner, flipping through one of his books while I work, hair pulled back and white gloves covering my hands.

"Do demons do any human things?" I ask him.

He quirks a brow. "Meaning?"

"I like reading as much as anyone, but I was curious if you ever use technology? Internet, social media, etcetera."

He smirks. "Why? Were you hoping to change your Facebook status to in a relationship with the prince of the Under World?"

I snort. "No."

"Do demons use technology? Sometimes. Do I? Rarely."

"So, if you needed to post to TikTok to save the world, you'd let us all burn?"

He chuckles. "How, exactly, would posting to TikTok save the world?"

"Hypothetical."

"I'm sure I could figure it out. I'm not totally oblivious; I just don't particularly like being connected all the time. Some of my contacts prefer that form of communication, though. I got one of your potion ingredients from Facebook."

"Which one? Take it back!" I joke.

"So hilarious," he mocks.

I continue working in the resulting silence, organizing my ingredients. I pull out a gemstone and set it in the center of the empty cauldron. I pour in a few more ingredients then begin my first spell over the spice, sage, and salt water.

The next time I glance up at the old Victorian clock on the wall, it's a half hour later. "Damn," I mutter. "Not much time left."

We're supposed to head up to the party in the next hour, and I'm going to need a shower first.

"There isn't any real rush, but I can help if you want."

"We're supposed to be there in an hour."

"Believe me, we can be as late as we want."

I grunt.

"But really, what can I help with? I'm terrible with potions, but if you tell me what to do..."

"Can you just separate the salamander skins?" I ask, nodding to the jar of slimy skins.

He grimaces, and I quirk a brow.

"Don't tell me the prince of the Under World is squeamish."

He glares. "It's not the kind of thing I'm usually expected to do."

"Too important to get your hands dirty, got it."

He grunts and begins sorting skins without another word.

"Thank you," I mutter softly.

"Anything for you, sunshine."

I finish up my work quickly and let the few ingredients simmer in the cauldron for the night. I'll have to be up early in the morning to add a few more and check to make sure the temperature in the room is right. This potion requires a low temperature. Luckily, it's not below freezing, but it's still chilly enough that my nose is red and cold by the time I move away from it.

Even despite the frigid temperature, the spell is already steaming.

"It will be okay for the night?" he asks as I pull my gloves off and shelve the unused ingredients.

"Yeah, I'll be back in the morning to check on it."

"I can join you," he offers. "If you want."

I raise my brows. "You enjoy watching me make potions?"

"I enjoy being around you. And I don't like leaving you alone. You're relatively safe in Minor Hall, and you have friends to keep an eye out for you. But down here, you're likely to face Superior or Elite students while alone. I don't like it."

I pause, hands resting on a small vial of sea salt. "Can I ask you something?"

"Anything."

"If we weren't pretending to date..." I pause, measuring my words carefully.

He waits while I work through my thoughts.

"This protective stuff," I finally continue. "Is it just to guard your reputation?"

I honestly expect him to say yes. Well, I expect a longer answer that eventually equates to yes. I understand the need to hold back any threats to his power by showcasing his dominance. He may be magically strong, but he'd be torn down quickly if he didn't have enough backbone. Allowing anyone to harm what belongs to him—whether he actually cares or not—is dangerous.

What I don't expect is for him to stop what he's doing and step in close to me. My heart thuds loudly as his dark eyes capture mine. "Publicly break up with me tonight if you want to see how I'd react tomorrow should anyone threaten you. Harm you. Speak against you." His voice becomes increasingly angered. "I would burn this school down if anyone were to harm you, girlfriend or not. You don't have to reciprocate any of those feelings for me to care."

My cheeks heat.

"The only thing I value over your well-being, Candice, is your free will."

I frown. One, what does that mean? Two, what about his kingdom?

He leans in so close I can feel his breath heating my cheeks and smelling of mint and darkness.

"What does that mean?" I whisper. He's so close I swear he might kiss me, and that thought sends my heart racing even faster.

It wouldn't make any sense. There are no witnesses.

"It means, I'd mark you," his voice is a low purr that sends warmth through my belly, "if you'd be willing, but I know better. It means, I'll allow you to stay in Minor Hall, even though you'd be safer in Elite Hall with me. It means, I'll let you fight against your unknown villain, even though it's dangerous. I'll let you put yourself at risk when you must. Because your will matters to me."

I blink. Only one response comes to mind.

"Why?" I breathe.

He lifts his hand toward my face and gently shifts my hair behind my ear. "Because I'm not the monster you think I am."

28

OLD HABBITS

I WALK into the room with Jarron's arm slung over my shoulder, the weight more comfort than hindrance. It's funny how easy it is to fall back into old habits.

Jarron feels natural. He knows me well. I know him.

Still, my heart races and cheeks warm when all attention shifts to us.

Trevor's room is a near replica of Jarron's. The bed has red sheets instead of black, with chains and handcuffs twisted around the metal bed frame—I refuse to dwell long on that—but the layout and shiny black décor is all the same.

There are maybe a dozen people in the room, with several more on the balcony.

Bea's shrill laughter rings out over the music. "You made it! Pay up, Kyler!"

Some random vampire groans and hands a stone to Bea. Making bets on our arrival. *Good times.*

"It's about time you made it!" Stassi leaps forward,

tongue practically hanging out of his mouth. "Is it possible? Stirring cauldrons all day has actually made you more attractive?" He smiles big and wide at me.

I snort a laugh. He's a bit odd, but people like him make me feel more comfortable in situations like this, so I appreciate his exuberance. Even if I don't know what to say to all the compliments.

"By the way, I call making a speech at your wedding, okay?"

I give him an incredulous look, but he's already hopping away into the crowd. "Is he serious?"

Jarron chuckles. "Yes."

We're greeted by several wolves, one witch, and a few fae. I've done a fair bit of research but it's still hard to keep track of everyone. Besides, I've now limited most of my research to particular castes of supernaturals.

I've decided that uncovering the identity of my sister's lover is the key to her death.

So, my focus is mostly on demons. If I happen upon a sphinx or a nightshade, I'll add them on. But as of now, my list of suspects consists of eight.

Jarron.

Laithe, his second.

Trevor.

Mr. Vandozer, the principal.

Jose, Emanuel, and Mohammed, three demons who keep mostly to themselves. I haven't learned much about them yet.

And Mr. Lee, a high-level magic teacher I've never seen.

There's been a shift in the way I'm regarded in Elite Hall

since the day Jarron nearly killed Auren. I'm more accepted. Or maybe more feared, now that they've seen I have some sway over Jarron's actions.

It's one thing to be an object he protects, it's another to be a voice of influence.

Even with that shift, there's still a gap between us. Maybe one of my own making.

I need to loosen up and at least pretend to be comfortable here.

Don't let anyone make you feel weak.

Jarron is hard for me to read. Or maybe it's just that I don't quite believe the vibes I'm picking up. All signs lead to: boy has legitimate feelings for me.

But that can't be true, can it?

The demon royalty book has been in my head for these last few days too. The overall gist I've discovered is that most demon species are ruthless killers, with little morality—they are eager to destroy anything and anyone in their pursuit of power. But the demon royal line is a different story. They also used to be ruthless and animalistic, thousands of years ago, but when they connected to the human world, they began softening. Humanizing.

For a long while, this change was regarded as the royal line weakening, but in truth, the world has flourished under the new leadership style. At the end of the day, it means, yes, some species of demons are heartless bastards, but demons like Jarron have a strong level of humanity in their blood. It's very possible for them to have affection for humans or other lesser creatures.

Jarron may be exactly what he appears to be.

But even a human could wear a mask to hide the darkness deep inside, so it's not impossible for my first theory to hold true. It's just a lot more complicated than that now.

I find a small glass filled with a dark red liquid right in front of me in the hand of a dark-skinned witch. I consider accepting the offering because it's clear to me that what's holding me back from getting the secrets I need is myself.

But before my fingers can grasp the glass, a rumble escapes Jarron's chest.

The witch stumbles back with an apology.

"What the hell was that?" I ask.

"You do not accept drinks from anyone," he tells me.

"Oh, come on, Jarron," a deep voice says. We spin to see Trevor scowling at his brother. "You don't really think I'd let anyone spell the drinks in my own room, do you?"

Jarron quirks a brow. "Like that black out night didn't happen last summer?"

"That was different."

"Jeremy laced our drinks, and you know it."

Trevor rolls his eyes. "All my canisters have protection spells on them."

"Good, then we will pour our own drinks."

The crowd parts as Jarron pulls me over to the drink cabinet. Twin witches squeal and flee the area.

"Okay, Mr. Growly. I thought today was about fitting in."

"You don't have to drink."

"I want to."

He quirks a brow, then after a beat, he slides two glass bottles forward. One is red, one is blue.

"Red is a mollifier, basically a relaxing potion with similar effects as alcohol. Blue has a mild hallucinogen. It usually takes four or more drinks to feel anything, but I don't know how quickly your body would metabolize it. It may feel stronger to you. So, blue just to loosen up a bit. Red to party hard."

"Red," I answer easily.

Without hesitation, he pours a few ounces of the red potion into a glass cup, drops a sugar cube into it, then hands it to me.

"Thanks," I say and take a tiny sip. It's sweet and sour and oh so smooth.

Jarron pours himself a glass of something black and oozing.

"What the hell is that?"

"Something I don't expect you to taste. I'm not sure it's even consumable for humans."

"Looks like tar."

He smiles. "It's not tar."

"Is it a hallucinogen?"

"No. Mostly, just calming. It's possible to feel a sort of high from it, not unlike marijuana, I'm told, but it would take a lot to feel it's effects in any strong way. And yes, it's completely legal."

"Even at your age?" I nudge him with my elbow.

"Even at my age."

I shrug and leave it at that. "Anything else I should know?"

"I'll be with you the entire night. Go nowhere with anyone alone. Ever."

I scowl at him. "I'm not stupid. But you don't have to be linked to my side. I need to make friends, right?"

He examines me closely. "Tonight is our first outing as a couple. We should stay together, most, if not all, of the night. This is a primer. A showcase for our relationship. Once that's solidified in people's minds, they'll begin to come to you on their own."

I frown but nod. All right, we'll do this his way.

We're inseparable and in love. Or at least in lust.

My heart skips a beat as I consider exactly what that means. Will he kiss me tonight?

I take a large gulp of my drink and wince; this time, the liquid has a harsher bite.

Jarron smirks. "I suppose I should have poured you a larger glass."

JARRON and I make our way through the pods of supernaturals. One group plays dart dodge—dodge ball with darts. Which is entertaining to watch for its high level of stupidity. But I suppose when you're a wolf shifter that heals in seconds, what difference does it make?

One dart is deflected and soars straight toward us. I yelp and throw my arm up, but Jarron disintegrates the projectile with a flick of his wrist.

"Maybe enough dart dodge for me," I mutter.

Jarron chuckles and curls his arm around my waist. He takes a seat in a cushioned chair near the low flickering fire and tugs me into his lap. My blush remains for the following thirty minutes as we chat with a female shifter and Manuela.

There is nothing overly sexual about the position. Yes, my butt is on his thigh and his arm is still hooked around my waist, but no one seems to bat an eye.

I nurse my second drink, not wanting to overdo it.

To be honest I was never much of a partier at my other schools. A couple of our friends would sneak a bottle of wine to share for movie night and we'd have spiked drinks during dances, but that was only a couple times every year.

I'm fairly certain this crowd does this nearly every weekend in some fashion or another. But supernaturals tend to have much quicker metabolisms than humans, which means the effects don't last as long.

The female wolf shifter across from us is a pretty redhead with ballerina-like grace. Manuela takes the opportunity to introduce her friend Lucille and brag about her abilities, telling me she's one of the most highly sought-after females in Elite Hall. That surprises me because I don't ever see her with us at lunch.

Jarron's right hand rests on my upper thigh casually; his left holds his tar-like beverage. He doesn't add much to the conversation, though. Only answering when spoken to.

"It's good to see him out," Lucille says, her voice low and sultry, but not in a way that makes me uncomfortable. I notice many of the wolf shifters watching her intently. "Jarron doesn't spend much time with us little people."

Jarron snorts.

"And to see him with a female," she raises a brow at him, "is even better."

His hand tightens on my thigh. I'm not sure what to make of the turn in conversation.

"Was he lonely before?" I ask.

"I suspect he likes his solitude. But we enjoy seeing him come out of his shell."

"Some were beginning to suspect I prefer men," Jarron tells me.

"Oh," I say stupidly.

"In truth, if I did prefer men, I wouldn't be bashful about it."

"Turns out he just prefers *humans*," a shifter behind us says then howls in laughter. I tense in Jarron's lap. He squeezes me tighter.

"Or perhaps he prefers non-douche bags," I say, quieter than I'd have liked.

Jarron's lips graze my shoulder, as he chuckles. "I quite agree."

"Busybodies, the lot of 'em," Manuela says. "Curiosity is a hard habit to quit, though."

I meet her stare. "Maybe so, but it doesn't need to be voiced."

Eventually, Jarron and I head outside, where it's a bit quieter and I ask him about the redheaded shifter female. He explains that Lucille is indeed strong and every wolf would give his tail to be with her. She doesn't like to be around the shifters at school very often because they tend to annoy her with their attempts to woo her.

He runs his fingers down my back slowly. "Would you like another?"

"Huh?" I squeak, distracted by the sensations.

"Drink?" he purrs. "Would you like another drink?"

Oh, right. "No. I'm good for the night."

"Thought that potion was supposed to loosen humans up," a wolf jokes. "She still seems so uptight."

My stomach sinks. Am I ruining this?

Jarron leans in close until his lips are at my ear. "You have nothing to prove to them."

"This is the same reason I never partied even at human schools," I say.

"Oh?"

"Introverts are always misunderstood." I shrug. "And when we do try to have fun, boys expect us to act a certain way. Like they want us to perform for them. It's annoying."

"Perform?"

"Dance, flirt, laugh, belly shots, flashing."

Jarron tilts his head. "What is flashing?"

I blush and don't respond. Does he really not know?

He gently pulls me to face him. "What?"

I cough awkwardly. "Oh, ya know, when a girl lifts her shirt to show..."

His eyebrows rise, but his expression is innocent curiosity. "Show what?"

"Jesus, you really don't know? Or you're just messing with me?"

His lips quirk ever so slightly. "Not messing with you, but I'm very curious now."

"They show their... boobs." God, why does that word sound so damn stupid?

"Humans are pigs," a deep voice says. I blink and turn to find Bea and Trevor standing in the open doorway.

"Human boys sound exactly like supernatural boys," Bea says with a smirk.

I blush as Trevor grabs Bea's right breast, full on.

"See?" she laughs.

Jarron appears less than amused. Bea and Trevor walk

away without another word and disappear around the bend to some unseen section of the balcony.

In the silence, the two wolves start chatting about which path they like to run the most. They point to the trees that are a blur of darkness to me. Apparently, they can see well enough to point out trails.

Jarron and I stand side by side against the banister, looking out at the darkness. I grow bored of the view quickly since I can't see much of anything beyond the torchlight.

There's barely an inch separating Jarron's chest from my arm.

He's watching me I realize, and I turn to face him as he examines every inch of me. *What's he trying to find?* I wonder.

He reaches out slowly until his fingers find my bare shoulder, then drift up my neck. I tilt my head, exposing more of my neck to him.

He freezes. His eyes turn to solid black and pin to my neck. I gasp, and Jarron doesn't so much as budge. Just below his top lip, two sharp, white points appear.

Fangs.

"Uh oh. Time to go," the dark wolf jokes and then pulls a blond back through the door to the crowded room.

"Jarron?" I ask, voice so small it makes me sick to my stomach. I'm helpless. Jarron's expression is one of hunger.

He blinks, and color returns to his eyes. "Sorry," he whispers, wincing tightly. "Want to go back inside?"

I peep past his arm to the buzzing powerful supernaturals in Trevor's room. I don't particularly want to rejoin that part of society. It's quiet out here. The cool air is heaven on my hot skin.

I don't respond, just settle back into a comfortable position nestled between his arms. "I'm sorry I called you a monster," I say.

His hand clenches over the metal banisher, caging me in.

"I'm sorry I left like that." It's something I should have said a long time ago, but I've been too proud. And too unsure. Am I beginning to believe in his innocence? That's the only thing that would make me say that, right? If I believed him. Trusted him. Cared for him.

He finally takes in a breath, long and slow. "If you knew my thoughts just now, I'd have proved you right." He sounds pained.

I bite the inside of my lip. "You wanted to bite me?" I ask. That had been a strange, tension-filled moment, and the way the wolves reacted was odd.

I watch his expression closely. He's focused on something in the darkness I'm sure I couldn't make out even if I were to shift my attention there. His jaw clenches.

"Do you—is that something you do?"

His gaze shifts to me, agony so clear in his eyes that I feel the urge to run my hands over his chest. To comfort him. Not that I'd have the slightest idea of how to do that.

"You think I go around biting innocent damsels for fun?"

I clear my throat, torn between awkward embarrassment and honest amusement. "Oh, well, I mean, demons in general. I skipped over the blood-drinking portions of my demon studies."

His lip quirks ever so slightly. "Interested in the inner-workings of demons, are you?"

I shrug.

He straightens, and all emotion disappears as he

explains, "Most demons you'd ever meet are carnivores. They'll eat anything with a pulse. Blood, organs, all of it. Even cannibalism isn't uncommon. Blood drinking is slightly different, but common among some species."

I purse my lips. That's interesting. But if there is one thing I've learned from my book about demons, it's that there is a big difference between the royal line and other beings from the same world. "The royal line?"

"We eat only from creatures without complex thoughts and emotions, as a general rule. We farm, much like in the human world, breeding our preferred meals. We avoid the blood of our prey by draining them completely before butchering."

"So, where does blood drinking come in, then?"

He admitted he wanted to bite me, so there's obviously some kind of precedent for it.

He runs his tongue along the edge of his canine, so much longer than just a few minutes ago. Do they elongate when he loses control? He seems pretty in control right now.

"Biting a living creature and drinking their blood is a very different act then consuming the flesh of our prey. We do not drink from the creatures we eat. In fact, that would be considered obscene. Blood is not a form of true sustenance. It's more of a pleasure than a need."

My heart skips a beat. "Like dessert?"

His gaze turns dark, and with each breath, he shifts closer. "No, not exactly." His hips are touching mine, and a tremor begins in my legs.

"Like sex?" I squeak.

A low vibration begins in his chest. "Yes." His whisper is husky.

I close my eyes and allow myself to feel these terrifying emotions for only this moment before I lock them away for good.

"It's an erotic sensation."

The pressure of his body increases, and a slight vibration begins in his chest. I grip his waist tightly. Then, finally, I force my eyes open.

"Let's go inside now," I manage to say with a surprisingly solid voice.

Without hesitation, Jarron steps back. My fists clench. *Calm down*, I coach myself.

"Are you okay?"

I nod quickly. My blood is heated, and I'm feeling things I most definitely shouldn't be, but I'm not afraid. That's the weirdest part about this.

Jarron just admitted he wanted to bite me. Suck my blood.

And I am not afraid.

I shake that thought from my mind and take his outstretched arm. He guides me back inside. Everyone watches as we make our way to the drink station. Is it my imagination or are they all staring at my unmarked neck?

Wonderful.

Jarron pours two new drinks. "You don't have to drink it," he murmurs. "It's just something to do with your hands until the attention dies down."

"Thank you," I say honestly. It's a thoughtful gesture because he's right. It does help to have something to hold on to while the entire room is focused on us.

"Anything else you'd like to do?" he asks. "We can call it a night at any time."

My body is still buzzing from our most recent conversation and dealing with the overwhelming attention from it. There are a few couples forming now. One wolf and a vampire are sucking face on Trevor's bed. Two male fae and a female wolf have made their way to the balcony and are getting a bit handsy. Who knows where Trevor and Bea went.

"Aren't we supposed to..." My heart races all over again.

"Supposed to what?"

"Kiss," I whisper, in part because people probably shouldn't overhear us chatting about a planned kiss and also because part of me is utterly terrified.

Jarron flinches, surprise lighting his expression. My stomach sinks. Is he dreading it too? I don't know why that bothers me. It shouldn't.

We're not really together. Not really dating.

He doesn't really like me like that.

"Come with me." He tugs me by my free hand to an open chair. He sits and pats the footrest for me to sit between his legs. I oblige with an awkward smile.

He keeps hold of my hand, as I sit. He watches me closely. What is he looking for?

"Is that what you want?" he asks softly.

I press my lips together. "I... no. I mean, it's what we talked about before, in the speakeasy. It's... for the—" I cut off my rambling.

He glances at the large group gathered in the opposite corner, chatting and laughing and occasionally sending glances our way. His lips are turned down, his jaw tight.

"Unless you don't want to," I offer, stomach sour.

He gives me a half-grin, his expression still slack. "What I don't want, Candice, is to kiss you if you don't want it."

My lips part. I hadn't expected that. "But I thought—"

"I was wrong. It's not fair to hold that over you." He looks away again. "I don't want to if you don't."

I lick my lips. There's a tension in my limbs that I'm unsure how to define. I'm confused to my very core. I want him. I don't want him. I desperately want him to want me, and I'm terrified of that very same thing.

"What about them?" I ask. "Aren't we supposed to sell this?"

"Believe me, we did that already. Maybe we'll just save the kiss for another time. This was plenty enough for tonight."

Disappointment swirls in my stomach. And shame at that same feeling. What the hell is happening to me? "You're sure? They believe you're really into me?"

Jarron chuckles, but his smile doesn't reach his eyes. "Yes, they are fully convinced. For now."

His fingers dance gentle circles on my knee.

"Tomorrow, you should spend some time in Elite Hall. We'll make it casual, not a date. You can have free reign. Go to the library, get a chai. Sit in the lounge. I'll be around, keeping an eye out, but we won't stay together the whole time. You may find opportunities to meet some new friends."

My brow furrows. "Friends?"

"When I offered to help, I told you I could make the Elite want to be your friends and tell you all of their dark secrets."

"You also said that would happen in a matter of days."

"Yes, well, it could have, but you were hesitant, and I didn't want to push you."

Fair enough. I was terrified of this place, of how it made me feel. I was out of my element, and they could all tell. Now, I guess I'm feeling more comfortable. "So, you're saying if I spend time here without you, Auren and Manuela and Mia, the wolves, and whomever else will spill their guts to me?"

"No, not all of them. Most likely the lesser females in the hall. The ones who want in but aren't quite there yet."

"None of the guys?" I ask, simply curious.

"Most of them will be too afraid to spark my jealousy."

"Except Stassi," I say. He's most definitely not afraid to make Jarron jealous.

He nods. "Except Stassi. He's like that with everyone. He would never overstep with you."

"Would it?" I ask. "Would other wolves talking to me make you jealous?"

"Maybe. Many of the wolves are already on thin ice with me. They're too forward, and I don't like how they look at you."

I frown. "How do they look at me?"

"Like a meal."

I grimace. I'm not sure which way he means that—they desire me or want to rip me apart? Maybe both.

My mind jumps to my potion brewing deep below us, and I long for it to be ready. I need more too. I need something offensive. Something to put those pups in their place if they do decide to push their boundaries when Jarron isn't around.

Jarron's thumb caresses my cheek. "What are you thinking about?"

I blink. "Ways to put them in their place if it comes to that."

"Good girl," he purrs. His words send a shiver down my spine. "And what did you come up with?"

"Not much yet. I'll look for another potion this week and see if I can find something."

"I have something that could help if you're interested."

"Oh?"

He nods with a mischievous smile. "We can go back to my room now if that's okay. I'll give you a little gift and then walk you back to Minor Hall."

I bite my lip, unsure how to define the feelings shifting through me. I won't give voice to the things swirling beneath the surface. I may be starting to trust Jarron more, but I can't let my guard down completely.

And, even if I did, all of this is pretend. Make believe.

We aren't really together.

Jarron wouldn't want someone like me.

29

TOO LATE FOR I'M SORRY

WE GIVE a few casual goodbyes to the party and head back to Jarron's room, which is right around the corner. In the hall, two boys leap back from each other with squeals of panic and then scramble away the moment they see us.

Jarron chuckles.

"Does it ever bother you, the way they fear you?"

"Why would it?"

I smirk and shrug. "It would bother some people."

"Would it bother you?"

"No," I say too quickly. My cheeks warm. "I'd enjoy it."

Jarron's eyes shine with some unknown emotion, then he pushes open the doors to his room for me.

His room is pristine, as usual. The bed is covered in smooth black silk without a wrinkle in sight. And yet, his pile of notes and books still sit in the corner untouched.

"What are behind those doors?" I ask, nodding to the two single doors on the left wall.

"That one is a closet. Nothing too interesting. This one,

though." He pushes open the door, and a warm light automatically flicks on, followed by purple and blue inlet lighting, revealing a massive luxurious bathroom.

"Wow.". There's a huge rainfall shower with slate grey tiles. A porcelain tub and double sinks.

"You're welcome to use it any time you like."

I step away from the massive bathroom, farther into his bedroom, because for some reason, that feels like the safer place. That shower looks to be made for more than one person to use at a time.

Or maybe that's just my dirty mind going there.

"What did you want to give me?"

"Right!" Jarron leaps into action and is across the room in an instant. He pulls open the top drawer of the table beside his bed and hands me a narrow black box.

"What's this?"

"Open it. It's a gift."

Frowning, I pull the lid open and gasp at the beautiful black dagger inside. The hilt has a spiraling design, and the blade is shiny black.

"It's spelled obsidian. It can kill most supernaturals, powerful or not."

I swallow. "How?"

"You might want to do a little research to fully understand how it affects different supernaturals. To kill a wolf, you'll need to pierce the heart. But even just a cut will weaken them significantly more than a regular blade. It would render vampires motionless for nearly a minute if you get it deep enough. It won't affect witches any more than any other material, though."

"Demons?" I ask, voice thin.

Jarron smirks. "Would you like to try it out?"

I blanch. "You think I want to kill you?"

He chuckles. "It wouldn't kill me. Even a direct shot to my heart, I could survive. Though, it'd hurt."

"So, it wouldn't do anything to you?"

"It would weaken me, but the effects would be limited. You could add additional spells to it, though. Coat it with a potion of some kind. Obsidian takes well to magical influence."

"How—" I shake my head, realizing how ridiculous of a question this would be to ask Jarron.

"What?"

"How do you kill a demon?" I ask, cheeks reddening. "Not that I'm—"

He steps closer. "No need to explain. It's a valid question."

"Okay," I whisper.

"You'd have to remove the heart completely. Or sever the head."

I suddenly feel faint at the thought of either of those things.

"Our healing abilities are quite significant, and we can heal from nearly all other injuries. There are many spells and potions that can weaken us, making it easier to do what's necessary to end our lives. There are also some illnesses that can take us out, and extreme temperatures could do it too."

"How extreme?"

"Very. At least double the cold or heat it would take to kill a human."

With deft fingers, he closes the lid over the blade.

"It's not technically allowed." He shrugs. "If you happen to get in trouble with it, call me and I'll clear it up. But feel free to flash it any time someone makes you feel uncomfortable, and definitely if you're ever threatened. It will be intimidating to any wolf or vamp, which is what I most like about it. Only use it if you absolutely must. Oh! And this is for you too."

He hands me what looks like black ribbon with something attached.

"It's a thigh holster. You can wear it under your skirt during school."

"Thank you." It's a kind gift. The kind that could give me a chance at evening the playing field between me and my masked villain.

"I want you to stay safe, Candice. I want you to feel as comfortable as possible. And most of all, I want you to learn just how powerful you're capable of being. You're beginning to see it. I'm eager to see how far you can go here. What potions you can create. One day, you'll put one of us in our place definitively, and I will love every second of it."

"Why?" I whisper. "Why do you care so much?" I don't even understand how he could be this kind and considerate to me after everything.

Without responding, Jarron takes a few long strides to his bed and curls his legs beneath him casually. I don't move, still holding tightly to the dagger box.

"One night on Myre Island, when we were young, there was a vampire on the beach. Do you remember?"

I nod.

"Trevor and Liz ran off the moment we saw him. He seemed peaceful, soaking in the moonlight, but we knew he was dangerous to all four of us at the time. He could have killed us all if given the chance. But you refused to retreat. We were building a sandcastle in the middle of the night—because somehow that made sense."

I smirk at that memory.

"I remember the way the moon reflected off your hair. The expression on your face as you focused so intently on our castle. You barked instructions at me, but most of the time, I didn't complete the task to your liking, so you redid it anyway."

I remember how no one ever wanted to build with me because I annoyed the hell out of them all. Except Jarron. He was impressively patient with me. Maybe that's why I was always closer with him than Trevor. Liz put up with my antics only as much as she had to. She'd go off and do her own thing, leaving me to obsess over whatever it was I was obsessing over at the time.

In this case, a sandcastle.

Myre Island was fairly safe. There were guards everywhere and only a few select families were allowed there. There weren't supposed to be any vampires, that's for sure.

"We should have run too, you know. A human and an underage demon prince? A prime meal for a vamp who'd just swam miles. But you refused to run. You were the bravest of us all."

I snort. "I wasn't brave. I was stupid."

He shrugs. "I was in awe," he says, voice distant. "You just sat there and continued to shift the sand beneath your fingers, crafting this ridiculously elaborate structure. I still don't know how you did it. It was like you were spelling the sand."

"I don't have any magic."

"Yeah, I know. But in my mind, it was magic. *You* were magic. Because that vampire never even looked in our direction. He saw Trevor and Liz run up over the hill and into your parents' house. But we stayed on the beach, and he didn't see us. I wondered what would have happened if he had seen us. I was convinced that you'd protect me. No one could ever stand against someone as brave and strong and beautiful as you."

I suck in a breath.

"That's why. That's why I'm so determined to help you, both in getting your revenge and gaining back the power I'm so convinced you could have. Should have. I know you're human; I'm not saying you have any hidden magic. But you didn't run when you should have. And I want to see that Candice again. I want you to believe you can be her."

My stomach twists. Tears sting the back of my throat.

I don't see that night the same way he does. Our parents came out within ten minutes, before I was even able to finish my project, and they flipped out that we were out alone at night. The authorities hunted down the vampire, and I was grounded for three days. By the time I was allowed back out, my castle was completely gone. It was pointless. Worthless.

I never realized he'd been impressed by my bravery or my determination. Both were stupid, in my mind.

"Thank you, for the dagger," I tell him. "I should head back now." My stomach aches, again unsure if that's actually what I want.

Jarron slowly rises to his feet and approaches the door. But I don't move, something sticking in my mind.

"That night," I whisper just as his hand lands on the door handle. "The night you changed. Do you remember that one?"

He freezes. "Not really. It's all a blur."

"You turned, exposing your true form while we were playing hide and seek. And you stalked Liz."

Jarron stops breathing. He still isn't looking at me; he stares down at his hand, squeezing the handle tightly. We were just playing. I don't know what triggered his manifestation or if that's just how it works. One moment he's basically a regular boy, if not a bit stronger and faster than usual, and the next, he's a literal beast with magic he couldn't even begin to control.

"You weren't you." My voice breaks the same way my heart did that night. "You hurt her. Did you know that?"

His head whips to me, eyes fully black. I stumble backward at the sight of those demon eyes that terrified me from that night.

But after only an instant, I recognize something more. It's pain. I swear I've never seen more anguish in my life.

"It wasn't deep, but your talons broke the skin on her chest," I whisper with a wobbly voice. "And our parents came running within moments. I was angry that you'd hurt her. But I was even more angry that I couldn't do anything to stop it. We knew your parents were magical, from a different world. We thought that was cool before we saw what it meant for ourselves. Before we felt your magic controlling us." I shake my head. I don't need to go into detail about how much I screamed and cried for him to stop or how I convinced myself I hated him because he wouldn't.

"But I thought you were gone. Or at least, that's what I

convinced myself. I mourned you like you died because in my mind, you had. And that's what I expected when I came here. I thought I'd have to look into the face of a boy I once cared about and see a monster, like I did that night."

Jarron's shoulders go slack, and he leans forward until his forehead is leaning against the door frame. "I'm so sorry," he whispers. "I didn't even…" He shakes his head. "Trevor told me that I'd changed in front of you. Scared you. But that you were fine. I came to see you the next day, and you called me a monster." His body shutters.

I don't say anything more because there isn't anything more to be said.

"My father had this long talk with us about how differently people react to what we are. Some will hate us. Some will desire us. Some will try to manipulate us. Only a rare few will accept us truly. When we find those people, we have to hold on to them."

I swallow, watching him force air through his lungs.

"I was determined you were that person. You had to be. But then, as time went on and you responded to my letters with that goodbye note, telling me you didn't want to have anything to do with anything magical—including me. I was angry. Hurt. Confused. But I never realized I harmed her. No one ever told me that."

He straightens but still doesn't look my way.

"Now, it's too late. I can't even tell her I'm sorry."

Jarron pulls open the door and steps into the hall quickly. He waits only a moment for me to join him. His gaze is set straight ahead, his arms crossed as we walk. I want to apologize again. I want to tell him I believe he's not really a monster. I want to tell him I can be that person, the one that accepts him and cares for him.

But I don't know if any of that is true. Or if it should be true. Can I be that person? Should I be?

After all of this is over, can I be his true friend? Because I really don't know.

We walk in silence, the weight of that conversation still hanging between us like a physical wall. I don't know how to bridge this.

And so, we say nothing. All the way across campus. Until the Minor Hall gate comes into view and he stops. When I turn, only to find dark, dead eyes watching me.

"Goodnight, Candice."

He walks away before I even pass through the gate.

30

BITE ME. JUST KIDDING, PLEASE DON'T

I TOSS and turn that night, thinking through that entire evening with Jarron. How his touch affected me. How he wanted to bite me—and I wasn't afraid. How he wouldn't kiss me, even though it made all the sense in the world.

His story about the nighttime sandcastle.

My story about his change. He didn't even remember it. He didn't know he hurt her. The injury really wasn't that big of a deal; it was more about the feeling behind it.

I tried to pull him off of her, but his magic sucked the air from my lungs until I couldn't move.

He grabbed my sister's throat and growled, a shrieking inhuman sound. Not at all like the warning growls he does now. His eyes were so black there were no whites to them at all. His bat-like wings curled over his hunched back.

Jarron was gone, replaced by something utterly alien. It was horrific. A moment I've never gotten over.

I could have watched my sister die right there and been powerless to stop it.

And it was him. Jarron.

How could I ever feel powerful again if I couldn't even stop someone who loved me from hurting me? It wasn't long after that my parents revealed the truth about the threats on our lives by the witch potionist. Honestly, I think they wanted us to be thankful to the Blackthorns for their protection, but it had the opposite effect.

Liz and I came to an easy conclusion. We would never be truly safe or welcome in the supernatural world.

Our parents were supportive of our decision to remove ourselves from their business and the world of magic completely, even though it harmed our relationship as a family.

Now, I wonder if that was the right decision. Was it short sighted and based in fear?

I finally fall asleep with one word on my mind.

Coward.

I WAKE EARLY, surprised to find my headache missing, despite the restless night I had.

"Good morning," Corrine purrs from the bed across the room.

I sigh. "Morning, yes. Good, no."

"Did your party go badly, then?"

"No, the party went well. Just didn't sleep well. How about you? You were hanging with that boyfriend of yours, right?"

Her smile spreads wide. She's been teasing us with hints of her *amazing* boyfriend but never giving us any information. It's annoying. It would bother me more, though, if I knew her better. As it is, we only talk occasionally.

She wants attention. She wants us to ask continuous questions and obsess over the mystery, but I have more important things to obsess over.

"Janet has a boyfriend now too. Did she tell you?"

I twist to face her. "No, she didn't. Who is he?"

She shrugs. "Ask her. She's your friend. Sorta."

I frown. I've been spending a lot of time working on my potions and doing my research. Not a lot of time talking to Janet and Lola about their own relationships. Does that make me a bad friend?

Corrine skips from the room, leaving me to dwell on my own concerns. I take a few minutes to play with my shiny new weapon. It takes me fifteen minutes to figure out the best way to strap it to my thigh beneath my skirt. I walk around, testing the weight and the tightness. I find a decent balance finally and head out.

I do a sweep through Minor Hall for Lola and Janet, Corrine's words still bothering me. But when I find no sign of them, I head to Under Hall to work on my potion. It needs to be done. Hopefully, I can find them afterward, before I go to Elite Hall.

There's no sign of Jarron in Under Hall or in my potions room, which I'm disappointed by. One, he told me he'd come. Two, I want to make sure everything is okay after our conversation last night.

I just told him the reason I avoided him for years. Now that I've had the chance to get to know him again, I wish I'd handled that situation differently. I shouldn't have fled like a coward. I should have... at least talked to him.

I called him a monster, but I don't think that anymore.

Maybe I should have said that last night.

I'd like to say it now.

Because unless he's a true psychopath and a fabulous actor, he really is the same Jarron as before.

And the horrible possibility that he's an emotionless killer just doesn't add up. Trevor would also have to be acting, and the people in school would be shocked at his change in behavior.

I still know he was capable of hurting Liz, but the worst thing I can imagine now, is that it was an accident or a stupid mistake that led to her death.

I finish up a few hours' worth of work on my potion and then head back to Minor Hall for an early lunch.

The tension in my chest eases slightly when I find Janet and Lola in the common room. They happily join me for lunch, and I ask all the questions about Janet's boyfriend.

"He's not my boyfriend!" she exclaims, but her cheeks are red.

"Well, tell us about him. We can help make him your boyfriend." I grin wide.

"I don't want to jinx it."

All I've gathered after our conversation is that he is not in Minor Hall and he kissed her on the cheek last night. She's planning to see him again next weekend, and they talk between classes sometimes.

Friend duty established, I ask them something that's been bothering me about my own boy troubles. "So, tell me about the biting situation," I say under my breath.

Lola's resounding giggle is like a tinkling bell, and it's sickeningly cute. Janet leans in, expression bright and excited. "Honestly, I'm surprised he hasn't bitten you yet," she whispers. "It's usually a pretty quick development."

She's been a lot more open with me this week. Maybe she's beginning to trust that I'm really here to stay.

"But you guys have taken things really slow, and that's totally okay. You have history, and he's obviously into you. I wouldn't worry about it."

Yeah, I wasn't concerned that he hadn't bitten me yet. I'm really only concerned what other people think about it. No demons will be sinking any teeth into me any time soon. I hope.

31
VIOLENTLY PROTECTIVE BOYFRIENDS ARE... KINDA HOT. SUE ME.

AFTER LUNCH, I head over to Elite Hall as discussed and pray Jarron isn't going to be MIA there too. The moment the archways come into view, so do three shifters. Two girls, one boy. Their bright silver eyes pin to me and don't let go.

I try my best not to act like a scared kitten, but I doubt I achieve it. I'm nervous about walking into Elite Hall alone and worried Jarron won't be around when I do. I know being alone was part of the plan, but not *completely* alone.

"Hey," one of the wolf girls says with a sweet smile. She has short dirty blond hair. "Candice, right?"

I swallow. "Yep, that's me."

"I'm Elyse. This is Charlene." She points to a Middle Eastern girl next to her. Her hair is braided intricately, and she has henna on her hands. "And Tommy." A tall, lanky boy with clothes that barely fit him.

I wave stupidly.

"You meeting Jarron?"

"Yeah." I force a smile.

"That sounds a bit uncertain," Tommy says with a flick of his brow. I don't like the expression on his face. Like a predator that's spotted a weakness and is eager to exploit it.

I decide for honesty because I'm not able to hide all of my insecurities right now. "He was supposed to meet me in Under Hall earlier but didn't show."

"Damn. Standing you up already," the boy says and then rubs his jaw in that stupid, arrogant way.

I nearly curl a lip in disgust.

"Is he done with you now? Can I have a turn?" He leans in, a predator sizing me up.

My stomach sinks.

"Shut up," Charlene says, smacking her hand against his chest. Her voice is low and sultry. "I'm sure it was a misunderstanding."

"Yeah, definitely," I say and point to the archway. Is it like Minor Hall, stopping certain people from entering? "I've never gone in without him, though. Is there a trick or something?"

Charlene smiles. "Anyone in his inner circle has access to Elite Hall. No trick, just walk through. If you want to send a message, though, just put your hand on the panel on the right column and a phantom will show up to help you out."

"Really?"

She nods.

"Thanks. That's helpful."

"Shouldn't he have told you all of this?" Tommy takes a step forward. My heart speeds up. The girls are nice, but if Tommy tries something, will they stop him? I don't know.

The strap over my thigh feels suddenly tight. A reminder that I do have some defense. Even if it's not much.

"I'm just saying. No committed boyfriend would leave her all alone to face the wolves." Tommy laughs.

I ignore the comment. "Thanks," I say, continuing to ignore the creep.

I look up at the intricate structure as I pass through the metal vines protecting the archway. They constrict the moment I'm under them. Nothing else happens, and I keep walking.

Once past the barrier, I rush forward, away from the wolves, and rush to find Jarron. He's sitting in one of the large armchairs in the sunroom, where the black willow hangs over the glass panels. Trevor, Stassi, and Bea are in the chairs surrounding him.

His posture is casual, slumped in the chair with an air of arrogance that gets under my skin in uncomfortable ways. He flicks a brow as I approach.

I'm one part relieved, one part annoyed as hell.

"My, my, candy—" Stassi says, his grin wide. "Can I call you candy? You are a snack, after all."

"No," Jarron and I say at once. Bea chuckles.

"I was wondering if you'd come," Jarron says lightly.

I cross my arms. "I thought you were meeting me to work on my potion, but I guess not."

He blinks, a sincere expression of surprise flickering across his face. He sits up straighter. "I totally forgot about that."

I consider saying more, but my stomach is still in knots from the trip in here. From the way that wolf looked at me.

Like a meal.

Jarron leans forward. "You all right?"

"Mhmm," I answer, unsure if that's actually true. We

talked last night about his concern for my safety. He said he doesn't trust the wolves, but the next day, he leaves me alone and I'm confronted by one. For some reason, that hurts.

He doesn't owe me anything, I remind myself. I won't have him to protect me forever, so I may as well get used to it.

"I'm gonna go to the library," I say and begin walking before I can expose any more of these stupid emotions. I walk quickly through the hall, passing a few supernaturals without so much as a glance to tell if I know them or what caste they belong to.

"Hey," Jarron calls.

I take in a long deep breath before he catches up. Determination fills me. *I don't need him. It doesn't matter. None of it.*

His hand wraps around my upper arm, and he pulls me to a stop. "What's going on?"

"Nothing," I say. Though, I meet his stare, my heart still beats unevenly. "This is what we planned, right?"

He frowns, looking me over. "You're mad. Is this about last night?"

I clasp my hands together "No."

"Then, what? Did something happen? Someone say something?"

"No."

"You're mad I didn't come to Under Hall this morning?"

"No."

He throws up his hands. "Then, what is it?" He's frustrated, but his voice is strained. He's also concerned. Some of my ice melts.

"Nothing. I'm fine. I was just a bit nervous coming here

today. And I had to walk in alone." I shake my head. I consider mentioning the wolves, but nothing happened there, and I don't want him to worry or get angry.

"We should have talked about this a bit more. I should have—" He run his hand through his hair.

I shrug. He steps closer and reaches out to touch my cheek with his thumb the way he does. I close my eyes.

"I'm sorry," he whispers. "I've been a bit off since—well, what you told me last night. I would have done things differently if I'd known, and I can't stop thinking about it all." He shakes his head. "It's not an excuse. You shouldn't have had to come here alone. That was stupid. And I'm sorry for ditching you this morning; I really didn't remember."

I nod. He leans in, pressing his forehead to mine. He grips my hand and curls his fingers through mine.

"I want you to feel safe here. That's important to me."

I'm not though, am I? Maybe I was beginning to feel something, but that was stupid too. I'm here for a purpose. I have a plan. I'm not here to reconnect with an old friend. While part of me is happy to have the chance to get to know him again, to learn he wasn't as gone as I thought, I can't let it derail me.

"I do really want to go to the library."

"How about a drink first? A chai, or maybe change it up with a cinnamon cider? It's the potionist's signature recipe for fall."

I force my lips into a smile. "Cider sounds good."

His shoulders relax. Our fingers stay interlaced as we walk together toward the speakeasy. He quickly pours us two glasses of cinnamon apple cider from the thermos container, and then we sit at one of the open tables.

I fidget with the glass.

"Is that really all?" His voice is hoarse.

"I'm not sure we're doing a very good job convincing people we're a real couple," I spit out. Which maybe was a stupid thing to say, but it's what came to mind.

He leans back, surprised. "What makes you say that?"

"Just something..." I pause. I probably shouldn't tell him this. I can't imagine it going over very well.

"Something what?"

"Something someone said."

His nostrils flare. "Who?"

I wave him off. "It's fine," I say quickly. "People talk. In Minor Hall, some people were talking about how it's weird you haven't bitten me yet. I don't care about that. I really don't."

"But that's not all," he says, his voice a low rumble. "Tell me."

I roll my eyes. "There were some wolves at the entrance to Elite Hall."

His muscles tense.

"A wolf boy made a comment about you leaving me alone. Can he have a turn." I bite my lip.

A growl rips from his lips, and I jerk back.

"Jarron," I say quickly, but he's already on his feet. "Jarron, stop please."

He turns back to me, his eyes fully black like the last time. "No," he says calmly. "Not this time. Maybe he's right that I shouldn't have left you alone, but it's still a challenge to me. I cannot let it stand, not when it comes to you."

My heart skips a beat.

"Do you know his name? It'll make this a lot simpler and save a lot of wolves pain if you do."

I frown. I don't want to throw some wolf under the bus, but if he means it—that he's not letting this go and he's going to tear through all the shifters here until he figures it out—then it's better if I concede now.

"If I tell you, you have to promise not to do any real harm." I cross my arms. That's my stand. "Scare him. Threaten him. But nothing more."

He clenches his jaw but then bows his head. "Fine." He's not happy about the concession, but he's willing. I'll take it.

"His name is Tommy. And I'm going to the library while you do your alpha thing." I wave him away, partially annoyed at his antics. But truthfully, I just don't want to be seen as part of it. When all of this is over, I don't want to be the girl that sent her boyfriend to pick on the other supernaturals. I really don't need an entire caste to hate me.

"Come with me to the main hall, then you can go to the library with Laithe. I'm not leaving you alone here."

I purse my lips but abandon my barely touched cider and follow him up the stairs.

"Laithe," Jarron calls once we reach the main hall. A moment later, a demon boy with thin, sharp features rounds the corner. His skin is a dark red, eyes pitch black, and he has two short horns on the side of his head. I haven't talked much with Laithe, so this'll be a first.

"Stay with her. I'll be back in an hour or so."

Great. A demon bodyguard.

Without a word, Laithe follows me to the library. A crash reverberates down the hall once we reach the stairs to the massive library. I ignore it. I don't want to hear the yelling or snarling as Jarron takes part in his pissing match.

"Does it ever bother you?" I ask as we descend the stairs toward the section of the library I intend to search.

"What?" Laithe asks.

"Doing his bidding?"

"Not usually," he answers in his quiet tone. "I'm not a fan of leaving him to fight while I play guardian angel."

I snort. "Guardian angel, huh?"

He shrugs. "Not that I mind guarding you. I don't. You're important to him, so you're important to me."

"Did it bother you when you were bumped down on the list?" I ask. I've never had the chance to ask that question to either him or Stassi. Or Manuela, for that matter.

"No. Stassi was annoyed at first but then immediately started planning your wedding when he learned the reason."

I chuckle.

"We've always known a lover would take the first place eventually. You were simply a surprise. Or at least, the timing was a surprise."

"Hmm."

"I'm sure Jarron would have liked to take a slower approach to your relationship—I'm aware you were as surprised as anyone—but royals don't always have that opportunity."

"What do you mean?"

"Well, the questions around your relationship put you at an increased risk. The moment it's clear there's interest, most royals slap a label on it immediately—usually involving a mark."

I groan. Not more talk about marks.

"It labels you as untouchable. That in-between time can be dangerous. Jarron has had to do a bit more work to make it clear you're his since you're opposed to it."

I grimace but ignore the comment. "But doesn't it bother you that your whole life has to revolve around him?"

"I don't see it that way, to be honest. We are linked but I am not a slave. I could choose to leave, if I wanted but I don't think you realize what my life would be like without him. Without this honor of being his second."

My lips part. "You don't have to tell me," I say slowly. "But if you're willing, I wouldn't mind hearing it."

He swallows. "I'll give you the truncated version. Two of my brothers starved the summer before I was chosen. The mountain range my family is native to had become barren after a conflict broke out between us and another family, destroying the land. So, we struggled. I would still be there, scrounging for scraps and killing for even a mouthful of food, if not for Jarron."

"Couldn't you leave that mountain range in search for something else?"

"We could, but it would have significantly weakened us. We are bound to the magic of the soil we were born to. We require an anchor. We can only thrive outside of our homeland if we find a replacement bond, but that is tricky business. Anyone with royal blood can become that source. There are thousands with royal blood but millions that desire the bond. It's an absolute miracle that I happened to catch the eye of the heir. The strongest in all my world. My family is doted upon now. My honor is high."

"How did he find you?"

"Well, in my world, there are fighting rings and traveling talent shows that serve this purpose. Many royals seek out servants or friends from these. Some royals prefer beautiful companions. Some search for artists. Some fighters. So, we present our talents in any way we can. I wasn't looking for a royal host; I was simply rebelling against my parents, to be honest. Part of me planned to die in that city. Without the magic of my home soil, I would have eventually withered away. There were gambling dens, where I spent too much of my time. But in that time, I learned many things. I learned to cheat. To misdirect and to lie. That was my talent. That was what Jarron chose me for."

My eyebrows shoot up. He chose Laithe for his ability to lie?

"He tells me he chose me for my intelligence. My shrewdness. I also know he likes that I wasn't seeking a royal host."

"I thought your world was thriving with the current king and queen?"

"Our world is large. Overall, things are well. Most have plenty, but it is impossible for every mile to be prosperous. I happen to be one of the unlucky ones."

"Thank you for telling me all of that." It's a lot to take in. I just imagined this black void with a few cities and monsters in the pits between. Obviously, it's more complex than all of that.

I come to the section I'm looking for and focus on my most pressing matter: potions.

After an hour of scouring through the few books I've found, I have a list of ten potential potions to try.

Offensive potions:

Stunning—something stronger than we brewed in class.

Confusion.

A weakening poison—not to kill, but to drain my opponents' strength.

Dizziness.

A speech stopper—for witches specifically.

All of these have instructions for skin absorption. I can't exactly force my opponent to drink something in the middle of a battle. I also have a book with detailed instructions of different ways to project these kinds of potions.

Defensive:

Invisibility.

Silencer—to go with my invisibility. Wolves have quite apt hearing.

Healing.

Mirror—will rebound spells, for a few minutes only.

Scent alterations.

THERE ARE ALSO a few more barbaric potions I jot down, just in case. These are the sorts I'd only use against my sister's killer, not some wolf shifter with too much attitude.

A rotting potion—basically leprosy in a bottle.

A mind eraser—spins the truth and mixes it up so rapidly it often leaves the victim mindless.

And of course—**instant death.**

"OMG," someone mutters nearby. "Did you hear what Jarron just did?"

My head whips in the direction of the two witches whispering a few tables over. "What did he do?" I ask loudly. Did he not follow my instructions to not harm Tommy too badly?

The girl with dark hair spins to face me, her lips parted. "Oh," she says. "Well, I kinda assumed you'd know."

I shrug. "I didn't want to be involved. But I'd like to hear the story if you don't mind telling."

The dark-haired girl glances to her redhead friend, who basically pushes her in my direction. "You too," I prompt, motioning to the open chairs. Laithe sits back, a knowing smile on his face.

I'm an hour into my library stay and still no takers on being my BFFs, so why not take matters into my own hands? At least I'll show I'm open to conversations.

The two girls sit across from me. The brunette keeps looking over her shoulder, at first fearfully, but then I notice how she seems increasingly disappointed, despite no one being around.

She wants to be seen talking to me.

I smile. "So? Spill."

The redhead leans in and eagerly, if not a bit frantically, starts telling me about how Jarron charged through the hall calling all of the wolves in for a meeting. Then, he asked for someone named Tommy.

"Do you know Tommy?" I interject.

"Oh, yeah. Everyone knows him. He's kind of a jerk, so I'm not even mad this happened to him. Probably had it coming."

I nod. *Good.*

"What happened to him?" the other girl asks, still looking around.

"So, Jarron starts asking all angry and sexy like—Oh! Sorry." Her eyes widen, looking at me.

I chuckle and wave for her to go on.

"'*You have something to say?*'" She mimics Jarron's deep voice. "'*What did you have to say to my girl?*' I'm pretty sure Tommy wet his pants right then and there."

The other girl giggles.

"He wouldn't answer, though, so Jarron started asking the other wolves if they heard anything. Elyse finally stepped forward and told him that he said something like '*a dedicated boyfriend wouldn't leave his girl to the wolves alone. Maybe he's done with you.*' Then, Jarron got super pale. Like those words really hurt him or something."

My eyebrows rise.

"Then, what did he do?" the dark-haired girl asks.

"He kind of snapped out of it and then flung Tommy against the wall with his magic. He held him like five feet up in the air and gave everyone a warning. Like, you mess with her, you mess with me sort of stuff. Then, he let Tommy go. He fell to the floor in a whimpering heap, and Jarron stomped away."

"Wow." The dark-haired girl sighs. "That's so romantic."

"Right?" the redhead says.

"You're so lucky that he loves you that much."

I flinch. They think he loves me? Laithe laughs under his breath, and I glare at him.

As if on cue, Jarron appears at the top of the stairs, descending toward us like a freaking king, his eyes glued to me. The two girls scamper off, and I frown. I didn't even have a chance to get their names. No secrets or anything.

Jarron approaches, his expression unreadable.

"Did you have fun?" I ask, arms crossed. His brows rise.

"No, I did not."

I shrug. "Sounded like you did."

"I don't like hearing about people threatening you or questioning my intentions, that's for sure. You left out some things in your story."

I scowl. "I didn't remember exactly what he said. I got the general idea."

He bends toward me, his face hovering just over mine. "You didn't tell me he implied I didn't want you anymore."

I blanch at that and look down at the table.

Jarron takes in the longest breath ever. Then, he plops into a seat beside me. "Maybe you're right," he says quietly. "Maybe they don't believe our relationship that much."

I purse my lips.

"Which pisses me off because..." He trails off, glancing to Laithe. "I've been trying."

Why do I feel like that was only half the conversation? These two don't have some kind of psychic link, do they?

"You wouldn't reconsider letting me mark you, would you?"

I grimace.

He pouts. "Didn't think so."

"It's fine," I shrug. "I'm gonna start another couple potions this week. I should have a decent stock before that fancy event next weekend."

Jarron gives me an impressed look.

"And..." I shove my shoulder into Jarron's. "You're supposed to be keeping your distance so I can make friends." I wave my hands dramatically.

He grunts and leans back in his chair. "I don't want to leave yet."

"Is the prince of the Under World pouting?" I make a baby voice, and he curls his lip at me.

"Aren't you two just adorable?" Laithe mutters.

I hold back an amused grin.

"You can come back tomorrow?" he offers.

"Nope. Tomorrow, I'll be potioning *all* day."

He wrinkles his nose. "I guess I better check out several books to entertain myself, then."

Jarron and Laithe both sulk off toward the shelves while I dive back into my research. Friends aren't actually high on my priority list, but I also understand how a set of loose lips near me could help.

A couple of wolves pass by the tables, but upon noticing me, they scamper off like I've got the plague. *Good times.* I was kind of hoping I might see Elyse—the girl who stepped forward to tell the story of what Tommy said.

Both girls were kind while Tommy was being a jerk, and now I'm concerned she'll be in trouble for tattling. But with the way all the wolves are avoiding me, I'm thinking I won't get the opportunity to find out.

I do end up catching the eye of someone unlikely, though—well, at least in my mind. Bea, Ms. Gothic Snow White herself, traipses up and sits in front of me. "Hey, Candice."

"Oh," I say, honestly surprised. "Hi."

"I'm surprised Jarron is even letting you out of his sight now."

"Oh, he's nearby somewhere." I wave vaguely.

"Hmm," she says. "We've never really had a chance to chat since you joined our circle, have we?"

"Nope, not really. You and Trevor seem to be distracted the times we're in the same general space." I note the very obvious puncture marks on her neck.

"Yeah, we're a bit more *affectionate* than you and Jarron. But it's still early days for you."

I shrug.

"Whatcha researching?" she asks, leaning over my notes.

I pull the book back instinctively, and her eyebrows rise. She suddenly seems much more interested. My instincts flare: *Danger, Will Robinson.* Good thing I'm not doing much.

"Just researching some potions." I hold up the book.

"Truth potions, huh?" she asks, despite the book being open to a stunning potion. She nods toward my notebook. Damn eagle eyes.

"You never know when you may need one." I make sure to give her a focused glare.

She smiles. "Don't worry, your secret is safe with me."

"I'm sure." I shut my notebook and textbook and lean in. "So, you probably have all the best gossip. What's up with Auren?" I decide to go for the obvious target first so as not to ping any more of her Spidey-senses.

Her face lights up, and she straightens. "Oh, she's a wicked opponent. But Jarron has never been too into her, so I wouldn't worry on that front. If you're checking out your competition, I'd be more concerned about Lucille."

I frown. "Manuela's girlfriend?" The beautiful

redheaded shifter that avoids the Elite groups because of how much she's desired by the wolves? I shift in my seat.

Bea's smile widens, obviously enjoying my discomfort.

"What about her?"

"She's been on and off with Manuela for a while, but she's secretly been into Jarron for years. He has no idea. She's *much* more his type than Auren."

"Who else has she dated?" I ask.

Bea shrugs. "One wolf shifter, but that went about as bad as it could. She's been quiet about her love life since. With the exception of Manuela."

"Wolf shifters seem like the epitome of toxic masculinity." I grimace.

"Nah, not really."

I flick a brow. I hadn't meant the comment to begin a new conversation, but I'm curious about her take.

She notices my curiosity and continues. "Wolves are family animals first and foremost. They're loud and strong, and that can sometimes come across as macho, but they're very sweet once you get to know them. We see the worst of their attributes here in the school, where there's a lot of mixed packs and other potential threats to their people, but don't let it convince you they're always like that."

Hmm, interesting. "Thanks. That's actually helpful." I'm honestly surprised by her insightfulness.

"I can be very helpful to those I deem worthy." She checks her nails casually.

I ignore that comment. It's either a dig at me or an offer. But I'm not too concerned about the details. "Do you have any close wolf relationships?" I ask, curious how she knows so much about them.

"Oh, not really close. Depends on how you define the term."

"How do you define the term?" I frown, confused about her meaning.

"They make wonderful lovers."

"Oh." I blink. "I thought you and Trevor..."

"Oh, well, when you've been with someone since you were children, it can get stagnant fast."

I don't point out the fact that they're barely more than children now.

"We've had a few breaks to explore." She licks her lips. "Plus, our relationship isn't always just the two of us."

"Oh," I say again, stupefied by this admission.

"Our culture is not as strict about sexual expression as most human cultures. There's only a species or two in our world that practices monogamy regularly."

My mind jumps to Jarron, which is about the stupidest thing it could do. My cheeks redden.

"Don't worry, Jarron's more reserved than most. I don't suspect he'd do well with sharing you."

Sharing me. I nearly gag at that thought.

"So, you've had flings." Is that the right word? It sounds so stupid, and I feel like a massive prude right now. "With other supernaturals? Like a lot?"

She shrugs. "Eh." Noncommittal.

I resign myself to this being the end of the conversation. She doesn't seem intent on giving me much more about herself, but then her smile spreads and she gets that dangerous glint in her eyes.

"So, when are you going to let Jarron drink from you?"

32
BEING BITTEN FEELS LIKE WHAT?!?

I NEARLY CHOKE. "WHAT?"

She chuckles, again enjoying my discomfort. She pulls back her long black hair, exposing several dark spots on her neck and shoulder. They don't look painful, exactly. "It's really not so bad."

"Does it hurt?"

"For a moment. But then, it's, well..." Her brow flicks up. "Ever had an orgasm?"

I cough.

"It's not precisely the same, but it's similarly intense and pleasant. And it lasts minutes."

I try my best to ignore the pattering in my chest.

I'm not sure what to make of my new *friend*. I don't trust her at all, but is she actively trying to freak me out or just telling me the truths I need to know with no regard to how I'd take it? I don't mind the latter, even knowing she'd turn on me any second.

"I know you're human and it probably seems pretty

intimidating, but it's quite enjoyable. And it would give you a significant level of protection. Not as much as a mark, which would give you access to Jarron's magic, but these kinds of marks would have the same effect on supernaturals you pass. They'd see it and know, without any doubt, that you are his. For now."

I wince, and she smiles.

But something new crosses my mind that pulls me from the spiraling thoughts she's dragging me into.

Bea is not just some mean girl. She doesn't create chaos around her; she simple revels in it. She's powerful and knows it, owns it. Loves it. I don't have the same abilities, but if I did, I'd certainly be more like her.

I seek control in the ways I can too. The only difference is, Bea actually has an immense amount.

There's still very little I know about the demon princess, and I don't pretend to trust her in the slightest, but right now, I feel like I understand her.

"What are you thinking about?" she asks, head titling curiously.

I smile. This thought process has certainly helped me overcome the freak-out worthy truth bombs she just threw at me. I contemplate telling her this, but I don't think she'll take it the same. She's still a supernatural that looks down on humans. That's not something I'll forget easily. And I doubt she'd take my revelation as well as me.

I just shrug. She narrows her eyes, and for the first time, I realize I have the upper hand in the conversation.

"Tell me about Jarron?" I ask.

She rolls her eyes. "I'm not just some encyclopedia for you to ask continuous questions."

I lean back and cross my arms. She's trying to regain control. "And see, here I thought we were building a friendship, chatting about relationships and drama." I shrug.

"I can tell when I'm being used." Her tone implies she doesn't actually mind. "Besides, you know as much or more about Jarron than I do."

I guess in some ways, I do. But not all. "I missed three big years of his life. Nothing important I need to know there?"

She picks at her perfect fingernails absently. "He's been broody since that summer. I think he internalized some of what you said—that he's a monster. Not very nice, by the way."

"I was wrong."

She shrugs, like it doesn't actually matter. "Trevor says he was heartbroken."

I freeze, all energy wiped from my body. *What?* I somehow manage to keep the exclaiming internal. Bea's face lights up again, realizing she's found that target needed to gain the upper hand once more.

"You look pale," she says, head tilted innocently. I know better. "Something about that bothers you?"

"Nope," I say in a near squeak. "Just surprising." I successfully even out my tone.

"He was waiting for his lost human friend. Hoping. Imagining. Trevor's told me Jarron has had many kinds of fantasies about reconciliations with the Montgomery sisters." She wiggles her eyebrows.

I flinch but recover quickly. "You're lying," I say with full confidence. "I knew Jarron when we were kids. He wasn't desperately in love with me. Or Liz. This isn't some Nicholas Sparks novel."

"Well, I hope not." She waves the thought away. "Don't those always end terribly?"

"He's big on bittersweet endings."

Bea gives me an annoyed looked. "I'm not saying he was pining for you, waiting for the day you showed back up—he never expected you to come back. But fourteen is the best time for an irrational romantic obsession, and when he found out Liz died. Well, he was pretty distraught. He doesn't have many deep relationships, so having you here, it gives him hope. All I'm saying is, he's clearly more into you than you are him."

Several emotions surge through me. "He has other relationships," I say, desperate to shift the conversation away from me.

She snorts. "No, he doesn't. Even Trevor's and Jarron's relationship is strained due to power struggles. Trevor wants the throne. Did you know that?"

I frown. I did not know that. I'm not even sure that Jarron wants it.

"So, yeah, he nearly flipped when you walked through those doors that first day."

My heart skips a beat.

"You don't really see me as a friend," Bea says, her tone dropping, "and I don't blame you, but I'm really not messing with you here. I've never seen Jarron like this with anyone." Curiosity flickers in her eyes.

My stomach twists.

"But the longer you keep him at arm's length, the likelier it is you'll lose the one chance you have to change your circumstances. You could be truly powerful if you played your cards right."

I frown at those choice of words. "That's not what I want."

"Isn't it, though?"

My brows furrow. Yes, I want to be powerful. She can see that. She's perceptive. But I don't want to be powerful just by being linked to someone else with magic. It's possible she knows that too, and if so...

"I don't want to have to rely on someone else's power. I want my own."

Something new shines in her eyes. Something knowing and ancient. Her demon?

"I didn't think so," she says. Then, she pushes from the table and walks away without another word.

33

THE FINE LINE BETWEEN FRIEND AND ENEMY

"WHAT WAS THAT ABOUT?" Jarron's baritone voice floats from a few feet behind me.

I spin to find him leaning against a bookshelf a few feet away. Did he listen to that entire conversation?

"Oh, you know, stretching my friend-making skills."

"With Bea?" he asks dubiously.

I shrug. "Beggars can't be choosers."

He pulls out the chair beside me and sits with no sound at all. "Bea is a dangerous choice for anyone."

"Oh, I know."

He nods. Especially considering how that conversation ended. She was a bit too pleased with my mention of wanting my own power. If she knows something about the Akrasia Games, would that be the kind of comment that would peg me as a possible contender?

"But," he continues slowly, "if you get her on your good side, she's incredibly influential. She's had her hand in

247

essentially every major event that's happened at this school in the last three years—good and bad. She's often underestimated."

"Understood." None of that surprises me. She comes across as a love-struck priss at first, a mean girl second. But there's certainly intelligence there too. She showed some of her hand during that conversation. The only question is, how much did she mean to show? Was it all a carefully orchestrated scheme to push me in one direction or another?

"I'm not a huge fan of Bea, personally," Jarron admits, leaning back in his chair. "But she's the kind of strong I'd like to find in a mate. Resilient, intelligent, tenacious."

I fiddle with my pile of books, unsure how to respond to that.

"Next week is the fundraiser. You need something formal to wear. I'm assuming you didn't bring anything?"

"Definitely not."

Jarron nods. "I can recruit someone to help. Manuela and Lucille would be my first choice, but Bea has more dresses than schemes, which is saying something. So, she's an option if you feel comfortable."

"I'd prefer Bea, I think." I'm not sure how I feel about Lucille after Bea's admission that she's secretly into Jarron.

His eyebrows rise in surprise, but he concedes.

Jarron and I take another public walk around Elite Hall, then he escorts me back to the potions study hall to work for a few more hours.

As I busy my hands with work, stirring the now frothing liquid, crunching leaves, and skinning a rabbit's foot, my mind spins through several things.

Mostly, my relationship with Jarron.

It began as a pragmatic solution to a problem. But now it has become a sincere friendship. To be honest, I'm not sure the relationship has helped the investigation much. I mean Jarron has helped, but being his "girlfriend" hasn't helped much beyond access to a few books and putting a massive target on my back.

So far, I haven't uncovered anything significantly helpful in my investigation, just more questions.

But at the same time, I'm so much more comfortable here than I'd ever expected. I feel comfortable around Jarron, which is mind blowing to me. I trust him to protect me, which gives me a bit more leverage to make risky choices.

I'm learning potions I never would have dreamed of trying, and they're going surprisingly well. I've started two more already and have three more planned—all to be brewed at the same time. The speed increaser, silencer, confusion, and dizzy potions all require a hot environment, so I put those to the side for now and try to manage the several I'm working on.

"This looks like a lot," Jarron comments eventually, peeking up over his book.

"I have a lot to overcome."

"I will keep you safe, you know. Even if..."

I consider asking him to finish that sentence, but after a long beat, I decide not to. "I don't want to have to rely on you," I say, not for the first time. "I appreciate the help, and I won't turn it down, but I want to know I can defend myself without you if I ever need to."

"I know," he mumbles. "It makes sense. I just don't want you to overwork yourself."

"I'm good. I thrive on this, to be honest." And I do. I feel more energized after my potions work.

I use a magical gemstone to increase the nullifier's development. It's not a requirement, but it does speed up its completion. Potions are not large magic users; they build on themselves to get stronger and stronger, which is often why they take a long time to be completed.

"Or is it simply that you're bored playing bodyguard?"

"No," he says quickly. "I wouldn't be doing much different if I weren't here with you. I'd be a bit more comfortable, but otherwise—"

"The poor demon prince wants his velvet throne back?"

I hide my shiver in response to his husky laugh.

I continue working for another hour before I pack up and leave my projects be. Three of them are coming along well. I should have my nullifier completed before the event this weekend, which is perfect. I did a shortened version of the invisibility spell first, so that should be done in time too. It'll have a large constitution, so each dose will be a large vial, but for all the potions, the dosage matters least. It will be me drinking it, not an opponent.

I'm also working on a stunning potion. It could be finished in a few days as well, but with this one, I'll have to be more patient. Though, it'll work on contact, without the condensing process, each dose will be around eight ounces, making it difficult to use. If only a little bit of liquid falls on the target, they'll feel next to nothing. And it's challenging to splatter a large portion of liquid onto someone in the middle of fight. I need a freaking water gun or something.

So, the more condensed, the better. I'll leave it for another week or more.

As we're closing up my little potions shop far below the school halls, Jarron tells me Bea is eager to help me dress for the formal.

"Eager?" I ask. "That sounds dangerous."

He chuckles. "Push back on her if she puts you in anything you feel uncomfortable in. It's not a Victoria Secret fashion show, as much as she'd like to think it is."

I snort. "Maybe I should have stayed with Manuela as my personal shopper."

He smiles. "Bea will be fine. She just needs a firm hand. I'm certain you can handle her."

"How does Trevor feel about it all?"

"He's vaguely pleased you're here and we're together. He doesn't show much emotion to anyone but Bea, though, so it's hard to gauge."

"Bea was telling me a little about their relationship. She implied it's more of an open relationship."

Jarron frowns. "Of course she'd tell you that."

"Yeah, she was trying to get under my skin any way she can."

"Sounds like Bea." He nods. "Demon relationships are a bit more varied than humans', generally, so it's not all that uncommon or surprising for us to not be so strict with our monogamy."

"Hmm," I say because I don't know how else to respond. Jarron doesn't elaborate what that would mean for him.

"You can meet Bea to get ready for the event at seven on Friday night. Does that work?"

"Sure," I answer quietly. We round the final corner, and

the gates to Minor Hall come into view. "I'll see you at lunch tomorrow."

He nods, a question in his eyes that I don't dare ask about.

34

WHO KNEW DEMONESSES COULD DOUBLE AS FAIRY GODMOTHERS?

THE UNICORN BONE crumbles in my fingers as I rummage through the large plastic bag. It's a bit softer than I'd prefer, to be honest, but when getting pre-prepared ingredients, that tends to happen. It's impossible to get it perfect.

I could have requested unicorn bone and cooked it myself, but I was a little unsure of my abilities. I glance at the three steaming cauldrons lined beside this one, all set to be ready tomorrow.

It's probably safe to say my concerns were unfounded. I could have easily cooked the raw bone myself. But now, I'll have to make do with what I have.

I hand mix the bone meal until it's powdery and then grab a thick handful and scatter it into the bubbling liquid. The potion will be finished in less than an hour.

I'm supposed to be meeting Bea to dress for the gala in forty-five minutes.

Dammit, I need it done before the gala. If I don't do it

now, it could be ruined. I can't leave it for the morning or the top will crust over and it won't be absorbable.

Timing is everything with potion making.

Bea is just going to have to wait.

"Where the hell have you been?" Bea shrieks through the door the moment I knock. She swings it open, and her lip curls as if she smells something sour as she takes me in. "You look terrible. What have you been doing? Slaving over a cauldron all day?"

"Actually, yes."

"Why?"

I roll my eyes. I may not be shouting about my potions work in the halls, but they all know I'm vulnerable and potions are my only means to magic.

"Come on, let's get started." Bea already has a face full of elaborate makeup and her hair tied into a lovely updo. She wears a black robe, ready to finish her look with a gown in a moment's notice.

I sigh and enter her room, almost as big as Jarron's and Trevor's with bright red silk sheets, just like Trevor's. She's only missing the balcony. On the far end of the room, though, is a large window with a lovely view of the mountains. The sky is orange and pink. Damn, this is a fantastic spot for a sunset.

"Do you plan to study at the gala?" Bea eyes the bag still strapped to my back.

"I didn't have time to take it back to my room." I shrug.

She nods to a chair next to a shiny black door. "Leave it there. Forget it exists until Monday. Got it?"

I obey, although I intend to retrieve my things first thing tomorrow morning. The rest of my potions will be finished tomorrow, and I need my notes to follow the final steps.

She walks to a door and holds it open for me.

Holy crap.

Bea's closet is nearly the size of the rest of her room. There are lines of rolling wracks filled with hundreds of gowns. The back wall is floor-to-ceiling shelves of shoes, and in the corner is a massive three way mirror.

"Take your pick." She waves to a rack on the right side of the room. There are at least a hundred dresses in the row, in order by color. "Those over there are dresses I've worn. I don't care if you take one of those, but there will be some people who notice that sort of thing."

"Pretty sure I can find something in this," I say, shifting through the massive rack of dresses. I'm overwhelmed already. What am I even looking for? I don't know what looks good on me or what kind of style people wear to these kinds of events. Jarron mentioned it's not a Victoria Secret fashion show, but considering they wear peacock feathers with lingerie, it really doesn't narrow it down much.

"Color preference?" she asks.

I shrug.

She looks me up and down. "Green?"

I grimace.

She chuckles. "I mean like a deep emerald." She walks over to the rack and pulls out a lovely long gown covered in panels of sheer lace over the stomach and twisting straps over a plunging neckline. "It's gorgeous on. Want to try it?"

I try to give the dress a full consideration but it's really not me at all. "Maybe something less dominatrix?"

Bea snorts. "That is nothing. All right, 'Miss Virgin' it is."

I resist the urge to roll my eyes or complain. Bea and I are on totally different planes when it comes to modesty. It's not that I don't appreciate the beauty—I'm sure Bea will look incredible—it just makes me uncomfortable when I get that kind of attention from men.

I'd like to be remembered for more than the way I look, so if I'm a bit forgettable in that regard, that's okay too.

"I'm going to pick four dresses, but you have to try them all on. Every one. If you don't like them, no big deal."

"What if they don't fit?"

Bea is a bit taller and lot bustier than me. Her waist is like Barbie small.

"I have a seamstress on hand to shape it perfectly."

Of course she does.

She looks me over. "Yours will need to be hemmed, of course. And maybe let out in the middle, but that's no big deal."

I shake my head at the massive selection of dresses. Does she have a full-time designer or something? And the fact that she'll give me free choice over them is wild.

She pulls out another dark green gown that's simpler than the last. Smooth silk with a low neckline—but nowhere near as deep as the last—and few embellishments. She also selects a black and white gown that I don't get a long glimpse at, a dark blue gown with sparkling jewelry—I pray they're not diamonds or gemstones—and finally, a nude tone gown with a corset top and scattered with glitter.

She holds them out. "Strip."

I'm not usually insecure, but with Bea's sharp gaze continually watching my every move, I find myself fidgeting a lot. It's like she's sizing me up, seeking weaknesses she can exploit.

She probably is.

I try on the blue gown first. It's lovely, with an embroidered halter top. The gems are not heavy enough to be gemstones or diamonds. It's already tight over my waist making my belly look even plumper than usual. Not the most flattering cut for me.

Next is the nude tone dress. It's honestly gorgeous, and with the corset boning, it smooths my belly nicely. It pushes my boobs up pretty intensely, but that's the point. "It's beautiful. But it's not me."

She nods. "Next."

I grab the black and white dress she selected in the beginning. On the hanger, it looks a little odd. The top is half-white, half-black embroidery in a crisscross over the chest. The handkerchief skirt is shorter in the front than in the back.

I suck in a breath as she zips it up. It hugs my waist and chest snugly, making me look curvier than the others. The top of the dress is simple white, lacey embroidery in a sweetheart neckline, but the black swirls up from the black skirt, like it's taking over.

"I like it," I admit.

"See." She wiggles her brows. "You don't always realize what is a perfect fit till you try it. I'm not one hundred percent convinced it's the best option yet, though. You?"

My smile widens. My shoulders relax now that I know I

have an option that will be appropriate and flattering. "I don't mind trying a few more."

"That's the spirit."

She throws another three dresses on the rack, the green dress left forgotten. One has a sheer bodice and a coral skirt. Pretty but back to that tad-too-sexy problem. Another is a simple black with an empire waist and sweetheart neckline.

"Too prom," I comment.

She nods.

Another is a beautifully draped light blue dress with gold jeweled embroidery under the bust that makes me look like a Greek goddess.

"I still like the black and white better," I say after staring at myself for a full minute. It's fun to play dress up, and with each new dress I see another version of myself. Which one will I be today?

She picks up the dark green gown and holds it out to me with a smug grin. "Try this one still. I've been putting it off 'cause I'm confident it's the winner."

She holds up the emerald gown. It has long sleeves, a low V-neck, and an A-line silky skirt.

I stare at it dubiously. It's beautiful, but it's much simpler than I'd have expected Bea to like.

I step into the silky material and pull it over my chest and arms. The moment Bea zips up the back, I freeze.

It fits my chest and waist perfectly, emphasizing every curve to precision, and the flowy silk skirt expands out, making my waist curves even more accentuated.

It's understated sexy.

My lips tilt up.

"You love it, don't you?"

"Kinda."

It's incredibly comfortable for a ball gown. The silk is so smooth I just want to rub my legs against it for hours.

She hops up on her tippy toes excitedly. "Is this the winner, or do you wanna try the black and white one again?"

I consider. This dress feels very me. Dark and elegant, but with a twist of malevolence. The other dress is different, almost quirky. It's me in a different way.

But which version do I want to be tonight?

"You think this one is appropriate? I'll fit in?"

"It's a little tame on the exposed skin." She winks. "But it's perfect for tonight if you're looking to impress instead of make everyone want to have sex with you."

"Are you hoping to make everyone want to have sex with you?"

"Obviously."

I snort. Then, I look at myself in the mirror again. It really is beautiful.

An uncontrollable smile spreads across my lips. "Okay, sold."

Bea makes me take a shower and condition my hair before she brings the seamstress in. Then, for a full hour I'm made to stand still in front of the mirror while a short fae woman with glowing skin and golden eyes measures and pins my dress. "We'll do your hair and makeup while she's sewing."

"Don't you need to get ready too?" I ask Bea.

"All I have to do is put on my dress."

She's being very attentive, which has surprised me. Other than the occasional wolfish grin, she's been very sweet.

I know better than to trust it, but I'm appreciative all the same.

"So, tell me about you and Jarron," she says as soon as the seamstress tugs the dress off of me. I quickly twist into the black robe sitting on the chair waiting for me.

"So, we've made it to the gossip part of the evening?" I mock.

"You knew it was coming, didn't you?" She stands and grabs two shoots of some sparkling liquid on the table near the wall. "I'm fairly certain it's why you even asked to have me help you prepare for tonight."

I bite my lip, trying to hide my surprise.

"Other than my impeccable taste." She winks again. "So, spill. You are getting a total makeover; the least you can do is start first. Tell me something juicy."

"I don't know. There's not much that's juicy about our relationship."

"Yet," she chides. "Besides, I don't believe that. There's plenty of drama beneath the surface. Tell me something."

Do I lie? Come up with something completely false and risk it biting me later? Or worse, her not believing me to start with. Or do I give her a bit of the truth?

"When I first came here, I wanted nothing to do with Jarron."

She snorts. "What?"

"I had some incorrect assumptions about what he'd be like as a demon. He's proved me wrong every step of the way."

"Hmm," she says. "So, you thought he'd be a violent monster ready to prey on the innocent human girl, did you?"

"Not exactly, but close enough, I guess."

"Yet, you began dating him within two days."

I freeze. Yeah, I guess that sounds a bit off. "He... Well, it's hard to say no to him. And I guess I was curious. He promised to take it slow, but announcing a relationship was the best way to ensure my safety."

"Did he confess his undying love? Tell you he's been obsessed with you since you were kids? That he's fantasized about you in the years you were apart."

I choke, coughing on my shock. "What?"

She chuckles. "No? Hmm. That's disappointing."

"What's disappointing?"

"Oh, nothing. I just had a bet going. Sounds like I lost."

She's betting about our relationship? "What else are you betting on?"

She runs her finger over her bright red lips. "You." There's that wolfish grin again.

I frown. What does that mean?

"I'm betting that you're ambitious and clever. You're going to win."

"Win what?"

"You'll understand eventually. Close your eyes."

I obey, wiping the frown from my face so she can swipe eyeliner over my eye.

"So, what are your intentions with my future brother-in-law?" she asks. "The only question I'm uncertain of is if you're gonna repeat the same disappearing act in a few weeks' time or if you're my future queen."

My lips part. *She's trying to get under your skin,* I remind

261

myself. And she's supposed to believe I'm into Jarron. At least a little. *Get a grip.* Just because I admit to feelings, doesn't mean it's real.

I pull in a breath, ready to commit to the act.

"I'm hoping for something in between." I force a smile. "The latter is a bit intense for me at the moment. But I don't plan on running any time soon."

She nods, apparently accepting my answer. She runs her fingers through my hair. "I'm thinking braided updo."

I shrug. "I don't usually do anything to it but a French braid when I'm feeling fancy."

"Of course you don't. It's no wonder Auren never had a chance."

"What?"

"Jarron likes low-key, non-materialistic. Humble." Her voice rises on the last word, a strange cadence like it means something more than she's letting on.

"Humble?" I'm not so sure that's something I'd define myself as. I mean, more so than Auren, sure. "Just because I'm powerless doesn't mean I'm humble."

"Perhaps not," she says, unconcerned. She pulls at the strands of my hair, parting it and spraying product in.

"I'm surprised you don't have a professional to do hair for you," I comment, hoping it's not rude to say. I'm impressed she even knows how to do hair, given she's been considered a princess most of her life.

"I could, I suppose. But I actually enjoy it."

"That's good. Makes me feel better about relying so much on your help tonight."

"Well, I also don't mind you owing me one." Her bright red lips pout, but her attention remains steady on her project. I don't like the thought of owing her anything, but I'm not naïve enough to think she holds anything over me. She may request a favor, and I may or may not oblige.

"Tell me about how you became connected to Trevor. You were an arranged marriage, right?"

"Oh, no, not really. My family has been close with the Blackthorns for centuries. Our parents certainly mused their son would marry their friends' offspring, but it wasn't forced. Actually, if it were truly arranged, it would be Jarron I'd be attached to, not Trevor."

My mouth goes dry.

"My parents imagined me as queen, so the eldest brother was their first pick."

"So, how—"

"We met first when we were young children. We played together. Jarron was always off on his own. He liked to build things and explore. He wasn't very social. It didn't help that he was groomed to be a ruler, so his education was much more stringent. Trevor and I were only friends for all that time. Our parents saw how Trevor and I got along so well, and they switched their ambitions from queen to princess. But Trevor and I didn't think much of that as children. It wasn't until I hit puberty that things changed."

I watch her fingers curling and twisting expertly through my hair. "How did they change?"

"He imprinted on me."

I straighten. "He what?" Why do I feel like that's all I can manage to say when talking with Bea? "Imprint like... the werewolves in that YA novel?"

She snorts. "No. Not even a little bit."

My brow furrows.

"In our culture, there is a tradition. It's specific for rulers but fitting for any demons in the royal line. This tradition states that at some point in a male's youth, their demon will choose a mate."

"Their demon?" I ask, confused. They *are* demons, right? How does their *demon* choose?

"Yes, it's a difficult concept to translate because the words are the same in English, but its…" Her fingers still, eyes narrowing as she focuses on the right explanation. "This instinct? The spirit of the beast inside, I suppose." She nods, content with that wording. Her fingers continue their dance through my hair.

"You see, we are a different breed than other creatures in our world. They are more animalistic. Violent and focused on the kill. Most species from our world are now creatures. They're intelligent and have languages and loved ones and even cultures, but they have little compassion or empathy. They do not care for anyone outside of their own. They don't think much of the future. You won't find stores of food or farmers adding substances to increase crop growth. They take what is available and move on. Or they stubbornly stay in ruins, never considering ways to rebuild what's been lost. Our family does that for them, for the betterment of the world. Most of our people, many different species included, do not understand our way of higher thinking or controlling, but they have come to realize the benefits."

I consider my conversation with Laithe and what I read in my textbook. This all fits into what I already know, but I'm not sure how it connects back to imprinting.

"So long as we benefit them, they will protect our rule. That is the way of lower-level demons. Without us, there would be no society at all. Only small factions hunting each other and warring for resources. They see us almost as alien rulers, so different from them but guiding them to be better. Some follow us like gods. Others, a form of being they simply accept. No matter how diluted our blood becomes, though, we have a form that is fully demon. My demon form is the same as any other females of our kind, even though my mother is fae. The skin is not muted, the scales and horns remain, and the wings are the same size, but we are able to switch into a secondary form using glamor. It feels more like a shape-shift than a glamor to me. I cannot change what I look like in human form in any substantial way. This is who I am as a human. But to our people, this duality is in spirit as well as body. We are alien beings with a demon soul. And it does feel that way often. Like I am me, but inside is a beast waiting to be freed. When I change my form, I see through the beast's eyes, not my own. The world is changed. It's simpler. We usually only transform into these forms during very instinctual events—sex and battle —because we can lose who we are. Our minds change along with our bodies."

"Okay," I say, trying to soak in every word. "What does this have to do with imprinting?"

"I believe the tradition began around the time we learned to use glamor, when more and more portals to other worlds began and our kind continued to change through intermarrying other worldlings. When our right to rule was questioned by lower demons. The tradition states that our logical, high-order forms cannot choose our mates. Our demons do. The base, instinctual being—the beast—will choose for us, and we must obey this choice. This is one stipulation for the lower-level demons to continue to trust us. We allow the part of ourselves that is like them to choose our future, our bloodline. They trust the beast, not the mind."

My eyebrows pull together as I take this in. I consider about twelve thousand questions, but most of them are things she's already answered that I just have a hard time fully grasping.

"But there is some truth to it; there is a raging instinct that rushes through young demons when they find a mate. From that moment, those instincts will pull us toward that being. It will never go away."

"Never?" I whisper. "What if—Is it always reciprocated?"

"No!" she says quickly. "That's part of the tradition as well. It is one sided, almost never two, especially when you consider other species who cannot experience the phenomena. A two-sided imprint is nearly unheard of. And so, you cannot guarantee your chosen one will even want you in return, and it is forbidden to force your chosen mate. In fact, it's even forbidden to talk about it until you've been accepted. You must earn them. To earn the love of your chosen is to earn your right to rule."

I frown. "What happens if you fail to earn them?"

"You are free to choose another, and most of the time, nothing changes. It really only matters for the next in line for the throne, but even then, unless a rival for the throne were to campaign against the ruling demon with proof of chosen rejection, the lower demons will not know and there are no real consequences. There's no easy way to prove who a demon's chosen is, so it's unlikely to have any legitimate consequences. We do care about it, but the chances of it affecting real world events are slim. It's simply highly personal to us."

I'm quiet for a while after this. It's a lot of information to take in.

My mind jumps to the one and only time I've seen a demon's true form. Jarron's true form. He wasn't himself. I knew that. I've always known that. When he was in that form, he was not the Jarron I knew. But when he changes to human form, he's back.

I suppose that makes sense based on my experience. But it also increases my fear of him ever shifting around me.

"So, if you're not supposed to talk about it, how did you know Trevor imprinted on you?"

"Well, being from the same world, I'm familiar with the signs, but also once he marked me and we began to share magic, I could feel it."

I blink rapidly, trying to wrap my mind around it all.

"Finished!" Bea announces.

I blink those thoughts from my mind and look at myself in the mirror. The loose braid wraps all the way around my head like a crown and then twists into more intertwining braids in the back.

"Now, let me check on the seamstress so we can finish up and turn some heads."

35

FUTURE QUEEN OR NO ONE. THERE IS NO INBETWEEN

My mind continues spinning through the information Bea threw at me. It wasn't the gossip I'd been expecting. It's not information I really need.

But it sure serves her purpose: it gets into my head.

The gala is being held *in* Elite Hall—because of course the only *important* students are here. Cue brain scrambling eye roll.

Which means when we leave Bea's room, there are already important supernaturals roaming around in the common rooms.

She hooks her arm in mine, now in her outrageously beautiful—and very revealing—black gown. The skirt is silky like mine, but there is a sheer panel from her left outer thigh that runs all the way past her hip, extending to expose nearly her entire belly, and her breasts are only covered by black lace appliques in a swirling pattern. It barely covers the bits humans don't like shown. She struts down the hall with me in tow.

"Come on," she says in a sultry tone, the hot demon princess persona already in full force. "You're one of the most important—and you certainly hold the most intrigue—of all the guests here. To them, you may be a future Orizian queen. Act like it." She hisses the command.

My knees begin to tremble. I wish I could be on Jarron's arm for this part. At least then, I'd have someone I trust to rely on.

Trust.

Do I trust Jarron? I swallow. I'm not supposed to. I'm supposed to still believe he may be guilty. I'm supposed to be preparing myself for the possibility that he either dated or killed my sister.

Yet, as I search my heart, I realize I do. I trust him. He would be my support. He would give me whatever I needed, without concern for himself. He'd whisk me away if I got too overwhelmed. I know it.

My heart speeds up, now eager for that safety net. His arms.

This is a problem.

It's all a game. I'm playing a part. I'm just lucky enough to have a friend playing the other side. That's all this is.

Friendship pretending to be more.

A tightness in my chest eases, and not just the anxiety of tonight. I'm relieved to admit Jarron matters to me. I'm relieved to finally believe he isn't the demon I was so concerned he'd be.

At least while he's in human form.

Now is not the time to think about his beast.

I force my shoulders back and chin up.

"Better," Bea says.

I do my best to keep my feet steady and expression empty of the panic coursing through my body now. We stop when we reach the end of the hall, standing in the opening to the sunroom, which is bustling with people. Most of whom I've never seen before.

Bea's red lips curl into a sly smile. She waits. And so, I wait too. Jarron and Trevor turn to meet our stares first, then like a cascade, more and more eyes turn to us.

Jarron is on his feet, strolling toward me, one hand in his pocket, in an instant. His entire demeanor is calm, relaxed, except the fire in his eyes. Wild and full of wonder, pinned to only me.

"You look incredible," he says when he stops in front of us. "I appreciate your assistance, Bea."

"Anytime. Princesses need to stick together." She winks at me, and I blanch. Jarron doesn't react, doesn't even look away from me as Bea bounces off to meet Trevor, who wordlessly takes her hand and brings it to his lips.

She's an accepted part of his life. Everyone is accustomed to her being with him.

The attention is all on me and Jarron.

"How are you?" he asks quietly.

"Secretly freaking out," I admit.

He smiles. "You look incredible, truly, if that's any help."

"A little, I guess."

He grips my hand tightly in his. "Let's say hi to Mom and Dad. That won't be too bad, right?" he asks, standing so close his chest brushes against my arm. "Then, we can go for a walk through the courtyard."

My mind peppers with dizziness. "Okay," I whisper.

He leans down and places a gentle kiss to my shoulder before guiding me through the room.

The King and Queen of Oriziah, the Under World, stare straight into my damn soul with their unnaturally dark eyes as we approach. Yes, I've met them on more than one occasion, but that was always with my mom and dad to take the attention off of me and before I'd seen a demon in true form or felt the immense overwhelming pressure of their dark magic.

Now, I'm dating their son. To them, I'm a potential future daughter-in-law. A future queen. I don't know what to expect from them this time.

Jarron squeezes my fingers, and it's then I realize my fingers are trembling.

I need a calming potion. I should have thought of that.

"Miss Montgomery," Emil Blackthorn says with a slight bow of his head.

"Hello." The word squeaks out. Dammit, why am I such a coward?

"You look well," the queen says. "I'm surprised to see you here at this school."

I press my lips together.

"Candice is still deciding her life's path," Jarron says. It sounds so much like a thing an adult would say that I wonder if the line is a relic from a past conversation between them.

"Seems to me she's made her decision," Emil Blackthorn says. Jarron's father is part-demon, part-dragon. A rare combination. His mother is the true ruler of their world.

My heart squeezes, but I force my voice to remain steady

as I respond. "Walking one path does not always negate others." *Ha*, that sounded grown up as shit.

"Indeed." Jarron's mother smiles. "There is nothing wrong with exploring options and discovering who you are before you commit to any one plan. I was impressed when you and your sister chose your own path in the human world. I am also impressed you've made the choice to come back after your sister's death. You are a strong woman."

"Well, I am less impressed," Emil says.

I blink. Jarron glares.

Jarron's father shifts from foot to foot, hands clasped behind his back, chin high. He has the demeanor of a foreign diplomat. Impersonable. "From what I understand, you are taking the most basic courses they offer at this school."

I frown. Who has he been talking to? My parents? Mr. Vandozer?

"You are significantly more talented than every other student in your classes. If that is true, you are taking the easy route rather than stretching yourself. That is what I find disappointing."

I swallow.

Jarron's shoulders relax. "Candice has a habit of underestimating herself. You should see the potions she's working on. I'm sure she'll downplay them to you."

I look up to Jarron, surprised. "I finished the nullifier. I never got the chance to tell you."

"A nullifier, huh?" Jarron's mother says. "Which class is teaching you that?"

"None. It's an independent project."

Surprise flashes in her eyes. "Oh? Well, isn't that interesting, Emil? Tell me, dear, what is the constitution?"

I'm surprised right back. I supposed she'd have to be somewhat knowledgeable in potions if they worked so closely with my parents for several years. At least enough to know the value of what they're getting.

"Only requires a few drops," I say.

"On the tongue?"

"Face."

She nods. "Impressive. If it works. Have you tested it?"

"Not yet. I collected it only this morning."

She nods again then turns to Jarron. "Perhaps you can help her test it."

"You want him to weaken himself?"

"If done wisely—his quarters are well protected—I don't see the harm. It couldn't last more than, what, an hour or so?"

"On someone as strong as Jarron, more like forty-five minutes." Maybe less because of the unideal unicorn bone meal.

"All right, young one," Emil says. "I take back my judgement. You are obviously not limiting yourself in all aspects here."

I give him a smile. "I'll consider taking some more ambitious classes next semester," I offer. If I'm even still here.

"Good." He clasps his hands behind his back.

"We're going to take a walk in the courtyard," Jarron says, his hand resting on the small of my back, guiding me in the direction of the door. "We'll see you at the banquet."

His parents bow their heads, and Jarron sweeps me from the crowded room, down a short hall, and out into the silent night.

I breathe in deeply, cool air coaxing the stress from my chest.

"Wasn't so bad," Jarron says, nudging me with his elbow.

"Not too bad," I agree.

The glass covering the courtyard reflects light from the building behind us. The trees are dark, rustling softly. A wolf howls in the distance.

I stare up at the massive full moon.

"They always schedule these near the full moon so most of the wolves scatter. Otherwise, they tend to overwhelm the guests."

"What about the alpha and his son?"

"There will be a few wolves in attendance today. They'll be easier to agitate, so I'd suggest you keep your distance."

"Oh. I thought shifters couldn't control themselves during a full moon?" It's well known that they spend the entire night out in the forest this time of the month.

"It isn't until tomorrow, technically."

I look up at the moon again. I can't tell the difference.

"And powerful wolves are still capable of controlling themselves during a full moon. The younger or weaker wolves, less so."

"Noted."

We continue a slow walk through the quiet space. We pass a couple kissing on the bench beneath the willow and reach a section of black flowers. There has to be a thousand of them in the hundred square feet.

They're dark calla lilies. The closer I look the more colors I see. Dark blues and purples, and a few deep reds. "These are the flowers you gave to me," I mutter.

Jarron nods. "This is my favorite spot at night."

"It is very beautiful."

His eyes cast down to me. "You'd fit right in. I'd like to plant a few more in this color." He slides the silky fabric on the cuff of my sleeve between his thumb and forefinger.

For some reason, I blush. He drops his hand and then bends down. He runs his fingers over a dark blue petal and then a purple. I just watch, letting the quiet moment stretch as long as physically possible.

Then, Jarron plucks a pure black flower and stands. He reaches out and tucks the short stem into the side knot of my curls. "Perfect," he whispers.

And holy crap-oly. I think I literally swoon. The powerful demon prince, threatening to disembowel anyone who'd dare threaten me, picking me flowers and putting them in my hair. How does a girl not fall for that?

The sizzle of magic tinges the air, and I find Jarron staring at me, eyes solid black. I should fear him, but I don't.

His thumb gently slides down the side of my jaw. "You're absolutely incredible, you know that?"

My stomach flutters. "I'm not all that convinced." But I can't keep my eyes from his, can't get over that look. There are a lot of questions that remain about our relationship, but there are a few things I cannot deny.

Jarron cares about me.

Jarron desires me.

My heart patters in my chest as he steps closer, our gazes still locked. He leans in but pauses a breath away from our lips touching. My lungs tighten, forcing shallow gulps of air, but I don't dare step back.

"There's no one around to see," I whisper breathlessly.

His lips tilt up ever so slightly. "Practice?" he asks, uncertainly.

Then, giving me every opportunity to step away, he ever so slowly bridges the distance between us until his lips graze against mine.

Instantly, there's a zing of pleasure—and panic and hope and fear. His lips are so soft, so gentle. He slides them against mine, barely touching, then presses in just a bit tighter. My hands find his chest; his find the back of my neck.

I expect him to deepen the kiss, to take more, to intensify, but he doesn't. He keeps at this leisurely pace as his lips explore mine. His hand is gentle on my neck. His tongue—

His tongue connects with my lower lip first, and I suck in a breath.

He pulls back immediately. *No, don't stop.* He searches my face, but I don't voice my plea.

He licks his lips, the color returning to his eyes. "Are you ready to face the wolves?"

My lips curl up, but the truth is, I'm internally praying for any excuse to stay out here. "Here is good," I whisper.

He leans his forehead against mine. "We don't have to stay long. Make an appearance. One dance. One kiss." He's whispering now. "Then, we can come back here. Or I can take you... wherever you want to go."

I bite the inside of my lip hard. Because my first thought?

His bedroom.

Yep. I'm in really big trouble tonight.

36

ARE YOU CONVINCED YET?

ALL ATTENTION TURN to us as we enter the packed banquet hall—yes, Elite hall has an elaborately decorated hall just for massive events like this one, and all the important alumni and the few invited students have now congregated here. We are, apparently, fashionably late.

There are world rulers here, politicians and celebrities—mostly fae—and others with more understated influence, but significant all the same. Inventors and warriors. Some of the beings here are over five hundred years old.

They are all in incredibly luxurious gowns and suits.

I feel beautiful in my green gown, but next to all of them, I'm nothing.

Except, when I'm on Jarron's arm.

I see the envy in several faces as we pass. No Auren, so far as I can tell, but an older female with a crown of literal ice is eyeing me harshly. Pretty safe bet that's Auren's mother.

Jarron guides me through the room, stopping to chat

with a few people. We meet a witch coven leader. A half-goblin advisor to the President of the United States. The oldest living dragon.

Jarron's mother and father nod their heads in greeting but have nothing more to say. They know me well enough, I guess.

They haven't passed judgement on our relationship. They treat me much the same as they did when we were only friends as kids. They are so casual about it all that I almost wonder if they know the truth.

Could Jarron have told his parents our relationship is fake?

My gut twists at that thought. Why does that bother me? I shouldn't care. It's true.

Right?

"Miss Montgomery," a husky voice says from behind us.

We turn to face Mr. Vandozer. I bite the inside of my lip. I still don't like him, and I'm certain he doesn't like me.

He studies mine and Jarron's clasped hands. "I see you are well. I heard there was an incident in Elite Hall recently."

I frown. The thing with Tommy? "All is well," I say, uncertain what he's looking for.

"Very good. I'm glad you are comfortable enough to be around such powerful beings. We wouldn't want any other students feeling unsafe at this banquet."

Jarron forces a stiff smile. "Auren chose not to attend?"

Mr. Vandozer nods. *Ahh that's what this is about.* I didn't even do anything to her.

"I always want to make sure our students feel safe," he says. "Powerful and vulnerable alike."

Is he annoyed my presence has made life difficult for

some of the Elite. "Which is more valuable to you?" I ask sweetly. "Minor students or Elite?"

Mr. Vandozer's lips part, then he looks down at me. There's a glint of something there, a shrewd consideration. A sizing up of an opponent. Jarron's arm stiffens ever so slightly. Does he see it too?

"Of course I care for all my students. We cannot ascend them all to greatness. But those few—" His smile does not reach his eyes. "Those few are my shining examples. The ones that bring the others hope. You could be one of those, Candice. If you accept the challenge."

My lungs stop breathing entirely.

"Thank you for the encouragement," Jarron says tightly and then pulls me away from that awkward conversation.

Ascend. He said ascend.

I know it's not much to go on. But that word gets under my skin as it is.

"You all right?" Jarron whispers against my hair.

"Is Mr. Vandozer of the royal line?" I ask.

Jarron's brows pinch. "Yes. Why?"

I force air through my tight lungs.

"Want to go somewhere to talk?" he asks. "We can get away from the crowd for a bit?"

I nod quickly. "Sounds good. Talking. Talking would be good." Maybe Jarron can help me make sense of the panic spiraling through me now.

He sweeps me quickly through the crowd toward the edge of the room, but just before we're free of the packed bodies, a large chest looms in front of me.

Jarron jerks to a stop, arm still tight around me.

I look up to a burly man with a thick beard and harsh

expression. The wolf shifter alpha. *King of all the alphas*, as he likes to call himself. His silver eyes cast severe judgement on me as we stand here unmoving. Awkward.

"Jarron," he finally says in way of greeting. "Who is your friend?"

"This is Candice, my girlfriend," he introduces me, as he has with every other supernatural we've spoke to. And unlike every other, the alpha does not try to hide his disapproval.

The alpha quirks an arrogant brow. "Indeed? I find that surprising."

"And why is that?" Jarron asks, his voice dripping with barely disguised anger.

"She is the weakest being in this room," he says matter-of-factly. "Possibly in this school. If I didn't know better, I'd think it were an almost pathetic choice of a partner for a future ruler."

Jarron bares his elongated canines, his fingers turning sharp against my waist, but before more can be said, the King of the Under World slips between the two. He places a firm hand on Jarron's chest and then turns to the alpha.

"My son's choice in mate is none of your business," he says smoothly, but with a distinct bite to his tone. "If you'd like to pass judgement, so be it. Let's hear it all out right now." He waves his hand, as if inviting the alpha to make a physical move.

The alpha glares in my direction.

"Call me or my chosen pathetic," Jarron growls, "one more time and I will tear you apart where you stand."

The alpha smiles. "Oh, you certainly misunderstood," he says sweetly. "I would never—"

"I'm certain he did," Emil says, chest puffing out. "Because if that's what you said, we will have a serious problem here, and it will not be the human girl looking pathetic tonight."

I gasp. The alpha grimaces, his eyes turn down. An act of submission.

He turns and marches away.

Emil turns a surprisingly soft expression to me. "Are you all right?" He gives my arm a reassuring squeeze.

I nod, although the anxiety in my gut is nearly overwhelming and my knees are wobbling.

"He's a dick," I mutter.

Emil and Jarron both chuckle, their shoulders relaxing ever so slightly. "He's never been our family's biggest fan. He thinks we should stay in our own world. He'd like any reason to turn others against us."

Jarron curls a lip. "If he's planning to use Candice as proof of our weakness, he is a complete fool."

"He was likely only trying to get under your skin. Perhaps instigate a reaction so he can claim you are unable to control yourself."

"It nearly worked," Jarron admits.

"You know better."

Jarron grunts but then nods.

"Where were you running off to?" his father asks.

"Just looking for a few moments alone." Jarron's voice dips again, this time with that husky edge.

My cheeks burn red.

Amusement shines in Emil's eyes. "Don't be long. And don't you dare run off before the meals are finished."

Jarron sighs. "Yes, Father."

We finally escape the crowd and find respite in the corner of the room. Eyes still scrutinize us, but at least I can breathe and I'm not expected to speak.

As we reach the wall, Jarron tugs at my hips so that I'm facing him, and he pushes me back against the wall gently.

My heart leaps into my throat.

His hands plant against the wall on either side of my head, caging me in. My whole body pulses with adrenaline. His dark eyes watch me. I peek under his arms to see several people glancing our way then back. Like they want to watch but don't want to be seen watching.

I shift my attention back to the predator caging me in, and yet I feel no fear. Jarron runs hands up my thighs, nails pressing against the silk fabric. I breathe heavily through my nose.

"Do you like this?" he whispers.

Yes. "No." I don't know why I lie. Maybe because nothing could scare me more than how much I'm enjoying this.

He smirks, like he knows the real answer. Can he feel my heart pounding rapidly? How I work to hide how breathless I am?

The pressure eases, and then his hands still, just resting against the outside of my thighs.

"So, what did you want to talk about?"

I can just barely make out his fangs as he murmurs the words. His face descends closer to my shoulder.

His nose grazes my neck, and I shiver.

He purrs in satisfaction, and my head falls back until it's resting against the wall.

"What are you doing?"

"Making it look convincing." Then, his mouth captures

my neck. This time, I can't hold back the breathless whimper. His sharp teeth graze over the sensitive skin.

He could rip me apart with just the wrong movement. I am entirely at his mercy.

And somehow, despite the fact that I am on the edge of death, it is not fear that fills me. A pulse flutters in my gut, drifting lower. I squirm against him, and he presses in tighter.

"Are you convinced?" he purrs.

"They seem to be." But I'm not actually looking. I'm too distracted to know if anyone has even noticed. I'm sure they have, given the amount of attention we've garnered just walking in together, but I can't manage even an ounce of energy to care about that now.

"So, what did you want to say?" he murmurs against my neck.

My eyes flutter closed, brain clouded with sensations I am totally not supposed to be enjoying. I'm supposed to answer. I'm supposed to say something, but his lips are on my skin and I'm burning in the best possible way.

"Mmm, uh, I wanted to..." I trail off as his lips meet the skin of my collar bone.

"Yes?"

"I, um."

"Very interesting."

I clear my throat and shift, forcing my brain to obey. "Mr. Vandozer. There's something off about him."

Jarron pulls back, his expression serious and completely empty of the heat I'm feeling. "There certainly is. But what exactly concerns you?"

"He said *ascend*," I mutter. I'm sure it sounds stupid.

Jarron doesn't respond or react; he only waits. I pray desperately for my heart to slow and mind to clear.

"Which maybe isn't enough to go on, but he fits too."

"You've lost me," Jarron admits. "What fits?"

"My sister," I whisper, trying to ignore his closeness, his smell, the way I imagine very inappropriate things I'd like him to do with his hands. I picture Liz, her smile, her bright hopeful eyes. Someone killed her. I can't let this—whatever it is—stop me from seeking her killer. "In her journal, she wrote about her new lover. That he 'ruled' the school and said he could 'ascend' her. Which is totally not like her. She made it seem like he could make her incredibly powerful, not just in a bond but something more."

Jarron's mouth twists as he considers all of this. "It's certainly not enough to implicate him."

I pull in a long breath through my nose. "But enough to make him a serious suspect."

He nods. "Fair enough. We'll begin looking into him tomorrow."

The pressure on my chest eases slightly. He doesn't think I'm delusional. He's willing to believe me, help me. And damn, I really kind of like that I have a better suspect than him.

I don't know if I could keep doubting him. Doubting this.

I trust him.

It's still such an incredible thing. To trust Jarron, the demon prince.

"But for now," he murmurs, stepping in closer again, "I have a few other things in mind."

"Jarron," I whisper, hyper aware of our nearness. His

warm breath against my temple, his hips against mine, his body towering over me.

"Yes?"

"I need to ask you something."

"Anything," he whispers, lips grazing against my ear.

"Is this real?" My heart thuds so loudly, and my cheeks warm. It's the question I've avoided for days now. Because dammit, it feels so real. So right. Is he just an incredible actor?

Is this really the game we've made it out to be? Or is there more to it?

I'm equal parts desperate for it to be real and terrified of that same thing.

He pulls back, searching my face. What does that reaction mean? My mind is racing, panicking. My hand fists his jacket as he delays his answer. The answer that's everything. The trajectory of my entire life.

Because if Jarron truly wants me the way everyone believes—the way I'm beginning to believe—I'm pretty confident I couldn't possibly escape this. Escape him.

I don't think I want to, not anymore.

"Candice," he whispers. "It's always been real to me."

A shiver cascades down my whole body.

"I just didn't think it was real to you," he tells me.

My eyes flutter closed, and I lay my head back against the stone wall. "It wasn't before," I admit.

His arms tighten around me, and suddenly his chest is rising and falling in rapid succession. He searches my expression. "Has that changed?" he asks. He sounds as desperate as I am.

Yes, my mind screams, but I can't make my lips form the

word. My traitorous, human heart is too terrified to trust itself. He studies me, though, and he must read the answer in them because he smiles.

Then, his lips are on mine. This is not the sweet, gentle kiss of an hour ago. This is the fulfillment of everything we've both been suppressing.

This is the kiss I was expecting. Hoping for. The one that tells me, without a doubt, that he is as desperate for me as I am for him.

His mouth claims mine, his fingers digging into my waist. I push my hips against his involuntarily, and a growl rips from his mouth. I gasp, pulling away for only a moment.

I meet his entirely black eyes, but he's still the Jarron I know. My Jarron.

Mine.

Aw, crap, I'm in deep. I grab the back of his neck and tug his lips to mine, demanding. His hands slide behind my thighs and lifts, until my feet are off the ground. I let one leg hitch up to his waist. He growls again, and this time it sends a wave of delight through me. His tongue finds mine, and the taste of him fills me. Becomes me.

I forget where I am, what's happening. I forget who I am. There is only my body and his, tangling and burning. Desperate and passionate.

I don't know how long it continues, his lips and tongue exploring mine. Tasting and memorizing. I'm lost in this moment. In him.

But eventually, he pulls back, gasping in breaths.

He presses his forehead to mine. "Candice."

I lick my lips, pulling in air to my starved lungs. "Do we really have to stay?" I whisper.

A low vibration begins in his chest, soft. Like a purr. Is he *purring*?

The absolute absurdity of that thought, mixed with my much too heightened emotions, causes a hysterical laugh to bubble up. I can't stop it.

"What's funny?" he asks.

I continue laughing, now just at the fact that I'm laughing.

"Candice?" he asks, near a warning, but there's also concern there. That's the thought that sobers my hysteria.

"You," I pant. "You were purring."

"Purring?" he asks, sounding offended.

"That's what it sounded like. I'm sorry for laughing. I'm just freaking out."

His fingers drift over my collar bone, up my neck, and to my chin. "I could show you where that sound comes from, but it would require me to change forms."

I gasp. "Yep, not ready for that." My conversation with Bea and flashes of the memory from my childhood charge into the front of my mind and sober me quickly.

Jarron tosses a glance over his shoulder, and that's when I notice everyone watching. Even the dancers have halted their rhythm to watch us accosting each other in a public place. Embarrassment sucks the air from my lungs. *Whoops.*

Chattering resumes, and the dancers restart their movement.

"After the conversation with my father and this performance, I suspect we won't get away with an early retreat." His lips curl into an amused smile.

"Right," I mutter. "So, now we've got to endure?"

He squeezes my hand gently. "Just for a little while. It'll be a sweet form of torture."

His chest still rises and falls in heavily, his eyes alight with equal parts curiosity and desire. His jaw clenches as he examines me head to toe. "This is going to be hard."

He pulls away from me, fingers clinging tightly to mine.

I find amusement in his discomfort, and I use it as a distraction against my own. We approach a round table, a floating flame as a center piece. Laithe and Stassi eye us as we take our seats.

"That was so hot," Stassi says seriously.

I bark out a laugh.

"Looks like you need to release a bit of energy," Laithe says, a smirk on his face.

"Want a tussle?" Stassi asks. "Lord knows I could use one. Wouldn't mind—"

"No," Jarron says. "But a bit of air would be good. Are you okay, if I..." he asks me.

"Oh," I say quickly. "You're going to leave?"

"Just for a minute. Only if that's okay."

I nod. "Sure." I guess. If he needs some space.

Jarron places a hand on Laithe's shoulder. "Guard her with your fucking life, you understand?"

Laithe bows his head. "Of course."

Jarron marches away from the table and disappears into the crowd. I bite the inside of my lip, mind spinning through too much.

It's real. Somehow... somehow this became real.

"It's for the best," Stassi says. "You two need time apart or you'll be humping on the table in a few minutes."

Laithe doesn't react but for an amused smile.

People still chatter and move about the room, and I try my best not to focus on any of it. I watch the dancing flames of the magical centerpiece, and I notice images, barely discernable, in the licks of fire. Couples dancing, a woman's skirt soaring.

"Well, if you wanted to avoid more attention," Laithe murmurs, "you failed on that front."

"I suppose so." I can feel so many eyes on my back, but I refuse to turn. I refuse to give any attention to it.

"Why would she want to avoid attention?" Stassi asks.

I roll my eyes. "Of course a wolf wouldn't understand that one."

He shrugs. "You bet I don't understand embarrassment after dry humping a super-hot prince of an entire world. That just solidified your place here in a way nothing but a mark could have."

Ugh, not more marking talk. "What if that's not what I wanted?" I whisper.

I want Jarron, that's something I've got to come to grips with. But the power moves and attention? Am I ready for all of that?

Stassi laughs. "You might not be prepared for it, but you want it. Bad."

I bite the inside of my lip. Maybe he's right.

"Maybe I just don't want it like this," I say. Because that is true. I don't want to be recognized as the girl on Jarron's arm.

I want them all to remember my name because of something I've achieved, not who I'm kissing.

37

WHO KNEW DEMON PRINCES COULD BE SUBMISSIVE?

Jarron and I are quiet as we walk through the dark hall toward his room. He'd been calm for the remaining hour we stayed at the event. We sat at the table with Stassi cracking jokes and Laithe being broody and otherworldly as usual. Jarron's parents joined us and acted casually cordial, with zero comments or judging glances about our moment in the corner.

The only hint that I hadn't imagined the whole damn thing was Jarron's fingers finding my thigh beneath the table, drawing little circles over my dress. Even as we chatted like nothing was unusual.

As if I wasn't burning from the inside out.

Now, it feels surprisingly awkward between us, probably mostly my fault because I'm honestly freaking the hell out. I can't leave this night where we are, and so, I'd agreed to go back to his room, but what does that mean? What does any of this mean?

I have no idea what I'm doing.

"Are you all right?" he whispers, his hand lingering on the handle of his door.

I nod tightly.

"You sure? 'Cause you look like you may pass out."

I bark out an awkward laugh. "I may not be far from that."

He pulls his hand back from the door. "We don't have to—"

"We do," I say quickly. "I mean, we don't have to, you know. And actually, yeah, I think that might be a bad idea."

"No more than kissing, then? I have no problems with that."

"Okay."

"So? You're okay with going in?"

I nod. "Get me out of this damn hallway. Now."

Jarron laughs and pushes open the door immediately. "Yes, ma'am," he purrs.

Once in his room, I take in a few deep breaths. Jarron casually removes his jacket and hangs it on a hook next to his door and then loosens his tie.

"Would you like to go outside?" He motions to the balcony. Out in the darkness, a few snowflakes flutter down.

"Looks cold."

"I can keep you warm," he offers.

"Maybe for a moment." The cool air would feel good on my tight lungs. I've had an intense day if I'm honest.

We quietly walk out to the patio, where the icy air stings my lungs but makes me feel alive. Luckily, the long-sleeved dress keeps me a tad warmer than most others would in this situation. Jarron steps behind me and wraps his arms around my waist, his cheek resting against my temple. His warmth quickly seeps into my skin, and I sigh.

"Tell me what you're thinking," he says.

"That this feels good."

"Tell me what you think about today."

I fight a smile. "I don't know."

"You enjoyed it, right?" he asks.

I recline my head against his shoulder. "Yes." I definitely enjoyed it.

"But it freaked you out."

"A little. I'm—I don't know. This is the last thing I expected when I came here, and I honestly don't even really know what I want. What any of this means."

"Well, then, start small. Tell me what you know you want. It can be anything. To pet a puppy. To be warm. To feel powerful."

"All of those things sound good," I agree. "Hmm, I want... to find my own strength. I want to figure out who killed Liz and make sure they're in the ground."

"What about before that? In the meantime? The little moments between the big ones."

I sniff. "I want to be comfortable. I want to be with you, near you. I want your friendship. I don't want to lose our talks. Our small moments together. Part of me definitely wants more, but that's what scares me."

"Why?" he whispers.

The silence stretches for several moments as I grapple with how to answer. "Part of what freaked me out was how out of control I felt. I was vulnerable in a way I've never let myself be before. It scares me."

Jarron is quiet, his body still against mine. A solid, warm comfort, but he waits.

"You were in control. I wasn't."

He huffs out a breath. "I was most definitely not in control," he mutters. "You have no idea how much power you have over me, Candice."

"You've said that before, but it always feels like me that's unsure."

"I'm terrified too," he admits. "Except, I'm afraid if I make the wrong move, you'll run from me again."

I swallow.

"I'd give you anything you asked for, even if it was space. I told you I'd make the world bow at your feet if you wanted it. But you keep telling me you want to do that on your own, and so I'll let you." He steps back and then around to face me. "How about we play a game? You can test me. Maybe it'll help you see how much control you have over me. Ask me for anything and I swear I'll obey."

My eyebrows rise as I consider this proposition. "How long does this deal last for?"

"Forever."

I snort a laugh, but his expression tells me he's entirely serious. I swallow down another wave of uncertainty.

"Tell me to do something. I'll do it. Anything."

"If I were to tell you to kill Auren?"

"I'd do it."

My lips part but then I shake that thought from my head.

"But I imagined this game going a bit differently. I have handcuffs and chains if you wanted to test my willingness to be submissive." His lips curl into a smug smile as my eyes widen.

"You're serious?" I ask, voice cracking.

There's a challenge in his stare.

"Fine," I say defiantly. Let's play this game, then. "Take off your shirt."

His jaw clenches, eyes turning fully black, and I'm suddenly very happy we agreed not to cross a very solid line tonight. His fingers quickly make work of the buttons down his front, and then he sheds the thin material. It flutters to the floor. Snowflakes stick to the material almost immediately.

My gaze roves over his body hungrily. Dammit, he's fit. Forget six packs; eight packs are the new thing. His skin is golden brown, and I long to run my hands over the ridges of his chest and stomach.

"Can I make a request?" he asks with an amused smile.

I put my hands on my hips, and he smiles. "Yes?"

"It's a bit chilly out here for much more nudity."

"You said you'd obey me," I chide. "If I want you to strip down and do snow angels—"

He chuckles. "I'd do it, but that doesn't mean I'd enjoy it. This is a request, not a command."

I press my lips together to hide the grin creeping up.

I grab his wrist and lead him back inside.

Somehow, in here, the game feels more real. More intense. Probably the fact that his black silk bed sheets are staring at me judgingly.

"Show me your magic," I command.

Jarron blinks, for the first time unsure. "Anything in particular?"

I shrug.

He peers around the room then stops on a glass of water beside his bed. He holds out his hand, and the water rises from the cup into the air. He pulls his fingers into a fist, and the water condenses in a swirling orb and drifts toward us.

His hand flings open again, and I flinch. But nothing happens. I open my eyes to find myself surrounded by little drops of water. Like rain suspended in air.

I breathe deeply. The little drops glitter in the candlelight. "Beautiful," I whisper.

I touch a drop, and they all fall to the ground, not one touching me. My smile grows wide, and his stare is one of absolute awe.

"Where are the handcuffs?" I need to keep this momentum or I'll chicken out and run away, just like he fears.

He walks into the closet and comes out with a handful of things. He drops them on the floor. There are silver handcuffs, black metal chains, and a whip. Holy crap.

Again, my resolve wobbles.

"Have you used these?" I ask.

"No," he answers quickly. "They've been in there since I first moved in. Never touched."

I lean down and examine the items, unsure how to even use most of them.

"Command me to chain myself and I'll do it," he offers casually. His hands in his pockets.

"Okay," I answer, still unsure. But part of me is enjoying this way more than I should. We made the deal that we wouldn't do more than kissing, and I still intend to keep that deal. So, is going along with all of this just being a big tease or something?

"Something wrong?" he asks, noting my expression.

"Maybe we shouldn't?" I say quietly. "I don't want to... take it too far."

"Then, don't," he says matter-of-factly. "You're in control, Candice. If you want me in chains, just to see it happen, tell me. You can let me down immediately or leave me up there all night and not touch me. Or you can break your own rules. I won't stop you. I give you unequivocal permission to do anything you want."

"Anything," I mutter, mind roving over all the options. Some things I'd never in a million years actually do, but I've read enough naughty novels to picture them way more explicitly than I should, and others sound quite interesting.

"Even if it's nothing. Begin, and then stop at any moment. This is all you. Torture me however you please. I'll enjoy every painful moment."

My cheeks heat but I force my mind to obey.

"Shouldn't we at least have a safe word or something?" I put a hand on my hip. I'm pretty certain there is nothing I'd be willing to do to him tonight that would cross a line, and I don't know much about this, but I'm pretty sure that's a basic rule.

He smirks. "Sure, if you want."

"What should it be?"

He considers for a moment. "vRta."

"What's that?" I frown. "I'm not sure I'll remember it," I say honestly.

"Okay, how about... root beer."

I snort. "Okay, I think I can remember that one. Handcuff yourself to the bed post," I order.

He nods sharply and then looks again at the chains at his feet. My heart pounds rapidly.

"Okay," I say slowly and gather the nerve to make that first move. "Chain yourself to the bed."

"Lying down or standing up?"

"Up," I say, mostly because the idea of lying on the bed scares me.

Without hesitation, Jarron swings the cuffs around the top railing of his bed and clasps one wrist into the cuff and lines up the other. With a bit of effort, he's able to clasp the second securely over his wrist.

He's standing, shirtless, cuffed to the top frame of his bed.

I'm breathless, staring at the now immobilized prince of the Under World and wondering how I got here.

How am I'm supposed to deal with the feelings rushing through my whole body? I'm terrified and thrilled and eager and overwhelmed.

I lean against the back of the chair and just look my fill.

Jarron is breathless too, his chest rising and falling in rapid succession. He watches me for a few moments, and then his head falls back as he works to keep himself calm.

"What do you want?" I ask him, voice near hoarse.

"This isn't about what I want," he answers quickly.

"I know that. I'm not saying I'll do any of the things you tell me, but I'm asking. What would you like me to do?"

He licks his lips and lifts his sharp gaze to examine me again. "I want you to touch me."

"Where?"

"Anywhere."

I look over his body. The sharp edges of his stomach muscles are quite tempting. I step forward slowly. His eyes flare, heat radiating from them.

I can't help but smile as he squirms.

He's right; this makes me feel powerful. And I really like it.

I wait, only because I like how desperate he seems. I run my tongue over my teeth, and his gaze snags there. His eyes are unfocused, clouded with near-pained lust.

Finally, I put him out of misery—just a little. The moment my fingers come into contact with his skin, he gasps, head lolling back. I follow each line of his stomach muscles up and down. Indulging in every moment, with no regard for him.

Finally, when I reach the ridge just below his pecs, I put both palms over his stomach and drag them down slowly. Jarron breaths through his teeth.

When I reach his pants, I hook one finger inside his waistband and still.

He shivers.

I consider the many, many other things I could do. Would like to do.

But I set my line, and I don't want to cross it now. My heart is pounding, thrill throbbing through me at this new game.

"Do you have a key for those?" I ask, eying the cuffs. I hadn't thought about the after part of this.

"Somewhere in that mess. If you'd like me released, though, just say the word."

"Okay, I want your arms released," I say, wondering what he intends to do.

His muscles tense, bulge, and with one twisting motion, the cuffs break free in a snap.

"You broke them," I complain.

"I can get more."

I narrow my eyes and cross my arms. "The cuffs didn't even do anything if you could get out with hardly any effort at any moment."

He smiles. "It was the principle. I'd do anything you want. And if you really want to have the upper hand, you can always use that potion of yours."

My eyebrows rise. That's a thought, isn't it? Then, he'd really be at my mercy. My lips curl into a cruel smile. "Another time." I left the potions in Bea's room anyway.

Jarron seems to like that answer. He steps forward, hunger in his eyes, arms just beginning to stretch toward me.

"Ah ah!" I chide, finger pointed at his chest. "Just because you're free from the chains, doesn't mean you're free from me."

He swallows, chin dipping so he's looking down at me, his eyes black. He waits.

"Pull me against you," I tell him.

A heartbeat passes before he obeys. He snakes out both arms, wrapping them firmly around my waist, and he tugs me against him. I fold into his chest, hands curled against his bare skin.

"This is what I was going to do anyway," he murmurs.

"I know."

He chuckles. "Am I allowed to kiss your neck?"

"Gently."

He leans down slowly. His lips just barely graze the skin at the base of my throat.

"Tongue," I command.

His tongue flickers out, tasting my racing pulse and then sliding against my skin, and then his mouth captures my neck. I whimper, pleasure and desire flooding me.

"Stop."

He freezes. After several beats, he pulls back to look me in the eye.

"Kiss me," I whisper. "Like in the garden."

His lips meet mine in such a gentle, reverent way.

The prince is going to be my undoing, I think just before I grip the back of his neck and tug him tighter against me to deepen the kiss.

A groan escapes the back of his throat.

I pull back from his mouth and his arms. He watches me closely. His breath heavy, and his eyes lidded.

I take an awkward step back from him. "Okay, um, I—I think that's enough for the night."

"Okay," he whispers.

"Do you have anything for me to wear?" I motion to my dress.

His eyebrows rise. "What do you need?"

"T-shirt? Shorts? Something to sleep in."

His lips part, and then he freezes, like his mind has short circuited.

I wait for him to kickstart back into motion. "Are you okay?"

He blinks then nods. "Yes, I'm sure I've got something for you." He walks into his closest, his movements smooth and casual, and returns with a few folded articles of clothing.

"You can change here," he says. "Or the bathroom."

I stare at him for a moment. Obviously changing in front of him is a really bad idea.

I lick my lips as I take the offering and then head into the bathroom.

After changing into Jarron's oversized grey T-shirt and athletic shorts, I re-enter the room to find him sitting on the armrest of the chair by the fire.

I pause for a moment but then walk toward the bed and motion for him to follow.

He does, of course. "Should I change too?"

"Oh!" I squeak. "Yes, you can change."

He smirks and then retreats to his closet. He returns only a moment later in grey sweatpants and holding a white shirt. "Shirt or no shirt?"

My mouth dries as I consider the thought of curling up with Jarron's naked chest to sleep. "Shirt," I say quickly.

I'm already questioning my resolve to keep this night tame. To take this slow. My heart and mind are still all twisted up in so many things. My body sure as hell knows what it wants, but the rest of me is less certain.

Jarron throws on the T-shirt and climbs into the bed first, holding up the covers for me to join. I crawl beneath them and his arms, twisting so my back is against his chest.

He settles in, one arm beneath my head and the other draped over my waist. "Is this good?" he whispers against my hair.

"Perfect."

He gives me a gentle squeeze.

"Lights?" I ask. The room turns pitch black.

I gasp, heart racing. My vision adjusts quickly, though, and I can make out most of the room in the darkness thanks to the moonlight streaming through the window.

My body is still entirely wound up, and I can't stop my mind from considering all the things I'd really like to do right about now. Like straddle Jarron, pressing hard against him. Like kissing him, deep and passionate like earlier tonight, and not stopping for hours.

Nope, not tonight.

Tonight, I will find a way to relax and deal with all these confusing feelings in the morning.

Somehow, in only minutes, the warmth and comfort of Jarron's arms lulls me into a deep sleep.

38
MORNING, SUNSHINE

I shift and become aware of smooth, cool sheets on my legs. Not the itchy, thick sheets I've been sleeping with for weeks now.

I twist, forcing my eyes open. Darkness casts eerie shadows over the massive bedroom.

Not mine.

My heart races then skips a beat. *I'm in Jarron's room.*

I stayed overnight in his room. *Nothing happened*, I comfort myself as flashes of the night come back. Well, kind of nothing. Jarron did handcuff himself to the bed while I touched him to my fill.

My cheeks warm.

Well, this will be a very interesting morning.

"Morning, sunshine."

Jarron is standing in the doorway to his balcony, a mug of something steaming in his hand. He leans against the doorframe, a lazy expression of contentment on his face. Dammit, why does he have to be so sexy?

How in the world did I end up in this situation? Worse than pretending to date a demon prince? Now, I think I'm actually dating him.

"What's that look for?" he asks.

I smooth out whatever strange expression I'd been wearing. "Just trying to figure out how the hell I got here."

He frowns. "Do you not remember?"

"No!" I say quickly, flopping back onto the pillow. "I don't mean literally. I mean figuratively."

"Oh, right." He approaches. "It's not that much different from where we were before, is it?" He sits on the edge of the bed.

"It's not much different and it's entirely different at the same time."

He smiles, still seeming incredibly at ease.

"You're a morning person, aren't you?" I complain.

Jarron laughs, full and hearty. I stare at him. *God*, he is a morning person.

"You've been getting up at the butt crack of dawn for weeks to work on those potions. You're a morning person too."

"No, I'm a stubborn bitch. I wake because I make myself. That doesn't mean I'm happy about it. People in Minor Hall are afraid of me during breakfast, and I'm pretty sure it has nothing to do with my boyfriend."

"Boyfriend," he whispers. "I think that's the first time you've said that."

My lips part, but I slam them shut.

"Are you hungry in the mornings? I can have food brought up."

"Starving. Make it lots of protein, and at least something tasty and carby."

He smiles. "Done. Coffee? Orange juice? Hard liquor?"

I grimace. I'm confident he's joking, but the thought of alcohol makes my stomach sour. "I'll take the orange juice. Hold the coffee and liquor."

"Your wish is my command," he says, bowing at the waist. Then, he walks straight out the door of his room.

We don't have much left to prove about our relationship. Now, it's about the real implications of these feelings because I have no idea what to do with them. I have a suspect for my sister's murder, but it's not a strong one. I no longer suspect Jarron was involved, but even that isn't based on evidence.

Is it wishful thinking?

I heave in a sigh, knowing it really doesn't matter. I don't have the emotional capacity to continue to doubt him. If I end up betrayed, then I end up betrayed, and I'll have extra motivation to chop off his balls.

Jarron comes back within moments and plops next to me on the bed. "Did you sleep well?"

"Mhmm."

"Good. You can stay here anytime you'd like. You can transfer to Elite Hall too if you wanted." He shrugs.

I frown.

"I know you said you didn't want that. Just a reminder that the option is always there. Say the word and I'll get it done."

I shake my head and force myself into a sitting position. "I'm a Minor Hall lifer."

"Because of your friends?" he asks.

I nod. "Partly. And I feel safe there. It's my break away from the madness and constant power struggles here." *And, I don't say, it makes me feel better to know I have a place to belong if this doesn't work out.*

Because even if this is real and Jarron does want me—for how long?

I'm a weak human in a world where power is value.

I know Jarron has other priorities, but that doesn't mean it'll always be that way.

It's been made very clear to me my value to the supernatural world. I'm of no consequence.

I'm the girl whose death the authorities would stop investigating the moment they suspected someone more important was involved. Change out me for my sister and the conclusion would have been the same.

Jarron could kill me in this bed, and Mr. Vandozer would brush it under the rug. He's done it before.

I wrinkle my nose. "We need to look into Mr. Vandozer."

"Right," he says, eyebrows high. "I'll put in a call and get him out of the school this evening. We'll search his office after dinner."

I nod sharply. "Alright."

A gentle knock sounds on the door, and Jarron hops up to retrieve a rolling cart steaming and smelling ridiculously delicious.

The golden lid slides back, revealing a massive amount of food.

"Is that eggs benedict?" I ask, peering over the tray filled with at least three dozen cooked eggs covered in creamy sauce.

"And bacon. And rolls."

I blink. All right, next time, downplay my hunger. Got it.

He piles the eggs onto a plate, followed by a side of like twelve pieces of bacon and two rolls, then hands it to me.

"You know there's no way I can eat all that."

My stomach growls. Jarron smirks, holding the plate out to me. "You told me you make up for your skimped lunches by eating a big breakfast and dinner. Prove it."

I roll my eyes. "Half of this would be a big breakfast." Still, I take the plate. "Should we go to the table?" I ask, looking down at my legs still covered in luxurious black sheets.

"Only if you want."

"What if I make a mess?" And considering the contents of my plate, it'll be a miracle if I don't.

He shrugs. "The sheets will be changed before tonight anyway."

If he doesn't care, I don't. I plop a pillow over my crossed legs and use it as a table. My first bite is bliss. Holy crapolio. I pause mid-chew, tastes exploding on my tongue.

"I may have changed my mind," I say, mouth full.

"About what?" he asks, now making his own plate.

"If this is what the food is like, maybe I should move into Elite Hall." It'd be worth the extra bit of stress for this.

Jarron chuckles, taking a seat beside me on the bed. "As much as I'd like that, if you want to stay in Minor Hall, you should. I'll have food sent to you if you want."

"Really?"

He nods. "Fifty eggs benedict for breakfast every day!"

I roll my eyes. "Make it six."

"What about your friends?"

I consider the way Janet eats. "Fine. Twenty."

"Done."

I shake my head, mind boggled by the thought of having catered food delivered to me every day. Don't get me wrong, I grew up with wealthy parents. I have so many privileges, some I don't even realize. But this is some next level stuff.

"Let me know when you get tired of it. You can get anything else you want. Omelets, chappatis, chicken and waffles, Haleem, crepes, macaroons. Anything really."

"You're just showing off now."

I shove more of the delicious meal into my mouth. He does the same.

I still have half a plate when my stomach begins to feel really full. "You're trying to make me gain weight so no one else wants me."

His eyebrows rise. "Does weight determine desirability to humans?"

I pause, surprised by his question. "Yes," I answer. "Our society tells us our value is in our physical appearance and the preferred shape is thin. A lot of boys make fun of bigger girls. That's not the same in your culture?"

"No. Desirability is usually determined by ability and brightness. Body shape is not a factor."

"Brightness?" I ask.

"Hmm, yes. For most supernaturals, the brighter the eyes the stronger the magic. For demons, that shows in our true form. We have dull-colored skin, but we have another sense that allows us to see a person's—well, the only translation I'm aware of is brightness. Some call it an aura. In our human form, it's more of a feeling."

That's interesting. I've heard of that idea before—people have like a glowing color around them or something.

"So I have an aura? What's is like?"

He gives me a half-smile. "Gloriously bright, like sunlight."

"Hmm," I say, unsure what to think about that.

I somehow finish my massive plate of eggs and then lie in bed like a stuffed pig for the next hour. Jarron finally prods me out, only to realize I have no clothes to wear. It's his T-shirt or my dress from last night.

So, we waste another hour waiting for one of the invisible helpers to bring me clothes. Somehow, they bring brand new jeans and a black T-shirt that fit perfectly. It's almost eerie. Did they take my measurements while I slept?

They also brought socks and boots and toiletries.

A few minutes later, I'm dressed and ready to face the scrutiny of Elite Hall. Well, as ready as I'll ever be.

39

THAT WAS NOT SOMETHING I WANTED TO KNOW

Sharp gazes follow Jarron and me as we walk through the halls toward the sunroom. There is a small layer of snow over everything in the courtyard, making the world so much brighter today.

"There he is!" someone calls.

Stassi rushes over and gives Jarron an excited fist bump. Then, he chuckles and runs back. What the hell is that about?

Laithe, Manuela, Lucille, Bea, and Trevor are sitting in Jarron's usual spot beneath the glass windows beside the courtyard. Bea claps once, twice. Trevor joins in, clapping faster. Then, the rest join in until it's a full applause.

I freeze. A slow clap? Are they serious?

I turn on my heel, ready to hide from the attention, but Jarron pulls me by the arm. "Nope, not getting away that easy," he mutters.

The group laughs at my blush, and then Laithe stands to offer us the seat. Jarron takes it without question and tugs me onto his lap, an arm wrapped around my waist. I settle into his warm chest and cross my arms stubbornly.

"It's about time," Trevor says with a wink.

Bea leans in, looking at my neck. I shrink back. "Still no marks, though."

"One step at a time," Jarron says with a fierce smile.

"But did you see that kiss," Stassi says, followed by a high-pitched squeal. "I honestly thought they might start humping right in the middle of the banquet."

A warning rumble reverberates from Jarron's chest.

"Oh, whatever," Bea says boldly. "It's true. *And* a good thing."

I sniff. "By the way, Bea. I left some stuff in your room. Can I get them back in a bit?"

"Sure thing, babe. Maybe you'll give me the sweet tea in private."

I blush again. *Dammit.*

I've never dealt with attention near as intense as I do here. At my old school, one glare would send most of the busybodies running.

Here, well, I'm less in my element. I'd like the opportunity to set them straight when I feel uncomfortable.

The question is, how?

I consider what more I can use to my advantage other than potions. Maybe I'll start looking into magical objects. Or better yet, ones I can create. If I can orchestrate some new forms of magical objects, I could not only become really powerful, but I could create a business even more lucrative and influential than my parents.

It'll take a lot of research, studying, creativity, and time experimenting. This isn't a few-months-long project. It's years.

Potions first, I tell myself. Maybe I'll look into a few objects, but creating my own will be a next step kind of thing.

The topic of conversation turns away from Jarron and me, finally.

"How was the other prince of the Under World's night?" Manuela asks.

"Perfect, as usual." Bea's marks have not changed, but my lips part when I notice Trevor has fresh puncture wounds. Guess I should have expected it goes both ways when the couple is two demons.

"Just the two of you? It's been a while since you left alone," Jarron asks.

Stassi pants. "I know. I'm so jealous."

Bea chuckles. "Yes, we were a little vanilla last night. What about you two, though? Did you finally break out those chains building dust in your closet?"

My cheeks burn.

Trevor laughs. "They're taking it slow, remember?"

"Mhmm," Bea answers, a knowing glint in her eye.

"I heard the big alpha gave you some trouble last night," Manuela says. "Rumor has it, you almost took off his head."

Jarron sighs. "He insulted us both. He's lucky he kept his head intact."

"Daddy saved the day." Trevor laughs.

"I remember the last person to insult our relationship," Bea purrs. "Don't you?"

Trevor snorts. "Don't tell that story."

"Yes! Tell the story!" Manuela says excitedly. "I love torture stories."

I flinch. Torture?

Bea grins at me. "We sometimes use our handcuffs in different ways." She wiggles her brows. "I was alone in the city, meeting a friend for business. A vamp told me I'd never keep Trevor's interest so I may as well give him a taste. He tried too. Idiot. Trevor was shocked when I brought him back to our apartment, strung him up, and bled him out while we—well, you get the idea."

I shiver. *Holy crap.*

She waves at me. "He was fine. Just really hungry when we finally set him free, with a spell that forbid him from feeding on anything but goats for a month. I'm sure that was fun for him." She licks her blood red lips.

"Not one vamp has looked in her direction since," Trevor says, voice low and full of pride.

All right, I may never be as extreme as Bea, but I do envy her reputation. The pride in Trevor's voice. If she were ever a target, she could handle the threat herself. Trevor didn't drag the vamp back to their room; she did.

"This conversation took a turn I didn't expect," Lucille says, looking at the ground uncomfortably. "I'm gonna go grab a bite... of food. Cooked... never mind." She skitters off, and the group giggles, including me. Jarron gives me an encouraging squeeze.

"Well," Stassi says, quieter than before, his eyes still wide, "if you do follow in Bea's footsteps, I'm just saying, we could make it a party."

"I didn't think wolves were into the blood and torture bit," I say.

He grunts, looking a little pale. "Well, no, we're more into pleasure indulgence, but we're also fatally curious."

"There will be no parties in my bedroom," Jarron assures the group.

"Well, on this amusing note." Bea hops to her feet. "Candice lets go grab your things, yeah? We have much more to discuss." Her lips slide into a wide grin, exposing her ultra-white teeth with sharp points.

I resist a sigh and stand. Jarron leans forward, eyeing Bea, his fingers still clinging gently to my thigh, like he's not ready to let me go.

"Settle down, big boy. I'll take good care of her."

His eyebrows rise at her tone, but then he relaxes back into his seat with a sigh. "I'll be here when you get back."

"So," Bea purrs as we head down the hall toward her room. It's only a few hundred feet from Jarron's and right across from Trevor's. They must have a sort of "demon royals suite" section of Elite Hall just for them. Being in Elite Hall makes me feel like I'm living in a luxurious hotel. "Tell me about you and Jarron. Something has changed, yes?"

I twist my lips. Something has changed, but I'm more curious about what she thinks it is. "Why do you say that?"

She raises one brow, like she's annoyed I'd bother denying it. Then, she sighs as she flashes red magic at her door. It swings wide, exposing her massive villa. "He's significantly more relaxed today," she says. "Before, it was like he was walking on eggshells with you."

I frown. "Really?"

"It was clear to all of us that he wanted you, but we could tell you weren't in it all the way. That's changed. Am I right?"

I lick my lips. "I suppose so."

"It was strange to see the powerful Orizian heir scrambling for the attention of a human when a thousand other girls have been vying for his attention—with no luck—for years."

"Scrambling?"

She smiles. "You didn't see him before," she comments as she grabs my bag and holds it out to me. "He was the king of this school, strutting around with his head high and no emotion. Not for anyone or anything. He didn't show interest in females or males, no matter how much they tried to catch his attention. Even when he enacted his punishment for someone who threatened his power, it was cold and swift. He didn't partake in conversations at lunch. He'd sit there with his arms crossed, mind somewhere else. The moment you walked through those doors, Jarron changed. It was quite impressive, the shift in countenance. Suddenly, he wasn't a king; he was a desperate suitor, tripping over himself to get to you."

I frown, taking the items from her outstretched arm. My clothes have been cleaned and folded neatly.

My lips part, unsure of her take on the situation.

"That's why everyone was so convinced you'd used a potion on him." She shrugs. "And now, after last night, his confidence is back. He's still significantly more open emotionally, not closed off like before, but he's poised again. Willing to examine everyone else instead of only you."

I look down at my pile of things, mind still spinning through her words.

"I don't know what you did, but you've got him hooked. Your life is going to change drastically from here on out."

I frown, her words fading out. I'm holding my folded clothes, still warm from the iron. I open my bag and check my items. Two potions books, my potions journal, with all my detailed notes of what I'm working on. My bottle of finished nullifier. But I'm missing something.

"It's so surprising that he'd be like this with you. I guess it makes a little sense; you're so much like her."

I blink. I had been barely listening to her. "What?"

"Elizabeth. You're a close second, I'm sure. And since he never really got a chance to get to know her, it—"

"What?" I say again more forcefully.

She stops, looking at me like I grew an extra head.

"Go back. What are you talking about Liz?"

"I'm saying that we were all surprised he moved on with you of all people."

My stomach sinks. "Moved on," I say slowly, trying not to show my horror. "From Liz?"

Her eyebrows pull down. "Ye—Wait. Did you not know?"

I close my eyes. I think I might faint. "Know what?"

She steps forward quickly, hands up as if surrendering. "Sorry. I thought you knew. They weren't ever together, not really."

"Please explain," I say, barely managing to control my voice from pitching super high, barely able to stop from screaming. "Now."

"Jarron always had a thing for Liz. They kissed the night

before he turned, and then, well, you know how that turned out. He's been Mr. Piney Pants since then. He was in love with her, I guess. Then, you know, she died and you showed up." She shrugs, like it makes all the sense in the world and there's no point in expanding any further.

My mind spins. In the library, Bea had implied Jarron had held a flame for me.

Or had I misunderstood what she was saying? I replay what I can remember from that conversation. Did she ever say me? She did say the Montgomery sisters.

"Are you okay? You look really pale."

Of course I'm not okay, idiot! I want to scream those words, but I can't. Don't show weakness. *Don't ever show them your weakness.*

My mind is spinning too rapidly. I don't know what to do or what to think. I don't know if I believe her.

This is Bea, the girl who will do anything to get under people's skin and into their mind. The problem is, this time, it's working. I find that secret place inside that's full of fiery rage and steely determination.

"Yeah, I'm fine. I lost my journal, though," I say, looking down at the pile of things.

"Oh, hmm." She looks around, her expression telling me she's not at all concerned about my book. I can't explain that it's actually really important. "Did you take it out of your bag at any point last night?" she asks.

I frown. I didn't.

This is something to focus on besides Liz and Jarron.

I wince. If I think about them together, I'm going to barf. Nope, not thinking about it.

Instead, I play through my actions from yesterday pre-gala.

I went straight from the potions room to Bea's room, then I had dropped my bag and forgot it existed the moment I walked into her closet. I shake my head. "No. I must have left it in Under Hall." But I can picture myself putting the journal in the bag. I remember doing it.

"Oh, yeah. You were late. You were probably flustered and missed it."

Right. Sure. My stomach is in knots for several reasons, but the last thing I want is to show weakness to Bea.

"All right, let's go find Jarron and let him know I'm gonna go back to find it."

"Mmkay," Bea says happily.

I refuse to even let my mind rove over the implications that Bea threw at me oh so casually. This was part of her plan, certainly.

Losing my journal is still nerve wracking, though. If someone were to find it, they'd get insights into some of my darker thoughts. Things I don't want anyone to know I've felt. The pouring of my heartbreak over my sister.

They'll also know why I'm really here. They'll know I'm researching all of them.

Every single person in Elite Hall has been under my microscope.

My heart is pattering as we walk back, mind running over the events of yesterday.

Someone rushes up the hall toward us and stops, panting. "Come get Auren," the young demon girl says. "Before she gets killed."

I frown.

Bea runs ahead toward the sunroom. I don't hear any commotion, nothing but silence and the now-pounding of Bea's and her friend's footsteps fading away.

But then, my breath comes out in a puffy white cloud.

I don't know what's happening, but Jarron is very unhappy.

40

KEEPING SECRETS WILL ALWAYS BACKFIRE

I STOP at the end of the hall. The room ahead is dark and shadowed, but I can see the silhouettes of several heads, watching the two supernaturals in the middle of the room.

Jarron's chest is rising and falling in rapid breath. There's another male with thick muscled arms and silver eyes staring him down. Behind him is Auren. She looks less confident than her wolf protector, her arms crossed tightly, shoulders a bit hunched. But she keeps her chin up.

The wolf shifter's attention darts to me. "Oh, good, here she is." Henry, I recognize. He's the alpha's son. The strongest wolf in the school. But he's still not nearly as powerful as Jarron, so what's he playing at?

Bea is already at Auren's side, pulling her by the elbow. Auren's expression is filled with quiet fear, almost sadness. "Let this play out," she whispers to Bea.

"Playing it out leaves you dead."

Auren shakes her head and turns to me. "Not yet."

Jarron is staring down at an open book in his hands. A book with a purple leather cover.

My heart plummets.

Mystery solved. I know who has my journal. And this couldn't be worse for me.

"Want to tell us all about your girlfriend's recent studies?" the shifter says.

Jarron frowns. "The hell are you talking about?"

I step forward, desperate to get that out of his hands. I don't know what I'd do with it after. The shifter has obviously already read it. Jarron has seen some of it—he's looking down at my scrawled writing now.

"Ask her."

Jarron doesn't turn. "No, I'm asking you. You're the one that came in here, spouting insults. You're lucky I haven't gutted you already. Give me a good reason I shouldn't string you both up right now."

There's a flash of fear on the wolf's face, but he recovers quickly, shifting foot to foot. "She's been researching us. *All* of us."

I cross my arms, trying to hide the rush of fear. Jarron grabs the wolf's collar, lifting him off his feet. "Your point?" He challenges.

Henry is no longer able to hide his fear. "She has profiles on all of us. Writing down our personal information."

Jarron pauses, but then he throws Henry to the ground. "Get out of here before I rip you to shreds."

"No, listen—"

"Enough!" Jarron shouts. "One more word against her and I'll kill you, damn the consequences. None of this is news to me. So, unless you'd threaten *me* if you found out I was taking notes on you, I suggest you shut the hell up now."

The wolf scrambles to his feet but remains in a crouch.

Auren takes a tiny step forward. There's no malice in her expression, only submission and a tad bit of determination. "Do you know that you're in it too?" she whispers.

Jarron clenches his jaw.

"Do you know she thinks you killed her sister?"

41

JUST A TASTE, AND THEN IT'S GONE

"If you already knew that, I'll leave now." Auren holds her hands up, talking gently. "But if you don't, you deserve to."

Jarron is still. The lights flicker. The chill drops even lower.

She takes the pause as permission to continue. "It's the only reason she came to this school—she hates us all. Thinks supernaturals are all evil. It says so in there." She points to the purple book still clutched between Jarron's fingers. "And she's only pretending to date you to investigate her sister's death. To investigate *you*." She shifts back and the whole room is still, not even a breath in those seconds after.

Jarron finally recovers from the surprise and then shifts his shoulders, standing up straight. His eyes are hooded, face slack. All emotion gone. The lights return, the air warms. "This is not news to me," he says again, his voice quieter. "Now, get out."

Auren stumbles back, lips trembling. "She thinks you're a monster," she whispers. "I just thought you should know that."

Jarron's eyes flash black, and Auren flees the room, gone in an instant along with Henry.

No one else moves. Trevor watches closely, his eyes dark. The wolves are crouched, waiting for an attack. Manuela sits cross-legged, seemingly casual but her muscles are just as tense as everyone else.

Waiting.

Waiting to see what Jarron does.

I'm waiting too, my heart throbbing. My hands are shaking.

True fear shudders through me for the first time.

Finally, Jarron turns and approaches me. His face is still blank of all emotion.

My heart clenches. He grabs my upper arm with gentle fingers, and he tugs me, urging me to follow him down the hall away from the prying eyes. My chest is so tight it's hard to breathe.

Too much is happening all at once; I don't know what to make of it all.

He stops in front of his bedroom door. "Do you trust me enough to be alone with me?" he asks. He pushes open the door and waits. Is this a test?

After a short pause, I enter his bedroom.

It's icy cold now. Darker than I remember it being.

The door shuts behind him, and I turn to find him holding out the journal to me. "It's not mine to read."

I take it quickly and squeeze it against my chest. It was

open in his hands before he realized what it was. Did he read some of it? If so, what?

"But will you tell me the truth?" There's a challenge in his tone.

I swallow, holding the book tightly. "I don't think you're a monster," I whisper. "Anymore."

He flinches, but that shouldn't be news to him, right? I told him I feared him. I told him I believed the Jarron I knew was gone, but I was wrong. He knows that, right?

"Are you sure about that?" he growls. His eyes are completely black, no whites at all. I barely restrain a whimper as sharp points grow from his hair line, twisting until he has full curling horns. I can't breathe.

I take a step back, unable to hide the horror. It's not his full demon form, just a hint of it. But I remember. Oh, I remember so clearly what he really is.

With every rapid blink, I see his massive wings in my mind's eye. His grayed skin and black scales. How he prowled toward my sister with sleek, predator movements on the haunches of his beastly talon-tipped legs.

If he's testing me now, I know I'm failing.

"Tell me," he growls, his voice echo-y and alien. I wince. "Am I one of your suspects, Candice? Is that what you did this for? Not to look for the real culprit, but to find proof that I did it? You think I killed her? Do you think I would?" His voice breaks at the end.

Tears well in my eyes.

Yesterday, it would have been easy to tell him no. I believe him. Trust him. Now, Bea's words rattle through my mind, casting doubt too thick to lie my way through.

I hold the journal against my chest and try my best not to freak out.

"You—you fit the profile."

Jarron barks out a laugh. "Right. The profile. I should have realized last night when you accused Mr. Vandozer. Those things you marked of him are true for me too."

Bea's words twist through my mind, full of thorns that carve so deep I can't help but bleed. "I had to consider—"

"Had to?" he asks, voice pitching high. Rage distorts his features as he stalks forward, and I shrink away from him. *"Being alone with a demon is the most idiotic thing I've ever done. I spend every moment terrified he'll kill me the way he killed her."* He whispers the cursed words without looking at me.

He did read some of it.

"I didn't—" I can't think. I know I have ways to explain all of this, at least mostly. I can tell him that, yes, I did suspect him but not anymore.

"I hoped I was wrong," I say. "I—I was afraid it was you, but that doesn't make all of this not real."

He doesn't respond. He doesn't move.

As the silence stretches, my heartrate slows a bit, my seizing lungs catch up. The ache in my chest doesn't ease, though. If anything, it becomes more and more painful.

He stalked her, carved his talons through her skin. That was long ago. A moment of passion.

Passion because he desired her? My stomach twists. If he wanted her then, what about now? What about last year when she was dating someone from this school?

"Is there something you want to ask me, then?" he says finally.

Did you kill her?
Did you date her?
Did you love her?

"Candice?" he asks, his voice quiet. I run through the events of that night, how he stalked her, cornered her. I tried to stop him, but he pushed me away. I wasn't hurt, but I couldn't stop him.

My best friend growled at my sister as she whimpered and cried for me to help while he grabbed her and sliced her open.

"Tell me about you and Liz."

"What?"

I look down at my own wrist, running my fingers over the veins. "Liz," I say, voice low. Defeated. "Did you kiss her?"

The room freezes in an instant, literal frost cracks over the walls. He stumbles a step back. He doesn't answer, but betrayal and bone-deep pain flashes in his pitch-black eyes.

"Yes," he admits with no emotion in his tone.

My face crumbles. "When?"

"Three years ago."

"Have you seen her since?" I wish I didn't have these doubts. I wish it wasn't carving its way through my body, but it is. I'm drowning in the fear that Jarron never wanted me. He wanted her. And if he wanted her—

"No," he growls. "Do you need me to say it? I didn't kill her." He shakes his head and then turns, running his hands through his hair between his shinning black horns.

I'm glad he said it, but it's not enough. There's too much swirling around in my mind. Too many questions.

"You used me," he says, head rolling back, staring at the ceiling. "Just like they all do."

"It was your idea," I mutter stubbornly. Stupid comment, I know. But still true.

Jarron barks out a bitter laugh. "You're right. It was my idea. I was trying to help! Unless you think that was all a ploy too. You think you are next?"

"No," I say, voice still quiet, heart still broken. "I don't know what I think."

He releases a breath through his nose. "You don't know what you think," he repeats incredulously. "Are you fucking kidding me? I'm asking if you think I'm a murderer, and your answer is *you don't know*? Why not?" he yells, spreading his arms wide. "I'm a demon. A monster. Eager to kill and destroy. Why wouldn't I kill the meaningless, weak human girl?"

His words hit like a physical blow.

Jarron freezes. "That's all you think of me, isn't it?" His body is so still. His words so low, they rumble. He spins to face me, his eyes entirely black. "That I'm some evil bastard that seduced your sister and killed her, for what? You think it's all a game to destroy *you*?"

"No," I say, but it's so quiet I don't know if he hears me.

"What about last night, then? What was that?" He analyzes my expression. "You—you were pretending?"

"No," I say firmly this time. "No, I believe you care about me. This is real, I believe that."

He scoffs. "You believe this is real?" He points between me and him. "But you can't look me in the eye when I show you even a hint of what I really am. You believe this is real, but you still don't know if I killed her?"

My lips part, but no sounds comes out. "I—" I stutter, trying to wrap my mind around it all. Trying to figure out all of those jagged pieces in my mind. Trying to catch my damn breath.

"I'm the big bad wolf out to steal your virtue and destroy your soul. You think I'm so terrible and immoral and that I'd do *anything* to lure in the weak human girl, including murder her own sister. How pathetic do you take me for?"

That's it. The moment my heart shatters.

My bottom lip trembles but I refuse to cry before him. "You think I don't know that?" My words tremble, too soft. I want to scream them. "You think I don't realize that I am *nothing*. I always knew that. You're this great prince, destined to rule an entire world, Jarron. And I am the weak little human. I know. I've known since the day my parents told me what you were. The day you showed us your true form. The day I couldn't stop you and couldn't save her. Not only could I never be worthy of the legacy you were born into, but I couldn't save the people I care about."

Jarron blinks, eyelashes fluttering. His face is slack, emotionless. Only his eyes flare wide. "That's not what—"

"It's doesn't matter." I step back. "It's true. *Two* investigators stopped looking into my sister's death because she wasn't as important as the suspects. I'm sorry I accused you in my journal. I'm sorry I can't tell you I believe your innocence without question." Tears threaten to well again. Jarron reaches for me, but I twist from his grasp. I don't know if he would have held me or hurt me. But I don't want either.

I expected it. Knew it would come.

Knew I wasn't good enough to keep his attention. I don't

know if it's better or worse that it's my own damn fault that this happened.

I just need to leave.

I charge past him and escape into the hall. I half expect him to come after me. But his door remains closed.

42

NOTE TO SELF: DON'T WALLOW IN DESPAIR. GET ANGRY

I STAND in front of the gates to Minor Hall, panting, heart aching, trying my darndest not to flip out.

"What the hell is this?" I whisper to the closed gates with a sign that reads: **temporarily closed.**

My dorms are closed? How? Why?

"Some pipe burst or something," a pixie mutters, flying over my head then down the hall.

"So, what are we supposed to do?" I call, but she's already gone and no one else is around. This is not the time I want to be displaced from my rooms. I can't go to Elite Hall because Jarron now hates me and who knows how everyone else will react to the news that I'm investigating them all.

I can't go to the public places in the school because that'll mean facing *everyone*. They'll ask me tons of questions—about the gala or the breakup, doesn't matter. Any questions at all will destroy me right now.

I turn on my heel and run.

There's only one place I can go now. It's not the best option, considering I have to go through the tunnels to get there, but it's Sunday. There won't be many students working now, and I'm hoping those that are there haven't heard any of the news yet.

My teeth are chattering as I rush through the cold tunnels, sniffing back the tears I know will fall the moment I'm safe.

I pass two witches who barely look in my direction.

My heart stutters when I see the silver eyes of a wolf shifter. I'm literally feet from my private potions room, so I pick up my speed. The wolf starts walking toward me. With shaking fingers, I open the lock and slip inside before they even say a word.

I pant, back against the door. I buckle every lock, and then I slide to the ground. For all I know, that wolf was friendly or didn't even know who I was.

You believe this is real, but you still don't know if I killed her.

I run my hands through my hair then curl them into fists. He doesn't understand.

I have to assume the worst so often because the moment I let my guard down, the moment one person means to cause me harm, I die.

That's how it works for us.

That's how it ended for Liz and how it very well may end for me too. Because I no longer have Jarron's protection, but I sure as hell have a massive target on my back. Not only do supernaturals have a sick obsession with picking through powerful being's leftovers, but now they all know I've been researching them. Spying on them, from their perspective.

I curl over my shaking legs, and one single sob breaks out of me before I control it. The potions room is cold and miserable. The ground hard and damp. There's one halfway decent chair, but it's across the room, and I can't pull my body that far right now.

All I can think about is how much I messed up.

I don't know.

How can you not know?

This time, I can't stop the sobs from rising. This is just like me, isn't it? Realize how incredible he is and the life I could have with him, just to lose it all.

And it's my own fault.

Because I'm the one that can't trust. I'm the one too blind to see what's right in front of me.

Horns or scales or fangs, whatever. He's still him. He's still Jarron. And it was real.

Was.

It's not real anymore.

My protector is gone. My friend is gone. My chance to find answers is gone.

My whole body is shaking now, tears streaming down my face. I'm so pathetic. So dumb. I've gotten nowhere on answers about my sister's death.

A random hunch about the headmaster that's probably a massive stretch. I lean all the way over until my forehead is pressed to the cold stone of flooring then tip to the side until I'm a ball on the floor. More pathetic tears and feeling sorry for my stupid, cowardly self.

I lie here, miserably cold and sad for, I don't know, around an hour? An hour of being the pathetic human they all expect.

The lost doe without her beast to protect her.

Screw that.

I'm shivering when I finally force my body up. My chest is still tight and aching. My eyes are red and puffy. I feel absolutely terrible in just about every way.

But this can't be the end of it. I look over to my line of cauldrons. A few of my potions are just waiting to be bottled.

I don't want to be the pathetic human. I don't want to be the doe waiting for her protector. With or without Jarron, I'm going to finish this.

Then, I'll deal with my shattered heart.

Did he love her?

I shake my head. Nope, not thinking about that.

I force myself to my feet and march over to the table. The work comes easy, my hands moving without much effort. I know what I'm doing and only need to focus enough to distract me from my spiraling thoughts.

Against my will, images flash through my mind. *Jarron kissing her the way he kissed me.*

I swirl the red liquid of my stunning potion in the cauldron. There are still flecks of silver settling on the top layer. Not ready yet.

His hopeful stare boring into her as they dance. Her beautiful blue eyes, blond hair framing her round face and rosy cheeks. She was so beautiful. Why wouldn't he have wanted her? Why wouldn't he have chosen her over me?

I move to the next cauldron, thick and silvery. Invisibility is ready.

Was it her that he was actually missing all those years? When I showed up here, was she the reason he chased after me? Was it her he was seeking information on?

Swallowing a lump in my throat, I grab a set of empty vials. I pour the liquid into three separate vials with trembling fingers, sniffing back tears.

I stack several of the ingredients I am finished with on the shelf, mind still spinning. Dammit, this is what I'm trying to avoid. These thoughts are killing me.

I picture the moment I told Jarron that Liz was dead. The despair in his eyes. The ice creeping up the walls. His fierce determination to help me find the killer.

I will welcome their death.

My hands clench into fists. I press them against my forehead so tightly that pain builds in my mind.

Dammit. How am I supposed to keep doing this?

It was Bea; she put those thoughts in my mind.

I don't even know if it's true, but damn did she find the chink in my armor. She waited until the right moment. She waited until I was truly vulnerable, truly hopeful that Jarron and I could have something real.

That's when she dropped the bomb she'd been holding on to.

And it was such a convenient coincidence it happened right when my journal went missing from her room. Just moments before I'd be confronted about the notes in said journal.

I slam my fists against the table and knock over one of my potions.

She did this. It was her.

Maybe I can still smooth things out with Jarron. Maybe he'll still help me.

Now that I've had time to really think about it, I don't believe he hurt Liz. I could tell him honestly and whole-heartedly that I don't suspect him. I don't.

But part of me really does believe what Bea told me. He wanted Liz.

I'm only a second choice.

And if that's true, there is no future for him and me. My heart cracks again, but this time, it makes room for the rage.

I don't know who killed my sister. Not yet. But I know who is deserving of vengeance all the same.

What else are you betting on?

You.

I stow away my few good potions in my bag, putting my three vials of nullifier in the small pouch at the top for easy access. Two vials of invisibility in the front next to the blood-clotter and floating potions I made in class. Then, I march out of the room and head back to the one place I should stay far, far away from.

Elite Hall.

43

JUST LIKE THAT, I FIND MY IN

HOLDING on to all my determination and rage, I march toward Elite Hall. There's a group of wolves standing just before the archways, as usual. A few of them jeer in my direction. I ignore them.

I also ignore the fear that my invitation to Elite Hall has been rescinded, but I charge right through like I belong here even more than the rest of them. Like those blinding gemstones aren't there just to show how unworthy I am.

For now, I'll pretend.

For now, I have reason to be here, and no manner of intimidation will stop me.

Several sets of shocked eyes, bright with unnatural power, flash to me the moment I enter the sunroom. I ignore them too.

No one approaches me. No one comments.

I take the hall toward the demon royals' rooms, and my heart shudders the moment I see his door. Still a hundred feet away but visible.

Is Jarron there? Pouting and feeling sorry for himself like I was?

My heart is aching but I need my mind focused elsewhere. I can't deal with that now. Soon, but not now.

I slam my fist three times against Bea's door. The door swings open in only a few seconds. She blinks.

"Candice," she says, surprised.

"You told me there was more than one way to be powerful." I rattle of the words quickly.

Her eyebrows rise, new interest lighting in them.

"Tell me how."

Bea sighs. "You sure about this?"

"You have a way, right?" That's what all of this was about.

I'm betting on you.

"I do. But—" She stretches her neck to look behind me, down the hall. "Come inside." She steps back, holding open the door for me to enter her room.

"There's—well, there's something happening tonight."

My heart races. "Tonight?"

She nods, but there's more emotion on her face than I can name. I half expected a villainous cackle and explanation. I half expected her to pull out the Akrasia Games calling card from her back pocket, but while I'm still certain I'm right, there's also some hesitation and uncertainty warring in her.

"What is it?"

"You and Jarron…"

"Over."

She pulls in another long deep breath. "There is an event taking place tonight. I don't know who all is involved, but

I've heard rumors to suggest you'll have at least one friend there."

My stomach twists. *What the hell does that mean?*

"I hear Minor Hall is closed for the day. Stay here, get some rest. I'll send some food up."

She's being suspiciously nice. I swallow. What if this event isn't what I think it is?

What if it is?

"Tonight might just change both our fates."

And with that ominous comment, she slips from the room, leaving me alone.

Anger is my only companion able to keep the anxiety at bay. I'm terrified that I know exactly what's happening, and it's all following Bea's plan.

She had a purpose for all of it.

She built me up. Tore me down in all the right ways, all in the right moment.

All for this.

I have a really good feeling I'll be coming face to face with the supernaturals responsible for my sister's death in only a few hours.

44

I HAVE A MONSTER TO FACE

I PACE in Bea's room, trying to keep my mind calm while I work through it all. Bea was building me up, grooming me for this. Is that what they all do? Select a weak being to manipulate into the games?

Did Bea do this to Liz too? It wouldn't matter who she was dating—even if it were Jarron, as much as that thought causes nausea to roil through me—if she used Liz's insecurities against her.

I shake my head. No, her journal made it clear that *he* told her he could ascend her. He knew a way to make her incredibly powerful. If she was in the Akrasia Games, it was his fault.

I just don't know who *he* was.

My teeth are chattering as I think through it all. It's too much. Too much without enough information. Which is the only reason I'm going along with this right now.

I need to know if this is what I suspect. I need to know who's behind it. I need the chance to figure out who else

340

was involved. We've gotten next to nowhere in this investigation, and now that I've lost Jarron—well, I'm ready to take some risks to get answers.

Maybe I'll get the chance to enact my revenge tonight.

If it's truly a jinn behind the Akrasia Games and winning grants me one wish, I could simply ask for the death of the person responsible for my sister's death. Of course, that would require competing and winning, which I realize is a long shot, but it is a pretty picture if I could pull it off.

No, I don't intend to compete in this messed up game. I'm just going to play along long enough to get what I need. Let my villains remove their masks so I'll have a target to strike.

Less than an hour later, a fae delivers a tray of pasta.

It takes me a few minutes to convince myself to calm down enough to actually eat. But the event is still a few hours away, so it is in my best interest to not freak out for eight hours straight. Even if I don't intend to compete, I still need to be ready.

If I'm hoping to come face to face with my sister's murderer, I need energy. Plus, I don't know if I'll have the option of backing out of the games. That's a risk I'm willing to take, and so I'll do what I must to make sure I'm prepared.

I pile a large portion of chicken parmesan with broccoli onto my plate. It smells incredible, and I moan when the first bite hits my tongue. Dammit, I'm going to miss the food here.

My stomach twists. The taste of the food is suddenly dull. Not supposed to be thinking about that.

Or him.

Nope, I have a monster to face tonight.

I force myself to take another bite of the frustratingly delicious food.

AN HOUR LATER, there's another gentle knock on the door, followed by the whoosh and trickle of magic. I jerk my attention to the door. But when I answer it, there's no one there.

I peer down the hall. Nothing. No one in sight. Only the dull shadows of the hall, as usual.

It's five p.m. now. No one told me what time the event would actually start. Is it soon? My heart picks up speed, and I close the door, but as I step back my foot slips over something. I look down to find a piece of paper on the floor.

No. Not a piece of paper. A card.

My stomach drops to my feet, even as adrenaline pumps through me.

A tarot card with the image of a jinn on it. The same card from my sister's autopsy.

I've officially been invited to the Akrasia Games.

I CLOSE my eyes and try not to flip out. Images flash through my mind. My sister's limp bloody hand. The card dropped on the forest floor. The destroyed clearing.

Am I really going to do this? Join the same games that killed my sister? Yes, it's in the name of revenge. No, I don't intend to actually compete, but I know so little.

I need to know who's behind this, other than Bea. It is

possible she's responsible for my sister's involvement, but I don't know for sure. If I could figure that out definitively, I could get my revenge now.

My heart races. My mind spins.

Jarron will flip out if he learns of any of this.

Assuming he still cares.

I shake my head. He cares. I believe he cares. He might be mad at me, but I know he'd protect me. And if I laid all of it out, how Bea manipulated me, tear her apart.

Which is also bad news because she is Trevor's chosen. It would crush their family if Jarron were to kill her. I pace in Bea's room, unsure what to do now.

I'm terrified of following the instructions that slipped through along with the card. That's my key to getting through the gates where they're being held. With trembling fingers, I examine the instructions.

Minor Hall. 7 p.m.

That's why Minor Hall is closed. But how? How would anyone have access to shutting down an entire section of dorm rooms in this school without the administration getting suspicious?

Unless...

My knees give out, and I slump to the floor. If I was right about Mr. Vandozer, if he's involved, all of it makes sense. Mr. Vandozer is the only one that would have access to Minor Hall, to adjust the spells to allow only certain powerful supernaturals in.

I bite my lip. It has to be him. He has to be the answer.

I work my jaw and flex my fingers, anger clearing my mind.

I'm ready to face them. Ready to kill them for what they

did to her, and all of the other young, low-power supernaturals they're getting ready to destroy right now. More parents desperate for answers, destined never to find them. More investigators to declare those young people are not important enough to fight for.

People of no consequence.

They chose me because I don't matter.

Shadow Hills Prep is hosting the next Akrasia Games. Who else is inconsequential? Who else are they going to destroy?

You'll see, I'll be as important as you one day soon.

I shiver. Corrine? With her secret boyfriend? My stomach sinks.

Janet? She has a secret boyfriend too. Shit, maybe I should have put more energy into figuring that out. It's so much like my sister's story, but I didn't pay enough attention because I was focused on myself. On Jarron. On Liz.

I spin to look at the clock. It's five-thirty. I have an hour and a half until the event.

I rush from the room with an odd sense of relief. I have a purpose, something to do while I wait for the games to begin. I just have to find Janet and make sure she's not part of this.

45

PANIC IS NOT MY BEST LOOK

I'D AVOIDED BEING out in public since this morning for good reason, *dammit.* Though, so far, no one has bothered to address me directly, the amount of looks and whispers I've been getting for the last half hour have been intense and unnerving.

I checked the courtyard first, maybe taking more time than I should have, but it was incredible to feel the freedom of the open air. It helped to relax my stressed lungs.

Then, I went to the lunch hall where most of Minor Hall has been hanging out. The administration has apparently provided food and drinks for the day, as well as a few comfortable chairs and pillows. I walk through the room, looking over the huddled groups. There are at least a hundred students here but no Janet.

Something buzzes by my ear. I spin, nothing.

"Lola?" I ask.

Then, she darts in front of my nose, her purple wings

beating hard. "OMG, are you okay? I keep hearing all these rumors."

My eyebrows pull down, and I look past her to the several students staring, even some pressing in as if to hear our conversation better. "Yep, I'm fine," I say with a forced smile. "Have you seen Janet?"

She shakes her head. "Not in a while. She was here for lunch, but I haven't seen her since."

I bite my lip.

"Why? What's going on?"

"Uh, I just need to talk to her about something. Did she say anything? Was she going to see her boyfriend or something?" I ask, hoping for something to reassure me that Janet isn't involved in this.

Her eyes widen. "She didn't say, but she did say she had something to do tonight, which doesn't really make sense since all of our hall is closed. Maybe there's a party in Major Hall or something?"

I twist my lips as I consider this. Not good news. Not at all.

"Do you think her boyfriend is in Major Hall?" I ask. That's news that would be a bit hopeful at least. It's unlikely a Major Hall boy would care much about her status.

She shrugs and twists around. "She doesn't say much about him. He's not in Elite or Minor Hall, that's all I really know."

"Does it concern you that she's keeping it a secret?"

She sniffs. "I dunno. It's a little weird, but what's there really to worry about?"

I bite the inside of my lip. "It's what my sister did before she died. If I knew who she was dating, I may have been able to do something about it, but now…"

"Oh, I'm sorry," she says. "I get why it would worry you. But I think—I think this is okay." She doesn't sound all that confident, but neither does she seem overly concerned.

"Yeah, thanks."

She darts forward and lands on my shoulder, whispering into my ear, "There have been some rumors about you and Jarron. Are you all right? Is this really about Janet?"

"I'm okay. Kinda. We did get in a fight, and I don't know —but I am concerned about Janet. If you see her, will you try to find me?"

She drifts up and away from my shoulder. "Yep. Do you need anything, though? We can go hide away somewhere. Get away from the looks."

I give her a sincere smile. Man do I wish I could do that now. "No. Thank you, though. It means a lot you'd be willing to do that. Maybe tomorrow? If things are still bad, I'd wouldn't mind some time away from everything with you guys."

"Sounds perfect! I'll do a quick sweep for Janet too. See if there are any parties going on."

"Great," I say with another forced smile, then I spin and head out of the cafeteria.

I've run out of places to look, particularly since I may not be safe if I come face to face with wolves.

Only an hour left before my meeting with fate.

I slip into the bathroom and hide in a stall. This is bad. All of it. I can't tell Jarron what's going on. One, because I'm a coward and not ready to face him. Two, because he'd stop me. And what then? We don't have enough to go on yet, and this is my chance to get the answers I need.

But—but what happens if I go and I'm trapped? What happens if I don't make it back out again? My parents will have lost another child to these games without knowing what happened or why. Jarron will never know the truth about my feelings or why I went to the games.

I swallow hard and turn to find my books.

I pick up my journal and write one more journal entry.

46

DEAR DIARY & EVERYONE ELSE,

I DON'T KNOW what's going to happen to me tonight, and that's the only reason I'm writing this. I hope I can make it out. I hope I can get the revenge I've been craving, or at least the information I need to get it. But if not, if I get roped into the same terrible battle my sister waged and I don't survive, I won't let the mystery remain. I won't let those that care about me live the rest of their lives not knowing.

I believe my sister was involved in the Akrasia Games, in which some mysterious, unknown parties manipulate weak supernaturals and convince them to enter a battle to the death—with the promise of immense power if they win.

I have become a target. That much I'm confident about, considering I got the invitation today.

I am a human, and it's always bothered me that I am weaker than other supernaturals. It's not just my lack of magic, though; it's how we're treated because of our lack of magic. My parents are influential but have still been the subject of threats and degrading comments my whole life.

After my sister died, and multiple investigators dropped the case because she wasn't important enough to risk accusing someone powerful, I had a reason to rejoin the community. Revenge.

I am a weak human among beings a thousand times stronger. I hate it. But since coming to this school, I've also found true friendship and deep relationships. Some of the beings I thought to be so inhuman they're irreconcilably wicked, I've learned are truly incredible, beautiful beings. I feel grateful to have had the chance to get to know them.

Despite what I've learned and how I've changed, this insecurity still apparently targeted me as the kind of person who would be willing to kill innocent people for someone else's entertainment all to gain magic. While it's true that I am willing—even eager—to kill, I won't be killing innocents and it won't be for anyone's entertainment. It will be for justice.

So, even though I don't want their magic and I'm not willing to play their games, I'm going to play along. I will walk through the gates to Minor Hall, where the instruction in my invitation told me to go. I'm going to figure out who's behind these appalling games. Then, I will do what I can to escape.

I will do what I can to make those people pay.

I may not succeed. But I'm going to try.

Unfortunately, I know very little about the games so far, and that's the exact reason I'm going. Because the only way for me to get the information I need is to put myself at risk. But here is what I know, in case I'm not around to keep fighting tomorrow.

Bea is the supernatural that set me up with an invitation to these games. I don't know how involved she is, but she left hints that there are ways for me to gain power without Jarron, and the moment I asked for her help, she told me there was an event happening tonight. She ordered me food and told me to rest.

An hour later, I got an invitation to the Akrasia Games, identical to the one in my sister's autopsy.

Jarron, I believe to be completely innocent and uninvolved. He cared for me in ways that shocked me, and I feel that I am the one undeserving of his friendship. He wouldn't put me at risk, I believe that. Which is why it's him I'll deliver this journal to—I trust you, Jarron. I do. And I'm sorry.

I also suspect Mr. Vandozer of being involved, but I have no proof. He has made comments to me about ascending—a word used in my sister's journal before she entered the games—and I wonder how the Akrasia Games could possibly take place inside the school without his involvement.

That's it. That's all I know.

I'll know more soon; I may never get the chance to share the information with anyone else but that's a risk I'm willing to take.

WITH ALL MY LOVE,
Candice Montgomery

47

FRIENDSHIP IS THE BEST COMFORT TO A SHATTERED HEART

I LEAN against the marble staircase at the barren entrance to the school. There are portals to a dozen different worlds down the hall, only a hundred feet away. There was a time that thought would have made me shake in my boots. Now, it's almost tempting.

To run away somewhere no one would ever find me.

Of course, if I did that, I'd probably be dead within hours, and that would solve literally nothing. But maybe not. Sometimes, the unknown isn't always the scariest thing. Sometimes, it's the most wonderful.

I don't suspect the unknown I'm about to walk into will be wonderful at all.

I stare down at the quickly scrawled letter in my journal, biting my lip nervously. I need to deliver the message to Jarron, which will mean going back to Elite Hall, but I need to think things through before I do it.

If Jarron figures out what I'm doing before I go through with it, he'll stop me. I can't let that happen. Which means, I can't just hand it to him. I can't just tear the page out and slip it under the door.

No one with any significant amount of power can pass through without an implicit invitation from administration. Which is why, I'm sure, they're using Minor Hall as the location.

This means, so long as I get past those gates before he finds out what's happening, he can't stop me from risking myself to get answers. But it also means he won't be able save me if I get into trouble. This is something I'm going to have to do for myself.

I need to get through the gates to Minor Hall before Jarron reads my note. It's a long walk from Elite Hall to Minor Hall, and he is a hundred times faster than me. I need to guarantee myself a head start.

I flip through my notes about my investigation. The mentions of how I suspect Jarron. He deserves to see it all. Even the parts that may be hurtful. He already knows I've suspected him, and I'd be willing to bet what's in his head is worse than reality.

Because logically, he made sense as a suspect. But in my heart, I always knew it wasn't him.

So, Jarron gets the whole journal. That will help stall him a little. It'll take him a while to get to the page with the incriminating information.

"Candice?" A tiny voice flutters through the air.

I spin to find a little dark-skinned pixie soaring toward me at top speed.

"Lola? What's wrong?"

She stops right in front of my face. "You said to come find you once I found Janet. You seemed so worked up that I figured it was important."

My heart lifts. "And you did? You found her?" Please let Janet be okay. Let her be blissfully unaware of the games and just crushing on some Major Hall boy.

"Yep!" Lola beams and motions dramatically to my half-troll bestie panting as she shuffles down the hall toward us.

I rush forward and squeeze my arms around her the moment she's in reach. "Thank God," I whisper.

She pulls back. "What is all this about? What's going on?"

I take in another breath. This will be a tricky explanation. I don't want them involved in the games. I don't want them to feel obligated to join me in my risky mission.

"Oh, Bea told me something bad was going to happen tonight, and she implied one of you might be involved." I grip the back of my neck. "She was just trying to get under my skin, obviously."

Janet frowns. "Yeah, I wouldn't trust that girl for anything."

My laugh is bitter. "Definitely not. But it still worried me."

"What about you?" Janet asks quietly. "Did you and Jarron break up? There are rumors everywhere."

I look down at my feet. "Uh, yeah. I guess, kinda."

"Oh no!" Janet pulls me back into her arms, and Lola squeezes between us, nestling against my chest. I hold on to them, my limbs trembling, and I take in every ounce of love and comfort I can get.

Friendship is the best comfort to a shattered heart.

Tears sting my eyes, and I sniff back an awkward laugh when they pull away.

"Are you okay?" Janet asks.

I nod quickly. "I am now. Could you guys do something for me, though?" Another part of my plan pops into my mind.

"Of course!" Lola asks, her purple wings fluttering.

"I have something to do, but I want this delivered to Jarron."

They eye my purple journal.

"I should probably tell you the reason we fought, 'cause it'll be everywhere too." They deserve to know. "I, uh, well I told you my sister died this summer. I didn't tell you that she was murdered."

They gasp, but I continue past their shocked expressions to get this out.

"She was secretly dating a powerful supernatural here at this school. I found out when I read her journal. I don't know who. That's the only reason I enrolled here—to find him. Because no one else was going to give my sister the justice she deserved. I was going to do it."

"Oh my god, Candice," Lola whispers. She sits on Janet's shoulder, and they lean in to listen to the rest of my story.

"I knew it was a high level supernatural. Probably a demon because Liz talked about becoming powerful through a bond in her journal." I wave my hand, trying to rush through all the finer details.

"Jarron?" Lola whispers. "Do you think it was Jarron?"

My lips part. "Not anymore. I have no doubts about him now. He doesn't know that, of course. He—" I shake my head. "Jarron knew that I was here to search for the killer. He was helping me. But he didn't know I considered him a suspect. He found out this morning."

They gasp. "That's why you broke up?" Janet whispers.

I nod.

They watch me, expressions a mix of incredulity and concern. The charged silence stretches for a few more moments before Janet's gaze turns sharp. "Is something else going on? You said you had to do something?"

I press my lips together and lie out of my teeth.

"I need to finish up my potions." I resist the urge to look down at my bag full of my finished potions. "Honestly, I really just need some time alone. I'm really glad you guys found me, though. Can we—can we plan to hang out tomorrow?" My heart gives a squeeze. Will there be a tomorrow for me?

"Yes. Of course. You sure you're okay?"

I nod, maybe too quickly. Can they tell I'm freaking out? Probably. But will they assume it's because of Jarron, or do they suspect something more?

I hold up the journal again. "Can you deliver this to him, though?" Is it too much to ask they go to Elite Hall?

"Of course."

"Can you wait like fifteen minutes?"

They both frown. That does sound a little strange, doesn't it? But if I let them rush to give it to him, he might get it too fast.

"He's, uh, in a meeting right now." Best excuse I could come up with to cover why I want them to wait.

They narrow their eyes at me. But then. Janet reaches out and takes the journal from my outstretched hands. "Yeah, of course. You sure you're okay?"

"Thanks. I love you guys. I... never tell you how much I

appreciate you enough. I really thought I'd hate it here, but you made it feel like home."

"Aww, we love you too, babe." Lola wiggles.

Janet's expression doesn't change. She's still examining me like a puzzle to be solved. "We'll see you tomorrow, right?"

"Yep. We can meet in the morning."

Her shoulders finally relax, and I take a step back.

"Thank you," I say one last time and then turn on my heel and head back the other way. I try to keep my same level of confidence as I head toward the most dangerous situation I've ever put myself in.

I'm going to face my enemies—my sister's killers—in moments. I don't know if I'm ready, but I need to be.

I will be.

Even if it's the last thing I do.

48

DON'T YOU DARE

My footsteps echo as I slowly walk toward what feels like my impending doom. I guess I'm feeling a bit melodramatic at the moment, but with my heart and mind racing in unison and the hair on my arms standing up straight and the silence of the empty halls pressing down, I don't know how I'm not supposed to feel like these will be my last moments alive.

Still, I walk with my chin up. I won't let them see my fear. They don't get to see me crumble. If I die, I'll be super pissed, but it's not the end of this. Not for Bea or Mr. Vandozer or anyone else involved in the Akrasia Games.

If I die, Jarron will hunt them down.

I bite the inside of my lip. Only twenty feet before I reach the point of no return. I stop, staring at the sizzling magic of the Minor Hall gates, much less subtle than Elite Hall's magic. It's a warning. This is the most dangerous spot in the whole school for anyone with significant magic.

It will burn the flesh from your bones, Lola told me. If you're too powerful, you cannot get past this magic.

Once, Minor Hall was my safe place. Where I could escape the high-level bullies and breathe. Now, they're using it against me, and isn't it ironic that my safety will lie on the outside of the barrier this time and danger will be on the inside?

Jarron is my safety. I sniff.

My heart hammers pathetically.

The burn of the magic warms my skin. I hold the jinn card tightly between my fingers and try to imagine Liz doing the same. Just before she died.

"This is for you, Liz," I whisper to no one. Then, I take my last step through the magic of the Minor Hall gates to face my worst nightmare.

THE MOMENT the magic zings over my skin, something wraps around my waist and yanks.

I squeal until my back slams against the wall and a hard body presses tightly against me.

"Don't you fucking dare," Jarron growls in my ear.

My stomach twists in all the best ways, which isn't the response I should have, but damn, I'm hyper aware of his body pressed against me. His warmth. His body trembling with some form of anxiety. Anger? Fear? I don't know.

My brain stalls for a moment as I breathe him in. *Jarron.*

How? What is he doing here? He couldn't have read the letter that quickly, right?

"What—what are you doing?" I ask, my voice unsteady. *Play dumb, good plan.*

"Me?" he asks incredulously. "What are you doing?" He pulls back enough to look me in the eye.

"Just heading into Minor Hall." *No big deal, right? Right. No big deal.*

Hips still pressed against mine, pinning me to wall, he holds up a purple journal.

"How?" I whisper. I blink three times then swear. "Dammit, you're fast."

His lips turn up into an arrogant smile.

"Did you even read it?"

"Your friends rushed to find me. I was near the entrance to Elite Hall. Thank God for that. I read your letter at the end and a few bits in between." He leans in closer, nose grazing my hair as he inhales.

I shiver.

"And you better believe there is no fucking way I'm letting you walk through those gates. Maybe ever again." His voice drops into a rumble, dripping with venom.

"I have to go." I don't try to push him off, for reasons. It's not like I'd be strong enough anyway. *Yeah, that sounds like a good excuse.*

"You do not. We'll deal with Bea and Mr. Vandozer."

"We don't even know if Mr. Vandozer is involved. And you aren't allowed to kill Bea for this. You're not allowed."

He frowns. "Not allowed?"

"Nope," I say with a simple shrug.

"Fine. Then, you aren't allowed to go in there." He nods to the gates only feet away. "I won't kill her if you agree to that."

I scrunch up my face and then lay my head back against the wall, looking up at the flickering overhead lights. "I have to," I whisper again.

"If you go in, you may never come out. If you go in, I cannot save you." He grinds his teeth together. "It would kill me. It would literally destroy me, Candice."

I shiver.

He places his hand right next to my head. Something red catches my attention on his arm. I glance at it and then jerk back. "What the hell?"

I quickly grab his upper arm, the first place his skin is smooth and unmarred. Everything beneath it is bright red. Oozing flesh covers a large portion of his forearm.

Jarron seems unconcerned. "What happens if I try to pass the magic," he says lightly.

"You did that stopping me?" I ask, voice thin.

He nods. "I'd do more. So much more. I swear if you go in there right now, I'll follow you."

"It would kill you."

"I'm not convinced it would. I may never look the same, but—"

I flinch. "Are you serious?" He's not serious, right? He's just saying what he thinks will stop me from trying.

"We can do this another way, Candice. You're not entering those games."

I swallow hard, mind racing. Dammit, this wasn't supposed to happen. He was supposed to find the letter *after* I'd entered. Preferably after I was either free or dead.

Now what? I'm not strong enough to fight my way out of his embrace. I'm not fast enough to trick him.

Breathing hard and thinking harder, I look him in the

eye. He'll know if I come up with a plan, he'll see it. So, I allow myself to show the insecurity. The confusion. The truth.

His body relaxes ever so slightly. I relax too.

As my body winds down, my teeth start chattering. "The person who killed my sister is in there."

Pity crosses his expression, but his body does not ease up on mine. "Which is exactly why I won't let you go."

"You care about who killed her too, right?" I ask uncertainly, fishing for confirmation of the second thing on my mind. Maybe it's just a distraction. Or maybe the thought of him having feelings for my dead sister is a thorn I can't loosen from my heart.

"Of course I do," he says seriously, eyes darkening. "I intend to find them and destroy them. But I won't sacrifice you to do it."

I bite my lip. "She mattered to you, right?"

"And you matter *now*."

Now. I matter now that she's dead? I shake my head. Nope, I need to move on from this train of thought. It was manipulation. Nothing more. Maybe. But either way it doesn't matter.

"You can release me now," I say softly, looking down.

He narrows his eyes, examining my face. He pulls his hips back, but his fingers tighten over my wrist.

I glare at him. "I'm not a child."

He shrugs. "I'm not taking chances."

I sigh. I hold up my free hand, palm up, a show of surrender. "I just want my bag," I say slowly. Fingers still around my wrist he steps back and stretches with long limbs to grab the bag discarded on the ground by the gate. He grabs it with ease and then hands it to me.

I place it on the ground and squat next to it so I can rummage around one-handed. He holds on tightly, still not trusting me enough to let go. I guess I can't really blame him.

I slip my fingers into the small pouch near the top of my bag and find the vial I need. It's small, only a few milliliters of liquid. I slip the tiny vial into my palm.

Then, I twist, and with all my might, I slam it against Jarron's cheek.

He reels back as the glass smashes and the liquid splashes. His hand is around my throat, pushing me back into the wall. I gasp and claw at his shirt in those terrifying seconds before Jarron calms, chest heaving.

"What did you just do?" he whispers, voice strained and full of terror.

Prince Jarron Blackthorn, Crown Prince of the Oriziah, is afraid. I think I'd like the expression on his face in different circumstances. But right now, it's from my own betrayal.

"Taking your mother's advice," I say quietly. Then, I kick, sweeping Jarron's feet out from beneath him. If he expected another attack, maybe he'd have been more prepared. Or maybe it's the lack of magic in his limbs that's left him weaker and slower than he expected. He twists and reaches for me as he goes to the ground, landing on his hip hard, but I rip out from his grip and leap straight through the gates into Minor Hall.

49
I WON'T LET YOU GO ALONE

I PASS through the magic and stand in the hall I've been in many times, adrenaline pumping hard. It's quiet and shadowed, no sign of anyone. No big bad villain ready to give his speech. No gloating Bea. No scared Minor Hall students. Nothing.

Just an empty hall of the school.

I turn back, looking through the magic barrier. Jarron is on his knees, panting. His head hangs down, staring at his arms, fingers splayed. The gory red mess on his forearm is already a bright pink, almost healed.

He's not screaming or begging or even trying to get through the barrier. I knew it was a bluff.

His head jerks up to me, eyes black as pitch. I stumble a step back, even though he can't get through to me now.

"I'm sorry," I whisper.

His nostrils flare, pure rage on his face. And the flickering of something else. He glances at the bag by his feet then back up to me. "You should take this with you," he says, voice smooth.

I frown. Not exactly the response I'd been expecting.

He grabs the bag with surprising calm then reaches it out to me. Through the magical barrier.

My eyes widen the moment his skin connects with the buzzing magic. Magic that just moments ago tore his skin apart... now does nothing. Jarron smiles, rueful and cruel.

He is angry at me but pleased with himself.

I rip the bag from his grasp.

"I guess we know now if your potion works," he murmurs. "Forty-five minutes, right?"

"That's a bad idea," I warn. He's planning to come with me.

"It's a bad idea for you too, but that didn't stop you. I will not let you go alone."

Chest heaving and fingers clinging to the bag, I stare at him, mind racing once again. "They're expecting me. Not you."

His eyebrows flick up like he could not care less and doesn't understand why I'd think he would. Then, another thought crosses my mind.

"Wait. I have another idea." It's obvious we're both stubborn fools and he is going to follow me no matter what. My choice is to abandon my plan and go back with him. Where? I don't know. But I'm pretty sure he wouldn't let me out of his sight until he knows for sure this is over.

Or I can accept that he's along for the ride. So, I fumble in my bag a second time, and I come up with a silvery potion. This one is thicker, the dose higher. Almost a full six ounces that needs to be ingested to work. I hand him the vial through the barrier.

He takes it with a frown.

"Drink it."

"What is it?"

"Invisibility potion."

He blinks, shock crossing his face followed quickly by resolve. He gulps down the contents of the vial and smacks his lips. "Minty," he remarks, and I almost laugh. Almost.

He looks down at his body. "Did it work?"

My lips part, about to say no, but then his skin turns luminescent. A moment later, his whole form shimmers. "It's working," I whisper.

I blink, and in that instant, Jarron disappears completely from view. I'm shocked at something that was entirely my own doing. I can't believe any of this is happening.

"That one will only last about thirty minutes," I warn. "Less than the nullifier."

I don't know if he acknowledges me because as far as I can tell, the hallway is empty. "Jarron?"

The gentle sweep of fingers crosses my cheek then down my jaw. I shiver against his touch.

"I think I like this potion," he whispers softly as his fingers drift down my neck all the way to my collar bone before I knock him away.

"You ready?" I ask.

No response.

"I'll take that as a yes." I turn and press deeper into the quiet, shadowed halls of Minor Hall, with an invisible demon prince beside me.

50

NO ROOM FOR FEAR

THE ENTRANCE LOBBY of Minor Hall feels tiny, with the shadows shifting and the air stiff and still. There's no sign of anyone or anything. I'm not even sure where to go. Where would they hold a competition like the one I saw in the my sister's report? Minor Hall is not big.

I walk forward slowly. I glance all around, waiting for a sign or someone to jump and drug me or something. I can't see or hear Jarron. The only sign he's still with me is the gentle caress of his breath on my shoulder when I stop at the first set of archways. To the right is the common room. To the left, the dining hall.

I peer into both—no sign of anything strange.

A few more steps until I reach the next set of open doorways. The game room to the left, the study hall is to the right, and at first, I think there is nothing out of the ordinary there either, but then I realize the tables of study hall are gone. The walls are still covered in shelves of books, but the rest of the room has been cleared out.

I walk toward the only room that seems to have something different about it. The moment I step inside, a flash of red makes me flinch.

Welcome, the words float in a sort of red liquid. It pops then forms into another word. **Candice.**

All right, guess I'm in the right place.

Movement in the shadows pulls my attention to the wall to the right. Three small figures sit up against the bookshelves.

"Candice?" a soft voice says.

I flinch, but I recognize the voice. "Corrine?"

I take three quick steps into the dark room. Corrine stands, shoulders slumped. There's a girl I don't recognize still sitting beside her. And a few feet over is a boy. More contestants, I guess? The people I'm supposed to kill if I'm not able to get out before it gets that far.

Corrine stares at me, eyes wide. "You—you're—" Her hair is braided, her face painted with dramatic makeup. I wish I could say I was happy to see her, but it's too late for that. Not here, not now. Not like this.

Her lips part, and her eyes flicker to the far corner of the dark room but then right back to me.

I follow her gaze to the corner but see nothing. Is there someone there? Is someone watching us? "What are you doing here?" I ask, head shaking. Maybe it's a stupid question.

"Me?" Her voice cracks. "What about you?"

I bite my lip. I have unfinished business here.

"You want everything, don't you? The powerful boyfriend and power beyond imagining. Of course you'd try to take it from the rest of us."

My eyes widen. "Leave now," I tell her softly. "You can still get out. You don't have to do this."

She sneers at me.

"This is how my sister died. Did you know that? She had a secret boyfriend too. Was yours the person who pushed you to do this?"

She bites her lip.

"Who is he? Tell me, please. Actually, I'll walk out with you. I'll plead and beg for information about your secret boyfriend. I won't enter if you don't." And I mean it. Corrine could very well be the key to my sister's death. Her story is so much like my sister's. She's been dropping hints about a powerful boyfriend. She's been talking about becoming powerful. And now, she's here. It's possible her boyfriend is the same one who did this to Liz.

And even if not, he deserves punishment too for what he's done to her.

Corrine crosses her arms, her face showing her embarrassment for a moment, then she straightens her shoulders. "I don't owe you anything, Candice. You don't get to know all of my secrets. Especially since you're keeping a ton of your own. I'd almost say I'm surprised to see you here, but Jarron saw the truth, didn't he? He never even wanted you; he wanted your sister."

Anger curls in my gut, but at the same time, I'm hit with pain. She's not wrong. Maybe. I shake my head. *Doesn't matter.*

Fingers snake between mine. A comforting hand. I look down but see nothing.

"You always thought you were better than us. Well, now,

I'm going to prove that you're not. Without him, you're nothing."

I look down at my feet, trying to keep my anger at bay.

"Corrine," I say softly, swallowing down the shame and pain. "Can't you understand my concern? You've got this secret boyfriend just like my sister did. A boyfriend who made her think she needed power. And now, you're here, entering the Akrasia Games just like her. Do you know what they'll make you do to earn that unimaginable power? Do you know they take bets on which one of us survives? My sister's boyfriend may not have killed her, but he's responsible. He did that to her. And what if it's the same man who's manipulating you now? They get something out of it, don't they? Getting someone to enter? It's a big game to them. And it's us who pays with our lives."

For a moment, her face is slack with shock, but she recovers quickly. "You ended up here too, so what does that mean? Maybe it was *your* boyfriend," she spits in response. "That makes even more sense. Jarron seduced your sister—she's the one he really wanted, you know—convinced her to do this competition so she could be worthy of him. But she wasn't strong enough. She was weak. Just like you. And now, Jarron's doing the same to you, and the result will be the same."

She knows so much. How does she know so much?

I can feel the tension radiating from the warm body next to me. I squeeze Jarron's hand. *Keep calm,* I mentally coach, wishing he could hear me.

"Corrine," I say again, throat tight. "You don't have to do this."

Fear flickers in her eyes. "What about you? You're here

too. You're going to—you—" She shakes her head, and a new wave of anger washes over me. Whoever did this to her, made her think she needed to do this... That person will die by my hand.

"I want to stop it," I whisper. "I want to stop you from getting hurt. I want to stop them from hurting anyone else. And if it *is* Jarron behind all of this? I'll fucking gut him."

Corrine frowns, unsure for the first time.

"I won't let you hurt him," she says.

"Who?"

"He's even more powerful than Jarron. He runs this school."

Fire burns in my chest, hot and scorching, tearing at my insides. *He runs this school.*

He rules supreme at Shadow Hills Academy.

My stomach twists. It has to be him, right?

"Mr. Vandozer?" I ask quickly. I just need that momentary lapse, enough doubt to confirm my suspicions.

Her eyes flare for only a moment. If it weren't him, she'd have scoffed, right? It would be a weird suggestion—unless it were true.

"I don't know what you're talking about," she says, looking down at her shuffling feet.

"Corrine, I'm your friend. Aren't we friends?"

She bites her lips, expression softening. She shrugs.

"I thought we were," I say. "We can be."

"But then, why are you here telling me my boyfriend is some master villain or something? Like I don't matter to him. You're the one manipulating me."

My heart aches for her. "Maybe he really does care for

you," I admit. "But if that's the case, would he really put you at risk like this?"

"He didn't—" she stutters. "I chose to."

"Then, he wouldn't care if you were to leave now, right? With me? We'll leave together." I hold out my right hand, the other still clinging to Jarron.

She blinks rapidly.

"It's not a trick. I swear if you leave with me now, I won't enter without you."

She frowns, and then her bottom lip begins to tremble. "I—we can't," she whispers. "It's too late. They won't let us leave."

I spin to find the way we came is darkened. "We can't leave?" I ask uncertainly, voice thin.

"Rebecca tried. It tossed her back, and then—" she pauses, looking to the dark side of the room. "A voice started laughing at her. Called her a coward and said she'd be marked as the first to die."

"Whose voice? From where?"

She shrugs. "It was a female voice I didn't recognize. Bodiless, like magic."

"So, what now, then?" I say, trying to keep the terror from my voice.

"We wait for our turn." She stares again at the dark spot at the end of the room.

"For what?"

"You have to pass a test to enter. One at a time."

I frown. "And then, when is the actual fight?"

She swallows. "I don't know. It's not here, though. They'll take us somewhere else."

"Okay, so we wait?"

Corrine nods and takes her place back against the wall. I sit too, a few feet from her. Jarron clings tightly to my hand. "This is good," I whisper. "Forty-five minutes."

"Huh?"

I shake my head. "Nothing. Just thinking to myself." I force a smile. If we can stall for forty-five minutes, Jarron's magic will be back. Even if the people behind the competition remain hidden—which makes all the sense in the world, now that I think of it—we'll at least stand a chance of fighting our way out.

The silence clings to everything, until all I can hear is the pounding of my own heart. Jarron is so quiet I sometimes forget he's still here.

There's a strange clicking sound, and the boy near the front of the room starts quaking. "Dominic is up next," Corrine says.

There's a crackling of light, which explodes into the room so quickly I throw my arm up over my eyes and shrink into Jarron's chest. His arms are around me.

"Dominic," a female voice calls.

Dominic stands on trembling legs and enters into the white light—a doorway, apparently. I'm half-tempted to rush past him and enter the room first. My answers are there. I want them now.

But instead, I release a shaky breath and force my shoulders to relax. We're stalling, I remind myself. If we can wait long enough, the nullifier will fade and Jarron will have his strength back. That will be good. Definitely good.

My heart might explode while I'm waiting, but I'll just have to deal.

The hair on my arms stands up as the white light flickers out, leaving the room in darkness.

"I'm next," Corrine says.

"Are you afraid?"

She nods. "I don't have room for that, though. I'm already here." She straightens her shoulders.

"How long between each person?" I ask.

She shrugs. "Maybe ten minutes."

I calculate quickly. Three more people before me, so thirty minutes. It's already been five. "The second potion will run out first," I whisper.

Jarron's chin rests on my shoulder, and he nods so that I can feel it.

The following ten minutes feels like an hour. Finally, Corrine is called. I'm so tempted to grab her and try to leave anyway. Call me a coward, stupid glowing light. I couldn't care less.

It feels so much more like cowardice to watch Corrine enter the light and disappear. I'm shaking now. The wait is killing me.

Another ten minutes. Bernard is called and enters the light. Another ten. Harold is called.

I'm the last one in the room, and Jarron scoots closer. "Trevor knows where we are," he whispers in my ear. He wraps his arms around me. "He'll be trying to find a way in."

My heart leaps but then drops. Do we trust Trevor? If Bea was involved, what if he is too? *Trevor wants the throne, did you know?*

I don't share my doubts with Jarron. If he trusts his brother, I'll let him hold on to that. I pull my backpack closer and pull out a second vial of invisibility. "I only have two," I warn. Worth it, obviously, but this will be my last one. "Only if you need it."

I also grab the few other potions. Two more nullifiers, a blood-clotter and a random floating potion I doubt will be any help at all but I'd rather have them just in case. I shove them all in my pocket and jus hope the vials don't break.

Finally, after nearly thirty minutes of horrible, awful waiting, the light glows and a voice speaks. "Candice."

I shiver at the sound. The voice is echoing and strange but almost familiar. Forcing myself to my feet, I walk toward the light. Toward those responsible for killing my sister.

Jarron holds my hand as we step through together.

THE GROUND RUSHES up at me, and I crumple to my knees. I grip something prickly between my fingers. Astroturf?

Above my head, I find a massive dome ceiling made of dark paneled glass and stands surrounding the large field we are now in the middle of. I work air through my stressed lungs.

The arena is familiar. I have class here daily.

I didn't know I'd be fighting to the death here within only weeks. Such irony.

A glowing white light appears in the center of the field a few feet in front of me. I stand and face the being responsible for my sister's death.

"Candice, I've been wondering when I'd see you," that feminine voice purrs.

I swallow, trying to place the voice. It's like a doctored version of someone I know. If I could figure it out—

"Another Montgomery in my clutches," the voice says with a chuckle. "Whatever will Mommy and Daddy do?"

My breath rushes out, and I curl a lip, barely resisting a snarl. "Who are you?"

The voice laughs.

"No?" I say between clenched teeth. "Too afraid to reveal yourself?"

"I'm the jinn, of course," she says sweetly.

"Jinn don't exist. So, you're probably actually a fae or something hiding behind a bit of magic and a whole lot of cowardice."

"You think you're very clever, don't you?" She sounds much less amused than before. Good. I cross my arms and flick a brow. *Maybe a little.*

Ten minutes. We have to stall for ten minutes until Jarron has his magic back. I don't know what kind of charms or protection spells they'll have placed over themselves or the exits.

In the distance, a wolf howls.

"Would you still feel that way after I kill your protector?"

I frown. What does that mean?

A blast of white-hot magic slams into me. The world spins, and the next thing I know, the ground crashes into me. There's a roar of rage that I can't place, but it sends a wave of terror through my whole body. It's inhuman. Alien.

With a groan, I force my body upright, and just a few feet away there's a man holding a sword piercing the Astro-turf, right next to where I was just standing. Where did he come from? Was he attacking me? Did the jinn just save me?

Another cry, this time of utter agony, echoes through the dome, and my blood turns ice cold.

"No." The word comes out hoarse and quiet, but inside my mind it's a scream.

Oozing black blood pools, seemingly from the fake grass beneath the man's sword. Right where the invisible demon prince had been standing next to me.

Jarron.

Ears ringing, I look up to his attacker and find the demon I'd anticipated from the beginning.

Mr. Vandozer pants and wipes a splatter of black blood from his cheek. "Hello, Candice."

51

I'M NOT NOTHING

"Hello, Candice," Mr. Vandozer says with a smug smile.

One heartbeat. That's all I allow for my shock to settle before I leap at him, nails and teeth flying. I roar in rage, desperate and wild. My mind only able to focus on maiming the man who hurt Jarron. Who hurt my sister.

With a simple flick of his wrist, invisible magic pushes me aside like I'm a tiny kitten. To him, I am.

I am nothing.

I land on all fours, eyes glaring daggers. *I'm going to kill him. I'm going to find a way if it's the last thing I do.*

My mind clears, and I force the rage into something more useful: determination.

Panting, I sit back on my knees. I take a moment to examine the bloody lump on the ground not far away. The blood makes his form slightly visible, but there's no sign the magic is fading yet. He's magicless. Weakened because of me. And because of the invisibility potion, I can't tell how badly he's hurt. But based on Mr. Vandozer's relaxed shoulders and proud grin, I'm guessing it's bad.

He was run through with a large sword. Jarron told me demons can heal from major wounds. But will that still be true without magic? I do have something that may be able to help. It's at least worth a shot.

"Ahh. Are you willing to cooperate now?"

I put my hand in my pocket and grip the vial tightly. I manage a short nod.

"Good girl," he purrs with a husky voice.

I stare at him. Was this Corrine's boyfriend? That would explain why she'd never tell us who he was. He's ten or more years older than her. Was this Liz's boyfriend too?

He has the sharp jaw and shadow of a beard I'd imagine on a grown man. Thick, muscled shoulders and dark eyes. He's handsome, in a way. He licks his lips, looking down at me. Is he attracted to me? Is that what gets him going—young girls?

Nausea clenches my stomach. Disgusting. My sister was legal, technically. She'd just turned seventeen. Corrine was only fifteen or sixteen, though.

I suppose, of all his sins, bedding students isn't as bad as murdering them. He's far beyond anything resembling moral.

"What do you want?" I say through gritted teeth.

"I was going to ask you the same," he says, standing up straight and wiping the hair from his eyes, blood crusted beneath his nails. "I want you to join my games; I'm just unsure if you're ready. If you want it enough."

"*Your* games?" I flick a brow. "Does the jinn belong to you, then?"

The magic behind the white light gives a low warning rumble. I resist the urge to smile. She didn't like that. *Good*. I found a soft spot.

"We're partners," he says quickly, voice too smooth.

"Are you sure? One of you must have a little more power, right?"

He curls a lip. "If you aren't going to cooperate, Candice, we can end this now." He crosses his arms like he's back into headmaster mode, disappointed in my insubordination.

I force myself to stand and then take a few steps closer to Jarron.

"You can't protect him, child. As much as you want to think you're strong enough to beat me, you are nothing. But I can *make* you into something."

I stare down at the bubbling blood, streaming quickly from nothing. I wish I could see him, look him in the eye. I don't know if he's being strong or if he's desperate or if he's already fading. Damn that potion. It didn't even help.

How long have they known Jarron was with me? Did they know he was weakened? He had to have known, right?

The dark blood continues oozing. Too fast. Jarron is bleeding too quickly. Mr. Vandozer is right. I turn my back to Jarron and face my enemy. The man I will kill.

I want to tell him that. I want to tell him that I will be the one to destroy him for what he's taken from me. But not yet. I can't tell him that yet. My heel slips on the black liquid. I wobble and then fall to one knee before I catch myself.

Warm, slick blood covers my hands.

I stare at my empty palm, and whimper pathetically. Then, I glance at the spot my vial had dropped.

Gone.

I can only hope Jarron took it. I stand again and wipe the blood on my jeans.

"You've given me the crown prince of my world on a silver platter. Mine to kill." He smiles at my discomfort. At my hands that are already bloody, and we haven't even started. "I almost feel indebted to you. Perhaps I should give you a gift to express my gratitude."

His smile boils my blood. "I want nothing from you."

He tsks. "If you don't want to play along, I'll kill you both right now. It won't even take much effort." He shrugs, like it makes no difference to him.

I bite the inside of my lip hard. "But if I play along, you won't kill him?" I ask dubiously.

"Oh, no, I still intend to kill him—if he doesn't bleed out before I get the chance. Your potion worked quite well, by the way. It's stopping him from healing." One brow rises high. "But you do have one small piece of leverage over me. I want you in these games. You're exactly what we've been looking for. Our betters will love to see the redemption story. A young girl desperately seeking revenge for her sister's death. It's precious, really."

Of course that's what he wants. Entertainment. I'm just a dog in a fight to them. May as well put a collar around my neck.

"So, if you play along, I won't shove another sword through him. Of course, that may only postpone his death, but..." He shrugs. "It gives you time, right? Hope for the hopeless?" He smiles because he sincerely believes it will make no difference. Jarron will still die. And he might be right.

He also knows I have to try.

I don't respond, and he just watches me as I examine the room, the situation. This is bad. Really bad. *Dammit, Jarron, why did you have to come?* At least before, it would have only been me that died if I got stuck here. Now, it's both of us.

"There's always a chance, right?" He smiles, but I can also see his mind working. He's confident but not entirely so. *Good. I hope he squirms.* But it's not enough to kill us both here and now.

"How long?" The magical voice echoes from behind him. The white light fades in and out but remains in one stationary spot.

Mr. Vandozer nudges the bloody pool. "Yes, good question. How long do you think you have until your potion fades? Twenty minutes? Thirty? How good of a job did you do, little potion master in the making?" He winks. He's taunting me, but there's a hint of strain in his voice.

He's concerned the nullifier will dull soon and Jarron will heal.

Time, yes, time is what I need.

"An hour and a half," I whisper, voice wobbling convincingly.

He grins. "Hmm, I don't think he'll make it that long, do you?"

Maybe not if it wasn't actually half that time. A blood clotting potion will also help—assuming Jarron took the one dropped. I won't let that hope show in my eyes, though. I need him to think he has me on the ropes. I'm near desperate anyway, even with the few bits in my favor.

"Well, maybe it's only your life you'll have to fight for then. There's no saving Jarron."

"She's misleading you," the feminine voice murmurs softly, the white light shimmering. "A demon as powerful as him will work past the barriers faster."

"How fast?" Mr. Vandozer asks quickly, angrily.

"Two thirds of the expected time," the voice answers.

Not many powerful beings know that much about potions. There's very little we know about the jinn, though. What caste is she? How old is she?

He snickers. "Little Candice, did you think you could fool us? Make us stall that long? Do you think you can drag this out for thirty more minutes?"

My teeth begin to chatter, and I don't make an effort to hide it. All right, so they didn't take my lie at face value, but they still think they have twenty more minutes than they really do.

Jarron is minutes from gaining his strength back—I hope. The invisibility potion has lasted a few minutes longer than expected, so maybe... God, please let my time estimate be right.

"What do I need to do?" I ask desperately.

"Sign a contract," Mr. Vandozer says with a cruel smile.

I frown. "A contract?"

"Indeed. It will bind you to silence about the games and those involved. It will ensure you show up. If you try to escape, you die. Simple." He shrugs.

"Show up? The games aren't now?"

"No, dear. They will take place in two weeks. We've held a spot for you if you want it."

I scowl. "And if I don't?"

"Well, one, Jarron dies. Here, now, because of you. And

two, we have a few of your wolf friends waiting for you. We'll simply open the doors."

There are more howls echoing in the distance. Tonight is a full moon. If they let wolves in here, they'll attack without conscious thought.

"Why not just kill me and be done with it?" I put my hands on my hips, feigning confidence. I'm sure he knows it's an act but it makes me feel better all the same.

"Oh, I could. But I'd like to get a little bit of entertainment out of it. Don't worry, we've got a plan for all contingencies. Sign and you can say nothing. Die and, well, it's a pretty believable story, isn't it? Potions master kid drugs and kills the prince of the Under World and then flees. In her panic, she accidentally runs into a few wolves. Wolves that will be wonderfully justified in shredding you to bits. And the school will remain as is. Your search for vengeance will be for nothing. So easy. So simple."

My vision peppers with black, panic pressing down even tighter. I have to master it. I have to be stronger than my own fear. I will be.

"Simple," I repeat through gritted teeth. "Tell me how she died?" I ask quickly. Something to distract me and him.

His brow quirks.

"Liz. How did she die?"

Mr. Vandozer smiles, and I almost leap at him again. I almost let my rage turn me into the animal clawing against my skin. If I could turn into that demonic form Jarron hides beneath his skin, I would. I'd tear him to bits with my talons. I'd carve into him, slicing his skin apart, ripping his limbs from his body.

I pinch the bridge of my nose. That'd be great, but I don't

have that ability. I have nothing. Nothing but my mind, so I have to keep it sharp. Rage can be as much of a weakness as a strength.

"Tell me," I demand.

"She wasn't a coward," he murmurs, the slight hint of pride in his eyes, "if that's what you think. She played. She fought. She was magnificent."

My hands curl into fists. "Did you love her?" I ask. Again, only stalling. I don't care if he tells me yes; there is no way in hell I'll ever believe him.

"Yes," he says.

Jarron groans, blood sloshing as he squirms. My heart lifts with the evidence that he is still alive. The shadow of a talon tipped hand reaches for Mr. Vandozer. Does it bother Jarron that he loved Liz?

"Liar," I spit.

Mr. Vandozer grunts. "I wouldn't expect you to understand."

"Right, because I'm too young to—oh wait, that's exactly what gets you off, isn't it?"

He growls, low and fierce.

"Corrine too, right? Do you love her too?"

"On your knees," he commands.

"No!" I won't submit to him, especially not like that.

"If you don't want to play along, then I'll end it now." He steps forward, sword in hand, and leans over the puddle of blood.

"No," I whisper.

"Then, get on your knees."

I whimper and then obey. Goddammit. My mind is spinning now, panic flooding every rational thought. *No, no, no. Keep it together.*

"I'm going to kill you," a low voice rumbles. Weak and pained. My head whips to Jarron. I can almost make out his silhouette lumped on the ground. The invisibility is fading. "For hurting her."

My stomach sinks. For hurting Liz or me? Maybe the distinction shouldn't matter, but for some reason it does.

"Yes, yes," Mr. Vandozer drawls impatiently. "Revenge and all that. You hate me for taking your chosen from you, don't you?"

My heart squeezes. Chosen?

He leans over Jarron, a taunting smile on his lips as Jarron's body slowly comes into view. His body is larger than I expect, though, and it takes a moment to realize his wings are out, tucked in behind his back. Twisting horns curl over the side of his head. He's in his true form.

"Don't you?" he asks again.

"I'll kill you for hurting her."

"What did you think you'd achieve, coming here like this, little prince? Did you think you could enact revenge on me in this state? The heart so often overrides our better sense. That tiny bit of hope did you in, didn't it? Did you come here looking for her? Your chosen?" Mr. Vandozer squats beside Jarron's body, trembling in rage and pain. "Oh, wait, no. You already lost her. She *never* wanted you. And now, it's too late. You'll never know what it feels like to be with her. To mark her. To bond her. To screw her."

A roar of wild rage rips from Jarron's demon form, but then Mr. Vandozer slams the blunt side of the sword down, and the monstrous beast slumps to the ground, limp. *No.*

My whole body is shaking uncontrollably now.

Mr. Vandozer is laughing, covered in Jarron's blood.

Keep it together. Please, I beg myself.

Even if the potion fades, he can't help either of us if he's unconscious. I clench my hands into fists. Hope. I can only focus on hope. Maybe it's useless. Maybe we already lost. But that won't stop me from fighting.

Determination overrides the pain of my shattering heart. Stall. Get information. Two birds, one stone.

"Chosen?" I force the question from my hoarse throat. I'm sure he can see the panic written all over my face now.

"You know what it means, don't you? Bea told you all about how demon males choose their mates." He smiles, heinous and horrifying. The light of victory shining in his terrifyingly black eyes. "Jarron chose his mate long ago. Didn't you ever wonder why he stalked her during his first shift on this planet?"

My stomach squeezes, and I swear I might throw up. I press my eyes closed, but that doesn't stop the tears from welling.

Mr. Vandozer's hand wraps around Jarron's throat and tugs him up. His body is entirely limp. "Pathetic prince," Mr. Vandozer murmurs.

Jarron gurgles out a quiet growl.

"Let him go," I demand with more strength than I even knew I had. "It's me you want, right?"

Mr. Vandozer drops Jarron, and he crumples into a heap, splashing blood toward me. My. Vandozer stands, predatory eyes pinned on his prey. How long has it been now? It feels like hours. It's probably been minutes.

"Yes, you're right. Now, it's your turn, Candice. The second-choice sister."

I flinch.

"That hurts, doesn't it? To know it was never you. Never the one anyone ever wants. Not really. You'll do, sure, but in the back of everyone's mind, they wish you were her. They wish it was you that died instead of Liz. She was the better sister. The stronger sister. The smarter sister. Your parents would have chosen Liz over you. Your *friends*." His gaze flicks to Jarron's form as he tries to rise but falls back on the ground. Mr. Vandozer winks at me.

"Enough," the magical voice demands. "The contract now."

A piece of paper forms a few feet in front of me. A pen falls to the turf in front of my knees. My heart races. If I sign, there's no going back. I'll have to fight. I'll have to kill Corrine and Dominic and Bernard and Herald to survive.

Time. I need more time.

I stare pathetically at the pen.

Mr. Vandozer drops to his knees beside the unconscious winged beast, dagger in hand and a look of determination on his face. Jarron is now completely visible. His skin is slate grey with scattered black scales. I try to ignore the claws and horns and the wings tucked against his back. There's a gaping wound through his stomach. He's covered in his own blood, and his breaths are shallow. I clench my jaw.

Mr. Vandozer presses the dagger to Jarron's jugular. "Play along, baby girl."

I gag. "If you kill him," I pant, "Trevor will just become the next king. What does it even solve?"

"Oh, sweet child. Don't you think that might be *entirely* the point."

My mouth falls open. "Trevor," I whisper. "Trevor is in on this? He wants to be king that bad?" My last hope crumples. Jarron is unconscious—for who knows how long. Trevor isn't coming.

I know Jarron and Trevor were brothers in competition. I knew Trevor wanted the crown. But part of me still expected him to come. Did Trevor choose the crown over his brother's life?

"We didn't set out to kill Jarron, just weaken him. Discredit him. Prove that his chosen rejected him." Mr. Vandozer's lips curl higher, his smile sickeningly smug. "She chose someone else. Chose death over being with him. It doesn't sound like much to a human, but to us, it's everything. The ultimate failure."

Anger pools in my belly, rage running so deep I know I must be broken. But this rage is strange because... it's not for me. It's for him.

"But well, killing him is a more finite plan. Trevor may feel differently, but I rather like it. We have you to thank for this, Candice. And I can lay the blame right at your little human feet which is just—" he puts his fingers to his lips and gives a chefs kiss.

I'd cringe if I wasn't so panicked.

Jarron. Weak and helpless, lying in a pool of his own blood because of me. And his own brother has abandoned him?

"Are you going to play along or not?" Mr. Vandozer asks, pressing the knife tighter against Jarron's throat. Black blood streams down his neck.

I don't know what to do. What to say. If Jarron is unconscious, it won't matter if his magic comes back. It'll take too long. Mr. Vandozer will kill him before then. "Tell me about Liz," I whisper. I don't even want to hear it, but I do. I don't want to have her memory tainted, but I also want to know.

If this ends in my death, I can at least get that much, right? Jarron is still motionless, other than a few shallow breaths. How much longer? How long can I wait? And will it make any difference at all?

Hopelessness digs its claws into my windpipe, making it hard for me to breathe.

"What do you want to hear, Candice? How Jarron imprinted on her when she was thirteen but never got the chance to woo her because you pulled her away from him? How when I entered her life, she fell at my feet in only days, begging me to bond to her so she could be powerful? How she was so thirsty, desperate for what I could give her?"

No, no. I shake my head but don't utter a word. Let him speak, let him give me the time. Time that may or may not make a difference. But I have to try.

"My sister was a fool," I say.

Mr. Vandozer curls a lip. He doesn't like that answer.

"Being thirsty for power makes you weak. Just like you."

A resounding boom shatters its way through the arena, and I gasp. The ground rattles. I twist to Jarron, but he remains an unmoving heap of grey-skinned limbs and horns.

"What did you do?" Mr. Vandozer whispers, his expression exposes his uncertainty for the first time.

My eyes widen too, and for a moment—a sweet, delicious moment—I can pretend it is my own doing. That I have some power hidden deep inside that would come out now when I need it most.

That I could destroy him. Rattle this entire academy down to its foundation and make this powerful man that hurt my sister—manipulated her, killed her—fear me.

God, there is nothing I want more.

Nothing I wouldn't give to make it true.

But it's not.

Whatever is happening, isn't me. It isn't my doing.

I don't even know what it could be. Jarron is so still he could already be dead for all I know.

Another shrieking crash shakes the walls. Mr. Vandozer stumbles back.

"Someone is coming," the white light says calmly. "From the outside. They're breaking down the barriers."

I scramble to my feet. If we make it out of this before I sign, Mr. Vandozer will be exposed. He needs me to sign.

Jarron is no help to anyone right now. He can't save me. He can't even save himself—and that's my fault. Mr. Vandozer grabs the fallen dagger and races to Jarron. There isn't enough time.

"Wait!" I call. "I'll sign the contract."

Mr. Vandozer shifts his attention to me, eyes fully black —no whites at all. Straight black horns have sprouted from his head. His skin shimmers and then loses its pigment, turning an icy white. His fingers elongate into sharp talons as he prowls toward me. I blanch from the horrible sight of his true form.

My knees wobble, and tears well in my eyes.

Once, it was Jarron prowling like this. He forgot who he

was. Who I was. I was terrified of him, and it wasn't even me he'd had his sights set on. He wanted Liz.

My broken heart aches.

I had no power then. And I have very little now. But I do have something.

After only a quick search of the floor I find the fallen pen and hold it up.

The moment it is in my hand, Mr. Vandozer stops. The rumbling has halted.

Whatever was happening on the outside of the building is either paused or finished. No help is coming.

Not fast enough, at least.

With a sharp stare, Mr. Vandozer in beast form inches forward on horrendous talon-tipped legs. "Sign," he says, low and serious.

The ground trembles ever so slightly. A panel of light from above swings haphazardly, sending an orange glow dancing across the field. The demon is inches from me when the contract floats up in front of my face.

"Now." He presses a claw against my throat. As I swallow, his blade-like talon presses against my skin. Warmth pools and slides down my neck. I wince then press the edge of the pen against the paper and begin to slowly scrawl the letters of my name.

Candic—

Then, with my left hand, I slam a glass vial against Mr. Vandozer's face.

His claw clips my throat as I dive away, and more blood splatters. Mine this time. His monstrous form lets out a shrieking roar. My whole body pulses with terror and pain and—God, I couldn't even name all the emotions. I can barely feel my own legs.

But damn if I'm not going to make this man suffer before I die.

"Kill the prince!" the jinn yells. "They're coming!"

But Mr. Vandozer is lost to the world now. His raging demon is not interested in the strategy. He wants to kill the weak human who dared to touch him.

I crouch, holding my dagger loosely in my right hand. I've trained with similar weapons before. Obsidian is heavier than steel, but I'm sure I can adjust for this.

"Come and get me, asshole," I taunt and grin.

My whole world is crumbling, but somehow, I'm pleased as a kitten that I got him in this position. The jinn must either have limited powers or she doesn't actually care about him. She isn't helping.

He's as weak as Jarron is now, and he doesn't even realize it yet.

The demon launches himself at me. Even without magic, he's fast as hell. I dive away, but his claws slice through my calf. I pull my leg desperately from his grasp, flesh tearing, because I know I can't let him catch me or I'm dead.

One well aimed slice is all it would take.

I right myself and breathe through the pain, readying for his next attack.

"Stop it!" the jinn yells. But there is nothing left of Mr. Vandozer. There is only the beast. And this beast wants to devour me. "Stop now. Kill the prince, you fool!"

The beast ignores her cries and comes for me again.

I slide forward as he attacks and shove my dagger into the thick skin of his stomach. He roars, but then his hand is around my throat, crushing my windpipe. I can't even cry out. Can't scream. Can't breathe.

It doesn't matter that he has no magic. He's still stronger and faster than me.

I am nothing.

Black peppers my visions. I'm going to pass out. *I'm going to die.*

A roar ricochets through the arena. Anger—so much anger. The monster's claws release me. The ground slams into my shoulder, and I cough in choking breaths. Acid scorches my stomach and throat.

Every breath is agony.

There are more growls and screeching rage from the alien beings, then a flash of light and the sounds stop, leaving only a ringing in my ears.

My vision is blurry, my pulse throbbing in my head, and then I look up into the pitch-black eyes of the monster standing over me.

His fangs and claws are dripping in blood.

There is no space left for the fear I'm supposed to feel when faced with not only death but the monster of my nightmares.

Again, I'm powerless as I look up into the alien eyes of the demon prince. Grey skin. Black leathery wings. Claws the size of my dagger.

He stalks forward, so much like the night that everything changed. Everything is changing again, I realize.

I'm helpless, just like that time.

Except, this time, I accept it.

There is no anger or defiance left in my body.

I've already lost everything. Liz. My revenge. It's all

slipped through my fingers. Maybe it's just poetic for it all to end like this, to be killed by *him*.

Maybe it's ironic that my nightmare has come to life, but I'm no longer afraid of it. Not afraid of him. Not afraid of death.

The monster places a claw under my chin. I tilt my head up to him, knowing I'm baring my neck to the beast. My eyes flutter closed, ready for death to take me.

At least, I think in the beat between realization that my death is imminent and the completion of the act, *I won't die with hatred in my heart.*

There is only sadness. And somehow, that's more beautiful.

I flinch when an explosion rattles the ground.

The world detonates, along with the ear-shattering crunch of twisting metal and the shriek of broken glass.

The monster flares his wings wide and bellows into the sky as the ceiling of the arena collapses—falling straight at us. I am rocked by sudden sharp pain, and my vision goes dark.

52

JUST A CASUAL CHAT WITH A SCALED MONSTER

EVERYTHING IS BLACK, but the pain is still as sharp as ever.

I'm panting, my lungs burning and nose filled with the acrid smell of dust and blood. I blink my mind away from the panic, but there is no new pain. The metal beams didn't smash my brain in. The glass didn't cut a thousand slices through me. The monster's talons didn't carve through my neck.

The weight of a heavy chest is pressing down on me and heaving just as desperately. His breath is warm on my neck.

His sweet smell blocks out all the others.

"Jarron?" I whisper.

A rumbling purr reverberates from his chest. *Oh shit.* The fingers at the ends of the arms holding me are sharp points. I squirm against the slight pressure at the bottom of my back.

The blackness surrounding me is not from or unconsciousness taking me. I'm in a cocoon of dark, leathery wings.

He saved me from the shattering arena. But now what?

The rumble is not a growl. Not a threat.

My fingers find their way to his shoulder and drag down to his chest, where hard-as-stone scales scatter across his thick skin. The scales vibrate beneath my fingers.

"Are you well?" His voice is hoarse and alien. It echoes like there are two beings, speaking as one.

"Uh, I'm not dead?"

He growls again. My head spins. That's when it hits me that I'm not talking to Jarron. I'm talking to his demon.

My heart hammers. *Right, yeah, no big deal. Just a casual chat with a scaled monster.*

"Calm, bright one," the demon holding me says. "It will take time for us to be released from this place."

"What?" I squeak.

"I'm trapped beneath the rubble. I don't yet have enough strength to escape, not without harming you."

Uh, since when do demons think about who they'll hurt by their actions? I don't voice that question. "How long?" I ask instead.

"Trevor and Laithe are digging to us now."

Trevor? "He came?"

"Yes. He was delayed by our change in location and the magic protecting the arena. But he did not abandon us."

Good, that's good. "I think we're going to owe him for this, then."

The demon rumbles out a laugh. "Perhaps I will not kill his mate for her role in your harm."

"I already said you weren't allowed to kill her." Not that I forgive her for this, but I don't want to be the reason Jarron destroys his brother's happiness.

"I did not agree to that," the demon growls. "But I will take it under consideration. *Only* if she is not a continued threat."

"That's fair," I say, as if this were at all a reasonable conversation.

Something vibrates and crunches over my head, and I shrink in closer to Jarron—the demon. My forehead presses against the leathery skin of his shoulder.

"Take your time, brother," the demon mumbles. "I am enjoying myself."

"Funny," I complain. "Can you change back?" It may be an unfair question, but I'd be significantly more comfortable with Jarron in human form.

"Not unless you don't mind being crushed by debris."

"Uh, right. This is fine."

"Are you unwell?"

"Well, your, uh, claws? They are kind of—"

"Oh," he mutters, then he shifts his hands, splaying them out so his tips are not digging into me. "Is that better?"

"Yes. Thank you." I relax a bit more. Still being cocooned by a literal monster, but I suppose it's better than the alternative—you know, dead.

"If you'd let me mark you, and establish a magical connection, those things would not happen. I could feel your pain as if it were mine."

"Uhhh, right. Yeah, it's not a big deal," I squirm and realize I should be incredibly clear about this topic considering I don't know how much I can trust a demon. "I don't want you to mark me."

This time, the vibration in his chest is clearly displeased.

"Thank you," I whisper. "For saving me."

"I will always protect you," he whispers. I don't fully believe that, but part of my heart thaws against my will.

I think it helps that I can't see him, but in the next few minutes, with our breaths mingling, skin touching, while we wait to be rescued, I find myself comfortable. At ease in my monster's arms.

"Cover your face with your hands," he instructs me eventually. I obey. The pressure on my chest lessens as he pushes away. Dust and pebbles rain down.

The groaning of shifting metal and stone sound just above me, and I'm secretly terrified something large will drop on me. I don't want to look yet.

"Come," the demon says. My breath is still labored, but I force my hands from my face and sit up.

I wince. Everything aches. Everything throbs.

Then, I move my legs and a cry rips from my lips. Crap. I forgot about Mr. Vandozer's demon ripping into my calf.

There's a hiss from above me. Jarron's demon growls, eyeing my leg. "I will kill him." I guess that means Mr. Vandozer got away?

"Pretty sure you already promised that," I say through my ragged breaths.

"Well, it will be slower than I'd intended before."

The demon leans over and gently shifts his arms beneath my body and lifts. *Oh, good, more demon cuddles.*

God, I think I'm delirious.

His body is hard, with sharp edges, but he's gentle as he carries me out of the hole they dug to get to us. He leaps over the fallen beams and piled stones from the ceiling of the arena.

His steps are slow but long, and he doesn't stop once we

escape the arena and enter the field outside. The moon is high in the sky. Wolves howl in the distance. Yeah, I guess stopping here would be a bad idea.

He marches into the school, still in his demon form, carrying me. He rushes up the stairs and then kicks open a wooden door. There's commotion on the other side of the room. Gasps and then pattering of feet.

The demon gently places me on a cot with white sheets. I'm in the infirmary?

"Rest. The nurses will take care of you, and I will keep watch."

"Wait!" I call before he walks away. "Mr. Vandozer. What happened to him?"

"He escaped into his jinn's power, taking him out of reach. We will find him again, and he will die a very slow, very painful death."

I blink. Fair enough. I relax into the cushions and allow the nurses to make a fuss over my shredded calf as the demon that haunted my dreams continues to protect me.

53

I WON'T BE A SECOND CHOICE

I MUST LOSE consciousness at some point, because my eyes fly open to find the infirmary dark and quiet. "Jarron?" I whisper hoarsely.

My head throbs. My leg feels like they're being ripped apart.

Footsteps approach. "It's Trevor," he says gently.

A shiver wracks through my body and I twist, pushing through the sharp pain and lift my gaze to look around. "Where is Jarron?" I ask, voice barely audible.

Trevor sits in the chair beside my cot. "He's resting now."

"Is he okay?" He brought me here but he was covered in dark blood. What happened after that?

"Yes. His heart will take a few days to heal, but otherwise he's fine."

"His heart?" My stomach sinks. Mr. Vandozer stabbed him in the heart? My eyes flutter closed for a moment, but I don't allow my mind to succumb to bonedeep weariness.

"The blow grazed his heart, yes. It takes more than that to kill us, though."

"He didn't have his magic. How did he survive that?"

Trevor shrugs. "My guess is barely. Even without magic we're more durable than humans. And the nurses said you gave him a potion to slow the bleeding? That may have saved his life."

I was so close to losing him.

"Your parents are here too. They arrived a few hours ago and asked me to watch over you while he rested. I agreed because I wanted the chance to apologize for Bea's part in all of it."

"No apology necessary. Her actions aren't your responsibility."

"Either way, I'm sorry. And I'm glad you're okay. We— we won't be seeing you for a while."

I sit up quickly and instantly regret it. My head spins and pounds at the same time.

"Easy there, killer." He grips my elbow, steadying me.

"Ow," I mutter, pressing my palm against my forehead. "What do you mean, you won't be seeing me?"

"Bea's already gone back to our world for a while. I'll go to join her. I—She's not going to be safe here for a while. If ever."

I sigh. "I already told Jarron not to retaliate against her."

There's a pause. "You did?"

I nod. "I think he agreed, if only because you saved us."

"Thank you," he says, looking down at his hands. "When I saw him not long ago—well, he wasn't in the talking mood. Some space between us is probably for the better anyway."

"Yeah. I guess I can understand that." I lie back against the pillow. "Thank you. For coming to help us."

He forces a smile. "All the teachers are going to be pissed I destroyed the arena."

I snort. "Right, cause our headmaster turning super evil villain and convincing his students to enter the Akrasia Games is your fault."

His chuckle is short lived.

"Hey, Trevor?" I realize I may never have another chance to ask about the elephant weighing on my chest.

"Mr. Vandozer said something. Something I'd like to understand more."

Trevor shifts uncomfortably. "Okay?"

"He said that Liz was Jarron's chosen."

Trevor's mouth falls open, a look of utter shock on his face. "That's..." He stares off past my shoulder, gaze unfocused.

I wait, as he works through his thoughts. Finally, he blinks and responds. "What did you want to know?"

"If it's true." I look down at my hands.

He rings his fingers together. "Has anyone told you what it means? To be a demon's chosen?"

I nod.

"Well, you should also understand that it's forbidden to talk about it. At least before the bond has been accepted. It's sacred." Trevor frowns. "Did Mr. Vandozer imply he targeted Liz because she was Jarron's chosen? That's a grave sin to our people if so."

I bite the inside of my lip. "I don't know but he said something about discrediting Jarron's right to the throne. I don't know if he planned that before or after Liz..."

Trevor nods absently, but his attention is cast to the floor.

"If it's sacred and no one is supposed to know or even talk about it, how would he have known?" I ask.

His smile is sad. "We don't talk about it, and the truth is Jarron will never admit who his chosen was. But there are signs. And those closest to him have a pretty good idea."

"He won't admit it?" I frown. "Ever?"

He shakes his head. "Especially if his chosen died before accepting him—"

So, Jarron will never tell me that he'd imprinted on Liz. He'll never admit that she was his first choice. "Is it bad that it changes my mind?" the words are bitter on my tongue. "I don't want to be a second choice."

Trevor frowns. "I don't think you're his second choice. Sometimes, what our soul chooses, isn't what we truly desire. Even if he imprinted on Liz, you aren't Jarron's second choice. You were just his demon's second choice. There's a difference."

Is there?

I rub my chest, that tightness back again. I don't see how that distinction matters, but I don't say it. Not now.

"I'll have to think about it."

Trevor nods and stands. "You should get some rest."

I force a smile, and ease back under the sheets, mind racing.

If my sister were alive, Jarron would choose her. Maybe he'd be happy with me now, but that's not something I think I can ever settle for.

54

THE DEVIL'S HEART CAN BREAK TOO

A SHINNING black talon is carving through my chest, piercing all the way to my heart. Burning pain clenches over my whole body and a scream rips from my throat.

I JERK awake to a pitch-black room, and agony clenches over every inch of my body. My panicked scream morphs into a pathetic whimper of pain.

The fear of the nightmare is already forgotten, replaced by very real physical pain.

I curl over and press my face into the itchy white sheets.

Tears instantly stream down my face. I can't define or explain any of it. There is only misery and grief and heartbreak.

So much heartbreak.

The door crashes open, but I can't even make myself face the intruder. I curl into fetal position and try to make it all go away.

Rough hands grab me by the upper arms and jerk me to face them.

Through my pathetic tears, I stare into a monster's void-like eyes. My body freezes. Leathery wings block out everything but the terrifying beast holding me.

"What's wrong?" The monster's voice is strained.

Confusion covers the anguish of moments before. Is the monster *concerned*?

"Jarron?" I whisper. Finally, some clarity has returned and reality settles in.

"What is wrong?" he asks again, louder now. "Are you okay?"

Though his form is terrifying, his expression is that of a lost child.

"I'm—I'm fine. I think I had a nightmare. And when I jerked awake, it—well, it hurt."

He looks me over again and then releases my arms. His chest rises and falls dramatically. "Are you okay?" I ask, remembering his injuries. He barely survived yesterday.

"Only if you are."

A nurse rushes into the room and freezes at the sight of the winged demon kneeling before my bed.

"You both should be resting," she murmurs frantically.

"She needs something to help her sleep," the demon's voice rumbles.

The nurse is clearly terrified but she nods rapidly and sprints off somewhere down the hall.

I take in a few long breaths and find that, though there are some major aches, so long as I allow myself to relax, my body isn't as hurt as it felt moments ago. The tension makes the pain exponentially worse.

Jarron remains kneeling on the ground by my bed. His eyes flutter, like he's barely able to stay awake.

"You can go," I tell him. "You—I'll be okay. And you need to rest."

He jerks his attention to me. "You want me to leave?"

I swallow. Yes. No.

"Tell me, bright one. Tell me the truth hidden in your eyes."

I press my lips together. This conversation seems better suited for Jarron in human form. If he hadn't just saved my life hours ago, I'd be utterly petrified. Not that it stops my chest from tightening when my eyes land on his sharp claws.

This is Jarron, I remind myself.

I don't want to fear him. I don't want to be disgusted.

But at the same time, I can't want him. Can't love him. I have to tell him it's over.

The nurse scurries back in. She scoots around Jarron's wings to drop a tiny vial of purple liquid on the table by my bed. "This will help you sleep." Her voice trembles slightly. "Um, do you—do you want your boyfriend to stay? He's— well he needs rest too."

My lips part, and my eyes dart to him. "He's not my boyfriend," I blurt out, not even thinking.

The nurse gasps. Then, after a beat of silent panic, she wisely skitters back out of the room.

Jarron's monster is watching me without emotion. "That's it? You're done with me now?"

"No. I didn't mean—" I swallow. "We're friends," I add stupidly. I don't know how to do this right. Maybe there is no right way.

He stands slowly, with much more effort than it should take a being as strong as him. Anger slowly drifts over his expression. "You deny me?" he asks, voice near a growl.

I try to hide my trembling fingers. I don't want to fear him.

"I'm sorry," I whisper. "But I can't—I can't do this."

His hand jerks out. I whimper but remain utterly still. His claw presses into the underside of my jaw.

"To you, I am not Jarron. You see me as something other." He speaks slowly, like he's working out a particularly tricky puzzle. "But I am not fooled. The Jarron you know and this being before you are the same. You desire him. Trust him. Want to be with him. Yet you will not."

His head tilts as he examines me.

I close my eyes. The sharp edge of his claw should be painful against my soft skin, but it's not. Still, my pulse races.

"Why? Is it the fear? You fear this version of me. Is that the reason? Or is there more?"

He releases me and stands straight.

"I will figure out it. I will uncover your secret, my bright one, and resolve this. I will fix it and claim you as mine."

He doesn't wait for a response or reaction. He simply turns on his heel and disappears into the darkness of the hall.

I close my eyes and fist the sheets while I let that new wave of pain flood me. Once the worst is over, I grab the potion and down it in one big gulp and pray that sleep takes me before I can think too deeply about what I just did or what his words could possibly mean.

55

I'LL BE BACK

SLEEP TAKES me moments after Jarron leaves the room and I only wake again when my parents arrive. They wrap me up in their arms with tears and whimpers.

"Are you okay?" my mom asks.

"Define okay," I ask, still groggy.

She shakes her head and tries again. "How do you feel?"

"My head hurts. My leg stings. But I'll survive."

"The nurses said you were okay to return home."

"Minor Hall is reopened?"

I consider how hard it's going to be to enter Minor Hall again. Will I forever be terrified of passing through those gates and looking into the study hall?

They pause, glancing at each other. "We meant, home-home."

"Oh."

I frown. I guess that makes sense. Things are—well, they're not exactly okay.

"You need to heal. Emotionally and physically."

I swallow. "Okay. But I want to come back here. Once things settle."

They glance at each other again. "We'll talk about it."

Something else crosses my mind. "What about my roommate?" I ask quickly.

"There wasn't anyone there when we went into get your things. We did see your friends Janet and Lola, though. Lovely girls. You don't mean them, do you?"

I shake my head. Corrine must have fled too. Did she sign the contract? If she did, she'll be bound to enter the games. I don't have much energy left to dwell on that now, but it's certainly something to worry about once I'm not on the verge of falling apart.

"Jarron's parents told us what happened," Dad says. "At least some of it. You—you went after Liz's killer?"

Yeah, they're totally not going to like this explanation. But, then again, maybe I have a better way of spinning it. "Kind of. I was just looking for answers, though. Mr. Vandozer tried to manipulate me into entering the games, but I refused."

Mom wraps her arms around me, jostling me just enough to send a ricochet of pain through my whole body. "I can't lose you too," she says, her lips trembling. I hold her tightly.

"I know."

After a little bit of small talk with the nurses, Mom and Dad help me out of bed. My body is heavy and my mind still groggy, but I'm able to get on my feet. Mom keeps her arm wrapped around me as we shuffle out of the infirmary. I don't actually need that much help—I'm not that hurt. But I let her anyway because I'm pretty sure they need the reassurance that I'm here and okay.

I meant it when I said I want to come back.

I want to stay with Lola and Janet. I want to brew potions. And I don't want to lose Jarron. Not all the way.

Who knows what our relationship will be like now, but I can't leave it like this. Our story isn't over yet either.

We stop just past the wrought iron gates while a few helpers load our car. "Do you think he's still going to come for you?" Mom whispers. "That headmaster?"

"I don't know," I answer, mostly because I don't have the heart to tell her that yes, Mr. Vandozer seemed very intent on getting me into his games. And he's prideful. Enough that he will try again.

"Maybe it'll be safer here for you, near Jarron," Mom says.

Mom slides into the back seat next to me, while dad gets behind the wheel.

"About Jarron," Dad says, voice low. "We also heard—"

"That's—that's over now," I say quickly.

Dad pauses another moment and must decide not to press the matter any further. Gravel crunches beneath the tires as he slowly pulls away from Shadow Hills Academy, a place that I know I'll never feel safe in again.

I curl my legs underneath me in the back of the car and run my fingers absently over my wrist. There's a slight burning sensation and when I glance down, my stomach sinks to my feet. Shimmering golden lines curl and twist over my veins.

The symbol is incomplete, and I pray that means the magic is also unbinding because the lines are faint, but I can follow the pattern. There's no mistaking the half-finished symbol of the Akrasia Games settling into my skin.

412

Note from the Author

Thank you so much for reading A Taste of Torment! This is the first book in a trilogy which means, yes—there's a lot of story left.

The next book in the Shadow Hill Academy series, A Drop of Anguish, is coming soon. And all I can say is—please trust me! I love putting my characters through the emotional ringer, it's kinda my thing, but there is a rhyme and a reason for all the heart break and I'm going to do my best to make it up to you & my beloved characters!

Until then, turn the page to learn more about my other (finished) series. Or find me on social media and vent all your feels about Candice, Jarron and all the others! I'd love to hear your thoughts.

If you enjoyed this book, I'd love it if you left a review or posted about it on social media. It helps us authors more than you realize!

If you want to be the first to hear news about my

upcoming books, please join my newsletter, which can be found at Www.StaceyTrombley.com

Follow me on Instagram and Tiktok @StaceyTrombleyauthor

Join my reader group Facebook.com/groups/StaceysPageTurners/

If you'd love to read another tear-your-heart-out but leave-you-happy-at-the-end series by me, please check out my Wicked Fae series!

All that's standing between me and freedom are eleven bloodthirsty fae

As a convicted assassin, I've been banished from the fae realm for years but now I have the opportunity to compete in a ruthless competition to earn a full pardon.

Dragons and twisted mazes are the least of my worries now.

I can handle a few bullies and death-defying challenges. The thing that will keep me up at night is having to face those I betrayed. Especially Reveln, the prince whose brother I killed. Every time I see the hatred in his eyes it reopens old wounds, a reminder of the destiny that was stolen from me. And I only have myself to blame.

But I'll find a new destiny—by winning the Trial of Thorns.

The whole realm thinks I'm weak but I'm stronger than they could ever imagine. By the time this is through—I'll bring them all to their knees.

ABOUT THE AUTHOR

Stacey Trombley is a casino pit boss by night, urban fantasy author by day. She lives in Ohio with her husband, son, and German Shepherd, Riley. When she's not writing or reading her husband is probably dragging her along on one of his crazy adventures for this travel vlog or competing against him about who can pick the most Survivor winners in the first episode (hint: she's winning). But mostly, she's probably reading.

Acknowledgments

Writing a book can sometimes feel like a solitary endeavor but it always utilizes help and support from so many sources. Thank you to my family, especially my husband Sean and my son Caleb, for being supportive and understanding of my deadlines and distracted moments. Also thank you to Tony and Kristie for helping whenever asked! We both appreciate it.

Thank you to my beta readers, Samantha R, Kay Hart and Danielle Oven, for the detailed notes and encouragement! Amy White and Deissy Hermunslie for typo hunting. And Kelly Burnette and Sabrina for helping with the Chapter titles!

Thank you to my writing group, the Queens of the Quill! You are all queens and it's a pleasure to be part of the group. You've inspired me, reassured me and taught me so much!

Thank you to my editor Caitlin Marie Haines, for your considerate and encouraging feedback! You always help my books shine!

And of course, thank you to my God. Help me to always remember, you are the one thing I seek.